MURDER BY MILK BOTTLE

A Constable Twitten Mystery

LYNNE TRUSS

D1334844

RAVEN BOOKS
LONDON · OXFORD · NEW YORK · NEW DELHI · SYDNEY

RAVEN BOOKS
Bloomsbury Publishing Plc
50 Bedford Square, London, WC1B 3DP, UK
29 Earlsfort Terrace, Dublin 2, Ireland

BLOOMSBURY, RAVEN BOOKS and the Raven Books logo are trademarks of
Bloomsbury Publishing Plc

First published in Great Britain 2020
This edition published 2021

Copyright © Lynne Truss, 2020

Lynne Truss has asserted her right under the Copyright, Designs and Patents Act, 1988,
to be identified as Author of this work

For legal purposes the Acknowledgements and Author's Note on pp. 300–2
constitute an extension of this copyright page

All rights reserved. No part of this publication may be reproduced or transmitted
in any form or by any means, electronic or mechanical, including photocopying,
recording, or any information storage or retrieval system, without prior permission
in writing from the publishers

A catalogue record for this book is available from the British Library

ISBN: HB: 978-1-5266-0979-3; PB: 978-1-5266-0978-6;
eBook: 978-1-5266-0980-9

2 4 6 8 10 9 7 5 3 1

Typeset by Integra Software Services Pvt. Ltd.
Printed and bound in Great Britain by CPI Group (UK) Ltd, Croydon CR0 4YY

MIX
Paper from
responsible sources
FSC® C020471

To find out more about our authors and books visit www.bloomsbury.com
and sign up for our newsletters

Milk bars!
I'd like to know just how they grow
And why we see them everywhere!
Milk bars!
Is it the dairies or the fairies
Who decide to put them there?

'Let's Have a Tiddley at the
Milk Bar' by Noel Gay, 1936

There have been, for once in a way, no serious mishaps this term, praise be. Little Joy Mowbray (*such* blue eyes) accidentally set fire to the Chapel last week, but apologised so prettily that I hadn't the heart to scold. I do feel the battle is won when they are genuinely sorry, don't you?

'Just an Ordinary Term' by Arthur Marshall, 1949,
collected in *Girls Will Be Girls*, 1974

Brighton Dairy Festival: Exhibitions! Shows!
Competitions! Real cows will live on the lawns of the
Royal Pavilion and be milked daily in public …
The **50-vehicle cavalcade** stretched for nearly a mile,
extolling the virtues of milk …
Several hundred people, told by Lord Rupert Nevill:
'We should and must drink more milk', took him at his
word and rushed for free samples at the mobile milk bar …
Lactic Lovely: the winner of the Brighton Dairy Princess,
a 19-year-old Eastbourne ledger clerk, drinks half-a-pint a
day!

Brighton Evening Argus, June and July 1957

To Gemma

The action of this book takes place over the
weekend of the August Bank Holiday 1957

One

Friday

Just before seven o'clock in the evening, Mr E. E. Hollibon of the Automobile Association took a last drag on his cigarette and stubbed it out in a nasty, overfilled ashtray. Then, muttering, he turned his chair away from the spectacular view of the Palace Pier silhouetted against the pinkly glittering sea. This being a warm August evening – the Friday preceding the 1957 Bank Holiday – he had earlier allowed himself to remove his AA uniform jacket, but now he stood up and put it on again, buttoning to the neck. Back in his chair, he sat up straight. It was time to radio a patrolman.

'Officer Inman? Do you receive me? Over.' Hollibon carefully enunciated into his microphone, using his best, brisk NCO speaking tones, and pressing a button on its base. When he released the button there was no reply. 'This is AA Brighton Control calling Officer Inman. Repeat, this is AA Brighton Control. Confirm position, please, Officer Inman. Repeat, confirm position. Over.'

He took his finger off the button, and a response came over the crackling airwaves.

'Just pulling in as it happens, Eddie,' was the affable reply. 'Here, I bet you put your jacket on just to do that, didn't you? I can hear it in your voice, mate.'

Hollibon huffed with impatience. *Mate?* Officer Andrew Inman never observed proper radio protocol. He always said he'd had enough of that malarkey in the war. But calling his controller *mate?*

'Confirm position, please, Officer Inman. Repeat, confirm position. This is Brighton Control. Over,' said Hollibon.

Sighing, Officer Inman (who preferred to be called Officer Andy) relented and confirmed his position in an acceptable manner. 'Arrived Hassocks address, Dale House, nineteen hundred hours,' he said. 'But for the last time, Eddie, why do you keep telling me you're blooming AA Brighton Control? I know it's you. I mean, who else is going to call me on this thing? Lord Haw-Haw?'

There was a long pause while Hollibon waited for his patrolman to say 'over'.

'You have to say "over", Officer Inman. I've told you a thousand times.'

'Look—'

'It's so simple! Any schoolboy can do it! In fact, any school-boy would love to!'

'My motorist is waiting, Eddie.'

'All right, but it's a good job you're my best mechanic, Andy. Over and out. Repeat, over and out!'

Hollibon leaned across his desk to make a note on the large, nicotine-yellowed wallchart ('19.00 A.I. Dale House, Hassocks'), and then – after a deep, steadying breath – shuffled his chair to the window to admire the still-warm evening sunlight dancing on the sea and enjoy a lovely, well-earned Weights pure Virginia cigarette (two and elevenpence for twenty).

Despite the insubordination he endured nightly from Officer Andy Inman, Hollibon did enjoy this job. He particularly relished peaceful, still moments such as this: the beginning of the night shift on a clear late-summer evening, with both patrolmen out and about in their shiny new yellow Land Rovers, selflessly serving the motoring public. On the small primus stove in the corner of his little office, a kettle was coming to the boil beside a ready-warmed brown teapot. The AA insignia on his lapel glinted in the low light. And best of all, the latest hit of smoke and nicotine was working its ineffable magic, as a really promising cough started to boil up in his chest.

Mr Hollibon was an ardent smoker with all the hallmarks of a man who has inhaled warmed-up toxins continuously for more than thirty years. The puckered skin, deep-stained fingers, disgusting cough: he flaunted them all with pride. An army doctor had once asked if his cough was 'productive', and he had replied, truthfully, 'Yes, *very*.' Leaning forward now, he alternately coughed and struggled for breath until (yes!) a veritable torrent of expectoration was produced. And then, pleased with himself, he lit a fresh fag to celebrate.

As it happened, on this same fine evening at the same serene hour, the young and smartly uniformed Constable Peregrine Twitten of the Brighton Police was making his methodical way through the nearby streets of Kemp Town.

He checked the shutters and gates of garages and goods yards; he hailed cyclists to inform them of lighting-up time; he called good evening to the drivers of the miniature trains on the Volk's Electric Railway who had just finished their day's work on the seafront; also, when summoned for the purpose by the dog-tired parents of scruffy street urchins, he would crouch down amid a group of overexcited six-year-olds and tell them, in all (mock) seriousness, that if they weren't well-behaved boys and girls he would arrest them on the spot, and march them off to prison.

All this warm-hearted *Dixon of Dock Green* activity might lead you to suppose that the twenty-two-year-old Twitten had been somehow demoted to the duties of a workaday constable, but in fact he was, rather, doing his 'rounds' – this being an enterprise of his own devising, conducted on his own time.

'The thing is, sir, I'm a young, fit policeman yet I've never experienced being on the beat,' he had explained to an unconvinced Sergeant Brunswick a couple of weeks earlier.

'Lucky you, son.'

'You don't understand, sir. I've been here nearly two months and all I've done is solve fiendish high-stakes crimes perpetrated by the worst kind of brutal criminal and psychopath. I've been on the spot when two individuals were shot in the head!' Twitten stopped talking and calculated. 'No, I'm wrong about that, it's three!'

'So?'

'Well, for one thing, it's not bally normal, sir. And for another, it isn't helping me be a good policeman.'

'No?'

'I want to serve the people of this town, which means I should be diligently pounding the streets with a notebook, pencil and whistle, absorbing all of Brighton's subtle diurnal rhythms. You know the sort of thing. How many pints of milk are delivered at number forty-two; what time does Mr Smith the grocer cycle home from the pub; how many people are sleeping every night beneath the Palace Pier? Instead of which it's been all *Bang! Bang! Bang!* and blood and brains and eyeballs and screams, not to mention people getting brained with giant bally humbugs.'

They were alone together at their desks in the police station when they had this conversation. Brunswick shrugged and took a sip of tea. On the whole, the sergeant approved of young Twitten, but he thought it a bit rich for him to complain of too much flaming excitement. Wasn't he the one who always stirred things up? Only last week, Twitten had started talking about the need to compile 'criminal records', claiming that this would 'revolutionise detective methods'! But luckily – since the actual work would involve typing cards and filing them – Inspector Steine had put a stop to that at once. 'Typing and filing are women's work, Twitten,' Steine had pronounced. 'Especially filing. It's bad enough that you insist on typing your own reports.'

Twitten likewise sipped his tea, made for him by Mrs Groynes, the cheerful cockney charlady. It was a very nice cup, as it happened, with his usual two sugars, but for historical reasons, he shuddered to think what else she might have put in it. Despite the short time he had been in Brighton, Twitten already had quite a history with Mrs Groynes, which could be boiled down to two essentials:

1) his discovery that Mrs-Groynes-the-charlady was in fact a cunning criminal mastermind (in disguise); and
2) Mrs Groynes's brilliant countermove, involving bogus stage hypnotism, which rendered it impossible for Twitten to convince other people that she wasn't what she seemed.

'I ought to arrest you,' he had said to her at the close of the last case he had been instrumental in solving. And she had patted his hand and said, 'I know, dear. That's your burden.'

Yet here he was, still drinking – and enjoying – the tea she made; still eating the currant buns. Talk about an ethical

5

pickle! And, as always, it had been his own bally cleverness that had produced this frustrating state of affairs. Why had he not been content to take Mrs Groynes at face value, as everyone else did? Look how happy the others were, living in the dark.

'Would you mind telling me something, Sergeant Brunswick, sir?' Twitten ventured. 'When *you'd* been in the force just a couple of months, what were you most afraid of?'

Brunswick thought for a moment and then laughed at the memory. 'I was scared of old Sergeant "Roly-Poly" Rowland waiting for me at the police box on the London Road, red in the face and with his hands on his hips.'

Twitten felt a pang of self-pity. Here, starkly, was the difference between them. The young Brunswick had feared being mildly ticked off by a comically fat police sergeant. Twitten's own worst fear was of being garrotted up a dark alley by a villainess masquerading as a Mrs Mopp.

They sat in silence and then Brunswick – in a rush of conscience – said sheepishly, 'I can't believe no one told you about the pay parade on Thursday afternoons, son.'

Twitten pursed his lips. This was a very sore point.

'Well, no one did, sir. Not even you.'

'I know. Was it really six weeks before you … ?'

'Yes, sir. Six bally weeks. I'd begun to surmise that the salary must be disbursed annually.'

Brunswick bit his lip. Was this perhaps the right moment to inform Twitten about the police canteen across the road from the station? It did seem unfair that the young constable still didn't know about it. But two months down the line, it was too late to drop it casually into conversation. Why hadn't Twitten worked it out for himself? That's what Brunswick wanted to know. Didn't he hear all the excited references to tripe and onions on Tuesdays? Didn't he notice how people disappeared from their desks at half-past twelve, crossed the road, entered an unmarked building by a side door, and came back thirty minutes later with custard stains on their trousers? If those weren't subtle diurnal rhythms, he'd like to know what was.

But somehow the observant Twitten had not yet postulated the existence of a police canteen. And now, a few days after his friendly chat with Sergeant Brunswick, here he was, thoroughly enjoying his nightly 'rounds' of Kemp Town and arriving at the AA Control Centre on Marine Parade just after seven o'clock – or 'tea o'clock time' as he had recently learned to call it.

'Good evening, Mr Hollibon, it's me! At tea o'clock!' he called, appearing at the open door just as Hollibon was pouring hot water into his teapot.

'Ah, Constable Twitten,' said Hollibon, looking up without enthusiasm. He rather resented the way police officers dropped in like this, expecting free refreshment. And there seemed to be more of them lately. 'Perfect timing,' he joked. 'You must have been outside, waiting for the kettle to boil.'

'Well, to be frank, I *was* lurking by the door,' admitted Twitten. 'But mainly so as not to intrude on that absolutely revolting coughing fit you were having.'

He pulled a chair towards him and sat down. 'I know it's not my place to say so, Mr Hollibon,' he said, 'but does it really *never* occur to you that inhaling the fumes from cigarettes is unbelievably stupid?'

With the August Bank Holiday approaching, the whole of Brighton was gearing up for visitors. While the high summer had seen record-breaking temperatures (with a consequent horrifying plague of jellyfish), the weather on the Bank Holiday was set fair again, and traders were rubbing their hands in anticipation, as were, of course, the tricksters, dodgy street-photographers and junior whizz mobs (juvenile pick-pockets). It was sometimes cynically suggested at Chamber of Commerce meetings that instead of 'Kiss Me Quick', the seaside straw hats sold in the little kiosks on the piers ought to bear the legend 'Fleece Me Fast', so as better to represent the true and somewhat alarming experience of the naive Brighton holiday-maker.

And on this Friday night, the weekend activities were all just about to start – the dancing, the bingo, the Ghost Train on the Palace Pier, the children's talent shows at the Peter Pan Playground, the Ice Circus at the Sports Stadium in West Street, with its breathtaking stunt skaters, clowns, performing chimps and high trapeze. At the Hippodrome, Winifred Atwell was warming up her knuckles for the piano; backstage at the Theatre Royal, a young Frankie Howerd was leaning against a distempered dress-ing-room wall, telling jokes unfit for public consumption.

The cusp of evening was a magical time here: an ending and a beginning. The day-visitors had made their way back to the railway station and the Southdown coach stops; the holiday-makers were tucking into their cooked dinners in drab boarding-house dining rooms. The children's entertain-ers were packing up, and the beach donkeys trailing back to their stables in Hove. But at the same time, the lights on the piers were starting to glow against the slowly darkening sky, and the juke boxes beginning to blare, and on the sea breeze you could catch tantalising hints of candyfloss, cockles in vinegar, Charrington's Toby Ale, infant urine, cordite from the shooting ranges, and seaweed.

Twitten wasn't the only policeman out and about tonight. At seven o'clock, Sergeant Brunswick was waiting outside the Sports Stadium with tickets for the ice show, wearing his neatly pressed collar open (no tie) under a light, three-buttoned jacket. He looked very handsome. He'd had a shave-and-hair-cut especially, at Rodolfo's in Western Road, and was even wearing a splash of Cossack ('for Men') from the bottle he'd got for Christmas from his auntie Violet. His gift to her had been a refrigerator, as it happens, but that's another story.

Annoyingly, he had bumped into Inspector Steine while dressed in this *mufti*. Steine was on his way to the Dome Theatre to take part in a live BBC transmission of the popular radio show *What's Your Game?* He said nothing about Brunswick's un-policemanlike appearance, but you could tell from the way he turned away sharply ('Brunswick, what on earth … ?' he rasped) that the throat-catching Cossack ('for Men') was not a male toiletry he'd be requesting next Christmas for himself.

'I take it you're meeting someone, Brunswick?'

'Yes, sir. A young lady. You've met her yourself, actually, sir, at the Lactic Lovelies beauty contest you helped to judge the other night.'

Steine cast his mind back. 'You secured a date with the *winner*?'

'Oh, no, sir!' Brunswick coloured a little. The winner had been a stunning girl with a waist the diameter of a drain-pipe and eyebrows modelled on Ava Gardner's. 'No, not the winner, one of the runners-up, sir. Barbara Ashley. Actually, you might remember her. She was the blonde in the red swimsuit who made the point that "Lactic Lovelies" was an offensive name, sir.'

'It was a *Milk Board* contest, Brunswick.'

9

'I know, but—'

'The winner was going forward to compete for Dairy Maid Miss of 1957.'

'Yes, but—'

Steine waved a hand. 'All I know is, she'd have stood a better chance of winning if she'd held her tongue. I hope the upcoming Knickerbocker Glory contestants show more sense.'

'Yes, sir.' Brunswick knew when it was time to stop arguing. 'Well, good luck tonight, sir. My auntie loves *What's Your Game?* She says it's very funny.'

'Really?' said Steine, puzzled. 'Oh, I'm sure it's not supposed to be.'

And so now Brunswick was waiting for Barbara Ashley, and feeling rather good about everything except, perhaps, the aftershave, which was making his eyes water. Barbara was *amazing*. A twenty-year-old clerk at a meat-importer's in Shoreham, she was blonde, measured 34–22–36 and wore coral lipstick – all fairly predictable in a beauty-contest entrant. But there was something unusual about Barbara. She was direct and bold and unsimpering. On top of which (and Brunswick's pulse quickened whenever he thought of it), she appeared to have a highly idiosyncratic psychosexual quirk that attracted her to older, injured men, especially those who'd been shot in the leg!

Naturally, this interesting facet of Barbara's personality hadn't come to light straight away. First, she had let him buy her a thick and frothy pink milkshake, and had told him this was her fifth beauty contest of the summer. And then, as they stood together with their drinks, she'd confided in a low voice that there was something fishy about the girls who always won. She had hinted that the fishiness in question might interest him *as a policeman*.

Brunswick had not wanted to hear this. Like most men, he was uncomfortable hearing a woman complain about anything; it made him defensive. So he had deliberately swerved away from the subject, chuckling, 'Blimey, there seems to be a contest for something every day of the week this summer, have you noticed? Dog shows, horse shows, flower shows! And everyone takes them so seriously! I don't get it; I really don't. My inspector's judging a Knickerbocker Glory competition for the local paper – it's only flaming ice cream – and he seems to think it's the most important job in the world! And then my barber's furious just because he didn't get selected to take part in something called Barber of the Year! It's out of all proportion, in my opinion. I keep telling both of them, these contests are *just a bit of fun.*'

Barbara had given him a steady look. She really was quite forceful. Her eyes – a deep blue – seemed to scour his insides. 'I'm not talking about barbers or ice creams or *dogs*, Sergeant Brunswick. I'm talking about girls with unnaturally large busts and missing ribs who are in fact models and escorts, going around the country winning all the local beauty contests! They receive coaching, Sergeant! They are *shipped in*, like – well, like so much Argentinian corned beef!'

He hadn't known what to say to that. But he did admire the way she so deftly reached for imagery from the meat-importing business.

'Can I take you out, please, Miss Ashley?' Brunswick had said, in a rush. 'How about the Ice Circus? It's fantastic this year. Clowns and trapeze artists and whatnot.'

She gave him a severe look, then set down her milkshake glass and, leaning close, took hold of his lapel. The movement was breathtakingly unexpected.

'Tell me what's wrong with your leg,' she whispered.

'My leg?' His eyes swivelled. Was this a suitable question from a young lady? She was standing so close, he could feel her breath on his face.

'You've got a limp, Sergeant. Don't deny it.'

'Oh. Well …' He glanced around to check that no one else was within earshot. 'Look,' he said, 'if you must know, I've been shot in the line of duty a couple of times. That's all.'

He expected her to laugh at him (or, at least, release him), but to his surprise, her eyes widened and she clung on.

'Shot!' she repeated with an intake of breath. 'I knew it. Go on.' Her whole manner had softened. Her pupils were dilated to a worrying degree.

He swallowed, but maintained eye contact. Whatever was going on here was completely new to him. If warning bells were also ringing, he didn't care. It was months since he'd been this close to a girl.

'To be honest,' he admitted, slowly, 'it's more than a couple of times. It's three … or *four*.'

Gasping again, she briefly closed her eyes (but in a good way).

'Look, all right. It's six.' At the word 'six' she actually let out a whimper.

Then she leaned forward and whispered, 'Shot … by criminals?'

He gulped. 'Yes.'

'Oh, my God, *six times*,' she breathed. 'And exactly … where?'

Brunswick wasn't sure how to answer. 'Well, mostly out of doors,' he began, but she held up a hand to stop him, picked up her pink milkshake and gave a loud, final suck on the straw. 'I'll meet you on Friday for your Ice Circus, Sergeant Jim Brunswick,' she said. Then she turned away, adding, 'Don't be late.'

But now, here he was, and Barbara Ashley was nowhere to be seen. At twenty-past seven, when everyone else had gone in, Brunswick saw a red American sports car draw up across the road and a tall, athletic man jump out and run to the stage door. But that was the only thing of interest. At half-past seven, he gave up hope. She wasn't coming. He tore up the tickets in a dramatic gesture, and crossed the road.

He was going back to the station. It was his best option. After being stood up like this, if he went to a pub, he'd feel conspicuously alone. The pictures? No, he'd seen four films this week already, and on Friday nights cinemas were packed with young couples.

Go home? Not likely. His dear auntie Violet would be tuned to *What's Your Game?* on the Home Service, which this week featured as guest-panellist Inspector Geoffrey Steine of the Brighton Police!

———

Across town, in the airless Green Room at the Dome Theatre, Inspector Steine was shaking hands with his fellow panellists and wishing he hadn't come. Evidently *What's Your Game?* was a beloved BBC institution, and all the other guests had appeared on it a hundred times. They were dressed in glamorous evening clothes, laughing urbanely together when he entered.

Seated on a stained divan were two coiffed and shapely women wearing crystal necklaces, evening gloves and off-the-shoulder satin; standing, two balding men in white-tie were smoking furiously, as if about to face a firing squad. Several bottles of spirits stood open on the various occasional tables, and half-finished drinks cluttered every surface. The scene was somehow classy and tawdry at the same time.

It was also both casual and frantic. The producer who escorted Steine from the stage door seemed extremely hard-pressed; the atmosphere was nothing like the calm of the inspector's weekly BBC recordings, in his sealed-quiet studio in Broadcasting House. And some of the anxiety, apparently, had been innocently caused by him. He should have reported for duty at half-past six at the latest – though to be fair to him, no one had said so.

'Our policeman's here at last!' announced the producer, rather gracelessly. Then, with an audible 'Tsk', he turned on his heel.

'Hello,' said Steine, extending a hand in the direction of the ladies. 'Geoffrey Steine, Brighton Police. So to coin a phrase, hello, hello, hello, what's all this then?'

He expected a smile, but none came. 'That's *it*,' said one of the women, opening her handbag to retrieve a silver powder compact. 'I'm telephoning Tony first thing on Tuesday. They can't expect us to work like this.'

'Now, Gloria, don't be such a beast,' said one of the balding men, waving a cigarette held elegantly between his middle and fourth fingers. This man's demeanour struck Steine as perfectly debonair – almost as if being debonair was what he did for a living (actually, it was).

'Hello, Steine, old boy,' he said, draping an arm round the inspector's shoulders. 'Look, you seem a bit lost, and I'm afraid we go on in ten minutes, and our poor highly strung producer is having a nervous collapse, so I'd better introduce everyone. How's that?'

Steine swallowed. What had he got himself into? Who were these ghastly people?

'Well, now, let's see. First of all, I'm Gerry Edlin. We judged that dog show together a couple of weeks ago, do you remember? Enormous fun. We disagreed over who should win the waggiest tail, but I bowed to your superior judgment.' He smiled as a joke occurred to him. 'Or perhaps I should say I *bow-wowed*?'

Such wordplay was lost on Steine. 'Oh, yes. I remember. That was good of you. But on the other hand, of course, you were wrong and I was right.'

'Well, Lord, anything for an easy life, that's me! So I'm in Brighton for the summer, doing magic and a few jokes in the big show down the road. For my sins, I'm the regular chairman of this silly game, and it's in my honour that they dragged everyone else down here tonight, can you believe it? Normally we do this up in town, and darling Frank Muir is in your seat. That's why the girls are so grumpy. Frank is *hilarious*. We *adore* him. He has the audience in *stitches*. But tragically he couldn't make it, hence your good self valiantly stepping into the breach when all the other chaps who'd been asked either got better offers at the last minute or found out how appalling the pay was.'

The others tittered. Steine smiled, weakly. Had Gerry Edlin just said they were going on in *ten minutes*? He tried to remember precisely how the invitation from the BBC had been worded, when they'd telephoned him. It was something like: 'You'll have heard *What's Your Game?*, Inspector. Honestly, there's nothing to it. Chap of your experience, you'll take it in your stride. And on home turf, too. Five guineas all right?' And just like that, he'd said yes.

'So this is Lady Prunella Cavendish.'

One of the women frostily raised a glass to him.

'Lady Pru is your teammate, and an absolute fiend of a quizzer. I advise you as a new bug to follow her lead in all matters. She gives the impression of not being competitive, but between you and me, if you outshine her in any way, she'll batter you to death with her stilettos.'

At this, the other balding male guest burst out laughing (a weird, high giggle), and Prunella shouted, 'You rat, Gerry!' – but affectionately and a bit too loudly, in a pointedly cliquish aren't-we-all-friends-in-showbiz kind of way.

By now, Steine was feeling giddy with panic.

'And here is Gloria Powell, famous comedy actress and fabulous raconteuse.'

Miss Powell grimaced. She was the one who had taken one look at Steine and resolved to call her agent.

'You might have seen her in *The King and I*. And finally, her regular teammate, Cedric Carbody, who does those screamingly funny skits on the wireless impersonating the headmistress of a girls' school. What's the school called again, Cedric?'

The other man pursed his lips and clasped his chubby hands together at his chest. His eyes twinkled with naughtiness. 'St Winifred's,' he trilled, in a well-practised falsetto that had the others spluttering their drinks with laughter. 'And *what* a term it's been!'

The door was flung open. 'Time, everyone,' announced a neatly ponytailed young woman in horn-rimmed glasses and a pencil skirt. Her words instigated a flurry of activity: the men stubbing out their cigarettes, adjusting cummerbunds, blowing their noses; the women standing up and straightening their nylons. Steine alone did not spring into action. In fact, he continued to stand on the spot he had first occupied.

'Inspector Steine! I'm so pleased you accepted!' said the young woman – who, now he thought about it, he recognised from his weekly trips to the studio in Portland Place. 'It's Susan Turner, Inspector. I assist Mr Douglas. It was my idea to ask you to stand in for Mr Muir when all the others dropped out. Don't worry, you'll be wonderful. So clever of you to come in uniform! Are you going to keep the cap on, or would you like me to look after it?'

As she led them towards the stage, they could hear the professional warm-up man welcoming the audience to *What's Your Game?* and getting them in the mood. '*So I said to the manager, I said, is that wallpaper flocked? And he said, what do you mean, "flocked"? It's good for another twenty years!*' Never in Inspector Steine's life had a gale of laughter sounded quite so terrifying.

———

Replete with tea and biscuits, Twitten was wondering whether to resume his rounds, but found he was curious about Officer Andy. A couple of radio calls from Hollibon had failed to raise him – although of course there was every possibility he was still busy on the Hassocks job, lying under a car.

'What was the nature of the call-out?' asked Twitten, picking up a Garibaldi.

'Well,' said Hollibon, excitedly, 'would you believe it? Only a *Thunderbird*!'

Twitten tried to look impressed, but didn't quite manage it. Cars had never interested him. *I-Spy Sports Cars* was the only *I-Spy* book he had failed to complete as a child. 'Look, Peregrine,' his father would say at Hyde Park Corner, on family educational trips to London. 'Over there! A Triumph Roadster!' But although Twitten politely said 'Gosh, sir', his heart wasn't in it. In the end, his mother had let him abandon *I-Spy Sports Cars*, and devote himself entirely to *I-Spy Antique Furniture*.

So was a Thunderbird something special?

'You'd know it was special if you saw one,' Hollibon assured him. 'Open-topped, long, shiny; this one's been imported especially by that famous Yank skater in the Ice Circus, Buster Bond. He got stuck out in Hassocks, see, when his Thunderbird wouldn't start. Andy was excited to see that car, I can tell you. It's got a record player built in. It plays LPs!'

Twitten made a mental note to look out for this special car while on his rounds. Buster Bond he'd certainly heard of. The local newspapers had printed several articles about him, on account of his brilliant skating, exciting bachelor status and devastating good looks.

'So you're not officially on this beat, then, Constable?' Hollibon asked.

'Not officially, no.'

'That explains it. Constable Jenkins still comes by at half-past ten, you see, and he's been complaining about you eating all the fig rolls.'

Guiltily, Twitten put down his biscuit.

'So if you don't mind me asking, Constable, what are you doing here?'

Twitten didn't mind at all. 'Well, firstly, I'm here because I think policemen on the beat build up a valuable amount of knowledge, while their very presence prevents any number of opportunistic crimes.'

'I see.'

'But at the same time ...' He faltered, and lowered his voice. 'Well, at the same time my walking the streets is slightly in the nature of a rest cure, Mr Hollibon. It's a quiet passage, if you like, after a spell of very high-pressure detective work.'

Hollibon was surprised. Twitten was surely too young to have seen a lot of criminal activity. This 'very high-pressure detective work' probably referred to early-morning stake-outs to catch children riding their bikes across the miniature golf course.

'How high-pressure do you mean?' Hollibon asked, with a smile.

Twitten wondered where to start. 'Well, do you remember those two men shot dead at the railway station last month?'

'Of course.' Hollibon frowned. 'But surely *you* weren't—?'

'I bally was, though. There was blood under my fingernails for *days*. And then I found some in my *ear*. And do you remember the man shot dead in the theatre, before that, in June?'

'Yes, but—'

'I was sitting next to him when the bally gun was fired!'

'*What*? But why?'

'And then there was the boy with his throat cut in the deck-chair, and the man knocked down and killed with a humbug, and the playwright slaughtered with a regimental sword, and the mesmerist fatally shot in a mutual death-struggle with a strong lady on the stage of the Hippodrome!'

Hollibon was horrified. 'Oh, my God!'

'I agree, sir.'

'I mean, sorry to swear, but …' Hollibon lowered his voice. 'I mean, *bloody hell*.'

'I know. You don't have to tell me, sir. And you needn't apologise. *Bally, bally hedgehogs* is what I often say about it all myself.'

Twitten took a deep breath and composed himself. 'But you did ask why I was sitting here having this jolly nice cup of tea with you, and that's the reason. I needed to opt for a lighter time of it. Between you and me, Mr Hollibon, I can't help feeling that another brutal murder in Brighton by an unknown hand with complicated motives would just about finish me off!'

<hr />

At eight o'clock, Brunswick said hello to the desk sergeant at the police station.

'Ah, Brunswick. There was a call for you.'

The sergeant handed over a note. It concerned Barbara. One look at it sent Brunswick racing down the station steps, attractive-multiple-gunshot-wounds-to-the-leg-while-out-of-doors notwithstanding.

'Agh,' he said, at every other step. 'Oof! Ow! Agh!'

Outside, he had a stroke of luck. A police car was sitting idle, the driver having just enjoyed his supper at the canteen across the road (the one Twitten didn't know about). The driver frowned when he realised Brunswick was wrenching open the passenger door and climbing in. He'd been expecting a few quiet minutes to complete his digestion of a delicious jam omelette.

'To the hospital,' Brunswick commanded. 'Quick as you can.'

A young blonde woman called Barbara Ashley had been found near the children's playground with life-threatening injuries; the caller had mentioned the words 'savage attack' and also (weirdly) 'milk bottles'. In the victim's handbag was a Regent Ballroom paper serviette with 'Sgt Jim Brunswick / Friday / Leg x 6!' written on it in coral lipstick.

<hr />

As the car sped eastwards towards the hospital, Brunswick spotted the roof of the Dome and wondered, fleetingly, how the inspector was getting on with his radio appearance.

In fact, against all the odds, Steine was doing well. It turned out that being clueless about the game was giving him an unexpected comedic advantage.

The format of the show was that members of the public turned up to answer questions, and the panel – seated in pairs at tables, behind state-of-the-art microphones almost as big as their heads – politely asked yes–no questions to establish what the person did for a living. 'Do you follow your profession indoors, Mr Gorringe?' they might ask; or 'Does your job require you to wear any protective headgear?' Traditionally, after a dozen or so questions, one of the ladies would be inspired to ask, in a clipped voice, 'Mr Gorringe, *do you test wellington boots?*' and receive a warm, congratulatory round of applause from the audience, who were always in on the answer.

Before going on, Cedric Carbody had leaned close to Steine and whispered to him, 'Now, please, don't look *quite* so worried, Inspector Diddle Dum-dums.'

Steine could hardly believe his ears. *Inspector Diddle Dum-dums?*

'Look, I wouldn't do this for just *anyone*, my darling,' continued Carbody, 'but I've been doing this show for a thousand years and I suppose I know my onions. So here's a tip, just for little old nervous you. If you can't think of anything else to ask, say, *Are you glad when it's knocking-off time?* It doesn't elicit any useful information, of course, but trust me, it's guaranteed to get a laugh.'

'Are you sure?'

'Positive!' said Carbody, a smile playing artfully on his lips. 'No one's said it for weeks; we save it up for special occasions.'

'That's very kind of you.' Steine thought about it. *Knocking-off time* sounded somewhat vulgar. 'Could I change it to *going-home time?*' he asked.

'Well, you could, if you were determined to ruin the joke and not get the laugh that I'm so generously bestowing on you.'

'Oh. Well, in that case, *knocking-off time* it is. Thank you very much.'

'Think nothing of it, sweet boy!' And then Carbody had emitted his high giggle, making all the others look round and laugh.

So Steine had thanked him again and, as he took his seat under the powerful stage lights, and controlled his breathing, he repeated the question to himself a few times. It helped. It was reassuring to know that when his own turn came to speak, he had something in the bag.

Now, the first subject for the panel's combined powers of deduction (introduced as 'Mr Jones of Brighton') was pretty clearly a fisherman. In fact, Steine recognised him as a fisherman from whom he'd bought mackerel just a few days ago. As each of the ladies asked Jones a question, it was established that he did indeed wear a protective hat on occasion, and that he was engaged in a seaside profession. Steine geared himself up.

But first it was Cedric's turn, and something extraordinary happened. Looking Steine directly in the eye, he asked, in a playful tone, 'Tell me, Mr Jones. Are you *very* glad when it's knocking-off time?' At which Jones exclaimed, 'Blimey, I'll say!' and the simple-minded audience roared with laughter.

'Now, Inspector Steine, welcome to *What's Your Game?*' said Gerry Edlin, warmly. 'Do you have a question for Mr Jones?'

Steine hesitated. What could he say? Thanks to the motive-less malignity of Cedric Carbody, he had nothing.

'Inspector Steine?' repeated Gerry with a little laugh to mask the pause in proceedings. 'We're all agog. We are mere amateurs at interrogation, but it's surely second nature to you.'

'Indeed it is,' laughed Steine, trying to ignore the feeling that his internal organs were fighting each other like weasels in a sack.

And then he saw his way out. He took a deep breath.

'Mr Jones, my question to you is this,' he said, sternly. 'In your capacity as a Brighton fisherman, have you ever sold me fish that you knew to be *on the turn*, contrary to section seventeen of the Shops Act of 1950?'

There was an awkward silence, and time seemed to stop. Gerry's easy smile froze on his face. Gloria Powell threw herself back in her chair. Lady Pru, sitting beside Steine, snapped a BBC pencil. The audience murmured. And up in the control box, the producer of *What's Your Game?* turned to Susan Turner and said, 'You're fired.'

But then Jones said, with a grin, 'It's a fair cop, guv'nor!' and the audience exploded with laughter, and started to applaud.

'Well done, Inspector Steine,' said Gerry, as Mr Jones got up and respectfully shook each of the panel by the hand. 'Well, that will teach us not to have a serving policeman on the show! Mr Jones *is* a Brighton fisherman! This is like working alongside the famous Sherlock Holmes!'

At eight o'clock, back in the AA control centre, the radio came to life, and Hollibon smiled at Twitten. But what they heard was not reassuring, because it wasn't Officer Andy.

'Hello, is there anyone there?' It was the voice of a young boy – a frightened young boy.

Hollibon grabbed the microphone. 'This is Brighton Control. Who is this? Over.'

He frowned at Twitten, who automatically produced his notebook and licked the tip of his pencil.

'My name's Stephen.'

'Stephen, this is Controller Hollibon.'

'All right.'

'Look, first of all, you should not be using this radio. I've got a policeman here who'll tell you the same. You could go to prison for this, my lad.'

He smiled at Twitten, as if to say, This is how to talk to naughty children! But Twitten, unsure, shook his head. It was certainly customary to threaten youngsters with a stretch in Wormwood Scrubs, but this boy on the radio sounded scared enough already.

'Where's Officer Andy?' said Twitten.

'I was out on my bike and—'

'Yes, but is Officer Andy with you, please?' demanded Hollibon. 'I'd like to speak with him. Over.'

'I just found him, I think.'

'Explain what you mean, please. Over.'

'You've got to call somebody. Look, it wasn't me! I swear it. There's glass and blood. And *milk*. There's blood and milk *everywhere*.'

Hollibon and Twitten looked at each other. Hollibon put his hands to his face. He had turned white. 'Oh, Andy!' he whispered.

'Hello?' said the boy, again, and Twitten gently removed the microphone from Hollibon's grip.

'Stephen,' he said. 'This is Constable Twitten of the Brighton Police. You're doing very well. It was clever of you to think of using the radio. No one thinks this is your fault, and I promise you won't go to prison. Please tell me where you are, so that we can come and help.'

'I think he's dead.'

And then the boy must have remembered what you were supposed to say when talking on a radio.

'*Over*,' he said, and started to cry.

––––––––––

At the hospital, Brunswick found to his dismay that he was too late. Barbara Ashley, recent runner-up in a grotesquely named beauty competition, had slipped away without regaining consciousness.

The news hit him hard, but possibly not so hard as it was going to hit Constable Twitten. A second murder on the same evening? Poor Twitten really did deserve a spell of peace and quiet after all that death-by-humbug and so on. And now, just ahead of the Bank Holiday, there were two new murders to clear up, both of which seemed to involve people being killed with milk bottles.

And then, to top it all, came a third. Because after the broadcast of *What's Your Game?*, as Steine was being hailed as an unlikely comedy hero by Gerry Edlin and the ladies back in the Green Room, the young (and rapidly rehired) Susan Turner had come in and whispered to Cedric Carbody that there was someone to see him – someone who apparently preferred to wait in the alley by the stage door. The others rolled their eyes. Carbody popping outside to meet an admirer was not unusual.

He affected surprise nevertheless. 'How *mysterious*!' he sing-songed. 'Well, I suppose I must comply.' He adjusted his trousers, and ran a hand over his thin head of hair. 'As I always impress on my girls,' he said, adopting his headmistress falsetto, 'we must grasp every opportunity that comes our way. You won't win Best Pony at the county gymkhana, Mildred, if you don't first saddle up Goldenboy.'

Steine didn't laugh at this. He didn't even turn to look. He had seen Cedric Carbody's true colours. Pouring himself a whisky, he felt the weight of the bottle and briefly wondered what it would feel like to say, 'Oh, Cedric?' and then, having got the vile man's attention, swing it at his head.

This thought would come back to haunt him. Half an hour later, Lady Pru asked where on earth Cedric had got to, and young Susan Turner was dispatched to look for him.

It was while Gerry and the ladies were all delightedly envisaging the scene of debauchery the poor girl might stumble on that they were silenced by something unnerving: the sound of her piercing screams.

Two

Saturday

Brunswick's barber Rodolfo was quite entitled to feel aggrieved that his application to take part in the Bank Holiday contest for Barber of the Year had been rejected. And he wasn't alone in his resentment: his whole clientele were up in arms. His not being allowed to compete was perceived as a gross insult to a man of his talent, standing and fantastic scissoring skills.

Rodolfo, aged forty-two, was not only a dedicated professional but the scion of a Brighton–Italian barbering dynasty stretching back nearly a hundred years. Romantic legend had it that his Tuscan great-grandfather Francesco had acted as official *parrucchiere* (hairdresser) to Giuseppe Garibaldi on his historic visit to England in 1864 – and that he had deserted the great man's entourage after falling in love with an English parlourmaid. But although this story was much repeated by subsequent generations, there was, sadly, no supporting evidence other than that, in all Garibaldi's pictures, you never saw a hair out of place.

Rodolfo was thus a proud man and a perfectionist from a long line of men with similar traits. His wife having died in childbirth seventeen years ago, when treasured son Carlo was born, he had for a long time sublimated all his passions into his work. Why shouldn't he be allowed to compete? Hadn't he broad-mindedly adapted his skills to every outlandish new trend in male coiffure? When the so-called 'duck's arse' first came into fashion in the early 1950s, hadn't Rodolfo been the first barber in the South East of England not only to conquer his horror and offer the cut, but also the first to say 'duck's arse' aloud in mixed company?

What hurt Rodolfo most now was his loss of face before his son Carlo. A handsome, charismatic boy, Carlo had already boasted to his friends that his father would come home from the Royal Pavilion with the title Barber of the Year. And now he had let the boy down, and it hurt. When that fateful rejection letter arrived at his shop, returning the costly studio photographs of perfect crew cuts, quiffs and pompadours, Rodolfo had for a moment actually considered stabbing himself to death with his own scissors, rather than confess his failure to his son.

If only the barbers of Brighton spoke to each other, Rodolfo might have learned the interesting fact that none of his rivals had been admitted to the competition either. All had met with the same curt rebuff. But sadly, the town's tonsorial practitioners were not on friendly terms, so none of them suspected there was something *going on*.

Which was a shame, because in regard to the inaugural Barber of the Year competition, to be held at the Brighton Pavilion on Bank Holiday Monday 1957, *going on* was exactly what something was …

———

At dawn on Saturday morning, Constable Twitten dressed quietly, and carefully collected from the neatly painted mantelshelf his notebook, pencil and whistle. Pale yellow light from the north-facing dormer window, with its view of tiled rooftops and seagulls, dimly illuminated the room, and he let out a sigh of profound satisfaction at the items he could see: tidy single bed with new chintz coverlet; antique nightstand; large wardrobe; tall oak bookcase crying out for the books being sent from home by Mother; pretty tiled fireplace; pegs on the wall from which to hang uniform and helmet.

Twitten loved everything about this place. It was the first room in Brighton that he had called his own; he had occupied it for a full week now, and he sincerely believed he couldn't have done better. How hard it was to tear himself away! But he must. As he made his way gingerly down the stairs, so as not to wake his landlady, Twitten gripped his helmet tightly to his chest, and dutifully turned his thoughts to what awaited him at the police station.

It was bad enough that one murder should disturb his self-prescribed rest cure; but *three*? Yet it was true: by the close of play the previous night it was clear that three people had been brutally murdered in Brighton within a short time of each other – and in a manner that suggested a link, despite the victims having nothing ostensibly in common.

One was a young beauty-contest runner-up barely old enough to have enemies; the second, a much-loved AA patrol-man of spotless record; the third, a visiting radio celebrity known for 'skits' involving female impersonation. But all had apparently been assaulted in the same way, and the murderer was still at large.

'Milk bottles? That's very suggestive,' Twitten had said, when the frightened boy on the radio had tried to describe the scene of carnage at the road junction north of Brighton where he had stumbled upon the lifeless body of poor Officer Andy.

'Milk bottles? People don't attack lovely young women with flaming milk bottles!' Brunswick had blustered, when he arrived at the hospital just moments too late to see Barbara Ashley alive.

'Well, I very much doubt this was done with *milk bottles*,' pronounced Steine, despite seeing the lacerated body of Cedric Carbody for himself in the dark alley, surrounded by glittering shards of glass in heaps, in a lake of milk reflecting the light from a street lamp, with a handful of tinfoil bottle-tops scattered on his chest, like petals.

But in all three cases, the murder did in fact seem to have been committed with milk bottles. Initial examinations at each scene suggested that first the victims had been stunned with blows to the head from full pints, then they'd been savagely stabbed to death with the broken bottle's remains. More bottles had then been smashed around the bodies, as if in a frenzy. It was certainly an unusual 'M.O.' – and had Twitten only been allowed to set up a criminal records system, murder-by-milk-bottle would have merited a card of its own, if not a whole drawer. As Inspector Steine had solemnly observed back at the station, this murder weapon new to the police certainly overturned one's complacent view of dairy delivery: it was as if a nice man with a horse and cart clip-clopped round the streets each morning and lawfully placed a loaded handgun on every doorstep.

'Up already, Constable?' called a kindly voice. It was Mrs Thorpe, Twitten's wonderful landlady. He was tiptoeing past her room on his way downstairs.

'Mrs Thorpe, I'm so sorry to wake you,' he whispered. 'I have to start very early today. Please don't get up.'

'Oh, you poor darling. On a Saturday?'

Mrs Thorpe opened her bedroom door. A wealthy middle-aged widow, and owner of this elegant period home on Clifton Terrace, she was wearing a sleek kimono-style dressing-gown and high-heeled velvet mules with feathery embellishments. She cast a loving glance down at them. 'Wouldn't you care for breakfast first?'

'I'm afraid there's no time, Mrs Thorpe. But thank you very much.'

'Perhaps tomorrow, then?'

'Yes, perhaps,' he said, agreeably, without meaning it. He doubted this multiple-victim case would be solved in a day. By way of apology, he turned to smile to her. 'Thank you again for having me, Mrs Thorpe. I do love it here. Living at the section house was *awful*. They turn the lights out at half-past ten!'

And then, even though he knew she was wide awake (and watching him go), he continued to creep downstairs. Once outside, he closed the front door as softly as he could.

How had Twitten come to be living in Clifton Terrace? Things had all happened quite quickly on the day, a couple of weeks before, that he'd accidentally walked in on a Thursday pay parade in the basement of the police station, and apprehended what it was. Constables were queuing up in silence, stepping forward when their names were called and signing for little sealed packets, which were ripped open at once to reveal amounts of money and printed payslips inside.

Twitten had experienced a mixture of strong feelings, including shock, bewilderment and visceral pain. Could this ritual of remuneration possibly take place *every week*? However, once he had calmed down and established that constables' salaries were indeed issued weekly, and that he had missed six already, and that there was even an additional rent allowance, he had promptly collected around sixty pounds in five-pound notes, and set his mind to finding digs where he could choose his own lights-out time – and a flash of inspiration had brought him up the hill to this attractive white-stuccoed house: to Mrs Thorpe's, formerly known as the best theatrical lodgings in the town.

And it was perfect. It was central, yet slightly removed from the hubbub; the rent was reasonable; and Mrs Thorpe, still traumatised by the fact that her last theatrical guest had been bloodily slaughtered in her front sitting-room, had leaped at the chance of having a representative of law enforcement as a full-time lodger. For it was in this very house, of course, that the Northern playwright Jack Braithwaite had been murdered in June by a professional strong lady using a regimental sword.

The life-or-death struggle in the front sitting-room had caused a terrible mess, with blood on the chandeliers, and so on. But at least it could be cleaned up. The emotional spattering received by Mrs Thorpe herself was a different matter: no amount of scouring with Handy Andy could set it right. In the weeks after the incident, she avoided the murder-room even after its complete redecoration. She stared out of the upstairs windows for hours on end. Eventually, with enormous sadness, she wrote to the managements of all the Brighton theatres, announcing she was closing her doors to her beloved thespian guests.

Several eminent actors sent much-appreciated letters of sympathy, but these were, of course, insincere: everyone in the business was livid at the inconvenience. Many years later, at the end of her life, she found out that her beloved Alec Guinness, whose letter she had framed and hung on the stairs ('I understand completely, my dear lady'), had in fact been extremely cross, and had slagged her off quite viciously in his diary.

This was a miserable and lonely period for poor Mrs Thorpe. She missed her thesps. Frightened to go out, she cancelled hair appointments and stopped going to the cinema. Mrs Browning, the daily help, often found her in the back rooms, checking the window catches. So it was kind and imaginative of Twitten to propose himself as her lodger, because the benefits were mutual. Since his arrival, she'd cheered up sufficiently to spend a whole afternoon in Hanningtons department store, first having her hair permed to a crisp in the salon upstairs, and then choosing three pairs of expensive fancy slippers that made her feel like Marie Antoinette.

On the corner of Dyke Road, Twitten passed the regular milkman, who tipped his cap.

'You're up early, Constable,' said the man, energetically jumping from his high seat, and lifting down a crate of chinking bottles.

'Yes, sir,' said Twitten, politely. 'I don't know how you bally do it every day.'

'Well, the horse does the hard part, bless him.'

As the milkman, whistling, set about delivering to the first house on the terrace, Twitten looked at the cart with its dozens of brightly shining bottles, and its less-than-catchy national marketing slogan, 'You'll Feel A Lot Better If You Drink More Milk'. A banner, draped along the side, advertised the new House of Hanover Milk Bar, which was due to open on the seafront on Monday.

This was a heyday for milk promotion, when you thought about it – what with milk bars springing up everywhere, and young people drinking frothy coffee and pastel-coloured milkshakes instead of the boring old lemonade and fruit drinks. Ever since Brighton's recent Dairy Festival Week, there'd even been a small herd of red-and-white Guernsey cows grazing in the gardens of the Royal Pavilion, as a sort of stunt. According to this banner, the opening of the new milk bar was to be graced by a visit from the good-looking young woman known nationally as the Milk Girl. All this young woman had ever done was pose for newspaper advertisements, and people were expected to flock in their hundreds to see her.

And now, it seemed, people were also being killed with milk bottles. As he walked briskly downhill towards the Clock Tower, Twitten fleetingly considered what milk actually *was*. Setting aside the obvious and alluring Freudian associations with breastfeeding, would you call it an opaque, fatty secretion? It was bovine in origin, obviously. Mammary came into it, too.

He pulled a face. Every single word so far had made his nose wrinkle. But as his celebrated psychologist father had so often told him: it was remarkable how readily the human mind blocked out unpleasantness. If you were to lift a jug of milk at a tea table and ask, 'Now, who takes opaque fatty bovine mammary secretion in theirs?' everyone would definitely say, 'Not me.'

—————

'Well, what about these nasty murders, then, dear?'

Mrs Groynes was already at the station when Twitten arrived, despite the hour. Did this astonishing woman never sleep? And what was she doing here on a Saturday anyway?

Hearing him come in, Mrs Groynes turned casually from locking the door to her built-in stash cupboard, slipping the key into the pocket of her overalls, and giving him a look that said 'our little secret'. He grimaced his pained collusion. It was in this cupboard that Mrs Groynes conveniently stored an armoury of weapons and ammunition, specialist burglary tools, full bank bags, a dozen packs of forty-denier nylons for pulling over one's head during an armed robbery, and enough gelignite to blow up the whole police station and everyone in it.

Twitten knew all this because he had once been locked inside it too – on an occasion neither of them was likely to forget. Now, on this Saturday morning, as he watched Mrs Groynes pocket the key, Twitten experienced his usual vivid mixture of admiration and revulsion: admiration for her sheer bally nerve; revulsion at her blatant villainy and careless storage of explosives. As she had once memorably observed to him, 'What am I like, eh? You don't get many of me for ninepence.'

'Cup of tea, dear?' she asked Twitten now. 'Two sugars?'

She bustled with the teapot and reached for a bottle of Sussex Dairies opaque cow secretion that had been cooling on the windowsill.

'That would be very kind, Mrs G. Then I'll go and see what the forensics chaps have come up with.'

He didn't need to explain himself further. Thanks to her extensive criminal network and her innate capacity for asking the right questions, Mrs G was always up to speed with police investigations. Indeed, she was usually ahead of them.

'And then – well, Mrs G, there are so many people to interview it's hard to know where to begin! The beauty queen's parents are coming in at ten o'clock; then there's the last person to call out Officer Andy, who was apparently an American skater in the Ice Circus with a glamorous imported sports car that *can play LPs*—'

'Really? What, while driving along?'

35

'Yes, apparently.'

'But the needle must jump about, surely?'

'Well, that's what I thought myself, Mrs G: why doesn't it? I mean, the needle on Mrs Thorpe's gramophone jumps if someone slams their front door three houses away. How could it *possibly* work in a car? But apparently it's the latest thing, and everyone's very impressed. Meanwhile, in connection with the death of Mr Carbody, I might have to interview the inspector as he was one of the last people to see Carbody alive – ooh, thank you, that looks lovely.'

Handing him his tea, Mrs Groynes decided to dispense advice. 'Well, make sure you get some bleeding help this time round, dear,' she said, sternly. 'Don't let the sergeant go undercover again and leave you all on your tod. You know what he's like with those undercover notions of his. He's undercover daft!'

This was not a bad point. Sergeant Brunswick was certainly governed by a powerful urge to rub shoulders with villains, especially if it meant disguising himself with a red wig, bushy beard or comical eyepatch. But why? By way of explanation he tended to say, 'I suppose it's the frustrated actor in me, that's all.' But Twitten was sure there was more to it, and would dearly love to probe. Was Brunswick's impulse perhaps rooted in his extremely low opinion of himself? Or was it sexual in origin? He resolved to raise these theories with the sergeant at the earliest opportunity.

In the meantime, he felt bound to agree with Mrs Groynes that Sergeant Brunswick's fondness for nose-putty was nothing but a burden on the department. It would be different if it actually achieved anything, but no criminal had yet been fooled by his disguises; meanwhile Twitten was left to do all the work. On top of which, the sergeant's adventures always ended in pretty much the same sequence of events: '*Take that, you lousy rozzer!*' followed by '*Don't shoot!*' and '*Bang!*' and '*Oh, no!*' as a body (Brunswick's) dropped once more to the ground.

'This is excellent tea,' Twitten said, brightly. And then, for the sake of conversation, he asked, 'Have you ever thought much about *milk*, Mrs G?'

She gave him a steady look, a lit cigarette clamped between her lips. 'No, I bleeding haven't.'

'I've been thinking about what Father would say – milk being a source of motherly nourishment; a staple of life, as it were. Freud's work on infantile sexuality was ground-breaking, as you know.'

Mrs Groynes shot him a warning look. Twitten ought to have grasped by now that when she heard the word Freud, she literally reached for her gun.

'No, really, it's jolly interesting. You see, by linking the oral stage, or *hemitaxia* as it's technically known, so overtly to murder, the perpetrator of these crimes is doing something quite new. Perhaps what we are dealing with here – meta-phorically, of course – is the work of a big unhappy baby exhibiting primordial fury against the parent.'

Mrs Groynes looked at him pityingly. 'Well, I'll tell you one thing for nothing. There's a very good reason people don't usually get killed with milk bottles.'

'Which is?'

'It's bleeding hard work, dear.'

'Oh. So you agree that the choice of weapon is significant?'

'Of course it is.'

'It tells us something?'

'Yes. But assuming this murderer is *not* a big unhappy baby – because I'm sure people would have reported seeing one, aren't you? – *what message are they sending, dear?* That's what you should be asking yourself. Here, do you think it's got something to do with that new milk bar down by the West Pier? After all, there's been all that hoo-hah and hulla-baloo about it, hasn't there?'

'That's true.' In the past two weeks, this new milk bar had been at the centre of a heated controversy. At issue was the fact that it was subsidised by the Milk Marketing Board. Nearby traders in cheese rolls and ice creams were suppos-edly angry to find themselves competing with it. When it had been announced that the milk bar would host the *Brighton Evening Argus* Knickerbocker Glory award ceremony (with Inspector Steine presenting the prize), passions had run so high that someone had thrown a brick through its window.

'But surely killing people with milk bottles would be a disproportionate way of objecting to unfair business practice, Mrs G?'

'Which is why I'm not saying that. I just think this might be a devious mind at work, who wants you to look for connections to that milk bar and all the hoo-hah, hullabaloo, and so on. And while you're busy doing that, well …' She waggled her eyebrows, suggestively.

'Well, what?'

'Perhaps he'll kill again.'

While Twitten absorbed this, she stubbed out her cigarette and lit a new one, sitting down at Brunswick's desk. 'But what do *I* know, dear?' she added. 'Not having a dirty-minded trick-cyclist for a father.'

Twitten put down his teacup. As usual, Mrs Groynes's air of authority in such criminal matters raised another question – a sensitive one for both of them.

'Look, Mrs Groynes,' he said, quietly. 'I have to ask.'

'Ask what, dear?'

She took a drag on the new cigarette, and smiled innocently.

'You know,' he said.

'No.'

'You're not … ?'

'Not what?'

'Did you … ?'

'Did I what?'

'Oh, flipping hedgehogs, Mrs G! You know what I'm trying to ask.'

'No, I don't. And there's no need for that kind of language.'

He accepted the rebuke, but still required an answer.

'I'm asking whether you or your associates are in any way involved in these bally murders!'

She let out a scoffing laugh – but then held up a hand.

'Shhh, dear.'

There was a noise outside in the corridor. Someone was approaching. From the slightly uneven footfall (implying a limp), it was Sergeant Brunswick. The silhouette that appeared behind the frosted glass confirmed it.

'To be continued,' said Mrs Groynes, cheerfully. She got up and took hold of a mop and bucket. But seeing the serious expression on the young man's face, she took pity on him. 'Of course I'm not involved in these stupid milk-bottle murders, dear. Hardly my style, are they? Ooh, is that you, Sergeant?'

And then, just as the door opened, Twitten was sure he saw a cloud pass across her face, as she muttered, 'I've got quite enough to think about right now without that as well.'

Out at Hassocks, the dashingly attractive American ice dancer Buster Bond woke to hear the telephone ringing downstairs

39

in Dale House, and checked his gold-plated travelling alarm clock. It was seven-twenty. The clock was the modern sort that folded up, with luminous numbers and hands, and he'd acquired it in Rome, earlier in the year, from a besotted *contessa*. Women often gave him such items by way of thank-you gifts. His stylish pyjamas, as it happened, had been given to him by the Duchess of Argyll.

'Mr Bond!' a voice called up the stairs. It was the lady of the house, Mrs Lester. 'Are you awake, Mr Bond? I'm afraid it's the police!'

The police? As he sat up in bed, his mind raced. What had he done? Checking his reflection in the mirror (and admiring what he saw), he quickly reconstructed the events of the previous evening. Reassuringly, nothing unpleasant came to mind. First, there was the problem with the Thunderbird; the AA man came and fixed it. Then a breakneck drive at seventy miles an hour into Brighton to the Sports Stadium, attempting to listen to Frank Sinatra's *Songs for Swingin' Lovers* on the record player, but giving up, on account of all the pot-holes on the road making the needle zigzag across the tracks; a sensational show to vast applause; free drinks at a late-night jazz club; praise, praise, praise, praise; illicit drugs; exciting multi-position sex with a pitifully grateful middle-aged woman in the dark back room of the club; maybe additional sex with the woman's younger, horse-faced sister (this, mercifully, a bit hazy); then the drive home drunk and happy; in bed by 3 a.m.! No, he thought, there was no reason for the police to take an interest in any of that.

Being an athlete at the peak of his powers was an asset at times like this.

'Be right with you, Mrs Lester!' he called, and was beside her in the hall in a trice, after virtually flying down the stairs.

She handed him the telephone receiver and retreated to the kitchen to light the range for his morning cup of coffee. Through the green baize door, he heard her conversing in a low voice with her daughter.

'This is Buster Bond,' he said, running a hand through his attractively sleep-tousled hair. 'How can I help you?'

Before Inspector Steine appeared at the station on Saturday morning to find several reporters waiting outside, two important aspects of the case had been swiftly established. First, all three murders had definitely been committed with milk bottles. Second, there was a suggested timeline. Barbara Ashley had been killed at around six o'clock, Officer Andy at about half-past seven, and Cedric Carbody at nine.

Steine pushed through the reporters. 'Not now, not now,' he said, waspishly. The insensitivity of newspapermen was always a shock to him. Didn't they realise people had been *killed*?

Once inside, he immediately bumped into Twitten, who handed him the forensic findings, with a proposed schedule of interviews and site visits.

'Ah, good work, Twitten,' he said. 'Where do we start?'

Twitten was surprised to find Inspector Steine so engaged – surprised but also anxious. What if the inspector actually took charge? Things went so much better for Twitten's investigations if Steine stuck to his broadcasts, ice creams and public appearances.

Yet here he was, studying a report as they made their way upstairs. He stopped on the first landing, and pointed at the second page.

'So these homicides were definitely committed with milk bottles?'

'Yes, sir.'

'Damn.'

'Pardon, sir?'

'It doesn't matter.'

'I know it seems like a not-very-serious murder weapon, sir –'

'You can say that again.'

'– but the victims are dead just the same. And the milk bottles are obviously significant, even if we don't know what that significance is just yet.'

Steine pulled a face. 'Significant' was an annoyingly vague and clever-sounding word he heard far too often from Twitten. He shuffled the papers and frowned at the interview list.

'What's this?' he said, pointing. 'You're intending to interview *me*, Twitten?'

'Well, yes, sir. Of course, sir. In turn, Sergeant Brunswick will interview *me* about what happened at the AA control room – it's quite normal procedure, sir. You were one of the last to see Mr Carbody alive and one of the first to see the body.'

'Just me? What about the others who were there? I suppose you let them swan off back to London?'

'Not at all, sir. They're on the list, too, look, for this morning. Mr Edlin went home to his usual digs in Hove, but I got rooms for the two ladies and the BBC production people. They spent the night at the Metropole.'

Steine stared at him. 'You got them rooms at the *Metropole*?'

'Yes, sir. I know it's expensive, sir–'

'I repeat. The *Metropole*?'

'– but the whole town is booked up, sir, on account of the Bank Holiday. And I just happened to know there'd been some cancellations at the Metropole because when I was doing my rounds last week, I got chatting to the night door-man who said there'd been an unusual block booking for this weekend, made about a month ago, for the whole sixth floor, which had thrown everything into turmoil; he said many regular guests were so upset to be moved to different rooms that they cancelled.'

Steine sighed and shook his head. It was at times like this that he wished he were deaf. And Twitten hadn't finished yet, either.

'Actually, sir,' he continued, 'I wonder if I ought to have inquired further into this booking. It's very suspicious to book a whole floor, and to instruct all hotel staff to keep clear of it! I'm wondering if it's someone extremely famous, such as Princess Grace of Monaco or perhaps even Sooty, sir, the glove-puppet bear-magician from television who is currently taking the world of family entertainment by storm. But anyway, the point is, it meant that when we needed to keep witnesses in Brighton for the night, the Metropole *did* have a couple of spare rooms, and we managed to secure them.'

Steine looked at him. 'Have you finished?'

'Yes, sir. I think so, sir.'

'Thank God.'

Steine huffed as he mentally sifted through what he'd just heard for anything of importance. 'What did you mean by your "rounds"?' he asked at last. 'You said you'd met this hotel doorman acquaintance of yours in the course of your *rounds*.'

Twitten bit his lip. 'Nothing really, sir. I've just been …' He faltered. He was aware that they were having this conver-sation on the stairs, where other officers could see them and might overhear.

'Been what?'

Twitten lowered his voice. 'Out and about, sir. Out and about, cultivating relationships with the everyday folk of Brighton, such as hotel doormen. I'm already on jolly good terms with quite a few shopkeepers, sir, and nightwatchmen and street traders. That's how I happened to be in the AA control office when the news came about poor Officer Andy. I was talking to Mr Hollibon and having a cup of tea.'

'But none of that is your job, Twitten.'

'Isn't it, sir?'

'No. If it were, I would know, because I would have been the one instructing you to do it.'

Twitten felt it was time to defend himself. 'Well, to be honest, sir, I would far rather have been in the office compiling essential criminal records files, but if you recall—'

'For the last time, Twitten, that's a job *for a girl*!'

Steine's raised voice drew an interested look from the desk sergeant downstairs.

'But, sir, it really isn't—'

'You've got to drop this criminal records nonsense, Twitten.'

'But how else can we hope to—'

'Men don't type! It's as simple as that!'

Steine turned on his heel and proceeded up the stairs.

'No, sir,' said Twitten, following. But he couldn't help adding, rebelliously (but under his breath), 'Men don't bally type? Try telling that to Ernest bally Hemingway.'

———

In the sunny breakfast room of the Metropole Hotel, the usually unflappable Gerry Edlin sat down at a corner table in a state of shock.

'Oh, my God,' he said to himself. He was shaking. 'Oh. My. *God*.'

'Are you unwell, sir?' asked a waiter, who was passing through, holding linen napkins wrapped around freshly polished cutlery. Breakfast had not begun, but being imbued with the spirit of service, he was happy to bring a cup of tea to any hotel guest in distress. Once, he had helpfully slapped a hysterical one (it was one of his happiest memories).

Edlin forced a smile. 'No, no,' he said. 'I'll wait for my friends; they stayed here last night. What time does breakfast begin?'

'Half-past seven, sir. Ten minutes.'

'Thank you, I can wait. You're very kind.'

'Excuse my asking, sir, but aren't you that man off the telly? With the magic tricks?'

Never known to disappoint a member of the viewing public, Edlin lightly pinched together finger and thumb and drew a string of coloured scarves out of the sleeve of his jacket. The waiter laughed appreciatively and resumed his work.

Edlin's brain whirred; he was in a state of panic. In the lobby he had spotted a familiar face from London – from the days when he had stupidly dabbled in nightclub ownership. This man had once threatened to break his fingers! He worked for the notorious Terence Chambers! Was Chambers in Brighton? Was he staying here, at the Metropole? Could Chambers's man be here looking for Edlin himself?

'Gerry!' Lady Pru's greeting made him jump. Smoothing her skirt, she sat down beside him.

'Ugh, you look as bad as I feel, darling,' she said, patting his hand. 'Poor Cedric! I couldn't sleep a wink.'

'I know. Nor I.'

'Whatever could the poor man have done to bring this on himself? He was such a pussycat!'

'A sweetie-pie.'

'A teddy bear.'
'A dear.'
'I adored him.'
'So did I.'

———

Out Hassocks way, on the main London-to-Brighton Road, Mr E. E. Hollibon of the AA stood smoking in silence at the minor turn-off where the body of Officer Andy had been found the night before. The police had impounded the Land Rover; all that remained was a leafy country-road junction, an old enamelled signpost with venerable rust spots, and a patch of trampled grass.

What puzzled Mr Hollibon was why Officer Andy had taken this route back into town. Seeing the place for himself, it still made no sense. Having completed the Thunderbird job at Dale House, Andy would surely have headed south again – but this was north-west.

Hollibon inhaled thoughtfully, and suppressed the gigantic bronchial spasm stirring in his chest. It was impossible to take in that Andy had gone. Everyone liked Andy! Hollibon wished he hadn't been so hard on him about the radio-protocol business. Because of course Andy had been right: life *was* too short to keep saying 'Brighton Control' and 'Over', and there *had* been enough of that malarkey during the war. Hollibon wished he'd asked Andy more about himself – about his wartime experiences in the Far East; his talents as a semi-professional musician; his passion for photography; his frequent day-trips to London. But now he never could.

Hollibon finished the cigarette, dropped it and stubbed it out with the toe of his shoe. Time to get back. He was glad he'd made the effort to drive here and see the site. But as he was turning away, something caught his eye. The signpost was wrong. It had been turned. The tiny Sussex village of Cantersfield was two miles down the smaller of the roads, but according to the sign, that was the way to Brighton. Anyone following the sign in that direction would end up at a farm-yard or a village pond.

'Kids!' Hollibon huffed.

But *was* it the work of kids? He put a hand to his brow, pondering the possible scene the night before. Had Officer Andy run into a gang of youths creating a nuisance to the great British motoring public, and told them off? Despite his laid-back approach to radio protocol, Andy took his uniform seriously: he was on the side of the great British motorist in all things. But telling off a bunch of kids for causing a bit of travel mayhem: was that enough to get him killed?

———

By now, Steine and Twitten had reached the top of the stairs – Steine briskly leading the way down the narrow corridor towards the general office shared by Twitten, Brunswick and Mrs Groynes (his own inner sanctum was beyond). They walked and talked in single file.

'I heard what you said about Ernest Hemingway just then, Twitten,' said Steine, over his shoulder. 'But luckily for you, the point you were making was both obscure and uninteresting.'

'Yes, sir.'

'On the other matter, however, I'd like you to curtail your rounds, as you call them. In fact, I want you to stop them at once.'

'Yes, sir. If you say so, sir.' Trotting along behind, Twitten hardly minded complying with this command, when there was so much else to do anyway.

'You should not be cluttering your mind with details of who booked how many rooms at the Metropole. It's not your job to seek out information of such a trivial nature.'

'No, sir.'

'I mean it.'

'Yes, sir. Ooh, but could I just say, sir—'

'I'd rather you didn't.'

'No, but could I just say, sir, I've remembered something. While I was out and about yesterday, I did learn one piece of information of a trivial nature that I think will interest you personally.'

'I very much doubt it, Twitten.'

'No, really, sir. It concerns the Knickerbocker Glory competition that you're judging. Is it right that you'll announce the winner on Monday?'

By now they had reached the door to the office. Steine frowned. He was getting irritated. It seemed that even when you didn't have to look Twitten in the eye, it was still annoying talking to him one-to-one. 'Yes. At this new milk bar,' he said, stiffly. 'I have that honour.'

Steine opened the door.

'Sir. Is it too late for you to withdraw?'

'*Withdraw?*' repeated Steine. With eyes narrowed and an expression of scorn, he turned to face his constable. It was such an accomplished move that any other man might have quailed, but not Twitten. On him, it made no impact whatsoever.

'Yes, sir. I'm sure they'd understand. You could pretend you're too busy with these murders. I mean, not pretend, that's the wrong word. I mean—'

'I shall not withdraw, Twitten. Judging these ice creams is a very important job.'

Twitten managed not to laugh – but only just. 'Gosh. With respect, sir, you surely see that it isn't? I mean, not really. In the scheme of things.'

'Well, that's where you're wrong, Twitten. Visitors to Brighton are presented with Knickerbocker Glories here, Knickerbocker Glories there, each claiming to be the best. How are they to know which *is* the best unless someone high-minded, trustworthy, impartial and famous for his appearances on the BBC takes the time to apply rigorous tests and announce his findings?'

'Yes, but still—'

'Perhaps you think it's easy.' Steine was becoming quite heated. 'Well, before you jump to that conclusion, consider the variables I have to take into account: the quality of the ice cream; the choice of flavours in complementary combination; the ratio of fruit to sauce; the sheer length of spoon, which sometimes, I regret to say, is *simply not up to the job*. I have already tasted every Knickerbocker Glory this town has to offer at least once, Twitten –'

'Gosh, sir.'

'– but over this weekend I intend to taste the front runners again. Then, on Monday, I shall announce the winner, who is likely to be Luigi, of course, because he's very good at everything, but I made a vow to judge this competition with my customary fairness, and *that's what I shall do*.'

Luigi's ice-cream parlour on the seafront was where Steine spent the majority of his time. He had taken his men there on the day of the famous Middle Street Massacre in 1951, when mutually destructive gang warfare had bloodily wiped out forty-five Brighton villains. Steine's unconventional decision to pause and consume a banana split, while a massive gun battle took place a hundred yards away, had been held up, then and since, as a triumph of imaginative modern policing.

'And you dare to ask me to withdraw?'

Twitten stood to attention. 'I'm sorry to speak out of turn, sir. But the word on the street is that it's a poisoned chalice, sir.'

'What is? A Knickerbocker Glory?'

'No, sir. *Judging* Knickerbocker Glories.'

'That's absurd. And what do you mean by *the word on the street*?'

'Well, to be honest, mainly Ventriloquist Vince, sir.'

'The Punch & Judy man with the Greek accent?'

'Yes, sir.'

'The one whose show is so graphically violent it causes hysteria in the mothers and gives the children nosebleeds?'

'That's him, sir.'

'Remind me, why does no one shut him down?'

'It's a mystery, sir. But anyway, Mr Vince told me yesterday that a previous judge of the Knickerbocker Glory contest had – well, he'd lived to regret it.'

Steine scoffed. 'Lived to regret it? Why? Too many glacé cherries for a delicate digestion?'

'Well, no, sir. It was more that when he went home afterwards …'

Twitten faltered.

'Oh, come on, Twitten. What happened to this poor unfortunate ice-cream judge? Did he *feel a bit full*?'

'Well, according to Mr Vince, when he got home, sir, he found that his bally house had been burned to the ground!'

Three

The Royal Pavilion in Brighton might seem an odd venue for a humble barbering contest. Nowadays we think of this overblown Regency extravaganza as a superior heritage attraction: an ornate seaside palace with a passing resemblance to the Taj Mahal, its ersatz minarets and domes outlined, incongruously, against a pale English sky. Why is it in Brighton? Its presence here is easily explained by history: in the late eighteenth century, the Prince Regent enjoyed the seaside; he was a keen Orientalist; he was fiscally irresponsible to the point of madness. And the Pavilion certainly suits Brighton in its sheer ostentation and inauthenticity. Over time, the building has been faithfully restored, with sumptuous replica carpets and gaudy gilding. People pay good money to go in. But when they come out again, they can sometimes be seen rubbing their eyes in wonder at the sheer oppressive tastelessness of what they have just seen inside.

But in 1957, this faithful restoration of the Pavilion was not yet complete. In the century since Queen Victoria had sold her uncle's extravagant beach hut to the local authority, the building had been neither quite one thing nor the other: open to the public, but not a proper museum; a place rented out for conferences, competitions and charity bazaars. It was certainly not sacrosanct, as it is now, and the Pavilion Gardens were not hallowed ground either: plans were often drawn up for boxy modern buildings to be erected in them; and as we already know, dairy cattle from the Channel Islands were sometimes grazed there for obscure publicity purposes.

So holding a barbering contest in the august Music Room on the August Bank Holiday 1957 was hardly sacrilege. But there was something noteworthy about it, nevertheless, and it was this: the mysterious 'Barber of the Year 1957 Ltd' (their only given address a Post Office box number) had booked the entire building for three whole days, despite being advised that this was both costly and unnecessary. A letter from the council had helpfully pointed out the perceived error, offering a rebate, but a letter had come by return from the secretary of Barber of the Year 1957 Ltd – a person signing herself 'Mrs P. Hoagland' – insisting that the initial booking should stand: the other rooms could be used for storage, refreshments, changing facilities, hair sweepings, supervised recovery from all the excitement, and so on.

No council staff need be present, Mrs Hoagland added, save for handing over the keys on the Saturday morning, and receiving them back on Monday night. Mrs Hoagland then casually mentioned that she had been authorised to enclose a hefty non-returnable cash deposit against breakages, at which point all bureaucratic interference from the council abruptly ceased.

But questions abounded, even if no one was asking them. For example, why would someone want to hire the whole of this building, which included the large Banqueting Room (ideal for conferences)? Why would they so blatantly bribe council officials to seal the deal? Who was Mrs Hoagland, and why does her name sound familiar? Was there perhaps any connection between this securing of the Pavilion and the booking – by the same mystery woman – of a whole floor of the Metropole Hotel for the same three days? And was there possibly a connection between these two things and the presence at the Metropole of a man employed by Terence Chambers? Put simply, *was it possible that the rooms at the hotel had been reserved for top villains from all over the country, who were convening in Brighton for a summit meeting to be held in the Pavilion's Banqueting Room on Bank Holiday Monday under cover of a bogus barbering contest?*

The simple answer is yes. Terence Chambers himself had called the summit, and not because he fancied a trip to the seaside. It was rare for him to leave his mum's small terraced house in Stepney, let alone travel to the South Coast. But there was an urgent and serious matter that needed top-level discussion: the issue of brash American mobsters threatening to take control of organised crime in Britain. Two casinos in Mayfair had already changed their allegiance. Chambers had heard rumours of incursions in other cities. Basically, could resources and information be pooled against a common Yankee foe?

All ten of the hardest regional crime bosses would be in attendance – plus, of course, Mrs Groynes, who had organised the whole thing, under an alias. When Constable Twitten had discovered her on this Saturday morning locking her stash cupboard, he had assumed she was tidying away red-hot jewellery or still-warm ballistic weapons. In fact, she had been hiding the seating plan she had worked on overnight. (It made her oddly happy to sign herself 'Mrs P. Hoagland', incidentally, even though circumstances had recently obliged her to shoot dead Captain Philip Hoagland, the only man she had ever bleeding loved.)

Mrs Groynes had been typically thorough in the arrangements for Monday's conference. It had involved a lot of work – not least setting up the fake organisation from whom all the genuine barbers applying to compete had received their rejection letters. Press photographers, and even newsreel cameras, would be allowed entry for a twenty-minute period to record what appeared to be a jolly, open contest, featuring in-the-know barbers from elsewhere; the press would also witness the crowning of Crouch End Billy Scissors (Chambers's brother-in-law) at the end. 'Who, *me*?' Billy Scissors would respond in mock surprise on being named.

Models for the haircuts would be insiders, too, while the security would be provided by her own trusted crew, including Birthmark Potter, Stanley-Knife Stanley and Barrow-Boy Cecil. It was a masterpiece of planning. As indeed it needed to be.

The one thing Mrs Groynes had failed to take into account was the potential for outraged honour in the local barbers. She perhaps assumed that rejected applicants would have a grown-up sense of proportion about it – but in this assumption she was wrong. As Sergeant Brunswick had remarked to Barbara Ashley, people really did take competitions too seriously. Twice in a week Rodolfo had shut the shop early and gone upstairs to his lonely flat to sit in silence. Meanwhile his brooding son Carlo, instead of helping him through his disappointment by diverting his attention to happier subjects, was actively looking for someone to blame. Carlo was an intemperate boy much influenced by *zeitgeist* movies from America concerning 1950s disaffected youth, and he welcomed any legitimate grudge. He sported an immaculate

James Dean quiff, wore stiff, high-waisted denim jeans, and his shirtsleeves were rolled up to the bicep.

'These so-called Barber of the Year people, Papa, who do they think they are?' he demanded hotly, studying the letter for the umpteenth time as he and his father sat over their pasta-and-meatballs one evening. 'How dare they do this to you? I'd like to go there and—'

'I know, I know,' said Rodolfo, shaking his head. 'So would I, Carlo. But look, no proper address. Just a Post Office box number.'

'And who is this Mrs P. Hoagland, telling you you're not good enough?'

'Again, I don't—'

'I hate her, Papa! I want to punch her stupid face!'

'Carlo, no.'

'I want to make her beg for mercy. It makes me so angry! All women are stupid, but this one – this *Mrs Hoagland* – she's the worst!'

Rodolfo had noted his son's growing misogynistic leanings over the years, but dismissed them as cause for concern – partly because his son was young, but mainly because they chimed pretty well with his own attitudes and everyone else's.

'I don't know about that, Carlo, although the idea of any woman taking decisions like this – yes, OK, it makes me sick to my stomach. But you have to calm down, because *there's nothing we can do*. When I talked about the injustice of it with Sergeant Brunswick, you know what he did? He laughed. He said competitions are *just a bit of fun*.'

Carlo said nothing. He pushed away his plate of food and brooded with the full force of his personality.

'Well, I say it smells, and I'm going to do something.'

'We don't know who they are, Carlo. And more to the point, we don't know *where* they are, either.'

'Yes, but we know where they are *going to be*, Papa. They'll be at the Royal Pavilion on Monday, and so will I.'

Rodolfo shook his head. 'Carlo, no. I forbid it.'

'You can't stop me, Papa. I'm seventeen. And those *bastardi* at Barber of the Year 1957 Ltd will find they have Carlo Innocenti to answer to!'

Saturday morning saw a certain amount of progress in the murder investigations, except in two respects. No one interviewed by Brunswick and Twitten could shed light on either a) the use of milk bottles as weapons, or b) anything connecting the three victims to each other.

Cedric Carbody's hifalutin' showbiz friends had insisted on jumping the queue and coming straight to the police station to give their evidence, in order to catch an early train back to the capital. But they had not been helpful, despite the unprecedented fancy tea and biscuits provided in the interview room. Lady Prudence seemed more concerned about Gerry Edlin's mood this morning, which was, apparently, unusually taciturn. Gloria Powell simply pursed her lips and refused to make eye contact.

But the sad truth was, they seemed to have little of value to say. Despite working with Carbody every Friday night on *What's Your Game?* for four years, they seemed to know – as Mrs Groynes might put it – sweet Fanny Adams about him, beyond what was common knowledge: his trademark sense of 'mischief', his popular headmistress broadcasts, and his far-from-secret sexual proclivities.

'Yes, but did he ever show any particular interest in *milk*?' Twitten asked.

A trio of stony, disdainful expressions met this question. Brunswick thought he'd never met more hoity-toity people in his life. They had even disdained the offer of tea. 'Could you answer the constable's question, please?' he said.

Grudgingly, Edlin relented. 'No, he never showed any interest whatsoever in milk, Sergeant,' he said, then raised an eyebrow. 'Now, *cognac* ...'

This made the ladies titter appreciatively. Brunswick, who was usually a sucker for theatrical types, was unimpressed. After all, this was a murder investigation, not a flaming panel game. He picked up a malted-milk biscuit from the plate and munched it crossly.

'I'm afraid we do need to ask these questions,' said Twitten, looking up from his notebook. 'Three people have been murdered, you see, so the stakes are abnormally high. And although you might *think* you can't help, it's been scientifically proved that in police interviews people who think they know nothing often provide invaluable clues. In my detective training we were taught that *people are generally wrong about not knowing anything*. The acronym is PAGWANKA.'

Brunswick nearly choked on his biscuit. 'Is that right, son?' he said.

'Yes, sir.' Twitten shrugged. 'Or WANKA for short.' In his own mind, Wrong About Not Knowing Anything was one of the top ten interview principles he'd learned at Hendon. 'Although I do recall they instructed us not to share this information too widely.'

'I'm not surprised.'

Looking at the stunned expressions on the faces of his interviewees, Twitten frowned, took a deep breath, and moved on. 'So,' he said, 'may I ask whether Mr Carbody could possibly have had any connection to the new House of Hanover Milk Bar on the seafront? Or the Milk Marketing

Board? Or the Dairy Maid Miss contests? Might he have met the young woman commonly known as the Milk Girl?'

'Look, despite the time-honoured principle of PAG—' With perfect comic timing, Edlin corrected himself. 'I mean, despite the thing that *you just said*, we really don't know anything like that about poor Cedric.' He waved an arm at the ladies, to include them. 'We met mostly "on the air", if you know what I mean.' Edlin seemed to be acting as spokesman, which was just as well. Lady Pru kept reaching into her leather glove to check her train ticket, and the beauteous Gloria Powell glanced down into her crocodile handbag at intervals, at an illicitly procured copy of Vladimir Nabokov's *Lolita*, which she was extremely keen to get back to.

'Although,' added Edlin, thoughtfully, 'the Dairy Maid contests might be worth taking a look at.'

'Ah-ha!' said Twitten.

'I do know Cedric used to judge beauty contests, because we did a few together. But he stopped a year or so ago. I wouldn't know if they were the Dairy ones. I suppose they might have been.'

Brunswick took over. 'Did the name Barbara Ashley ever come up?' he asked, hopefully.

'No,' said Edlin, shrugging. 'I'm afraid not. I'm pretty sure he didn't know anyone called Barbara.'

Lady Pru sighed with impatience.

'Or Officer Andrew Inman of the Automobile Association?' said Twitten.

Lady Pru huffed and rolled her eyes. 'Of course he didn't know a man from the Automobile Association! For heaven's sake, Cedric was a bosom friend of Noël Coward! He holidayed each summer in America with the Lunts!'

'Pru, that isn't helpful, my darling,' said Edlin.

'Well, really! As if Cedric Carbody rubbed shoulders with any of these – these common people!'

Brunswick was inclined to let them go, the principle of PAGWANKA notwithstanding. It was clear they knew nothing about the milk bottles. The list of people to interview was long. But Twitten had one last question.

'Do you mind, sir?' he asked.

Brunswick nodded. 'Go ahead, son.'

'Well, Lady Prudence, Mr Edlin, Miss Powell, I appreciate that you're all in a terrific hurry to leave,' Twitten said, pleasantly, 'and you've helped me realise that show-business people are bally awful as witnesses, being by nature shallow and self-centred, which I shall certainly remember to take into account in future.'

Brunswick, impressed by Twitten's astonishing candour, cast him a supportive glance.

'But there is one more thing I'd like to ask. The inspector told me this morning that on his *What's Your Game?* debut last night, Mr Carbody deliberately tripped him up, quite unkindly, with the intention of humiliating him.'

'Really?' said Edlin, suddenly interested.

'I was very touched that the inspector shared this sensitive anecdote, but on the other hand I suppose he had no other insights into Mr Carbody, having only just met him.'

'Yes, but what did Cedric *do*?' Edlin grinned. 'How did I miss it? Oh, good old Cedric!'

'Look, this isn't funny, sir,' warned Twitten.

'Oh, I bet it is,' piped up Gloria. This was the first time she had spoken.

'What happened, then, Twitten?' asked Brunswick.

'Well, it seems that Mr Carbody, spotting that the inspector was nervous as well as unclear about the rules of the game, generously supplied him with a question to ask in the first round.'

'Nice of him,' said Brunswick.

'Yes, but, you see, it meant that the inspector focused entirely on remembering that question, and therefore didn't prepare anything else to ask.'

'So?' said Brunswick, puzzled.

Smiles of happy anticipation broke out on all the faces of the *What's Your Game?* panellists. They liked where this was going.

'But then, you see, just before it was the inspector's turn to speak—'

'Oh, Cedric, you *cad*!' laughed Gloria, interrupting. 'You didn't?'

'Yes, he bally well did!'

'What?' said Brunswick, mystified.

'He stole it from him, sir! He asked the exact same question he'd given to the inspector!'

'Brilliant!' shouted Edlin, as they all burst into laughter.

'Genius!' said Lady Pru.

'Cedric, you utter bastard!' chuckled Gloria.

Twitten shook his head. 'Well, I'm glad you're all enjoying it so much, but from the inspector's point of view it was very, very mean!'

'I'm shocked by that,' said Brunswick. 'Really shocked.'

'So was I,' said Twitten, pausing to let the others simmer down. 'Look, I didn't tell you this to entertain you. The inspector thought this story wasn't of any use to us, and when I said I thought, on the contrary, it was probably quite significant, I'm afraid he just ticked me off again for using the word "significant", because he regards it as annoying as well as vague and a bit clever-sounding.'

'If it helps,' said Brunswick, 'I think so too.'

'Thank you, sir. Perhaps we could come back to that. But I think this anecdote tells us something important about Cedric Carbody. I can tell from your reaction that you might not be the right people to ask, but what I want to know is: was Mr Carbody a cruel man? Might he have made enemies by *being mean*?'

They seemed confused by the question. Edlin in particular didn't know what to say. Was Cedric 'mean'? Of course he was. He was vicious! He said vile, unforgivable things, which brought the house down! How else did he get to be the Duke and Duchess of Windsor's favourite house guest? But what could this possibly have to do with his being killed?

At last, Lady Pru spoke up. 'Look, Cedric was *brilliant*. And he wasn't "mean", Constable. What a silly, schoolboy word! No, Cedric was *crushing*. And he would use *anything* as material for a joke. The way he stole even one's most private confidences was shameless. Nothing was sacred to Cedric!'

The others laughed.

'But I suppose it's possible,' Lady Pru went on, more seriously, 'that he didn't always judge very well whether people could take it.'

'Ah-ha!' said Twitten, again.

'So, yes,' her ladyship continued, 'there probably were people – people who, and I emphasise this, *did not matter one iota in this world* – who did bear him a smidgen of ill will.'

Everyone was impressed. Lady Pru had performed quite a mental leap to consider the 'crushing' Cedric from the point of view of the unimportant crushed.

'Did he ever receive threatening letters?' Twitten asked.

Lady Pru looked thoughtful, as if she wasn't sure, so Edlin answered instead. 'Do you know, I think he did.'

'Bingo,' said Brunswick.

'And I've just remembered something – the reason he stopped judging contests. It was his agent.'

'Do you know the name of the agent?'

'Tony,' piped up Gloria. 'Same as me. Tony Sayle. Dean Street.'

Twitten made a note.

'Yes, it was Tony who stopped him,' Edlin went on. 'And when Tony Sayle puts his foot down, believe me, that's it. Cedric really missed travelling all over the country every weekend, judging dogs, and flower shows, and – well, anything. Children's paintings; short stories; best hat at Doncaster. He could be so *cutting* about anything at all. He particularly enjoyed judging vegetables …'

The others laughed.

'Look, I do these contests myself, and they're joyous. Children in talent shows, singing "Sally in Our Alley" horribly off-key, and doing Highland dancing but tripping over the swords and cutting their toes. It's money for jam. The prize goes to someone, youngsters burst into tears, everyone's happy. But I think with Cedric there were complaints …' Edlin hesitated, trying to remember.

'Complaints?' said Twitten, writing it down. 'What was the nature of these complaints?'

'I'm not sure. Do you remember, Pru?' asked Edlin.

'No,' said Lady Pru. 'Not the details. I just remember poor Cedric was very hurt. I can hear him now, saying, "I don't see what all the fuss is about. It was just a bit of fun!"'

She looked sad and angry (and vaguely bereaved) for the first time.

Gloria Powell pulled a face and got up. 'May we leave now?'

Twitten deferred to Brunswick, who made the decision and stood up likewise. 'Yes, you may, and thank you for your time. But make sure you leave an address and telephone number in case we need to speak to you again.'

They readied themselves to go.

'And between ourselves,' Brunswick added in a low tone, 'if you happened to hear any surprising police training acronyms by accident today, we'd appreciate it if you'd keep them to yourselves.'

Brunswick led the way out, while Twitten looked down at his notes. But when he looked up, he realised that the interview wasn't completely over.

Having held the door for the ladies to exit, Gerry Edlin had lingered behind. 'So, Constable Twitten,' he said, with affected nonchalance, 'you don't think Cedric's murder could have been *a professional hit*, do you?'

'No, Mr Edlin,' said Twitten, surprised. 'Not with a milk bottle. What makes you ask?'

Edlin laughed. 'Nothing at all, Constable,' he said. 'No, nothing at all.' But he hesitated. Part of him dearly wanted to report the London thug he'd seen at the Metropole Hotel.

'Are you all right, sir? Lady Prudence said she thought you were a bit preoccupied this morning, as if you'd seen a ghost. That's what she said, I think. I made a note somewhere.' Twitten checked through his papers. 'Yes, here we are: *seen a ghost*. She said you'd been odd since she met you for breakfast.'

'No, I'm tickety-boo, thank you. I suppose it's just beginning to sink in, that's all – you know, that poor, poor Cedric has gone.' Edlin shrugged. 'And I suppose, to be honest, well …'

Twitten waited.

'Well, I suppose we might have been a bit blind to his – well, his meanness, as you put it.'

Twitten nodded. He wanted to approve of Gerry Edlin, but something prevented it. With his open smile and perfect manners, the man was just too good at being charming.

'Ooh, and look, old boy,' Edlin said. 'Between you and me, don't forget to talk to young Susan Turner. She's the assistant on *What's Your Game?* She was always wary around Cedric, I noticed.'

'She didn't like him, you mean?'

'That's right.'

'But you don't think she killed him?'

'Oh, God, no. Although she did deliver the message that there was someone outside at the stage door, and she also found the body afterwards, of course. But no, not in a million years. The main thing is, she dealt with all the correspondence, and it was her idea to invite a policeman on to the show last night, too. I just wonder if she had an inkling of what was going to happen.'

He left, shutting the door behind him. Twitten, alone, looked with satisfaction at his notes. His excellent police training had been vindicated yet again.

'WANKA!' he said, triumphantly, to himself.

———

At the Metropole, villains were arriving thick and fast. Any schoolboy equipped for the holidays with a copy of *I-Spy Criminal Underworld Vehicles* would have had a field day, getting extra points for spotting suspicious tinted glass; bullet-proof windscreens; telltale holes in the doors; extra-large boots for transporting trussed-up members of rival gangs.

You might think that such an unusual influx of hoodlums would be picked up by the press, but no. For one thing, some of the villains had the good sense to enter the hotel by the back entrance; for another, the local photographer assigned to the Metropole this morning by the *Evening Argus* was cleverly intercepted en route by a nice-looking child in shorts.

'Mister! Over here!' shouted the boy, waving a copy of the *Beano* to get his attention.

The *Argus* man was on his usual route through the Lanes, walking at a smart pace on account of being late, hanging on to his hat. This tow-headed street urchin looked familiar (it was in fact Shorty, comic-book enthusiast and dependable runner of errands, in the permanent employ of Mrs Groynes). Even so, he did not stop walking.

'Mister, wait, I got something for ya,' said Shorty, running alongside to keep up, and grabbing the hem of the photographer's jacket. 'Wait, mister, you'll want to hear this.' The man looked down into Shorty's upturned oh-so-innocent face, but kept walking. He doubted he wanted to hear anything this little scamp could tell him. 'Look, mister,' said Shorty, a bit out of breath. 'It's only Diana flipping Dors!'

This information brought the walk to a halt. 'Diana Dors? Where?'

'She's here!'

'Where?'

'Here.'

The photographer narrowed his eyes. '*Diana Dors?*'

'Yes, Diana Dors. Blimey, mister, how many more times?'

'You seen her yourself? Listen, you'd better not be spinning one.'

'No, but the word is she's up Saltdean! At *Butlin's*!'

The Butlin's holiday camp was a tidy way out of Brighton, along the coast. But the lie was clever: recently the successful camp had been in the practice of importing celebrities at short notice, with the local press being alerted only at the last minute, which left the picture desks fuming.

'*Butlin's*?' The *Argus* man narrowed his eyes. He was weighing it up. On the one hand, Saltdean was a long way off; on the other, it was donkeys' years since he'd had anything on the front page. 'Diana Dors, you sure?'

'Worth a couple of bob, ain't it?' urged Shorty, with his hand out. 'Look, mister, they only asked her to bring her fur bikini!'

'The one she wore on the Grand Canal?'

Shorty wasn't sure. 'Is that in Venice?'

'Yes.'

'That's the one, then.'

'Oh, fuck me,' muttered the photographer, removing his hat and rubbing his brow. What to do? It sounded like cobblers, but could he take that risk? If he deliberately passed up a shot of Diana Dors in a fur bikini on a Bank Holiday weekend, he'd never live it down.

'What do you say, mister?' said the boy, still with his hand out.

The photographer dug into a pocket and tossed the boy a sixpence, then set off at speed in an easterly direction.

Having been woken early, Buster Bond decided to freshen up and head into town. There was a new jump he wanted to practise on the ice, and early on a Saturday morning was a perfect time to do it – before the place was packed with noisy clowns, and hungover orchestra members, not to mention all the trapeze artists and acrobats and performing poodles. God, he hated those dogs. They couldn't even skate! They pooped on the ice! And yet, night after night, show after show, they got the loudest cheer.

Stage Door Ernie let him in, wheezily remarking on how early it was. Bond explained that a brace of policemen would be visiting him at about midday, and Ernie, coughing, made a note. It was unclear whether Ernie ever went home, or actually lived in his little cubbyhole. Interestingly, his twin brother Albert was employed at the nearby Hippodrome, doing the same job, with the same respiratory problems. And since the brothers were almost identical to look at, and were equally ancient and deaf, visiting stars who appeared at both venues were starting to believe that Stage Door Albert and Stage Door Ernie were in fact the same man, collecting two salaries and communicating between the theatres by means of a private tunnel.

The Sports Stadium's ice rink was not the most beautiful arena Bond had ever played, but it was impressive. The vast, deep building – flat-fronted and monolithic – dominated the southern end of West Street, and the auditorium seated 2,000 people.

Originally designed in the 1930s as a sea-water swimming pool, it had been converted to an ice rink once the owners reluctantly accepted a disappointing fact: that most people who wanted to swim in sea-water at the seaside simply went down to the beach and *swam in the sea*.

But the decision to convert it to ice had been inspired. Twenty years later, the 'S.S. Brighton' was not just the busiest venue in Brighton, but the biggest attraction on the whole South Coast. In the winter months, ice hockey drew thousands of local fans; and all year there were spectacular ice shows, with lavish costumes and full orchestras. The current circus featured a novelty poodle act, glamorous trapeze artists and an internationally famous family of Italian clowns, not to mention a daily exhibition of superlative skills by one of the finest skaters in the world.

As Buster Bond slid out on to the perfect, gleaming, unsullied ice this Saturday morning, he felt he was king of the world. He glided to the centre spot of the vast arena, and stopped there: erect, poised, breathing the cool air into his lungs, listening to the pristine silence. In this moment, he felt pristine himself – which was quite a feat, considering the murky sexual shenanigans of the night before.

'Hello, *Brighton!*' he hallooed to the empty seats.

'Hello, Buster,' replied a familiar voice from the darkness.

He spun around in alarm.

'No!' he said. Instinctively, he held up his hands. 'Let me explain!'

Then there was the sound of a gun being cocked and a bullet being fired, and Buster Bond collapsed on the ice.

———

The interviews at the station having thankfully picked up pace a bit, by late morning Brunswick and Twitten were able to report a few findings to Inspector Steine. Their next scheduled interview had been arranged at the Sports Stadium, but they had a few minutes before they needed to leave.

'Miss Turner was the most helpful, sir,' said Twitten. 'Fortunately, she kept a lot of the letters listeners sent to Mr Carbody, so there's a good chance we'll find a lead there. She's gone back to Broadcasting House and has offered to telephone once she's located them.'

'Did she explain why she deliberately placed me in such a hateful position last night?'

'I think she genuinely thought you would enjoy it, sir.'

'Pah.'

'And she insisted that you were very entertaining. The producer is already considering you as a permanent replacement for Mr Carbody. It seems he liked your particular quality of "deadpan", sir, especially when you deduced people's occupation just by looking at them, and threatened to arrest them if they didn't cooperate with your inquiries.'

Steine considered this. The notion of joining this tawdry comedy show was preposterous, and yet, deep inside, a little part of him brightened at the prospect.

'As you know, I don't like to speak out of turn, sir,' said Twitten, in a confidential tone, 'but the sergeant and I agreed that the other panellists were vile.'

Steine beamed. 'They were, weren't they?' He looked down at his list, which was now decorated with a few ticks. 'So, Brunswick, what about the others? What about the girl's parents? You've seen them?'

'Well, sir,' said Brunswick, 'Mr and Mrs Ashley are convinced her death is related to the rigging of beauty contests, about which Miss Ashley had very strong feelings.'

'Very strong,' confirmed Twitten. 'I would go so far as to call it an *idée fixe*, sir.'

'Would you indeed?' said Steine. He waved at Brunswick to go on.

'Well, they were pretty fixed on it themselves, sir. When we asked them about anything else, they were unhelpful, but of course they are upset. Fortunately they gave us the names of some friends, including an old boyfriend of Miss Ashley's who is a skater in the Ice Circus, which is a nice coincidence, as we are going there shortly to talk to Buster Bond, the star of the show and the last person to see Officer Andy alive.'

69

'Mr Bond owns a Thunderbird, sir,' Twitten piped up, 'which is apparently a highly distinctive vehicle from America, which doubles as a gramophone.'

'I saw that Thunderbird last night!' exclaimed Brunswick.

'Did you, sir? Golly. And you recognised it?'

'Of course I did. You don't see one of those every day, son. It drew up outside the Sports Stadium at about twenty-past seven. When I was waiting for Barbara Ashley. That must have been him.'

Steine held up a hand to stop the flow of conversation. Glad as he was to know that investigations were ongoing, and that Brunswick could recognise American sports cars, there was something essential missing from his desk.

'Does either of you know how to make a cup of tea?' he asked, at last.

The others exchanged glances.

'No, sir,' said Twitten.

'Afraid not, sir,' admitted Brunswick.

'And Mrs Groynes isn't ... ?'

'She was here earlier,' said Twitten, 'but it's the weekend. And she intimated she had a very busy day ahead. Friends visiting, she said.'

Steine considered this surprising information. 'Mrs Groynes has *friends*?' he said.

'Yes, sir,' said Twitten, carefully. 'Hard to imagine, isn't it, sir? Mrs Groynes having a life *outside of being a charlady*?'

Steine shuffled some papers on his desk. This was a dangerous moment, as all persons present were aware. But he was in no mood today to discuss Twitten's irritating delusions concerning Mrs Groynes.

'Impossible, I'd say,' he pronounced, with an air of finality. He looked up. 'So, what else? Carry on with your report. Anything on that poor AA man, Twitten?'

'Not really, sir, to be honest.' Twitten raised his notebook and flipped a couple of pages. 'We've had much less luck with him so far. Mr Hollibon at the AA control room gave us an address for Officer Andy's sister in Hove, which is where Officer Andy lived, and also told us a curious thing about a signpost on the London road near to where Officer Andy's body was found, which had been *turned around*.'

'How odd.'

'Yes, sir. Of course, this detail might be unrelated, but it also might be—' Abruptly Twitten stopped talking. He'd been about to say 'significant'.

'It might be *what*, Twitten?'

'Well, you know, sir. It might be …' He tilted his head to one side, as he searched his mental thesaurus. 'Ooh, I know. It might be bally *germane*, sir.'

This was enough for Steine. He raised his hand again and looked out of the window, as if in thought. It was something he often did. It was, if you like, his trademark move. When they made a film about the Middle Street Massacre, the actor playing Inspector Steine (the great John Gregson) had done it too – very brilliantly. In close-up, you felt you could see the cogs whirring in his mind, as mighty deductions were made and mighty plans were hatched. When Inspector Steine sat unmoving like this, the only thing you could do was wait.

Finally, he spoke. 'Look, going back a bit, I don't understand what you said about beauty contests being rigged.'

'Really, sir?' said Brunswick. 'Why?'

'Because it simply doesn't happen. I've been a judge myself and the most beautiful girl always wins, just as the best Knickerbocker Glory will win on Monday. That contest last week had a stunning winner – you saw her yourself,

Brunswick. Well-defined eyebrows, hourglass figure, creamy skin. Knocked your girl into a cocked hat.'

Brunswick looked pained at this gratuitous slur, but said nothing.

'I think the point is, sir,' said Twitten, 'that such a beautiful woman should not have been allowed to enter.'

Steine huffed with impatience. 'That makes no sense, Twitten. Of course she should be allowed. It was a beauty contest! And she was a local girl, I remember that.'

'But even if the winner *was* a local girl,' said Brunswick, 'Miss Ashley's point was that she was a professional model, while the other girls – like herself – had normal nine-to-five jobs, or were at school or secretarial college, and didn't get free make-up and training and expensive costumes.'

'All right. But are you suggesting that Miss Ashley was actually put to death for saying such things?'

'I agree it's far-fetched, sir,' said Twitten. 'But at least with the Dairy Maid contests there's some kind of link to milk bottles. Possibly the thing all the victims have in common is these never-ending bally beauty contests sponsored by milk marketing. I looked in the paper, sir, and there are five milky beauty contests being held this weekend, one of them for girls under nine! Evidently Mr Carbody used to judge them until a year ago, when he was obliged to stop. People said he was too harsh in his comments.'

'I bet he was, that horrible man,' said Steine, shuddering at the mention of Cedric Carbody's name. He turned to Brunswick. 'Did Twitten tell you what Carbody did to me last night?'

'Yes, sir.'

'He tried to sabotage me on the wireless! What had I ever done to him?'

'Perhaps he hated policemen in general, sir,' said Brunswick. 'It's not unknown.'

'That's very true, Brunswick. And yet all we do, day after day, is work our fingers to the bone, wearing out shoe leather, enforcing the law for their protection! Which reminds me, Brunswick.'

'Yes, sir?'

'I absolutely forbid you to go undercover in this case.'

'Right, sir. To be fair, though, sir, I don't think there are any organised villains involved, so—'

'Yes, yes, I understand that. But I can hear you now, Brunswick! "Permission to join the Ice Circus, sir"; "Permission to pose as a kindly Automobile Association patrolman"; "Permission to infiltrate the beauty contest business posing as a shorthand-typist from Crawley who loves animals and dreams of becoming an actress". I just won't have it! You and Twitten will work jointly on this. You will ask questions, you will walk about, and you will solve these murders *like police-men*. Understood?'

'Yes, sir. Understood, sir.'

'And Brunswick.'

'Yes, sir?'

'For goodness' sake, don't start talking about organised villains again. If I've said it once, I've said it a thousand times: there are no organised villains in this town. The Middle Street Massacre wiped them out!'

Four

Nineteen-year-old Pandora Holden had been the Milk Girl for just eight months when she was dispatched by train to Brighton for the August Bank Holiday, but she was already convinced she'd made a questionable life choice. Being the Milk Girl was not as nourishing a job as the name might suggest, and she often felt lonely, despite being accompanied everywhere by the doughty Mr Henderson from Milk Promotion HQ.

'Remember you're the Milk Girl, Miss Holden,' he would exhort her, brightly. 'And milk is sunny and healthy and packed with vitamins!'

'I always do remember, Mr Henderson,' she would reply in a correspondingly positive tone. But though there was a plucky smile on her lips, there was sometimes a lost, faraway look in her fine grey eyes that didn't say 'packed with vita-mins' at all.

As it happens, Mr Henderson had cause for discontent on his own account. When he had chosen milk marketing as a career, he had hardly expected the knocks and disappoint-ments it would deal him. Recently he had learned that the slogan he had himself written – 'You'll Feel A Lot Better

If You Drink More Milk' (elegantly worded; quite musical; based on observable fact) – was about to be replaced. Very shortly, on posters, on milk-carts and in doctors' waiting rooms, people would find the crudely imperative 'DRINKA PINTA MILKA DAY' – and if there was an uglier set of words, he'd never met them. Those four thumping beats! The mere word 'DRINKA'! On his journeys with Pandora, when he was quietly pretending to read *The Times*, he was actually asking himself, over and over, how 'DRINKA PINTA MILKA DAY' could possibly be an improvement on 'You'll Feel A Lot Better If You Drink More Milk'. How could the public be expected to remember a slogan made up of such tuneless, invented words?

Mr Henderson therefore had his own good reasons for disgruntlement, and it irked him that Pandora – with her youth, beauty and sensational overnight celebrity – should be the one with the sulky face. As he sat across from her on the Brighton express on the Saturday morning before the August Bank Holiday – both of them wordlessly watching picturesque Sussex downland flash past the window – it was with a twinge of deep exasperation that he noticed her perfect poster-girl face settling once again into a frown.

From Pandora's point of view, however, the dissatisfaction was more than justified. How had it happened? How was being the Milk Girl even a *job*? Would the name stick to her all her life? This time last year, she'd been a happy school-girl at home in North Norfolk, with no connection to dairy products of any kind. On weekdays she had studied towards her Oxbridge Entrance; on Saturdays she'd played netball in a county league (goal shooter); and on Sundays she'd painted dark Expressionist landscapes in oils, with flashes of orange on purple and black, as a means of letting off steam.

Looking back on it now, what an enviable and promising life it had been – with Lady Margaret Hall beckoning, her bedroom smelling so innocently of library books, turpentine and plimsoll whitener, and her parents' moody Juliette Gréco LP revolving, with crackles, on the portable record player.

Yes, Pandora Holden, the only child of two enthusiastic Cambridge academics, was handsome, clever and a little bit spoiled – and she was also (obviously) a devotee of Jane Austen's *Emma*, with whose principal character she had so much in common. Unlike Austen's heroine, she was brilliant at making an adroitly propelled netball drop vertically through an elevated hoop, and her dark hair had been cropped short to her shapely head, giving her an air of continental chic; unlike Emma, too, she had already, in her young life, experienced the exquisite pain of unrequited love. But it would still be accurate to say that, up to this point, there had been very little to distress or vex her.

And now she was the Milk Girl – famous all over the country, but not for any personal achievement, just through the power of advertising, and to Mr Henderson's profound annoyance, frown lines were beginning to take up permanent residence on her universally celebrated face.

'What's wrong with being famous, Miss Holden?' he would ask. 'What's wrong with everyone loving you?'

If only the milk-marketing people had found a girl less precociously intellectual for the job. But Pandora had studied *Doctor Faustus* at school, and she worried that by selling her face, she had sold her soul. After all, how would you describe Pandora Holden now? Not as a netballing genius; not as a proto-beatnik; not even as a *gamine* with a dark romantic history. No, ever since she'd agreed to pose for a few harmless photographs to promote the virtues of milk, that real Pandora had been disappearing behind a big smiling face – the face that launched a thousand milk-carts.

'It's the Milk Girl!' people literally yelled with excitement sometimes, when she was spotted buying a magazine at a station bookstall, or trying on shoes in Regent Street. Sometimes small crowds would gather; at Liverpool Lime Street once, there had been a dangerous stampede. Externally, she dealt with all this beautifully – she was a polite girl with a *very* sunny smile – but inside, she was increasingly troubled by many questions, some of them deep and existential. And when she reached for a word to describe her unusual predicament, it simply didn't exist.

'Miss Holden, we're here,' said Mr Henderson.

Their express was drawing into Brighton. Pandora hadn't noticed. Other passengers were flinging open the doors and leaping out while the train was still in motion, then streaming off towards the ticket barrier, as if in a race to the sea. Henderson had already put on his jacket and hat, and reached down their suitcases from the overhead racks. He was not only her constant travelling companion; he was in charge of logistics, and custodian of the typed itinerary. '"Eleven-fifteen, welcome from Mayor of Brighton on concourse",' he read aloud, and consulted his watch. 'It's ten minutes past. We've only just made it. Are you ready?'

Pandora smiled up at him. 'How do I look?'

'Better now,' he admitted. Then, seeing her face fall, he rushed to explain. 'You looked a bit sad again, miss, that's all; a bit thoughtful.'

'Sorry.'

'You're a very lovely young lady, miss.'

'I know, Hendy.'

'Beautiful.'

'I know.'

'Frowning could result in permanent lines, and we wouldn't want that.'

'You're right.'

She stood up and smoothed her dress. She had given up discussing with Mr Henderson the metaphysical draw-backs of being the Milk Girl. There was no point. However articulate she was, she always hit the same brick wall. From Mr Henderson's point of view, you see, she wasn't a clever young person expressing legitimate philosophical doubt; she was just a needy female fishing for compliments.

'How many?' she asked, briskly.

Now that the train was stationary, Henderson opened the door and jumped down, holding his briefcase. He was pretty fit; in his early thirties, but balding, which made him look older. Looking up the platform, he could see a crowd of people in holiday clothes, the glint of brass instruments, and a hand-painted banner with 'Brighton Welcomes the Milk Girl' on it. Also, something else – something it was hard to miss.

'About a hundred,' he said. 'Some of them with their Box Brownies ready. A reporter and a photographer, presumably from the local press. Plus a band and a banner, and … um …' He hesitated.

'Is there a cow again, Hendy?'

He gave her a steady look. 'There is, yes.'

'Ugh!'

'Look, Miss Holden, it's no easy matter getting a cow on to a station concourse.'

Pandora laughed. 'I'm sure it isn't.'

78

'Those slippery hooves! It will have taken four strong men to manhandle her. They'll have had to hold up traffic.'

'Don't worry, Hendy. I'll be suitably impressed.'

'The cow *is* part of the story, after all. We can't ignore the cow.'

'No, we can't.' It was endearing how Hendy always flushed when the subject turned to dairy animals. 'But if anyone ever asks me to pretend to milk one again …'

'I know. I won't let them. I'll punch them on the nose.'

She laughed. 'And what's after this on our order sheet? Is there anything *without* cows?'

Opening the briefcase, he produced the itinerary again. 'Well, the main event, on Monday, will be the House of Hanover Milk Bar grand official opening, complete with announcement of the winner of the Brighton's Best Knickerbocker Glory competition. That's on the seafront, at beach level. So there will definitely be cows present there.'

'Really?'

'Oh, yes. They've been grazing in the town all week. But again, it will have taken serious organisation to get them down to the beach, Miss Holden, given that cows can't manage flights of steps, so—'

'I know, Hendy. I know.'

'But there'll be no cows at the Balmoral, I promise. It's a small quiet hotel in Hove. Or at the beauty contest today at five, which is in an upstairs ballroom or I'm sure they would have tried.' He waved the itinerary. 'More?' he said, slightly irritably. 'Or is that enough for your pretty little head to take in?'

She winced at this, but let it pass. She honestly wished she could make a better connection with Hendy; wished she didn't notice when men said stuff like 'pretty little head'. Her friends thought she was weirdly exacting. Isobel from netball had recently said to her: 'Pandora, if you keep letting men's *attitudes to women* get in the way, you'll end up an old maid!'

Pandora held out her hand for him to help her off the train.

'Here we go again,' she said. 'This is it, Hendy. You know the drill.'

'Yes, miss. But—'

'Say my name, Hendy.'

'Yes, miss. Pandora Holden.'

'Louder.'

'Pandora Holden.'

'Thank you.'

She took a deep breath and exhaled, then turned to face the crowd waiting at the end of the platform. How long would it be before the cry went up? Fifteen seconds? Thirty? Would she have taken one step, two steps, three?

It was no time at all.

'It's the Milk Girl!' someone yelled. And then the cow mooed, and the band struck up, and there was the usual charge in her direction, accompanied by excited cheers.

———

It might seem odd to spend so much time on this young woman's arrival in town when there are urgent gruesome murders languishing unsolved. After all, there is quite a lot to remember. For example:

> three people are dead in the morgue from frenzied milk-
> bottle attacks last night: an obscure young would-be
> beauty queen with unaccountable erotic interests; a highly
> respected AA patrolman; and a viciously witty monologist
> beloved by millions;

a world-famous skater still lies undiscovered on the ice at the Sports Stadium;

there is a puzzlingly reoriented road-sign north-west of Hassocks, which might (or might not) prove *apropos*;

unprecedented numbers of top-level villains are milling about on an upper floor of the Metropole Hotel, some of them openly toting weapons;

a hot-headed barber's son is bent on disproportionate revenge for a perceived slight to his father's honour;

a popular debonair magician is fearful for his life;

a photographer has been sent on a wild goose chase to a far-flung holiday camp;

a police inspector is beginning to panic about the possibly dire consequences of judging a Knickerbocker Glory competition;

a villainess who poses as a charlady is making last-minute arrangements for a secret summit;

and above all, two valiant and tireless policemen are out and about on the streets of Brighton, acquiring relevant information regarding the first three murders (*see above*) as quickly as they can, to the selfless neglect of both their breakfasts and their elevenses.

So, it is natural to ask: how does the lovely, troubled Pandora Holden from rural North Norfolk fit in with all of this? At first sight, she doesn't. And yet it would be foolish to imagine she will have no role to play in subsequent developments, because, for one thing, she's the Milk Girl.

As it happened, this was not Pandora's first visit to the town. She knew Brighton well. For a whole academic year, when she was eleven, she had boarded at the famous girls' school on the cliffs to the east – Lady Laura Laridae – while her parents travelled abroad to study Pacific South Sea Islanders. They were professors of social anthropology who worked and published together, as a pioneering team.

It had been a long year of separation for an eleven-year-old, and afterwards – back in Norfolk – she had tried mostly to forget it. But there were nights at home when the wind blew inland from the sea that she had flashbacks to that great draughty gabled school on the cliffs, with the old sash windows rattling in the dormitory, and her fellow Upper Thirders yelling hysterically that the building was about to collapse. Most of what happened during her year at Lady Laura she kept secret from her parents, for fear of alarming them. Some of it was too naughty; some of it *much* too embarrassing; some of it the stuff of nightmares. On the latter count, incidentally, all she had said on her return was, 'Daddy, if you love me, I don't want to see a Punch & Judy show again, not *ever*.'

By chance she had fallen in with a colourful crowd of fellow pupils that wouldn't have been out of place in a girls' novel – the sort of *Michaelmas Term for Moira* book skewered so brilliantly by Cedric Carbody's headmistress impersonations. First among them was Parvati, a rich and dignified Indian girl, brilliant at maths; then Diana, an absent-minded duffer whose hair-parting was *always* a zigzag, and whose ribbed school stockings bagged at the knees; athletic June, who was nimble of foot and good at archery (a skill that came in handy surprisingly often); and finally the tomboy-ish Wanda, who kept a pony called Rags and loved to cook up mischief.

The five of them got into trouble having midnight feasts (poor Diana, caught red-handed with a jam tart!), or making gunpowder in the chem lab without permission (poor Diana's eyebrows!), or going AWOL on Sunday afternoons to watch the talent show at the children's playground on the Undercliff (poor Diana, getting locked out for the night!).

Pandora had not only joined in with such escapades: thanks to the boldness of her personality, she had sometimes starred in them. One Sunday, at the theatre in the children's playground, when all five of them were overexcited, Wanda had dared Pandora to go up on stage and sing the old music-hall song 'Let's Have a Tiddley at the Milk Bar' – a song that the girls had all recently learned from an old 78 r.p.m. record discovered behind a curtain in the Upper Third Common Room.

But despite having sung along with it a dozen times at school, Pandora forgot the words halfway through, and the performance ended badly. The usually placid pianist actually told her off for wasting everyone's time, and a man in the audience even booed. Of course, the other girls turned it all to a joke in no time, and they laughed so much about it back at school over the next few days that Diana (it was always Diana) was sick over a banister into an antique Chinese pot.

The incident got them all into trouble, but it was worth it. For the rest of term, Pandora achieved a position her class-mates could only dream of: she was the most popular girl in the school. And all because of 'the Stoat' (as the girls all privately referred to the headmistress).

'I have been advised,' announced Miss Stoater, solemnly, the next day in assembly, 'that yesterday, Pandora Holden of the Upper Third not only left the school grounds without permission, but gave a public recital of—' She stopped. She couldn't believe her eyes. 'A public recital of a song entitled "Let's Have a Tiddley at the Milk Bar".'

She scanned the hall with beady eyes, ready to admonish any girl who tittered.

'I need hardly remind you girls that such a breach will not be tolerated. Pandora will write out one hundred times, "I must not bring the school into disrepute." Do you hear me, Pandora? Where are you?'

She peered out over the assembly hall.

'Here, Miss Stoater,' said Pandora.

The headmistress then studied the name of the song again. 'What is a tiddley anyway?' she asked. 'What can this song possibly be about? Anyone?'

Several girls put up their hands.

'Yes? Marjorie?'

'A drink, Miss Stoater.'

'Really? But how?'

'It's cockney rhyming slang, miss. Tiddley-wink, drink.'

'Cockney rhyming slang?' repeated Miss Stoater, in horror. And then she gave vent to the memorable exclamation that all the delighted girls would all repeat to their loved ones for the rest of their lives. 'Oh, Marjorie!' she groaned. 'Marjorie, Marjorie, Marjorie, *Marjorie*!'

Pandora sometimes wondered what had happened to the other girls from Lady Laura. Did they know she was now the Milk Girl? On the station concourse, as she approached the welcoming committee, while the band played a rousing 'Sussex by the Sea', and the attractive cow shuffled impatiently, she looked around in hope of spotting a familiar face – but, as usual, there was none.

'Mr Mayor,' said Henderson, as they arrived. 'May I present the Milk Girl.'

A cheer went up again. She saw in people's faces how thrilled they were to see her in the flesh – as if she were an actress, or a princess. Luckily, she was never required to make a formal speech; she just had to say hello to everyone, in a manner to inspire them to go away and drink more milk. And she had to pose for the photographs, of course, which would appear in the local press, so long as they didn't involve any udder-touching, which was disgusting. But to the Mayor, she couldn't help saying, out of politeness, 'I've been so looking forward to revisiting Brighton, Mr Mayor. I was here for a year as a girl, at school.'

He smiled, and shook her hand. 'You're here to open our new House of Hanover Milk Bar on Monday, I believe?'

'House of … ?' Pandora was about to query the ridiculous name, but was beaten to it by Mr Henderson. This often happened on their travels.

'That's right,' said Henderson, pleasantly. 'The House of Hanover. That's on Monday.'

The Mayor leaned closer. 'You're aware, of course, of a certain amount of bad feeling locally towards that milk bar?' he said, quietly. 'The brick through the window, and so on? The daubed paint?'

Pandora's eyes widened. No, she wasn't aware of this. No one had told her about any bad feeling.

'Yes, yes,' said Henderson, airily. 'But we're sure it's nothing to worry about. The opening will go ahead regardless. We've been in contact with the local police.'

'Have we, Hendy?' queried Pandora, sweetly, suppressing her annoyance.

'Later,' he said. 'I'll explain later, I promise. There's going to be a police presence. It's all arranged.'

'Could the Milk Girl stand beside the cow, please?' said the photographer from the *Argus*.

'Of course,' said Pandora, and – with one arm draped round the animal's neck – struck one of her lively signature poses, her face alight with fun, suggesting that standing beside a cow in a busy South Coast railway terminus was a totally normal and wholesome thing to do, just like drinking milk.

It was while she was thus occupied that the Mayor spoke privately to Henderson about the events of the previous night.

'I suppose you haven't heard yet about our sensational milk-bottle murders?' he said in a low voice.

Henderson blinked. '*What?*'

'Happened last night. Not everyone knows yet. Three slain! We're all so shocked. Bodies found covered in glass and milk – and blood, of course – and festooned with those little foil bottle-tops.'

'But … ?' Henderson, who had spent all his professional life thinking up new ways to associate pints of milk with life, health and happiness, was having trouble with the concept of people being heinously slaughtered with them.

'They'd been *killed*?'

'Yes, they had. With milk bottles!'

'Oh, my God.'

Henderson looked up to see Pandora returning from the cow photo session, with an expression that said 'We should go.' She had noticed that members of the public were already drifting away. The band had stopped playing. Even the cow was bored. The allure of the Milk Girl always seemed to wear off quickly. Henderson nodded and held out his arm to escort her.

But before they could go, the reporter had a question. Henderson prayed it wouldn't concern how Pandora would set about killing someone with a milk bottle.

'Did you just say you were at school here, miss?' he asked, with pencil poised. 'Was this at Lady Laura on the cliffs?'

She smiled. 'Yes. It was. But I think we're leaving now, I'm sorry.'

His eyes lit up. 'Here, Bob,' he said. 'This young lady only went to Lady L.'

The photographer pulled a face. He didn't care.

But the reporter wanted to pursue it. 'When was that exactly, miss?'

'Well ...' She hesitated, and turned to Henderson. They both knew she wasn't supposed to talk about herself.

He shook his head. 'I'm afraid the Milk Girl can't answer personal questions.'

'Yes, I'm sorry,' said Pandora. 'I spoke out of turn. I just wanted to say I liked Brighton, that's all.'

The Mayor glowered at the reporter. He hated the press, and with good reason (he had a lot to hide). 'All right, sonny. You've got your answer.'

'I only asked what year she was here, Mr Mayor. I was thinking, she might have known the schoolgirl who fell off the cliff!'

Pandora turned pale. 'What?' she said. 'What schoolgirl?'

'Oh, *yes*!' said the photographer, suddenly seeing what his mate was driving at. 'Good point, Jimmy.'

It was as if everything had gone dark. Pandora grasped Hendy's arm; she felt she was falling.

'What schoolgirl?' she said, again.

'Oh, you don't want to know about that, miss,' the Mayor assured her. 'That's a very tragic story.'

'And I'm afraid we *must* be going,' said Henderson.

'Diana something,' said the reporter. 'She was only about twelve. Messy-looking, the other girls said. Always in trouble, apparently. Diana Carmichael, was it?'

'Think so,' said his friend, who was leaning in to take pictures of Pandora's stricken face.

'Did you know her, then?' the reporter continued. 'Think she might have jumped? Here, Bob, quick! Take the picture! Look at her eyes glazing over! Milk Girl passes out! That's a front page if ever I saw one!'

'Diana,' said Pandora, staggering.

'Miss Holden, please,' implored Henderson quietly, leaning close and holding her elbow.

'Some help here!' called the Mayor, at a loss. At which a constable on duty outside the station was summoned to assist, but managed only to add to the mayhem.

'What's going on here?' he demanded. 'And whose is this flaming cow?'

'Please, Miss Holden … Pandora … let's get you outside. Can you walk?'

'And what about these people getting murdered with milk bottles last night, miss?' said the reporter, excited at the effect his questions were having – and belatedly making the obvious connection to a major news event. 'Care to comment on that?'

'*What?*' She looked in bewilderment at Henderson.

'I'll explain later, Pandora. I only just heard myself.'

'Ooh, I sincerely hope you've got a permit for this animal, sir.'

'Please, Constable, help the young lady! Who cares about the ruddy permit?'

'I do, sir. The laws governing the permissible movement of livestock in a built-up area are very clear.'

'I'm sorry, Hendy.' Pandora was inexorably sinking to the ground. Henderson lost his grip on her elbow.

'She's going!' yelled the reporter.

'Brilliant!' said Bob, still taking pictures.

'Get it?'

'Getting it now, mate.'

'Pandora, mind the cow!' shouted Henderson, in despair. And, fittingly enough, those were the last words the Milk Girl heard before she completely lost consciousness.

―――――

There is one last thing we need to know about Pandora Holden before returning to police matters. When she was fifteen, a keen young man with an academic interest in the kinship systems of the Fens had come to lodge with her parents. Just out of school, he wasn't yet precisely clear about his future, but social anthropology interested him greatly, and his father was acquainted with the Holdens through high-table circles in Cambridge. This young man sat at the feet of Pandora's parents, asking them gratifyingly intelligent questions, and helping them sort their findings as they prepared to write a major study. This young man, for whom Pandora conceived passionate schoolgirl feelings, was, of course, Peregrine Wilberforce Twitten.

He had stayed just three months, arriving on 23 April – a day whose recurrence each year still made Pandora's heart leap within her. It was a momentous meeting. She had opened the front door on a rainy afternoon to find this tall, lean, keen-faced young man drenched with soft spring precipitation, a damp suitcase on the ground beside him. Tucked under one arm was an attractive small ginger terrier, who caught her eye immediately and wagged its tail. We would recognise this young man instantly as Constable Twitten except that he was a bit younger, and had floppy hair, and was wearing everyday civilian clothes. He had been about to knock on the Holdens' door, and had been caught, surprised, with his knuckles raised, which made both him and Pandora laugh.

'Gosh. Hello,' he said, smiling. What an open manner he had! 'Are you Miss Pandora Holden? Oh, good, it's the right house.'

She had nodded, but not said anything. She couldn't take her eyes off the dog.

'Ooh, look, gosh, I'm sorry about him, but I think he's injured his paw. He was heading this way from the main road, and he appeared to be in difficulties, so after he'd limped along beside me for a while, I just decided to pick him up and bally well carry him.'

The dog, clearly enjoying himself, wagged his tail again.

'May I put him down now?'

Pandora wasn't sure. 'Well, you may if you like.'

'Thank you.'

It was a relief to him to put the dog down. It was small, but stocky. 'What's his name?' he asked.

'Oh, he's not ours,' said Pandora, not knowing whether to laugh.

Twitten groaned. 'Really? Oh, no.'

'Sorry.'

'But I've just carried him bally miles!'

They both looked down at the dog, who promptly ran indoors and scampered up the stairs.

Just then, Pandora's mother opened the door to the study, and took in the puzzling scene: a drenched young man on the doorstep; April rain gusting in; paws thundering up the stairs in a blur of wet intruder fur.

'Why on earth did you bring a dog with you, Mr Twitten?' she demanded. 'And where's it going?'

'He didn't really, Mother,' said Pandora.

'James!' Pandora's mother called. 'Did we know the boy was bringing his dog?'

In the end, the dog (a two-year-old drop-eared Norwich Terrier named Blakeney) spent a happy afternoon snoozing beside the range in the Holdens' cosy kitchen, waiting to be picked up by the station-master, who was his devoted, long-suffering owner. Evidently Blakeney was always tricking people into taking him home with them, a custom the station-master found entertaining but also hurtful. Twitten soon recovered from the embarrassment of his mistake, and everyone agreed that the dog possessed an unusual capacity for bending soft-hearted people to his will.

Meanwhile the fifteen-year-old Pandora had no sooner seen the hapless Peregrine Twitten on the step, with his damp hat and raincoat, and the cheerful little dog under his arm, than she had fallen deeply and forever in love.

For his own part, the eighteen-year-old Twitten had relished his time in Norfolk – but not for any corresponding romantic attachment made. The reason he later remembered Norfolk with such affection was that his sojourn with proper anthropologists cleared up, for ever, the issue of his vocation. He discovered he was simply too clever, and too impatient, for academic research. He certainly liked organising data and extrapolating from it ('Sir, I think I can see a pattern!'), but when it came to collating it from transcribed interviews with the entire native population of Rarotonga – well, what a waste of time.

Twitten was at a turning point in his life: too old now for schoolboy *I-Spy* books, but still avidly curious to observe, to spot, to draw quick deductions. He wanted to solve crimes. When he tried to explain this impulse to his grown-up hosts over convivial suppers, they would first heartily blame the works of Arthur Conan Doyle (which, it was true, Twitten had consumed at an impressionable age), and then gently remind him that he'd failed to spot the truth in the case of the malingering canine (it transpired that the dog's pathetic limp had been an act).

But he was not deterred by such well-meant teasing. His vocation was growing within him. When one day the Holdens heard about a robbery at a nearby seaside hotel, he borrowed a bicycle and rode there against a powerful wind. The local sergeant was at first annoyed by Twitten's unsought contributions ('Excuse me, sir, but did you notice this bally huge footprint?'), but in the end was obliged to thank him for his help. The culprit was a well-known local criminal; in fact, he was the first person everyone had thought of. He had boasted about the crime both before and after committing it, and had also left an abundance of clues. But still, with Twitten on hand, the case had been wound up in a quarter of the usual time, and the stolen goods recovered *in toto*.

'So you want to be a *policeman*?' Pandora had asked Twitten one day, as they walked down a dusty cart-track together in the light early evening. It was Twitten's last week in Norfolk, in late June. He was going to miss this wonderful county. He had volunteered to accompany young Pandora to the station after school, to collect a parcel of books and papers for her parents, and also to shake Blakeney's paw if he happened not to be out on an opportunistic jaunt.

'I think so, yes. I want to be a police detective. I've decided there's nothing I'd rather do.'

'Won't your father be disappointed if you don't get a degree?'

'Well, the way I see it, I'd just be taking his work a step further. Father wrote *Inside the Head of the Law Breaker*, and so on. I'd be applying the criminal psychology he writes about; putting it to real use. It does make sense, in a way. Rather than do an academic course, I could spend my time reading the sort of books that will help with the job. And then I can bally well do it.'

'Yes, but you'd be a *policeman*.'

'That's true.'

Twitten couldn't see the problem with being a policeman, if it meant he could work out who'd committed crimes. Perhaps Pandora was too young to understand what a valuable job a policeman did.

'What would you like to be when you grow up, Pandora?' He felt it was polite to ask the question.

She blushed. 'Well, an artist, eventually.'

'Really?' He let this sink in. 'Gosh. Well. Good for you.'

'There's no need to say it like that. I'm very good at art.'

'Sorry, I meant—' Twitten stopped talking. He was a little out of his depth. And perhaps he'd misunderstood. 'I mean, do you want to be an artist every day? Not as a hobby, but as a sort of profession?'

'Yes.'

'Well, gosh. Do your parents know?'

'*Yes.*' Her voice had hardened slightly.

'And they don't mind?'

'No.'

'Well, that's … No, gosh. No, really. Good for you.'

'Why are you so surprised?'

'I'm not. Not at all.'

'Then why do you keep saying "gosh"?'

Twitten bit his lip. He had started this conversation innocently, and now young Pandora seemed quite distressed. He saw a safe way forward.

'Will you go to art school, then?'

'No, not straight away.'

'Oh.'

'No, I'll do Classics first. At Oxford.'

'*Classics?*'

'*Yes!*'

Pandora stopped walking and looked at her companion. She had never felt such burning disappointment. In bed every night for the past three months, she had lain awake concocting a wonderful shared future of glittering prizes for herself and Peregrine Wilberforce Twitten – or 'P.W.' as she sometimes imagined calling him once they were on a more intimate footing. She would follow him to Oxford, then they'd get engaged. Eventually they would have a little dog of their own, just like Blakeney.

But Twitten seemed to have other ideas. For a start, he wasn't even interested in academia. Moreover, while he had decided on a highly idiosyncratic career path for himself, he'd clearly never thought for *a single second* about what the future might hold for her; never registered her precocious twin passions for classical literature and Expressionist art.

Tears welled in her eyes. Twitten, feeling that some sort of comforting gesture was called for, took her arm and said, 'I'll come and visit you at Oxford, if you like.'

At this, Pandora broke down. '*Will you?*' she wailed.

Twitten had no idea what was going on. 'Of course I will, Pandora,' he said, encouragingly. 'I mean, assuming your bally boyfriend doesn't mind.'

Her face dissolved in misery. 'My bally boyfriend? Oh, *Peregrine!*' she howled.

They had walked on to the station, and collected the parcel, but not seen the dog – it later transpired he'd managed to wangle a ride to King's Lynn in a baker's van. It was the last time Twitten and Pandora were alone together.

But now, four years later, Twitten was investigating milk-bottle murders in Brighton, and Pandora was fainting nearby on the station concourse, and frightening a cow. Fate – and more importantly, *milk* – was bringing them together again.

Five

The opening of the House of Hanover Milk Bar being just two days away, its manager and staff were anxious and confused.

This much-discussed public hostility towards the new venture – what could they do about it, and how had it arisen? For the past two weeks, the opening had been the subject of warm debate in the letters columns of the local press. Paint had indeed been daubed on its walls; a brick had indeed been lobbed through its window; moreover, the mild-mannered manager had been roughly jostled one day on his way along the seafront.

But why? Received opinion was that well-established local traders objected to this new, unfair competition: they demanded to know – in the strongest possible terms – why they should be undercut by a business subject to public subsidy. But when the manager, Mr Shapiro, bravely canvassed the existing tea-stall holders and ice-cream vendors in the area, asking how he could accommodate their objections, they all happily shook his hand and said – bafflingly – that they bore no ill will towards the House of Hanover Milk Bar; if anything, they expected it to draw more trade to their particular stretch of the seafront – and by the way, poor you, what an awful name you've been lumbered with.

It wasn't as if ugly new premises were being plonked down beside the West Pier, either: the milk bar occupied an existing building on the Lower Esplanade – a low, wide single-storey edifice that had recently stood empty but had started life in the 1930s as a 'bathing pavilion', where modestly inclined swimmers could – theoretically – pay a small fee to change their clothes in private. Needless to say, it never caught on, thanks to the peculiar dual nature of Brighton's holiday-makers: shrewdly tight-fisted, and at the same time brazenly exhibitionist. They spurned the offer of such facilities and continued to change out of their wet costumes on the beach, flashing bits of intimate flesh at each other in the wriggling, squealing process, and doing it for free.

So the House of Hanover Milk Bar was not, it seems, causing legitimate resentment from competitors, nor was it an eyesore. Its only mistake was to choose the afternoon of the August Bank Holiday Monday for its grand opening. This fact alone was the cause of all the paint-daubing and brick-throwing, and strongest-possible-terms correspondences. Because as we already know, something else was planned for Brighton on that Bank Holiday: a historic summit of out-of-town villains at the Royal Pavilion, which needed to take place below the radar. How convenient it would be for those villains if all police and press attention were focused on a different part of the town – for example, on the new (blameless) milk bar on the seafront. All it required to achieve this massive feat of cozening was a bold local criminal organiser capable of:

> initiating baseless rumours;
> writing strongly worded letters to the press under
> assumed names;
> committing reprehensible criminal damage without
> turning a hair; *and*

personally misdirecting a key member of the police force with a drip-feed of gossip at the station.

''Ere, have you read about all these ever-so-credible threats to that new milk bar on the seafront, dear?' Mrs Groynes had said in the office one day a couple of weeks ago, while delivering tea and biscuits to the inspector and Sergeant Brunswick. 'Outrageous, I call it, and I'm not the only one.'

'Milk bar?' Steine had responded. His newly adopted policy towards Mrs Groynes's constant wittering was to focus on just one fragment of it.

'Mrs Groynes means the House of Hanover Milk Bar, sir,' Brunswick explained. 'Due to open on Bank Holiday Monday. They've got that lovely Milk Girl coming to cut the ribbon, or that's what it says on the posters. Oh, thank you, Mrs G.' He reached for his tea.

'I put four sugars in.'

'Ooh, lovely.'

'Oh, yes. I know the one.' Steine sighed and put down the draft of the radio talk he'd been perusing. It seemed they were discussing this tedious subject whether he liked it or not. 'It used to be a glorified bathing hut that no one patronised. But what's the problem, Mrs Groynes?'

'Well, the opposition, dear! The hoo-hah! They're saying there's that much genuine and not-at-all-bogus-or-trumped-up opposition, they might not dare open it at all!'

'Really? Why is anyone opposed to it?'

'Oh, search me, dear.' Mrs Groynes started vigorously polishing Twitten's desk. 'Something about a commercially divisive, publicly subsidised business destabilising an

otherwise competitive free market. But it's much too complicated for my old loaf of bread, that's all I know!'

She laughed; they laughed as well. 'Loaf of bread' was
(presumably) cockney rhyming slang for 'head', and it was
true that an empty-headed charlady could hardly be expected
to grasp something as complex as this.

'All I *do* know is, they're in a right two and eight! Vandalism
and I don't know what all. Jostling is what I heard. Can
you believe that? *Jostling!* But hark at me, wittering on. The
sergeant here knows as much as I do about it, don't you, dear?
Weren't you our very own man-on-the-spot the other day?'

Steine turned to Brunswick with a questioning expression.

'Well, sir. That's right.'

'You tell him, love,' urged Mrs G.

'Tell me what?'

'I saw it for myself, sir. When the brick went through the
window a few days ago. I was only thirty yards away.'

'Were you? At what time was this?'

'Around dawn, sir. Of course, when I heard the smashing
glass, I ran to find out what was going on and found a brick –'

'An actual house-brick, dear!' exclaimed Mrs G, shocked.

'– wrapped in a piece of paper with "YOU HAVE BEEN
BLEEDING WARNED" written on it.'

'*You have been bleeding warned,*' repeated Steine. 'Ugh. No
signature, I suppose?'

'No, sir.'

'But how on earth did you happen to be on the seafront at
that ungodly hour, Brunswick? You're sometimes not at your
desk until half-past ten.'

'Anonymous tip-off, sir.'

'What, informing you of the precise time and place the
incident would occur?'

'Yes, sir.'

Mrs Groynes concentrated on a particularly energetic bit of polishing.

'And yet you didn't apprehend the culprit, Sergeant?'

'He just vanished, sir. I'm sorry.' Then Brunswick brightened. 'But do you remember, Mrs G, how I bumped into *you* as I was coming away? That was such a nice surprise.'

She laughed and patted his hand. 'It was nice to see you too, dear. I'd only got up to watch the sun rise, and suddenly there's poor Sergeant Brunswick, all shook up and in need of a reassuring cuddle from good old Mrs Groynes.'

'Do you know, sir,' said Brunswick, leaning back in his chair, 'it's amazing how many times I've bumped right smack into Mrs G just when I was in pursuit of some villain who then got away.'

Mrs Groynes frowned, as if needing to consider the truth of this remark. And then she smiled. 'Blimey, you're right, dear. It *is* amazing.' She laughed. 'The number of times I've heard you yelling, "*He's getting away! He's getting away!*" Here, do you remember when you were chasing one of those villains of yours and I nearly ran you over in that car that turned out to have brakes after all, when I thought it bleeding didn't?'

Brunswick burst out laughing. 'I was just about to arrest Stanley-Knife Stanley, sir. And suddenly there's a *parp-parp-parp* and people are shouting, "*Look out!*" Blimey, Mrs G, you nearly flaming finished me off that time!'

'Ah,' said Steine, starting to gather his things. 'The laws of probability in action, you see. I've been thinking about writing a talk on this very subject, as it relates to police work.'

'Probability!' scoffed Mrs G. 'Pull the other one, dear, it's got bells on. No, it's nothing to do with any of that with this lovely sergeant and me.' She put her arm affectionately round Brunswick's shoulders. 'It's fate with us two, dear. It's kismet!'

At which they all laughed and sipped their tea, and Mrs Groynes opened the biscuit tin, and at the smell of fig rolls Brunswick quickly banished from his mind the hilarious memory of how – accidentally, of course – he had once nearly been killed in the course of his duties by the comical station charlady at the wheel of an ostensibly brakeless vehicle.

It was at this moment that Constable Twitten had returned to the office from one of his secret rounds and found the conversation concerning the new milk bar in full flow.

'So, anyway,' said Mrs G, pouring Twitten a nice cup of tea, and casually resuming her theme, 'what on earth can be done for those poor people, that's what I'm wondering? What with all that nasty opposition hoo-hah and hullaba-loo; and what with the grand opening on Bank Holiday Monday.' She picked up a feather duster. 'I mean, you're the police, not me. I wouldn't stick my oar in; I've got enough to do, thank you very much, keeping up with all my mopping and polishing and swabbing, and fretting about the future of the monarchy since that awful Lord Altrincham wrote that article about our poor defenceless young Queen the other day. I mean how does he sleep at night, dears, that's what I keep asking myself? But I can't help thinking there must be *something* ... ?'

'Police protection, perhaps?' said Brunswick, as if the idea had come to him entirely unprompted.

'What's that, Brunswick?'

'It just came to me, sir. Could we offer police protection, perhaps? At least for the grand opening?'

'That's not a bad idea,' conceded Steine.

'Thank you, sir.'

Twitten, quickly grasping what they were talking about, put down his cup and saucer and said, 'Ooh, sir? Sir?'

Steine stiffened. The others watched with interest. The inspector had a very short fuse where Twitten's clever-cloggery was concerned.

'Sir? Sir?'

'Yes, Twitten?'

'May I say something pertinent, sir?'

Steine huffed. 'Well, that rather depends.'

'On what, sir? I've already said it's pertinent.'

'On whether it concerns, as usual, how you know more about everything in the world than anyone else.'

Brunswick and Mrs Groynes exchanged glances.

'Oh.' Twitten considered this. 'I'm afraid it might do, sir.'

'Well, in that case—'

'But it's about the famous hoo-hah and hullabaloo, as Mrs Groynes called it, surrounding the new milk bar. You see, according to Mr Shapiro's own inquiries, the hoo-hah and hullabaloo in question are in fact strangely baseless—'

But he got no further.

'Thank you, Twitten,' interrupted Steine, 'but I've heard quite enough about milk bars and hullabaloos for one day.' And then, with a curt 'Excuse me', the inspector gathered his tea and biscuits and retreated to the privacy of his own office, where he worked for the rest of the morning on his tricky radio talk about a fictional Everyman who – amusingly – keeps violating arcane laws such as the Registration of Business Names Act (1916). In his own opinion, the piece was the best he'd ever written. It both informed and entertained. No wonder it immediately put thoughts of offering police protection to a troublesome beachside milk establishment out of his mind, and in consequence he did nothing about it.

A few days later, however, his attention was properly caught. He was informed that the Knickerbocker Glory contest winner would be announced as part of the grand opening at the milk bar – thus placing himself at the scene. It was at this point that he had arranged, grudgingly, for a minimal police presence on the day.

But ever since Twitten had planted the absurd idea in his mind that judging the Knickerbocker Glory competition was a job that came with associated dangers of reprisal (namely, arson), he had wondered if he should do more. As he sat at his desk now, on the Saturday before the Bank Holiday, he tried to dismiss the notion as ridiculous: this was *ice cream*, he assured himself. But then he made a decision, picked up his peaked cap and left the building in search of the Punch & Judy man.

He found Vince on the seafront, talking to young Maisie, the buck-toothed stall-girl who had until recently been the entire focus of Sergeant Brunswick's pitiful and self-defeating romantic ambitions. Regrettably, he seemed to be a sucker for any girl in bobby socks.

'Mr Vince?' Steine said. 'May I have a word?'

Vince looked around and made a face. 'Oh, iss you, Isspector. Look, Maisie. Ratbag policeman rozzer ponce come to see us.'

Maisie looked the inspector up and down, but said nothing, which was a bit rude. Though to be fair, she was already fully occupied, resting a hand on her hip and chewing gum.

'It's about the Knickerbocker Glory competition,' said Steine, quietly.

'Oh, that.' Vince hitched his thumbs in his braces, made a rough sound in his throat and then spat on the ground. 'Blimey Riley,' he said, wiping his mouth with the back of his hand, 'you tooka time, mate.'

'Mr Vince,' Steine said, as calmly as he could (and avoiding looking down at the spittle), 'my constable tells me—'

'Looka, mate, iss up to you what you do, right?' The Punch & Judy man paused for an answer. '*Right?*'

'Yes.'

'But your Constable Twit-face, he says you doing the Knick-bocky Gloria competish – ass right?'

'That's right. And that's why I—'

'Hah!' Vince clapped Steine hard on the shoulder, making him stagger slightly. 'Well, it was nice knowing you, mate! Thass all.'

'But—'

'Nice to fucking know you. I s'pose you don't know 'bout last bloke what done it?'

Steine gulped. 'That's why I've come to see you. Something happened to his … house?'

'Nah, thass the one afore last.'

'The one before last? So what happened—?'

'Last one? Last one dark alley, mate.'

'What?'

'Forget setting fire to poncey house, this one dark alley, fucking cosh, mate, fucking blackjack.'

'No. But surely—'

'What for should I lie? Fucking *cosh*.' Vince mimed the action of repeatedly striking a person prone on the ground. 'Whack, whack, whack! Tell you what, he screams like a girl, mate!' He laughed. And then, adopting a playful, high-pitched Punch & Judy voice, added: '*Stop! Stop! What I do? At least tell me what I done!*'

'Well, I—'

Vince leaned closer. 'Bloke got *twitch* now, mate,' he whispered. 'Yeah. Everyone call 'im Twitchy Pete.'

Steine considered this. 'Well, thank you. Perhaps I should talk to him.'

Vince laughed. 'Ha! Good luck! Twitchy Pete don't say much nowaday. Don't say raspberry ripple, don't say cherry-on-a-top. Show him tin Del Monte fruit salad and he fall down, curl up, like dead.'

Steine bit his lip. 'And all because … ?'

'Ass right. All for giving fucking *second prize* Knick-bocky Gloria a Metropole Mike.'

'Metropole Mike? But I've never even *heard* of—'

'Ice-cream people no soft, Isspector. You think they soft coz ice cream all nice a sweet a creamy? No!' Vince spat again, and this time Steine made the mistake of following the trajectory. 'They like animals, mate.' He laughed. '*Animals!*'

'Well, thank you, Mr Vince. That's been … um, very helpful.'

Steine was about to leave when Vince remembered something else, and stuck out an arm to stop him.

'You know *scoop*?' Vince said, meaningfully.

'You mean … the ice-cream scoop?'

'Yeah, *scoop*. You know why iss that size? That essact size an' shape an' 'andle an' evyfing?'

'No,' said Steine.

Vince laughed again. 'Scoop your fucking eye out, mate!' he said.

And that very afternoon Inspector Steine ordered that the House of Hanover Milk Bar on the seafront should receive extra protection from the Brighton Police on Bank Holiday Monday, even if it meant removing men from their usual posts around the town.

———

Young Susan Turner of the BBC was as good as her word. On Saturday morning, at eleven-thirty, just as Brunswick and

Twitten were setting off to the Sports Stadium to interview Buster Bond (who was, of course, already dead), she rang from Broadcasting House in London. Twitten took the call, and expressed polite surprise that she had managed the journey from Brighton so quickly. He had interviewed her this morning at about half-past eight.

'I was lucky with the trains,' she said, modestly. 'And after all, it's a very urgent matter. Whoever killed Mr Carbody needs to be caught.'

Twitten visualised her: a fresh-faced young woman with a ponytail and an air of being highly organised. The sort of person whose pride in her own sheer competence might actually hold her back in her future career. She would doubtless remain an invaluable assistant producer for the next forty years. 'Miss Turner is our lynchpin! Where would we be without her?' they would say, while more ambitious people leapfrogged her easily on their way up the BBC pay grades.

'That's exactly right. Thank you, Miss Turner, for your helpfulness and efficiency.'

Susan, who was using the telephone at her desk in the deserted and oddly gloomy *What's Your Game?* production office (there was bright sunshine outside), glowed with pleasure. Being called helpful and efficient was fundamentally what she lived for. Being called those things by the attractive young constable in a sensational murder case made them all the sweeter.

'So …' she resumed, glad that he couldn't see her blush. She donned a pair of reading glasses and opened a dog-eared manila folder. 'So, I've got the file here of the letters I mentioned. And there are plenty from people who had been emotionally scarred by Mr Carbody, and there are some that are frankly obscene, and there's one we probably should have contacted the police about, as it's a direct death threat. But there's also one that – well, it leaped out at me for a different reason.' She sounded excited.

'Why's that?'

'Because it's from Brighton, and it's from a disgruntled beauty-contest entrant called Miss B. Ashley!'

'*What?*'

'Isn't Miss B. Ashley one of the other milk-bottle victims from last night?'

'Yes, she bally well is!'

'Oh, goody-gumdrops. That's what I thought.'

Brunswick, who had been loitering by the door, came to join Twitten at his desk.

'Oh, good work, Miss Turner,' Twitten said, with genuine warmth. 'What does the letter say? And when did she write it?'

'The letter isn't dated, unfortunately, but its arrival was date-stamped by someone – probably me – in August last year. She accuses Mr Carbody of being in cahoots with the rigging of the contests, and claims that professional models are taking part.' Susan paused. 'Isn't that allowed, then?'

'I think it probably is, actually; but Miss Ashley thought it wasn't fair.'

'Really? Why?'

'I don't quite understand it myself, but she felt very strongly, and from what I'm hearing, some of these women's eyebrows alone—'

'But there's no such thing as fair competition. Everyone knows that.' Susan's voice had changed, grown harder; the subject had clearly touched a nerve. 'Feeling hard done by is the most tiresome emotion there is, in my opinion.'

'I tend to agree,' said Twitten.

'Anyway,' said Susan, glancing down at the letter she was still holding, 'you're right that Miss Ashley was quite passionate about all this. In particular she seems to cast blame on Tony Sayle, Carbody's agent. She says she will be writing to him, too, in the same vein.'

'Tony Sayle.' Remembering the name, Twitten flipped open his notebook to where he had written, 'Tony Sayle, Dean Street'. He remembered the suave Gerry Edlin saying, in a knowing tone, *When Tony puts his foot down, that's it.*

'Didn't Tony Sayle ban Carbody from judging bally beauty contests at around this time?'

'That's right. He did. Mr Carbody wasn't happy, but he did what he was told. Mr Sayle tends to get his own way. He represents quite a few BBC performers, and between you and me, we all loathe him. He's a pig.'

'And she implies it's Sayle who's rigging the contests?'

'Yes, I think so.'

'Gosh.' Twitten made some rapid notes. 'Miss Turner, I hate to ask you to do more for us, but is there any way you could get that letter down to me today? Right now, we need to conduct more interviews, or I'd come up on the train and collect it myself.'

Susan didn't hesitate. 'I could bring it down, if you like.'

'But you just got back to London.'

'It's all right. I could bring the whole file. After all, I might have missed something. If I leave now, I can be with you again in a couple of hours.'

'Oh, Miss Turner, you're a bally saint. Thank you.'

'Well, my pleasure.'

Twitten hung up, and pulled a face at Brunswick.

'Do you think it's a lead, son?'

Twitten stood up. 'I think it might be, sir. It's a connection, anyway. We definitely need to find out more about this agent Tony Sayle.'

He looked at his list. 'But first we should go to the Sports Stadium and see Buster Bond and that local skater who was Miss Ashley's old boyfriend – that should be pretty straight-forward, I think – then on to Hove for Officer Andy's sister. We know so little about him, but if there's any link to beauty contests …' He stopped talking. Brunswick was giving him a funny look. 'What is it, sir?'

'That BBC girl. Miss Turner, is it?'

'What about her?'

'You do realise she fancies you, son?'

'What? No.'

'Tearing up and down on the train like that. She's not doing all that for the sake of flaming justice, is she?'

Twitten shook his head; he refused to listen to such soppy stuff. 'I'm sure you're wrong, sir,' he laughed. 'I think in Miss Turner's case it's nothing to do with being attracted to anyone; it's more about a classic female desire for approval.'

'That's baloney, Twitten.'

'And without wanting to be cruel, she just said "goody-gumdrops".'

'So?'

'Please, sir. We need to get on.'

Brunswick looked at him in wonder and amusement. 'You really don't ever notice it, do you, lad?' he sighed.

———

As it happens, the visit to the Sports Stadium was not as straight-forward as Twitten had imagined. On arrival they learned from Stage Door Ernie that Buster Bond had arrived quite early for a spot of rehearsal, and had not left. But when they went in search of him, his dressing-room was empty, and the rink was busy with other acts rehearsing. Buster Bond had vanished. To make things worse, Barbara Ashley's old boyfriend Graham had not yet arrived. His main part in the show being a sensational high-speed obstacle race against Bond (which he was contractually obliged to lose), he tended to skip rehearsals. With Bond missing and Graham absent, there was really no reason to stay.

But Twitten needed a moment to take it all in. He'd never seen inside the stadium before, and the sheer scale of it took his breath away. Also, the skill of the skaters whooshing past – so fast that they created a perceptible vacuum – was astonishing. The cold was bracing, the talent outstanding; it was like a bolt of ozone to the brain and the body. Why had he never been to see the ice show? He'd lived in Brighton since June! And the weather had been so hot!

'You were planning to bring Miss Ashley here last night, weren't you, sir?'

They were standing at the edge of the rink. Brunswick pulled his light raincoat tighter, to quell the shivering.

'Yes, well. Don't remind me.'

'Was it her idea to come, or yours?'

'It was all me. She wasn't too keen, as I recall. Probably because of her old boyfriend Graham. Of course, I didn't know about him when I suggested it.'

On the far side of the ice, a female skater attempted a complex jump and stumbled on landing, making Twitten scream slightly. But she got up and carried on, no harm done.

'Do you know who any of these skaters are?'

'Of course I do. The same ones tend to be in lots of the shows. Aside from Graham, of course, they go all over the world. We should pick up a programme; that'll tell us.'

Brunswick surveyed the scene: skaters weaving across the ice, turning to skate backwards; launching into jumps and spins; stopping on a sixpence, with a spray of ice, then accelerating off again. In one corner of the rink, a troupe of ice-clowns practised pratfalls around a miniature fire engine, while blowing whistles and honking horns held in their armpits; in another, a woman worked with a set of trained poodles.

'The dog lady's Russian, I think,' said Brunswick, pointing. 'And the clowns are Italian, all one family – three generations. Grandfather, three grown-up sons, three boys plus another kid not old enough to perform yet. When they're on the Continent they can use the little kid as well: apparently the audiences love him. They complain like mad that they have to leave him out when they're here. Actually, we were called in once because someone reported them for bringing the kid on. They denied it, of course.'

Twitten had forgotten that show business was the sergeant's pet subject. In his desk were umpteen copies of *ABC Film Review* and *Picturegoer*. He often borrowed Mrs Groynes's *Tit-Bits* as well, and was unashamedly agog for news from Hollywood. It was an unwise person who said 'I wonder what Debbie Reynolds is up to at the moment' in Jim Brunswick's presence if they didn't really want to know the answer.

'Is Buster Bond always the star?'

'Yes, when they can get him.'

'And why did you say Graham doesn't have an international career like the others?'

'Because he's just the local boy who steps in. It's a lovely story – heart-warming. A couple of years ago, one of the skaters broke his leg just before the opening, so they advertised for a last-minute replacement and got Graham. He normally works as a porter at the veg market but he's a good-looking boy and goes like a bomb on the ice. When that show was over, and everyone packed up and left for the next place, Graham went back to the market. They'd kept his job open.'

'Gosh.' Twitten surveyed the buzz of the rink, and thought about poor Graham trading his spangly costume for drab porter's overalls; swapping his skates for wellingtons; trundling sacks of muddy spuds about while his co-stars decamped to Vienna, or Paris, or Rome. 'That must have been hard for him.'

'Well, I suppose.' Brunswick had never thought about it. 'But this year, you see, he was in luck again.'

'You mean, someone else had a convenient accident?'

'Exactly. And yet again our local boy came to the rescue!' Brunswick sounded quite moved. He was a sucker for a Cinderella story. Being dramatically plucked from obscurity ('Who, me? To play *the lead*?') was something he quite often secretly dreamed of for himself.

As the two men made their way to Hove along the busy Western Road, both were rightly focused on the job at hand. Images of the three bodies covered in blood, glass and milk were still fresh in their minds; and Twitten could hardly forget the dread words of Mrs Groynes: *Perhaps he'll kill again.* So it was understandable that neither of them had yet cared to acknowledge how unusual this morning was – it being the first occasion since Twitten's arrival in Brighton that they had actually worked a case together.

They were friendly enough at work, of course: Twitten had loyally visited Brunswick in hospital when he was shot in the leg (both times); Brunswick had occasionally patted him on the shoulder and said 'Well done, son.' But after two months as close colleagues, they scarcely knew each other. Brunswick's auntie Violet had encouraged him to invite Twitten home for supper one evening, but although he had agreed, he'd never intended to go through with it. In the end, his auntie stopped asking. A woman who spoke her mind, she upbraided her nephew for not extending a bit of hospitality to a friendless young man on his first posting away from home. 'People were kind to you when *you* started out, weren't they, Jimmy?' she said, reprovingly. 'You should do the same.'

There was irony in this. Brunswick had, in the past, often fondly pictured having a fresh young constable under his wing. In this fantasy, he and the grateful young shaver would go out after work for a pint of Watneys, and stay late, flirting with women. Perhaps they'd go and watch Brighton and Hove Albion on Saturday afternoons. The younger man would be of similar working-class background to Brunswick (perhaps also, like him, an orphan) and be intelligent but, crucially, not *too* intelligent. He'd have done his National Service. His name would be something simple, like Bob.

Sometimes, at his desk, Sergeant Brunswick still dreamed of this companionable fledgling PC – and then Peregrine Wilberforce Twitten would bounce into the office announcing that he'd uncovered something bally significant; something that had been *under their noses all along* – and the dream of Bob the Perfect Constable would crumble and drop to the floor, like ash.

'We've never done this before, sir, have we?' said Twitten, now, as they proceeded smartly in a westerly direction. 'I mean, we've never been ordered to work together on an investigation. We've never pooled our brains, as it were.'

Brunswick shrugged. 'Let's hope it pays off.'

'Between you and me, sir,' Twitten lowered his voice, 'I think the real reason the inspector suggested it was because he wanted to prevent your going pointlessly undercover again and wasting a lot of valuable time when you could be helping solve the crimes.'

'Did you just say *pointlessly*, Twitten?'

'Well, yes, sir.' He was puzzled. Didn't Brunswick *know* that his undercover exploits had never led to an arrest? 'Ooh, and to prevent your getting pointlessly shot again, of course! Going undercover and getting shot, both to no good purpose – it seems to really annoy the inspector when you do either of those things.'

It hardly needs saying that PC Bob would never have said anything remotely as cutting as this.

'Well, what *I* think, son,' replied Brunswick, sharply, 'is that the inspector didn't want *you* jumping into the investigation feet-first as usual, involving the flaming press and resulting in people getting shot in the head in broad daylight.'

Twitten accepted the rebuke. People had indeed been publicly shot in the head the last time he tried to handle a case alone. In his defence, though, he'd involved the crime reporter from the *Brighton Evening Argus* precisely because Brunswick was nowhere to be seen, too busy posing as a trumpet player in a nightclub.

In an ideal world, Twitten would have liked to form a closer connection with Sergeant Brunswick, but – sad to say – he could never imagine them becoming friends. For one thing, Brunswick was simply far too emotional to be a good policeman; his moods flapped about between euphoria and despair. You never knew which version of him you would discover each morning – the one who avidly scanned the *Police Gazette* while humming to himself, or the one who sat mournfully at his desk with his head in his hands. Just last week, Mrs Groynes had offered the sergeant a piece of his favourite gala pie, and he'd asked, pathetically, 'With a bit of hard-boiled egg in it?' and she'd said, 'Ooh, sorry, dear; but look, you can see the hole here where the bit of egg formerly was' – at which he had nearly burst into tears. 'That's my life, Mrs G!' Brunswick had exploded. 'A hole where the bit of egg formerly was!'

Twitten suspected these extreme emotional states directly reflected the sergeant's up-and-down success with women, but he didn't inquire. Brunswick's untamed libido was another obvious personality flaw, making him fall in love with everyone from the unattainable Maisie the buck-toothed beach-ball seller on the seafront to the equally unattainable (but for different reasons) Debbie Reynolds. Twitten didn't object to the sergeant's romantic inclinations per se, but he firmly believed that a policeman should be equable by nature. He should be calm and unflappable, like a flat lake. Sergeant Brunswick was, by contrast, a boiling tide with treacherous undercurrents.

However, the main stumbling block between them was that Brunswick was such an idiot in regard to Mrs Groynes. True, Twitten's own position vis-à-vis Mrs G had become less of a torture to him as the weeks had passed. It was amazing what the human mind could get used to – on the one hand, knowing for a certainty that the charlady was a master criminal; on the other, accepting she had brilliantly stitched him up like a kipper so that no one would believe him.

Luckily, the whole issue had now died down. The inspector no longer tested him every morning on a scale of one-to-ten over the strength of his 'delusion' – and Twitten was glad. Mrs G had been right to warn him that the more he insisted 'But the charlady is behind all the crimes, sir!', the more it undermined his own credibility and made people cross.

Better to appear to let it go. In the long run, he would find a way to expose her, but at the moment she most certainly had the upper hand. She also had eyes and ears everywhere, not to mention loyal henchmen who – as she had memorably described it – would slit your gizzard as soon as look at you.

And yet, despite the highly mature way Twitten was coping with his predicament, there was one thing that still drove him to despair, which was observing how easily Brunswick was manipulated. How could *any* policeman be so blind?

'Tell me about these rounds of yours, then, son. Who was this Mr Shapiro you mentioned to the inspector?'

Twitten was surprised by the question, but happy to answer it. They had quite a long walk ahead.

'Mr Shapiro is the manager of the new milk bar, sir. He previously worked in Hastings at a similar establishment. He brought his wife and daughter here to help, uprooting them from friends and family, and they're all fearfully upset by the unwanted attention.'

'And you learned all this on your rounds?'

'Yes, sir. I know you don't approve, but you see, people do tell you such useful things if you ask them. All this so-called opposition to the new business – Mr Shapiro is baffled by it. He hasn't been able to identify a single person who feels strongly. Ooh, we're here, sir.'

They stopped. Evidently Miss Inman lived above a barber's shop – and not just any barber's, either. It was Rodolfo's. Realising this, Brunswick tapped on the window and gave the barber a friendly wave. Rodolfo signalled at him with scissors to come in for a trim; Brunswick mimed – pointing to Twitten – that he couldn't, he was out on business. It was true the sergeant liked to have his hair cut as often as possible – but in all honesty, he was sick of hearing Rodolfo complaining about being snubbed by that Barber of the Year competition. Also (could this really be the case?) he'd last had it cut less than twenty-four hours ago, before setting off to the stadium to meet Barbara.

What Twitten and Brunswick saw when they walked into Officer Andy's room was a game-changer, to say the least.

Up to this point, Twitten would gladly have averred that Officer Andy was by far the least interesting of the three milk-bottle murder victims. Compared with a paranoid would-be beauty queen writing wild letters to the BBC and a waspish celebrity with thousands of enemies, this humble, well-liked AA patrolman was a pretty thin proposition.

But that was before Miss Inman said, sadly, 'I suppose you ought to see this,' and opened the door. 'It began properly with the Middle Street Massacre,' she said. 'And then … it got worse.'

It had been a normal bedroom once. Now it was dark and musty and full of paper: the walls were hung with overlapping charts and pictures, all annotated by a frenzied hand; the bed, with its tired, threadbare candlewick bedspread, was stacked with thick scrapbooks, bursting with yellowing newsprint.

Miss Inman switched the light on. Large format black-and-white photographs were piled on the cluttered dressing table alongside an open diary covered in spidery handwriting. On every surface were rusting pairs of scissors and hardening pots of glue, plus binoculars, cameras and notebooks. The person who had lived in this room was obsessional, clearly – obsessional to the point of madness. And the subject didn't take a genius to discover.

'That's Terence Chambers, sir,' said Twitten, pointing at one of the walls.

'Those photographs are all of Chambers and his gang,' said Miss Inman. By her tone, you could tell only that she'd become inured to her brother's unsavoury hobby. 'Chambers was his special interest. On his days off Andy used to go up to London and follow him about, taking photographs.'

'Really?' said Brunswick. 'That's insane.'

'My brother had his camera taken away from him and smashed against a wall more than once. He found it exciting.'

'Crikey,' exclaimed Twitten. 'It's a wonder he didn't get himself killed!' And then he realised that, since Andy *had* got himself killed, this wasn't perhaps the most intelligent remark he could have made.

'Look at this, Twitten,' said Brunswick. With an effort, he was sorting through the heavy scrapbooks. 'He seems to have filled three of these on the flaming Middle Street Massacre alone.' He made a stack, and reached for more. 'Here's one on that Kennington Butcher of yours; this one's the Brighton Trunk Murders.' He put his hands to his face; it was all a bit overwhelming. There were fifteen more scrapbooks, at least.

'What's this one?' Twitten asked Miss Inman. It was marked merely 'Diana'. Opening it at random, he found pictures of schoolgirls – judging by the uniform, they were pupils at the famous Lady Laura Laridae on the cliffs. He was unfamiliar with the story. The cuttings – all from seven years ago – referred to a death plummet.

'Andy knew that schoolgirl Diana who died,' Miss Inman explained. 'He was furious that you police never got to the bottom of it.'

'This all happened before my time, I'm afraid,' said Twitten.

'That's no excuse,' she snapped back, with feeling. Her older-sister attitude to Officer Andy's appalling true-crime fixation was evidently not clear-cut. Now that he was dead, it was her instinct to defend it.

'Look,' she said, as if reading Twitten's mind. 'Of course I wished he would take up a nicer hobby like birdwatching. He was a lovely pianist years ago, you know – he could have done more with that. But I did think he was right to be upset about that girl.' She opened the scrapbook and showed Twitten a picture. 'These were her little friends. Andy always believed one of them had done it, had pushed her.' She flipped some pages. 'He's been keeping tabs on them all ever since. He told me he'd been planning to talk to one of them this weekend, but now …' For the first time, Miss Inman sounded emotional.

Twitten gently took the scrapbook from her, opening it at random, and turning the pages. Pictures showed a girl whose name was given as Parvati Kapoor transform, over time, from gawky schoolgirl in school uniform and spectacles to a smart young woman photographed at home with society friends in Bombay. There was also a girl called Wanda Grey, now married to a Conservative MP with a West Country constituency. Twitten was certainly impressed by Officer Andy's thoroughness (where did he find this stuff?), but otherwise not particularly interested in the girls themselves. Until he opened the page for Pandora Holden.

'Crikey, sir, I think I know this girl,' he said. 'I met a Pandora Holden in Norfolk four years ago.'

'Let me look,' said Brunswick, mildly curious. Then he turned a page, and looked at Twitten in disbelief. 'This is the flaming Milk Girl, Twitten! Are you saying you know her?'

He showed Twitten a double-page spread of glued-in milk advertisements, all featuring the fresh-faced Pandora smiling next to a glass of milk, or taking milk from the refrigerator, or pouring a foot-long stream of milk from a bottle into a blue-and-white striped jug.

Twitten was astounded. 'It *is* her. She looked very different when I knew her, sir. Her hair was in plaits. I've seen pictures of this girl everywhere, and it never occurred to me that she was Miss Holden.'

Brunswick was about to put the scrapbook down, but something made him turn a few more pages. And then a shiver of excitement went through him.

'Twitten, look.' He indicated a picture of a stunning, shapely woman in an expensive French swimsuit. She had luxuriant black arched eyebrows. 'That's June Jackson, the girl who wins all the beauty contests.'

'What? The one who was always being accused by Barbara Ashley?'

'The very one. And this picture was taken outside the Regent Ballroom by Officer Andy just last week, look.'

'How do you know it was last week, sir?'

Brunswick shrugged and pointed. 'You can tell by the film poster.'

'Really?'

'Yes. Look. That's *The Sweet Smell of Success*.'

'But how … ?'

'That was only on for a week. Blimey, don't tell me you didn't go to see it?'

Twitten grimaced. 'Of course I didn't, sir.'

'Well, you missed a good one,' said Brunswick. 'It's a flaming masterpiece. Burt Lancaster as you've never seen him before! But the point is: this week they've got *Beau James*. So this was definitely taken last week.'

'Gosh, that's very clever, sir. So what this picture proves is that Andy Inman *did* have a connection to the beauty contests and their possible rigging!'

'It looks like it, yes.'

Twitten turned to Andy's sister. 'Miss Inman, do you know which of these girls Officer Andy was hoping to talk to this weekend?'

'I'm sorry, no. But I suppose if the beauty queen one has been here a few days already, it must have been the Milk one.'

'She's appearing later at that final, Twitten. She might be in danger!'

The look of joint excitement that passed between Twitten and Brunswick made this a special moment indeed, which was only enhanced when Twitten took a proper look at the picture and said, 'Those eyebrows really are a travesty of nature, sir; Miss Ashley might have been on to something.' And Brunswick, clapping the constable on the back, said, 'Thank you. I agree.'

Six

It was late morning on Saturday before the people of Brighton were fully aware of the Milk-Bottle Murders.

On the front page of the *Argus* was the sensational headline 'Murder by the Pint – Three Slain by Killer Milk Man', and alongside unflattering library photos of the three victims, a picture of Pandora Holden fainting at the feet of a cow on the railway-station concourse. 'Is Brighton the new milk-bottle murder capital of Great Britain?' asked an alarmist editorial (answer: almost certainly). On an inside page a Brighton milkman, aged forty-nine, gave his reaction to the news, declaring that this was the worst thing that had ever happened to him, except for the day his horse had turned around without warning and bitten him on the face.

Meanwhile, for anyone whose life's work was the promotion of milk in a positive light – such as the conscientious Mr Henderson, escorting the Milk Girl – murder by milk bottle was a PR challenge beyond anything ever anticipated at the monthly board meetings. To put things in perspective, in both June and July the main subject for discussion at Milk HQ had been how to stop blue tits sticking their heads through the foil tops and filching all the cream.

In the visitors' lounge of the comfortable Balmoral Hotel in Hove, Henderson and Pandora took it in turns to stare in horror at the newspaper and then let it drop in their laps. Finally, Pandora spoke.

'Should we go back to London, Hendy?' she asked, gently.

Henderson put a hand to his face. 'I'm thinking, Miss Holden. Give me a moment.'

'Should we still go ahead with the beauty contest?'

'I'm thinking!' His voice was shaking slightly. 'Please. I just need to think.' But in truth, he wasn't planning what to do. His thoughts were merely running to the new campaign slogan (slightly adapted): *Drinka Pinta Deatha Day, Drinka Pinta Deatha Day*. He found it strangely comforting.

The shock reverberated through the town. At his AA control post, Mr Hollibon read the account in the paper with a Weights cigarette dangling unlit from his lips.

At Mrs Thorpe's in Clifton Terrace – where the paper was delivered every lunchtime – the lady of the house let out a cry of horror and nearly lost her footing in her fancy feathery mules. 'Oh, Constable! Is this why you left so early this morning – without breakfast?' she gasped.

Barbara Ashley's father went out to buy the paper, but when he saw the headline on the placard, he couldn't go through with it. He told his wife he couldn't find one.

Gerry Edlin, at the railway station, bought the paper, neatly folded it and tucked it under his arm before lightly hopping aboard a cross-country train, his hat tipped suavely to one side. He had left a charming note in his dressing room at the Hippodrome, excusing himself for a few days and implying that that his beloved father in Devonshire was unwell. Of course, his life-preserving flight from Brighton was completely unnecessary (Terence Chambers was in town for different reasons), but on the plus side, he did it with great panache.

In Rodolfo's barbershop, the customers quickly put two and two together about the morning's visit from the police to the flat upstairs, and were too excited to sit still, resulting in painful nicks to their necks and earlobes.

Meanwhile, at the Ice Circus, the skaters – including local boy Graham, who had now turned up, but not including Buster Bond, who remained unaccounted for – gathered round in the dressing-room corridor while the poodle lady read the articles aloud in a strong Russian accent.

True to form, Inspector Steine had issued an official press statement that had perfectly missed the mark in terms of reassuring the public.

If murderers are choosing to use bottles of milk as deadly weapons, I'm afraid the police are powerless to stop them. I need hardly point out that bottles of milk are everywhere. Unlike guns or knives, they can be found on every doorstep. But what I would say to an anxious public is this: if you spot someone brandishing bottles of milk, do not stop to ask, 'Excuse me, my good man, what do you think you are doing?' Run away as fast as your legs can carry you, shouting the words: 'Murder! Murder! Police! Help!' Unless of course he is a milkman carrying out his professional duties.

By the time Twitten and Brunswick returned to the station with all of Officer Andy's scrapbooks and photographs, Steine was perusing the file of letters helpfully brought from London by Susan Turner – and also enjoying the splendid cup of tea she had made for him in Mrs Groynes's pot. This young woman was very impressive in many ways, it seemed – not just in her mastery of railway timetables.

'But what I don't understand, Miss Turner,' Steine said, indicating the quantity of hate mail, 'is why that producer of yours continued to employ that loathsome man, when the listeners clearly despised him.'

They had sorted the letters into degrees of aversion to Cedric Carbody: from slightly disliking him (one out of ten) to actually threatening his life (ten out of ten). The majority of the letters were sevens and above.

'But everyone who appears on the wireless gets complaints written about them,' she explained. 'It's quite normal.'

'Is it?'

Steine was startled. Was she saying that his own talks attracted such poisonous responses? How was that possible?

'May I ask, do you mean everyone in the literal sense?'

She smiled. 'I'm afraid so.'

He sat back in his chair. 'Good heavens.'

There was a noise from outside the door, which was then flung open.

'We're back, sir,' said Brunswick, puffing from carrying boxes of evidence up the stairs. 'We had to stop on the way to take a roll of film into the Polyfoto shop in Western Road. Oof, this is heavy.'

Steine watched with amused interest as Brunswick held back the door with his left leg while straining under the weight of three heavy boxes, stacked higher than his head. It looked quite difficult to manoeuvre them through the doorway.

'What is all this, Brunswick?'

'Mostly scrapbooks, sir,' he replied, awkwardly, over his shoulder. 'It turns out – oof, sorry, sir – that Officer Andy was a bit of a busybody when it came to the world of true-life – oof, hang on – of true-life *crime*.'

'There's a strong link to the beauty contests, sir!' called Twitten, who was out of sight, waiting to bring in the rest of the boxes. 'We might have cracked the case!'

'Well, be that as it may, that's too many boxes to carry at once, Brunswick. You'll hurt yourself.'

'Yes, sir. We summoned a police car to bring us here. I hope that was all right, sir.' Brunswick was beginning to break out in a sweat. 'Sir, I don't suppose you could—?'

'Let me help,' said Susan, springing up.

'Oh, yes, that's a good idea,' said Steine. 'Would you mind?'

And thanks to Susan simply holding the door open, the boxes were finally delivered without mishap, and the two out-of-breath officers rewarded at their desks with cups of tea of such outstanding quality that it was instantly understood between them that Mrs Groynes must never, ever, know.

And then they brought Steine up to date with their discoveries, while he twiddled a letter-opener and nodded. At the end of their account, he sighed.

'So what you're saying,' said the inspector, 'is that our killer is trying to cover up the rigging of beauty contests, even though I assured you from my extensive personal experience as a judge that such rigging does not and cannot take place?'

'Yes, sir,' said Brunswick, and then frowned. *Was* that what they were saying?

Twitten stepped in. 'But I think, sir, it might be immaterial whether contest-rigging *actually occurs*.'

'Immaterial, how so?'

'It's more that if people start *saying* the contests are fixed, and casting doubt on them, it undermines confidence, in which case there are dangerous people who stand to lose a lot of money; they might act with disproportionate violence. Would it help, sir, if we referred to it as *alleged* contest-rigging?'

Steine considered this. 'Yes,' he said. 'Do that.'

'Well, sir, we know that Barbara Ashley talked about this alleged contest-rigging rather too much. It was virtually the first thing she said to Sergeant Brunswick, who was a complete stranger to her.'

'That's true, sir,' Brunswick chipped in.

'We also know that Cedric Carbody was banned by his agent – a very shady character named Tony Sayle – from attending the contests any more. Sayle's given reason was that Carbody was too cutting in his comments to the contestants – but what we're learning about him is that he was cutting *all the time*. This man used to make small, untalented children run crying to their mummies, sir.'

'Did he?' Steine was shocked.

'I'm afraid so, sir. For failing at Highland dancing and so on.'

'What a swine.'

'But also, he was a liability. Anything he learned in confidence he might use as the basis for comic material. Do you remember what Lady Pru said, Sergeant Brunswick? She said that with Cedric Carbody *nothing was sacred*.'

'She did say that, sir,' agreed Brunswick.

'So perhaps the real reason for the ban was that he was starting to ask awkward questions. As for Officer Andy – well, sir, our friendly AA man had apparently been hanging around the stunning June Jackson, and taking pictures of her. As it happens, his reason for tracking her was nothing to do with her career as a model and beauty queen: he was obsessed with this, sir.'

Twitten reached for the fat scrapbook labelled 'Diana' and handed it to the inspector.

'It's an unsolved case from nineteen fifty, when a twelve-year-old girl at Lady Laura Laridae fell to her death from the cliff in front of the school. This June Jackson, now a beauty queen, was a contemporary of the dead girl, and also one of her best friends. Andy knew Diana personally, apparently. Hence his interest.'

'So there *isn't* a link to the contests with him?'

'No, not a direct one. But what I'm thinking, sir—' Twitten stopped, glanced at Brunswick, and corrected himself. 'What *we're* thinking, sir, is that possibly Officer Andy took a picture this week of Miss Jackson that would have incriminated someone such as Sayle, sir, and was seen doing it.'

Steine looked out of the window. He knew he ought to congratulate his men. To find out so much about the victims in the space of just a few hours was impressive. But on the other hand, he had always upheld that the true measure of good policing was his own magnificent handling of the Middle Street Massacre, and this was negligible by comparison.

'So why the milk bottles?'

'Don't know, sir; it's unclear,' admitted Brunswick. 'Except that so many of the contests are related to dairies. You remember how Miss Ashley objected to being called a Lactic Lovely.'

'And who do you think, specifically, is behind the murders?'

'Well, everything seems to point to this beastly Tony Sayle, sir,' said Twitten.

'All right. But before you go arresting him, take a look at this, please,' said Steine. 'It might be – as you like to say, Constable – *significant*.'

He handed the death-threat letter to Twitten, who held it out so that the sergeant, still engaged in drinking his tea, could read it as well. It was so graphically anatomical in its threats that Brunswick, caught mid-sip as he read the worst part, spluttered and choked, and needed to be patted on the back. The writer warned Carbody that he should never show his face again in Brighton. The only line that bore repetition was the somewhat clue-heavy opening: 'I saw what you done at the children's playground that time.'

'Gosh,' said Twitten. Was this a hint at very dark matters indeed?

He turned to Susan. 'Miss Turner?' he said, making her jump with surprise. Everyone seemed to have forgotten she was there. 'Miss Turner, is this the letter you said you should have told the police about?'

'Oh. Yes. That's the one.'

'May I ask why you didn't draw it to their attention?'

'Oh.' She gave this some thought. 'I suppose because it's not BBC policy. I mean, it's hardly our responsibility, is it?' It was clear she had worked long enough at the BBC to absorb its defining trait as an employer: institutional heartlessness. From the Corporation's point of view, if Carbody was attracting death threats, that was entirely his own concern.

'Was Mr Carbody even aware of the letter's existence? Did you show it to him?'

'Probably not. Think of the risk. If he'd taken it badly, it might have endangered the smooth running of a very popular programme, leading to the disappointment of millions of listeners.'

'I see.' Twitten looked at the letter again, where the writer threatened to cut out Carbody's tongue, slice him open down the middle and then gut him like a fish. 'You think he might have taken this badly?'

'The best policy when dealing with artistic or theatrical types is to encourage them all the time,' Susan continued. 'You have to assure them constantly that they're brilliant and popular, otherwise they sink into a state of despondency that affects their performance. Our job is to keep them up, up, up!'

'Well, I honestly don't know what to make of this, sir,' Twitten admitted, handing it back. 'It doesn't fit the beauty-contests theory, certainly. But the murders are so strongly linked by the milk-bottle method – and this letter doesn't relate in any way to Miss Ashley or the AA man. True, the children's playground was where Miss Ashley's body was found, but I don't see any other link. What do you think, Sergeant Brunswick?'

'Oh. Me?' Brunswick cleared his throat to cover his surprise at being asked his opinion. 'Well, son, what do I think? I think it can do no harm to investigate the beauty-contest angle further.' He addressed Steine. 'Sir, permission to attend tonight's beauty contest and question Miss Jackson and Mr Sayle?'

'Very well. Permission granted.'

'Thank you, sir.'

'But no undercover stuff, posing as a security guard.'

'No, sir.'

Steine seemed satisfied. 'It's good to see results from you two working together.'

'Thank you, sir,' said Twitten.

'Which was at my own insistence, if you recall.'

'Yes, sir.'

Steine placed the death-threat letter back into the file, and then – instead of dismissing them – folded his hands and looked briefly out of the window. Twitten and Brunswick exchanged glances. As experienced Steine watchers, they knew he was about to speak to them in a serious manner. He might even address them – ignoring the presence of Susan Turner – as 'men'.

'I suppose you haven't had a chance to read today's paper?' he asked, at last.

'Not yet, sir,' said Brunswick. 'We were too busy with the boxes.'

'Well, men, I'm afraid I have to tell you something rather grave. They are calling Brighton the milk-bottle murder capital of Great Britain.'

Twitten started to laugh, but stopped when Steine held up a hand. 'This isn't funny, Twitten.'

'No, sir.'

'I think I kept the reporters at bay for a while, but mark my words, they'll be back. As far as the press is concerned, with the Bank Holiday on Monday, the town is expecting its largest crowds of the year; meanwhile it also has a deranged killer slaying people seemingly at random, using the nearest weapon that comes to hand. The press will whip up panic in the streets. So, I need results quickly, men. The sooner we can solve this case and apprehend the culprit, the better for us all.'

'We'll do our best, sir,' said Twitten.

'You can count on us,' said Brunswick.

Susan Turner smiled encouragingly.

'Good.' Steine got up to go back into his own office, and was then apparently struck by a thought. He remembered what Susan had said about keeping people up, up, up. Did it apply to managing policemen as well?

'Um … but there is something else.' Steine waved a hand at them, and they looked back with attentive but puzzled expressions. 'Look, men, I just wanted to say … well done. That sort of thing. Well done on what you've achieved so far.'

'What, sir?' said Brunswick. He was stunned. In seven years working for Inspector Steine, these were words he had never before heard.

'I said, well done, both of you.'

'Gosh, sir,' said Twitten, pleased. He nudged the sergeant to add something, but nothing came out beyond a small strangulated sound.

'Thank you very much from both of us, sir,' said Twitten. 'It means a lot – in fact, I think Sergeant Brunswick is quite moved.'

'Is he? Good grief.'

'No! No, I'm all right, sir,' said Brunswick, quickly, with his hand to his face.

'Good. Because we certainly don't have time for anything like that. I'll just say, up, up, up! And carry on.'

───────

At the Metropole Hotel, all ten regional delegates for Monday's conference had arrived by Saturday lunchtime, and were safely ensconced in light and roomy suites over-looking the sea. In many ways, the weekend was proceeding according to plan, and yet Terence Chambers was still annoyed. He had promised these people a raft of tawdry, illegal seaside entertainment – much of it too unsavoury to name – but now, with the outbreak of high-profile murder in the town, it looked as if they would be confined until Monday to their rooms. Naturally, Chambers focused his anger on Palmeira Groynes. She had assured him Brighton was the right venue for the summit. She had promised to have everything under control. And now she had let him down.

'Milk bottles, Pal?' he said quietly to her now, as she walked into his room at midday. He was seated in an armchair wear-ing a short maroon dressing-gown. On his wrist was a gold link-bracelet, and his thinning hair was combed back with

Brylcreem. The Brighton paper, its pages in disarray, was on the floor. A henchman hovered behind him.

'Calm down, Terry,' she said, perching on the arm of a smart little settee. She was dressed in a rose-pink sleeveless dress with tailored matching jacket. It was astonishing how feminine she could look when she threw off the dowdy char-lady disguise. Just removing the thick grey army socks made a world of difference.

'It's some nut with a grudge,' she went on. 'Look at the M.O., dear. Talk about pathetic.'

Chambers regarded her, then looked down admiringly at his own fingernails, which had just been manicured. Part of what had always given him the edge in the hoodlum business was this practised air of suppressed, pent-up violence. He almost never swore, and he disapproved of his henchmen doing it. It was as if, the more he kept the violence down, the more of it there was available when he really needed it. Everyone knew that the more softly Chambers spoke, the more likely he was to jump up, drive a fork into your neck and then watch you bleed to death.

'Pal, what do I care who done it?' He smiled. 'All I care is that I've got a dozen mugs here in their best whistles all scared to put their boats out of doors.' (Terence was very fond of cockney rhyming slang. When he said 'whistles' and 'boats' he meant *whistle and flute* = *suit* and *boat race* = *face*.)

'I know. It's a bleeding shame. But look, Terry, in a way it's good for us.'

He folded his arms. 'I don't see that,' he said.

'It really is.' Mrs Groynes sounded firm and in charge. She had learned how to stand up to Chambers after the war, when they had been in the same East End gang, specialising in the raiding of city banks and bullion vans – and then, later, when they lived together without getting married. She knew all about the soft voice and the reasonable manner. And she made a point of never talking to him in the vicinity of cutlery of any kind.

'Listen, it just so happens I've been directing all their attention for Monday on to a bleeding milk bar, dear. I admit this Milk-Bottle Murderer bloke wasn't in my plan, but we can't ignore him. We have to adapt to prevailing conditions, don't we? If something interferes with the plan, make a new one. You taught me that.' She gave Chambers a meaningful look. 'You've got to trust me, Terry – or else, well, you know …'

'Or else what, Palmeira?' Chambers asked. The hoodlum behind him stiffened and reached for his waistband.

'Oh, for gawd's sake, Terry. I meant *or else send everyone home*, dear.'

This was clever. As they both knew, sending home those ten mugs in their pricey whistles would entail a tremendous loss of boat. Plus, more importantly, Chambers would fail to get the support against the Americans he desperately needed. A moment's thought, and all objections to staying until Monday had been dismissed.

'No, no,' he said, shaking his head. 'All right, you win.'

'Good,' said Mrs Groynes, standing up to leave. ''Coz I got my barnet done 'specially.' It was a rare pleasure for Mrs G to be able to talk cockney with a fellow speaker. (*Barnet fair = hair.*)

'But stay where you are, Pal, there's something else,' said Chambers. 'I've got a little job for you.'

'What's that, then?'

Chambers turned to the young man lurking in the background and summoned him forward. 'Nicky, tell Mrs Groynes here what happened on the road down last night.'

She frowned. Why would an incident on the road to Brighton have anything to do with her?

'Well, I ain't drove this way before, OK?' said Nicky. His tone was both defensive and agitated. Mrs Groynes sensed trouble.

'So, like I say, I don't know the road. And I was bringing that Geordie 'Ardcastle from up North; picked him up from Euston, like Mr Chambers told me, and drove him the rest of the way. And this 'Ardcastle, he's never been south of Leeds, he says, so he don't know the bleeding way neither. So we're only a few miles from here and there's this signpost.'

'A signpost?'

'Yeah. It points *off* the road, like where the road forks, but it's a proper signpost so I follow it, don't I? It says "BRIGHTON 10 MILES", so I turn off and follow it!'

Mrs Groynes was aware that Chambers was staring at her intently, as if he suspected her. She pulled a face at him. She genuinely had no idea where this unusual travel anecdote was going.

'Well, it's a trap, innit?' said Nicky.

'What do you mean, a trap?'

'A trap, like an ambush. We follow this road for a bit, and it's narrow, and I keep saying, "This don't look right, Mr 'Ardcastle; we should turn round." And then there's another fork and another sign to Brighton, but the road gets proper narrow down there and we get to this dead end, just a village pond, and I say, "I'm turning round; there's something fishy about this," and then these kids – a bunch of *kids* – jump out of the bushes, dressed up like Red Indians, shouting and whooping and whatnot and firing catapults at the car.'

'It was kids, Pal,' sighed Chambers. 'Kids playing Cowboys and Indians.'

'And the stones are hitting the car, and I'm trying to turn round, and Mr 'Ardcastle only gets out his gun!'

'What?'

'And he opens the window and he fires it!' Nicky was by now quite worked up, but was doing brilliantly. Not only was he telling the story well, but, cognisant of Chambers's feelings on the subject, he had shown incredible restraint in not resorting to the intensifier 'fucking' fifteen times at least.

'So I finally get the car turned round and I'm shouting at him, "Don't shoot! Stop ruddy shooting!" And the kids have all run off, wailing and screaming and diving for cover, and I drive back up the road as fast as I can, and then when we get back to that first signpost, by the main road, there's something going on.'

'What do you mean?'

'Wait for this,' said Chambers, raising an eyebrow.

'For a minute I think it's a different place. 'Coz earlier, there was just this signpost, right? But now there's this *scene*, with one of them AA Land Rovers sitting there, and a bloke in uniform laying on the grass by the side of the road, covered in glass and blood, and a van driving off in the direction of the town!'

'Oh, my God, that was Officer Andy,' gasped Mrs Groynes. 'So you were there, Nicky?'

'Yeah. Well, I wish I hadn't of been.'

'What sort of van was it?'

'A small blue one, I don't know. I only saw it for a fuck—' He stopped and corrected himself. 'I mean I only saw it for a blinking second!' Nicky was quite distressed. For a young man who had volunteered for a life of violence in the pay of a notorious hard man, it was interesting how shaken he was by this encounter with a dead body. It was also plain to see that the instinct to swear was becoming overwhelming.

'Anyway, I don't know why, I stop the car. Mr 'Ardcastle's yelling at me to keep going, and threatening me with the gun! But I think I see the bloke move, so I don't know, I tell 'Ardcastle to shut up, and I get out. And what do you know, the bloke isn't quite dead.'

Nicky had been speaking with his head down. Now he raised it and found that his audience was agog.

'So I says to him, "Who done this, mate?" And he puts a hand up, and I leans in close and he whispers in my ear.'

'And what does he say, dear?'

'Ugh!' Nicky's entire body gave way to a massive spasm. 'That's the point, ain't it? He don't say nothing. He fucking *sings*.'

'What? No.'

Nicky looked at Chambers. 'Sorry I said *fucking*, sir. It slipped out.'

'That's all right, Nicky,' said Chambers, magnanimously. 'Tell her about the singing.'

'Well, it was just faint, like, but it was dead creepy. It's been giving me nightmares, I tell you.'

'What did he sing?' asked Mrs G.

'I can't.'

'Yes, you can, boy,' said Chambers, patting Nicky on the back. 'Just one more time. Go on. Tell her like you told me.'

So Nicky took a deep breath and sang Officer Andy's last words for Mrs Groynes, complete with racking gasps and simulated death rattle. At the end, a shudder went through all three persons present.

'So I says, "You need to explain that a bit, mate" – but all the light's gone out of his eyes, so what can I do? I jump back in the car and drive here as fast as I fuck—' He stopped. 'I mean, as fast as I can.'

There was a thoughtful silence. Nicky looked for guidance to Chambers, who waved at him to sit down.

'What do you make of that, then?' said Chambers.

'Good gawd,' said Mrs G.

'The point is, Pal, *my boy was never there.*'

'Oh, that's understood, Terry.'

'Nicky arrived here with the bloke's blood on him.'

'It's all right. It's all right.'

'So if the police get any reports of gunfire in some country village … ?'

'I get it. Don't worry, dear. I can handle all that, piece of cake.' She turned to Nicky. 'But as for this swan-song, what the bleeding hell am I supposed to do with that?'

At the offices of the *Brighton Evening Argus*, young Ben Oliver knocked on the editor's door.

'What?' was the shouted response. But when the reporter put his head in, his boss said, warmly, 'Ah, you, good. Come in, then, lad.'

Fred Ackerley, who hailed originally from Yorkshire, was a hardened newspaperman who had made a considerable mistake in assuming the editorship of a paper in the balmy south of England. It was not the most comfortable fit. Ackerley loathed the namby-pamby donkey shows and la-di-da celebrities-outside-nightclubs stuff: it was no accident that his favourite film was Billy Wilder's gritty and cynical journalism drama *Ace in the Hole*.

But despite his open contempt for the town whose paper he was running, and for most of his own staff, Ackerley found he was daring to put faith in young Ben Oliver, who seemed to have good instincts, and whose most outstanding quality was not taking no for an answer. Oliver had managed to wrest a statement from Inspector Steine. He had also written the front-page story and got the angle right first go: that the murder victims seemed to have been randomly targeted; that the killer might strike again at any minute; and that everyone in Brighton should live in mortal fear of the innocent-looking milk bottles in their own larders and refrigerators, or risk expiring in a pool of blood, milk and shattered glass.

'Good stuff, Oliver,' the editor said, happily holding up the front page. '*Is Brighton the new milk-bottle murder capital of Great Britain?* Bloody fantastic. And the wife wonders why I don't retire and keep whippets. How's that police source of yours, then? Constable Twit-twat.'

'Twitten, sir. He's proving difficult to get hold of today. But I wouldn't call him a source. When we worked together last month, I'd say Twitten used us quite as much as we used him.'

'Ah, but we doubled our sales, lad.'

'Well, that's true. Anyway, the thing I wanted to talk to you about, sir, is Inspector Steine.'

'Steine? What about him?'

'I've been thinking about it for a while.' Oliver took a deep breath. 'I'd like the paper to run a campaign.'

'To say what?'

'To say *Steine Must Go*, of course.'

His attention caught, Ackerley folded his arms. 'I'm listening.'

'It seems to me that these murders provide us with a perfect opportunity, you see, because if the Brighton Police can't even solve a crime committed with a milk bottle—'

Ackerley waved at him to stop. 'Hang on, lad; hold your horses. On what grounds *must Steine go*? I don't understand. Steine's a very well-loved public figure.'

'Oh.' Oliver realised he had started in the wrong place. 'Sorry, sir, I thought everyone knew. The thing is, he's completely useless as a policeman.'

'Is he? Are you sure?'

'Absolutely.'

'But doesn't he win awards? He was even on *What's Your Game?* last night. Mrs Ackerley and I agreed he was a bloody breath of fresh air. And Mrs Ackerley used to be lady president of the Hebden Bridge Frank Muir Appreciation Society.'

'Inspector Steine has a lot of luck, sir. It's hard to explain, but things just tend to turn out well for him. Like the Middle Street Massacre, for example. I mean, that was a terrible piece of policing, but it was the blasted making of him!'

The editor narrowed his eyes. 'Has he pissed you off in some way?'

'This isn't personal, sir.'

Ackerley chuckled. He reached into his desk drawer for a packet of cigarettes. 'Believe me, it wouldn't bother me if it was. A personal vendetta can be a beautiful thing in our line of business.'

'No, really, it's not personal, although I have to admit it does annoy me that someone so ineffectual is held in such high regard. But I'm not the only person who's thinking this way.'

'How do you mean?'

'I happen to know that there's a major reassessment of the Middle Street Massacre being written right this minute by one of Fleet Street's top crime reporters, Clive Hoskisson of the *Mirror*, sir. It's going to appear in his next book. So I would propose that we at the *Argus* get in first, linking it to the inspector's inevitable failure in the milk-bottle case, and make it clear that on the day of the Massacre, Steine could have caught and brought to justice forty-five villains, and instead he took his men for an ice cream.

'As a direct result of this negligence – and it *was* negligence – forty-five men killed each other. And yet, instead of being called to account, Inspector Steine got credit for supposedly clearing up local crime!'

'So you want the *Argus* to tell its readers that the Middle Street Massacre was – what? A disgraceful bloodbath?'

'Yes.'

'Well, I'll think about it. He's a popular man, lad. That film of *The Middle Street Massacre* is still playing somewhere every week in this town. But on the other hand, well, I don't like the sound of that Hoskisson fella leaving us to follow in his wake like a bunch of ninnies.'

Oliver waited while his editor fully absorbed the obnoxious idea of a despised Fleet Street newspaper breaking the story. No one in journalism wanted to look like a ninny.

'All right,' he said. 'Let's see how this milk-bottle investigation works out. If Steine doesn't get results soon, well …' Ackerley trailed off, eyes narrowed, as he weighed up the various pros and cons, newspaper-wise, of destroying Inspector Steine's reputation.

'You were saying, sir?'

'What? Sorry, lad. I was just picturing the front page. *The* Argus *says, Steine Must Go: Brighton Police a Laughing Stock for Too Long.* Oh, yes, all right. If they don't get results on these murders soon, lad, let's do it.'

'Really, Mr Ackerley?'

'Yes, really. Let's crucify the ineffectual bastard.'

Back at the station, at 2 p.m., Twitten excitedly turned the pages of the 'Diana' scrapbook for the umpteenth time. He was alone. Brunswick had headed back to the ice rink to pin down Buster Bond, and Steine had gone to Luigi's to reassure himself about the proper, non-violent applications of the ice-cream scoop, and perform his final taste test. It occurred to Twitten that the inspector's lack of proportion in regard to the Knickerbocker Glory competition was both a help and a hindrance where the current investigations were concerned.

Susan Turner, meanwhile, had left at the same time as Brunswick, ostensibly to catch a train back to London, but actually with less fixed intentions. Back in London was a modest room in Camden with net curtains and a small scarlet geranium on the windowsill. In Brighton there was life, noise, a sea breeze wafting heady smells, and an exciting homicide case whose every detail she had just been privy to.

'Please don't mention to anyone what you heard here today, Miss Turner,' Twitten had said to her as she left.

'I was very glad to help, Constable.'

Twitten noticed she was pink in the face as she said this, but couldn't account for it. Perhaps she was coming down with a summer chill.

'I was very glad,' she added, 'to help *you*.'

Brunswick pulled a conspiratorial face at Twitten, who ignored it. 'Well, goodbye, Miss Turner,' he said, shaking her hand. 'There's bally well mountains of stuff to do.'

Outside, Brunswick had said goodbye to her as well, but added in a kindly way, 'It's not a good idea to pin any romantic hopes on young Twitten, miss. It's like water off a duck's back with him.' And then, having dropped this bombshell, he'd struck off for the Sports Stadium, with Susan trailing a few yards behind. As far as he was concerned, she'd gone back to the railway station, and then home.

In West Street, she'd just lost sight of Brunswick in the crowds when something happened: a man, appearing out of nowhere, thrust a ticket to the matinée of the ice show into her hand.

'What's this?' she said, puzzled. 'It's not mine, I'm afraid. Is it yours?'

'You can have this if you want it, love,' the man said. 'I just heard Buster Bond's not skating today, and he's the only reason I came.'

'Are you sure? Can I pay you?'

'No, dear. Forget it. Have a nice time.'

Normally, she would have refused, but this was not a normal day. There was something in the air, she felt. As if her life was changing; had already changed, in fact. So she accepted the ticket graciously and joined the queue to go inside.

Knowing none of this, Twitten was glad to be alone with his thoughts at last. It was true that he and Brunswick had made laudable headway with the case, but was it possible things had progressed too quickly? Had he been too hasty in assuming this beauty-contest connection? The discovery of Officer Andy's dangerous hobby of stalking big-name criminals opened up so many other possibilities; likewise the death threat to Cedric Carbody should not be dismissed.

And at the heart of the case was the method. Hadn't Mrs Groynes advised him, quite forcibly, on a previous occasion that it was a waste of time working out motives if the method didn't make sense? A London agent with famous clients might have a serious reason to silence all three of these victims, but why would he kill them with milk bottles?

He was just thinking about all this – and staring blindly at an image of the Milk Girl – when Mrs Groynes came in.

She looked so different in her smart pink costume that he physically started in his chair.

'Only me, dear!' she laughed. 'I was just out having a tiddley at the milk bar, and I thought, I know, I'll see if I can be of any help to that young constable of mine! So how goes the case, then, dear? And what the bleeding hell is all this toot cluttering up the place?' She indicated the heaps of boxes.

'They came from Officer Andy's sister's.'

'Well, you've done *her* a favour, that's for sure. She'll be dancing a jig to be rid of these.'

Then she noticed something else: telltale cups and saucers left around on the desks.

'Here, have you been interfering with my teapot?'

'No, of course not, Mrs G. The girl from the BBC made us all a cup. It wasn't nearly as good as yours.'

Placated, Mrs G sat down and picked up a scrapbook from the file. Then she set it aside. It was obvious she had come here to tell him something.

'Look, dear. This is awkward. I've got some information for you, but the trouble is, you can't tell anyone where you got it. And I'd get into boiling hot water myself, come to that, if anyone knew I'd told you. So, what do you think?'

'Does this information concern the murders?'

She rolled her eyes. 'No, dear, it concerns who's got his hand up Sooty's backside. Of course it's about the bleeding murders!'

'There's no need to be sarcastic, Mrs G. I just wanted to be clear. So I'm assuming this information comes from a criminal?'

'Yes. And for a lot of reasons he can't come forward.' She considered. 'A lot of reasons.'

'Oh, lumme. But he's not the killer?'

'No.'

'Would this information help me identify the killer?'

'Not exactly. It's not quite as good as that. Ooh, and I ought to mention there's a bit of a quid pro quo attached.' She indicated how small the quid pro quo would be by putting thumb and finger very close together. 'Just a tiny bit. Like that?'

'Oh, Mrs G!' Twitten was shocked. 'You know I can't agree to that.'

'Not if it helps you solve the case and possibly prevent another murder?'

'No.'

'Well, you're a fool to yourself.'

'So be it, then. But in any case, Mrs G, I've got a very good working thesis already, which the sergeant and I are going to follow up as soon as he gets back from the Ice Circus. Have you heard of Tony Sayle? He's a London theatrical agent and impresario, who'd been harassed by Barbara Ashley for his part in rigging beauty contests. And by all accounts, he's a man who's very hard to stand up to.'

'And you really think this poofy agent is the sort to kill people with milk bottles?'

Aside from the gratuitous 'poofy', this question went straight to the heart of Twitten's own doubts, but he hardly had time to answer before there was a knock at the door, and a small man in a white suit came in. He had a neat moustache and wore a Panama hat, and also carried a cane. He looked, for all the world, like Hercule Poirot, but smaller.

'Hello, we've never met,' he said, in a high voice, extending a hand to Twitten, and ignoring Mrs G. 'I'm Tony Sayle, Cedric Carbody's agent, and I demand to know what you're doing to find his killer. And I warn you, if you don't tell me everything at once, I'll scream.'

He presented such a freakish figure that Mrs Groynes let out an involuntary 'Ooh-er' and started laughing. 'I'll leave you to it, dears,' she said, collecting up the cups and saucers and piling them on a tray.

Meanwhile, the tiny Mr Sayle drew a large white handkerchief from his jacket pocket and used it to flick dust from a chair before sitting down.

———

Half an hour later, Twitten's working thesis was in ruins, yet when Mrs Groynes came back with the washing-up done, he seemed strangely relieved.

'He obviously didn't do it, Mrs G.'

Her eyes twinkled. 'You think not?'

'I mean, he obviously didn't club anyone to death personally. He couldn't bally reach! But I don't think he had any motive, after all. Barbara Ashley wasn't the only person whining about unfairness in the beauty contests; he says he's got box after box of letters from disgruntled losers.

'On top of that, the prize money is negligible, apparently – did you know the winners get two guineas at most, and a fashionable swimsuit alone can cost three pounds, nineteen shillings and sixpence? He does represent Miss Jackson, but only because she pretends to be his girlfriend. But the main thing is, he loses a fortune with Cedric Carbody's death. He was on a twenty-five per cent cut! And Mr Carbody had just been signed up to appear in a new programme on ITV. Mr Sayle was planning to back a West End show with the proceeds and put Miss Jackson in it.'

'You don't seem too upset, dear,' she observed, 'that your working whatsit has collapsed.'

'No.' This was odd, but true. 'I'll just have to bally well start again, I suppose. Sergeant Brunswick will be disappointed, though. The inspector said "Well done" to us both earlier and the sergeant nearly broke down in tears.'

'Well, if you want my advice, stop a bit to think about it first this time. About the bleeding method.'

Twitten shrugged. That was exactly what he'd been trying to do. 'But it's hard to read anything into a method that no one's ever done before,' he said. 'As far as precedent goes, there isn't one. Ergo, *anyone* could have done this.'

'No,' said Mrs G, firmly. 'Not anyone. Ergo the bleeding opposite, dear. This method speaks volumes about the person who did it.'

'Does it?'

'Of course. It eliminates nearly everybody! I mean, for a start you can rule out anyone who's got a smidgen of power or influence. They're all out.'

'Are they?'

'Yes! Most of them have never even *touched* a milk bottle! Then you can rule out anyone who's ever committed violence before, as well. This is someone who thinks of himself as a nobody – in fact, you might well be looking for a woman, dear; that would fit. Women kill their husbands all the time with rolling pins and frying pans, and people laugh. But think about it. A rolling pin or a frying pan is, I grant you, just the blunt instrument a woman is likely to have convenient to hand. But when she uses it to kill, dear – when she lashes out with it – it feels *right* to her, do you see? She hates that frying pan as much as she hates that hubby. I bet if you stepped in and gave her a gun or a crossbow instead, she'd be much less likely to use it.'

Twitten had to admit this made a lot of sense, although he flinched at how blithely Mrs G had reached for the idea of a crossbow.

'So who would hate bottles of milk that much, Mrs G?'

'Ah, that's for you to find out. I can't be doing everything for you, can I? I've got things of my own to do. But look, this information I mentioned. I'm sorry, dear, I do have to tell you. But obviously you can't tell anyone it came from me.'

'Listen, Mrs G—'

'No, I've made my mind up. Forget about the quid pro quo.'

'No, wait—'

'Shhh, dear. So it involves a van seen driving away from the scene of Officer Andy's killing. A small blue van.'

'Who told you this?'

'I've already explained. I can't tell you.'

'But—'

'But listen, dear. This person who saw the van, he also heard Officer Andy's bleeding last words. He said to Andy, "Who done this, mate?" And do you know what Andy did, with his dying breath? He sang!'

'He *sang*? Oh, please stop. Unless you can tell me who told you this—'

'He sang the first line of a popular song, dear, and then he croaked. And what do you think the song was?'

'I don't know,' said Twitten. 'Please don't tell me.'

'Oh.' She grimaced. 'If you say so, dear. My lips are sealed. I'll be like Dad and keep Mum, how's that?'

This was an agonising situation. It might be a very important clue. But if it came from a criminal who would never agree to testify, courtesy of Mrs Groynes who would never admit she had passed it on, what bally use was it?

But on the other hand, how could Twitten resist?

'All right,' he said. 'Tell me!'

'Good decision, dear.' Mrs Groynes leaned forward and attempted – in muted tones – the same ghastly, last-gasp impersonation she'd heard from young Nicky. '"If you [*cough, wheeze*] were the only [*wobbly voice*] girl in the world; and I [*groan of agony*] were … the only … boy … [*trailing off, silence*]".'

She leaned back in triumph, her arms folded. 'How about that, then? And don't tell me you aren't bleeding intrigued by that, dear, because who in the world wouldn't be?'

Seven

Predictably, the reunion of Peregrine Wilberforce Twitten and Pandora ('The Milk Girl') Holden on Saturday afternoon was not a smooth one. In their defence, Twitten and Pandora were young and shy; the last time they'd seen each other, they'd been even younger.

Four years before, when he had taken his leave of the Holden home in Norfolk, Twitten had looked – with his floppy hair, grey flannels and tweed jacket with leather patches on the elbows – for all the world like a bright Oxbridge student off to conquer academia and eventually become Home Secretary. Meanwhile Pandora, summoned to the front door by her parents to wave him goodbye, had been, in Twitten's eyes, a mere enthusiastic schoolgirl in a paint-smeared artist's smock, with a copy of Ovid's *Metamorphoses* in the pocket. She wore no make-up; her eyebrows were slightly inclined to meet in the middle; her long dark hair was in plaits; she wore brown Clarks sandals with ankle socks; and crucially, she was not identified in any way with the dairy industry.

'Thank you again for having me, Professor and Professor Holden,' Twitten had said, at the front door, picking up his suitcase. (The joint form of address when a married couple were both professors was problematic for everyone.) And then he had walked away, and the Holdens had laughed and pointed, because under his free arm Twitten was carrying Blakeney – the scamp-ish dog he had arrived with – delivering him back to the long-suffering station-master after he'd been found snoozing again beside the Aga in the Holdens' kitchen (he had apparently caught a bus). So although the parting was a sad one for Pandora, it was difficult afterwards to be fully tragic about it. Every time she pictured Twitten's departing form, the sense of teenaged bottomless woe was annoyingly undercut by the memory of that little golden tail waving jauntily beneath her loved one's arm.

'Hello, Miss Holden. It's me, Peregrine Twitten, I wonder if you remember me? I'm a police constable now. I work here in Brighton!'

Twitten had practised this careful overture en route, but as he walked towards Pandora, he was still nervous. What if she didn't remember him? Backstage before the beauty contest – at around half-past four – she was sitting with Hendy discussing something serious with her head down, while in the background twenty slim young women with not much on, and their hair in tight curlers, milled about in bare legs and white high heels. Pandora, by contrast, was fully clothed in a crisp white blouse and mid-calf polka-dot pink skirt, with a little red scarf knotted at her throat. The image of the Milk Girl might be vivacious and attractive, but it was resolutely clean-living.

At the sight of the two policemen approaching, the underclad beauty contestants scattered – and clattered – as fast as their mad, tarty shoes could carry them. But on hearing Twitten's words Pandora looked up, clutched at the little scarf, and gasped with such emotion that Henderson instinctively leaped to his feet to protect her.

'Do you know this policeman, Miss Holden?'

Did she know this policeman? In an instant's stricken gaze, she assimilated the following about the young man standing before her: his clever face (still adorable), his policeman's uniform (horribly real), his regulation haircut (revolting), and his expression of total amazement at how much she had changed (hugely gratifying).

'Peregrine? No!' she exclaimed. 'No, no, no! I mean, it can't be you!'

'Miss Holden, I could bally well say the same thing. You're transformed.'

'Oh, Peregrine!'

Mr Henderson didn't know what to do. Should he drive this constable away? He had never seen Pandora in such a state, and the sight filled him with concern.

'Oh, Peregrine!' she repeated, her eyes wide – and again Henderson dithered. For a man who secretly adored Pandora and hoped one day to marry her, it was highly confusing to see this rapturous expression on her lovely face, caused by another man.

Brunswick, by contrast, was enjoying the scene, and for less complex reasons. He had never properly appreciated before how funny Twitten's first name was when spoken aloud. He stepped forward and offered his hand. 'An honour to meet you, Miss Holden. I work with Peregrine. I'm Sergeant Brunswick, but call me Jim.' How good and solid the name Jim sounded by comparison.

Henderson duly performed his own introductions, but kept them short. 'Are you all right, Miss Holden?' he wanted to know. 'Would you like me to ask these men to come back later? You look upset. You've turned a funny colour.'

'Please, I'm all right.' She knew she was blushing, but she would have to bluff her way through it. 'Hendy, I had no idea that Peregrine was in Brighton or that he'd really gone ahead and become a policeman!' she said, in a rush. 'I knew that's what he wanted to do, but what are you doing *here*, Peregrine? I mean here, at this ballroom, this afternoon? I can't get over it. It's too much. Oh, Hendy, don't just stand there: get them some chairs. I can't believe it's you, Peregrine! I just can't believe it!'

'We're investigating the murders, miss,' said Twitten, quietly, as he sat down. 'These are early days but—'

'Did you know I was the Milk Girl?'

'No, not until today. Actually—'

'You didn't recognise me in all the pictures?'

'No. But—'

'I thought you would have recognised me. I imagined you thinking, *That's Pandora*.'

'I'm sorry. But about these murders—'

'Oh, these murders! We've been so worried, haven't we, Hendy? Since we arrived this morning. We were saying – I mean, it's awful for the people who've been killed – but it's like someone has set out to destroy the good name of *milk*!'

Twitten would have liked to agree with Pandora, but he couldn't let this pass.

'Well, possibly, Miss Holden. But I think mainly he wants to kill people.'

'Yes, but also to make people think differently about milk! Don't you see? Poor Hendy is the man who wrote the slogan: "You'll Feel A Lot Better If You Drink More Milk". He wants the world to think milk is good for you! He's taking these murders very badly. It feels somehow personal, doesn't it, Hendy?'

'It does.'

'All the same …' Twitten began, but stopped. It was obviously pointless to argue with her.

'I always liked that slogan,' said Brunswick. 'By the way, do you happen to know where the girls went?'

Pandora shrugged. She never took much interest in her surroundings. Her job was to turn up with nice clothes on, receive applause and adulation for holding a shiny glass of milk with a straw in it, and do her best to personify in female form an everyday liquid staple of life.

'So how did you work out that I'm the Milk Girl, Peregrine?'

'It's quite interesting, actually,' he said. 'One of the victims had a private obsession with unsolved cases, and he had a scrapbook concerning a schoolgirl called Diana.'

'Oh. Oh, poor Diana.'

'So you knew about her accident – or whatever it was?'

'No. Not until today. It was a horrible shock. A reporter told me. She was a friend when I was at Lady Laura Laridae.'

'Well, in this scrapbook he had pictures of all Diana's friends at school, and you were in it. You were in a school photograph, aged eleven or so. And there were some snaps Officer Andy had taken of you and your school friends in various locations around Brighton – you might like to see those. But he'd put two and two together about your being the Milk Girl – otherwise I shouldn't have realised, I'm afraid.'

'One of your other friends from school will be here tonight,' piped up Brunswick. 'June Jackson.'

Pandora's eyes lit up. 'Is June here? She must have got married. Her name was June Lester at school.'

'Stage name, I expect,' said Brunswick. 'She wins every contest. Hourglass figure, wavy hair, chalk-white skin. She looks like a film star.'

Pandora smiled. She seemed to have calmed down at last. 'Oh, June was always the fearless one,' she remembered. 'She was our ringleader, like a girl in one of those school stories. She named the five of us the Black Sheep Society!' Pandora laughed. 'Oh, I thought she was wonderful. She won all the archery competitions. But I was only at Lady L for a year, you see – while my parents were away collecting all that data in the South Pacific. After that, we lost touch. But we had some extraordinary times, our little gang, sneaking out of school, having midnight feasts and getting into scrapes.' She sighed. 'We were so young,' she said. 'So confident!'

'Look, Miss Holden, I feel I have to say this. Part of the reason I didn't recognise you as the glamorous Milk Girl on all the posters was not only because your appearance has changed so radically.'

'No?'

'It was that whenever I thought of Pandora Holden, I'm afraid I assumed she'd be at Oxford by now, in cap and gown, pedalling a bicycle with a Greek–English Lexicon propped up in the basket on the front.'

'Oh,' gasped Pandora. On the one hand, it was touching that Twitten remembered her schoolgirl academic dreams; also, that he appreciated the supreme importance to a Classics student of owning a Liddell & Scott. On the other hand, was he criticising her?

And he hadn't finished yet. 'You had such strong views about me not squandering my talents by joining the police, I hope you're not squandering your own, miss. That would be an irony as well as a tragedy.'

'Oh!' said Pandora again, biting her lip as tears formed in her eyes.

'Now hold on,' said Henderson, but Twitten hadn't finished. 'I mean, of course you make a bally lovely Milk Girl, but to be honest, so would plenty of other young women, wouldn't they?'

Henderson could take this no longer. 'How dare you talk to Pandora like that? Good God, man, you've made her cry!'

'Have I? Gosh. Miss Holden?'

'And I'll have you know that plenty of other young women *couldn't* have made such a lovely Milk Girl!'

'Calm down, sir,' said Brunswick, taking charge. 'There's no need to get worked up.'

'But your colleague—'

'I said, calm down, sir, thank you. Blimey, Twitten, did you have to say all that? Can't you see she's upset? This young lady values your opinion and you just told her she's wasting her flaming brain!'

'Well, as it happens, Peregrine,' Pandora said, with a sniff, 'I'm not going to waste my flaming brain much longer. I'm so sorry, Hendy.'

Henderson frowned. What was she saying? What fresh hell was this? Why had today gone so badly in every conceivable way?

'I wasn't going to tell you yet, but I am still planning to go to Oxford.'

'What?' said Henderson. 'But you're the Milk Girl, Pandora.'

'I know.'

'You're by far and away the best thing that ever happened to me, I mean the best thing that ever happened to milk.'

'I've got a place at Lady Margaret Hall for October. I've been meaning to break it to you, but I've kept putting it off.

In the contract I signed, I need give only a week's notice, you see, so I felt I still had plenty of time.'

'A week? That can't be right.'

'It is, though. My parents had it checked by their solicitor. The Milk Board made it short notice on both sides, presumably so that they could drop me easily. I suppose they didn't think the Milk Girl would want to give up the job voluntarily.' She started to cry. 'But I do, Hendy. I've had enough. You've been so kind, but I want to stop ... all this.'

Henderson glared at Twitten. 'What have you done?' he demanded.

'Me?' said Twitten.

'It's not Peregrine's fault,' she blubbed.

'Yes, it is.'

Henderson put his head in his hands. Pandora sobbed noisily into a pretty white handkerchief. Brunswick pulled an expression of polite concern while darting sideways looks to see if any curvaceous bare-legged young women in high heels had ventured into sight again yet.

'Well, I say that's excellent news,' said Twitten, getting up. 'Well done, Miss Holden. I don't know why you're crying: it's definitely the right decision. And now we need to talk to June Jackson. Does either of you know where she'll be?'

June Jackson had been dreading the inevitable visit from the police because she hadn't yet decided what to tell them. Backstage at the Regency Ballroom, she sat at one of the dressing-room mirrors and concentrated on pencilling her eyebrows, while humming 'Que Sera, Sera' to get herself in the correct mood for the show.

All around her, nervous girls in cheap undergarments fought for mirror space and spat inexpertly into little boxes of cake mascara; they shrieked in excitement; they panicked about lost shoes; they wailed when their hair hadn't curled properly; a few silently wept in corners because of the unbearable pressure, and because they were only fourteen. Over the whole scene hung the throat-catching scent of cheap setting lotion.

But the statuesque June was calm. If you hadn't known she'd been Sussex County Champion with bow and quiver, you'd have been able to guess from her magnificent bare shoulders. By comporting herself like a film star, and also having an ostentatious tiny agent who brought her orchids and dressed like Al Capone, she had achieved a special status back here, and in all the hubbub, no one jogged her elbow, not once.

But what *should* she tell the police? Earlier, Tony Sayle had returned from the police station, having answered questions about those ridiculous contest-rigging allegations. Perhaps she should limit herself to talking about those baseless allegations, too: send them off on a wild goose chase. June had hated and distrusted the police ever since the unexplained death of her friend Diana; why should she help them, when they hadn't helped her? Sometimes she wondered what she would do to the person who was responsible for Diana's death, if she ever found out who it was. Lashing them to an archery target would be the obvious first move.

But these three – who cared? What had the world lost? A paranoid flat-chested meat-packer. A busybody AA patrolman, always taking intrusive pictures. A mean-minded broadcaster who'd hung around Lady L schoolgirls for years, pretending to make friends with them, but patently collecting material for his 'comic' radio monologues. June's fearlessness – such an asset among fellow schoolgirls bent on adventure – was a rather worrying trait in her now. Her mother often cried herself to sleep, frightened of what June was turning into.

She had already argued with her mother about talking to the police. Mother – who was Mrs Lester, Buster Bond's respectable landlady in Hassocks – wanted to come forward and report what she'd seen last night. Bond had come off the phone white as a sheet, calling to her in the kitchen, 'That AA man from last night, Mrs Lester? Can you believe someone killed him? They want to talk to me because I was the last man to see him alive!' And Mother had whispered to her, 'Oh, my God, June. Did you hear that? I should call them straight back. Shouldn't I? Shouldn't I call them straight back?'

But then Mother was like that: a goody two-shoes always volunteering for unnecessary tasks. June found this intensely annoying. She had much preferred the years when they were apart: herself at boarding school in Brighton; Mother alongside Father at the Embassy in Washington.

But since Father died, she'd had Mother night and day, and they had argued constantly. Last night, when Mother had insisted on telephoning the AA on behalf of Buster Bond, June had said, *Let him do it himself, Ma!*; when Mother had personally made a cup of tea for Officer Andy, June had argued, *What for? He's just a mechanic!* And when Mother felt compelled to report something to the authorities, June had replied, hotly, *But it's nothing to do with you, Ma!*

'But we can't have the police suspecting dear Mr Bond of anything, darling,' her mother had pleaded.

'I don't see why not. Bond's a creep, Ma.'

'How do you know that?'

'I just do.'

'I wish you would tell me where you go in the evenings, June!'

'I told you! Secretarial classes!'

'You get home at two in the morning!'

But it amused June to think of Bond being under suspicion. She'd seen him so many times in the nightclubs around town. He'd even tried to pick her up once, not recognising his own landlady's daughter underneath all the slap.

'What I saw might be important, dearest,' Mrs Lester had protested. But June said no. She didn't want her mother talking to the police. For one thing, they might just tell her what her beautiful daughter got up to in the evenings.

On such a glorious afternoon, it seems a shame to confine ourselves indoors backstage at the Regent Ballroom. But we are remaining indoors, this time plunging instead into the proper darkness of a cinema auditorium. The editor of the *Argus* was not wrong when he said the film of *The Middle Street Massacre* was always showing somewhere in Brighton – usually as a B-feature supporting new releases such as *The Yangtse Incident* or *Doctor at Large*. What he didn't know was that, more often than not, Inspector Steine was in the audience for it – not only because he adored seeing himself depicted by the young John Gregson as handsome, staunch and twinkly, but because (fair point) each screening of this unexceptional film had the potential to be its last.

Often, he was virtually alone in the stalls. Other regular cinema-goers in Brighton being sick to death of *The Middle Street Massacre*, they timed their arrival with commendable precision in order to miss it. Even when it was snowing they preferred to wait outside until they received the signal that the coast was clear. So it was usually in dusty and echo-ing auditoriums that Steine got to watch, on his own, all the dismally faded and crackly adverts for local shoe shops and family restaurants, and the trailers for hastily made comedies starring Norman Wisdom. But then – well, then things improved tremendously as the screen darkened and a near-naked muscle-man struck an enormous dimpled gong, and the film he'd been waiting for began.

Steine knew every shot by now: over light woodwind music the black-and-white panorama of the Brighton seafront in early morning, with a calm, sparkling sea lapping on the shiny pebbles; then the central clock tower striking the hour of seven; then a tabby cat jumping up on a low wall, and a woman in a floral apron reaching for a bottle of milk on a windowsill.

Then the music changed to something darker, and a street sign that said, worryingly, 'Middle Street' was passed briskly by a man in a hat with his hands in his pockets. Seen walking down the street from behind, the man stopped and stared down. But at what? The music intensified as a close-up showed his puzzlement, then alarm, then horror. At his feet, a dead man with a gun in his hand! Then the brass section blew a discordant Pa-pa-PAAAAH! and up came the legend *Croydon Pictures Presents THE MIDDLE STREET MASSACRE*, and Inspector Steine prised open his box of Bassett's Liquorice Allsorts and settled down to be thoroughly entertained.

This Saturday, however, he had not been sure whether to come. After all, there was a vicious murderer at large in Brighton, and visitors were arriving by the thousand. What if he were spotted at the cinema? Even without a murderer to catch, this was a big day for the Brighton police. Holiday-makers who had no rooms for the night would be sleeping on the beaches, endangering public morals. In the absence of municipal car parks, motorists would abandon their Ford Prefects on main thoroughfares and cause obstructions in direct contravention of the Road Traffic Act (1956). And on the subject of obstructions, Steine had also noticed with a twinge of concern on his way to the cinema that a large unauthorised crowd had gathered in the Pavilion Gardens just to stare at a herd of red-and-white cows.

But he soon forgot these distractions once the film began, and barely noticed, either, when he was joined in the stalls by a young man with a notebook who chose a seat near the front.

The Middle Street Massacre wasn't a truly bad film, to be fair. The comic relief provided by the obtuse Sergeant Brunswood (a depiction that the real Sergeant Brunswick had never quite managed to live down) was cleverly handled, especially his famous cry of frustration about eating flaming ice cream at a time like this. Meanwhile Brighton itself looked marvellous, with shots of the flower gardens and fountains, trolley-buses and coaches, and children building sandcastles – all set in sunny contrast to the darkly dramatic gang tension (fictionalised) building to the famous shoot-out.

Steine loved it that the interior of the police station looked like a slightly bigger version of the Palace of Versailles, and that they gave him a huge Humber car with running boards. But his favourite scene came at the end, when John Gregson viewed the pile of dead gang members in Middle Street through a thick cloud of cordite and declared, 'I have no blood on my hands this day, just a smidgen of raspberry sauce.'

Today, however, that moment was ruined: when Gregson pronounced those words, there was a shout of laughter from the unknown young man at the front, who then got up as soon as the credits began, closing his notebook and donning his hat.

'Inspector Steine?' he said, as he passed by. 'Is that you?' The young man leaned close. 'Ben Oliver from the *Argus*, sir. Just refreshing my memory for an article I'm planning. How perfect that you're here too.'

And before Steine could demand an explanation, Oliver had pushed through the heavy swing doors to the blindingly bright afternoon outside, and disappeared.

So, all in all, it had been a busy Saturday afternoon. But at least the Milk Bottle Murderer was taking a rest, wherever he was.

Perhaps the crowds were simply getting too big. On the beaches, families had pitched camp from early morning; by 3 p.m. every deck-chair was in use on the two piers and the Esplanade; at the children's playground boys and girls excitedly boarded the gentle roundabouts, and got candyfloss in their hair, and lost their sandals, and bawled. On the stage of the Children's Theatre, a dapper man wearing a striped blazer and waving a cane encouraged children to take part in the talent shows where he was the master of ceremonies. (A placard alongside the stage declared it to be *Brighton's own 'Have a Go'*.) Meanwhile, in the centre of town, Steine had been right to take note of the crowd surrounding those cows outside the Pavilion: it was getting dangerously large. The farmer kept pleading with people to stand back. What the milk-marketing men had failed to provide when devising this grazing-cow stunt was any sort of fencing. They would later have cause to regret this.

When Mrs Groynes checked back with Terence Chambers at the Metropole mid-afternoon, he assured her that all his guests were obediently keeping to their rooms, but he was wrong. One of the regional crime lords had decided he could take it no more, and had slipped through a service door and down some back stairs in search of fresh air, fish and chips, and a bit of female company. Chambers would have been alarmed if he'd known – especially as the escapee was Mr Hardcastle, who, as we know, was irresponsible with weapons, never went anywhere unarmed, and tended towards jumpiness when geographically south of Leeds.

———

And what of Susan Turner? While everyone at the police station assumed she had gone back to London, Susan had attended the Ice Circus, and thoroughly enjoyed it despite the non-appearance of the famous Buster Bond. In fact, she felt that she'd been fortunate to see this particular performance, and when she emerged from the Sports Stadium mid-afternoon, she couldn't wait to tell Twitten what she'd learned. Thank goodness she *hadn't* gone straight back to London! Twenty-four hours ago, she'd been a contented but taken-for-granted assistant producer on a popular radio panel game. Today she was helping to track down a murderer. She had never felt more alive.

So what had made the afternoon's performance so special, and so useful? It was the controversial promotion to the starring role of local boy Graham Goodyear.

'What's happening?' Susan had asked, when the audience reacted with equal cheers and boos to the loud tannoy announcement that Graham would be replacing Bond for the afternoon's show. 'Why are they booing?' she asked the woman sitting beside her, who was sensibly wearing a tweed coat firmly buttoned up to the neck (it hadn't occurred to Susan that it would be cold in here).

'Aw, because they love that Bond bloke, don't they?' said the woman, surprised. 'It's him they come to see. He's lovely.'

'Oh. But in that case, why are they cheering as well?'

The woman gave her a steady look, and turned briefly to her husband, on her other side. 'She's asking why they cheered, Don.'

'Huh!' he said, putting his gloves on.

'You're obviously not from Brighton, dear. Look, Graham Goodyear's a local boy, works at the veg market carting sacks of carrots. But he dreams of stardom, don't he? Or that's what he told the *Argus*. The papers love it; call it a Cinderella Story – *From spuds to spangles*, it's that kind of thing.' She turned again to the husband. 'What was that one we had to look up, Don? Do you remember? That headline about Graham Goodyear? Like *From spuds to spangles* but something else?'

'You joking, Em? Why on earth should I remember that?'

The woman turned back, still smiling. 'Well, I wish I'd never mentioned it now. Anyway, the point is, Graham got called in this year when one of the professional skaters broke his leg – which, funnily enough, happened once before, the exact same thing, two years ago, so it all looks a bit fishy to some people, like lightning striking twice! That's his mum, look, down the front, waving the little Union Jack. She's Graham's biggest fan. She comes to every show, apparently, and cheers and cheers.'

'Is he any good?'

'Well, you'll see. He's no Buster Bond.'

Another woman leaned in. She'd clearly been eavesdropping. 'I heard the bloke who broke his leg *skidded on some loose peas left at the top of the stairs.*'

There was a ripple of laughter.

The first woman turned to her husband again. 'Did you hear that, Don? They say the bloke what broke his leg skidded on some peas. Like Graham got him out of the way!'

'Wouldn't surprise me,' he replied, lighting his pipe. 'Many a true word spoken in jest.'

'And Buster Bond's probably pinned down under a ton of King Edwards!' joked another man.

'Well, I say good luck to Graham,' said yet another woman, sitting behind. 'In case you haven't heard, an old girlfriend of that boy was murdered with a milk bottle yesterday. I say he's brave to go on.'

'That young beauty queen was his girlfriend?' said the first woman. 'I didn't know that.'

Again she turned to her husband, but he was deliberately looking in another direction now, so she turned back to Susan.

'Aren't you feeling cold, love?'

'I am, a bit.'

'Should have brought a blanket. Here, I just thought, though. I bet them two lovebirds – Graham and the beauty queen – I bet they met at that talent show down at the kiddies' playground. He was always there, Graham was. His mum made him do a turn every week for years.'

'What, skating?' asked Susan, puzzled.

'No, singing! He did it right up till he was fifteen, and they had to bar him in the end, he was so much bigger than the other kids. I bet that beauty queen Barbara used to do a turn down there as well, see; she was just the right type – you know, a proper little show-off. I know her mum. And I'll tell you what. That AA bloke that got killed as well – he used to play the piano for the kiddies down there and all, didn't he? He done it for years.'

But before the woman could elaborate, the house lights were extinguished and the orchestra struck up, and everyone stopped talking. In the crowd there was a murmur of anticipation mixed with the rustling of a thousand paper bags of loose sweets.

'Sugared almond, dear?' whispered the woman next to Susan. 'Or a pineapple chunk?' She rummaged in her handbag. 'I got some lemon sherbets in here as well.' And then she exclaimed, '*From rhizomes to rhinestones*! That was it. Thank Christ, it was driving me mad!'

———

After the ice show, Susan emerged from the Stadium with a bit of a sugar rush, ice-cold legs and feet, a slight headache from all the sheer spectacle, and a clear sense of purpose. Along with everyone else, she had applauded the success of Graham Goodyear with enthusiasm. 'A star is born, dear,' commented the woman beside her, as they were standing up to leave. 'Buster Bond might as well stay buried under all them spuds.'

But Susan's main emotion was pride: she was going to help Twitten with his inquiries! She was sure no one had mentioned the children's playground link before – that Barbara Ashley would have sung or danced there, while Officer Andy played the piano. And hadn't the threatening letter to Cedric Carbody begun: *I saw what you done at the children's playground that time*? As fast as she could, she made her way to the police station, only to discover that Twitten and Brunswick were both currently at the Regent Ballroom on Queen's Road, where the beauty contest was due to take place later on.

It was Inspector Steine she spoke to. He had just arrived back from the cinema, and was (understandably) looking very preoccupied. Why had young Ben Oliver been to see *The Middle Street Massacre*? What did he mean when he said it was for an article he was planning? Why had he loudly laughed at the best line ever spoken by a policeman over a pile of dead criminals?

'Is there something the matter, Inspector?'

Steine and Susan were in the outer office, where every surface was covered with Officer Andy's scrapbook collection.

He considered the question. 'Yes, I think there might be, Miss Turner. But it's nothing for you to worry your pretty little – excuse me, I mean there's nothing for *you* to worry about.'

'Oh. Oh, good.' Susan decided not to take notice of how he had so pointedly swerved away from the compliment. 'The thing is, Inspector, I've got some important information linking the victims of the milk-bottle murders.'

'Really?' He smiled indulgently. 'Well, I don't suppose your information *is* important, Miss Turner, but bless you for thinking so. Where did you obtain this so-called important information?'

'At the Ice Circus.'

Steine threw up his hands and laughed. 'There you are, then.'

'Perhaps I should tell Constable Twitten nevertheless. The thing is, it concerns—'

'Well, if you must,' he interrupted. 'You'll find Brunswick and Twitten at the Regent Ballroom. Ogling the girls in their swimsuits, if I'm not mistaken! Some of them are absolute stunners, I must say. A real class above the sort of drab young woman one meets normally.'

The way Steine managed to insult Susan with virtually everything he said was quite impressive, but she continued to rise above it.

'Would you like me to tell you first, Inspector?'

'Me? No. Tell me what?'

'The information.'

'Me? No, tell Twitten.'

'Are you sure?'

'Perfectly.'

'Then I'll be off.'

'Good, good. Thank you, Miss Turner. You're very ...' Steine couldn't think of the right word.

'Helpful?' she said.

'I was going to say you're very nosy. But I suppose helpful would be a kinder way of putting it.'

As she opened the door to leave, Steine remembered something, and called her back. 'Could you take these with you? Twitten was keen to see them as soon as possible.'

He held up a packet of photographs that had been delivered by the Polyfoto shop's boy and left with the desk sergeant. It contained eight paparazzi-type pictures taken by Officer Andy in the last two days of his life. Steine had intended to glance at them, but had forgotten. In date order, these showed:

June Jackson trying on a fur coat in a shop on Western Road, under the gaze of a small rat-faced man in a white suit;

a new poster advertising milk, with Pandora's face on it;

Terence Chambers outside the Metropole, watching his suitcases being unloaded from a car with plainly visible bullet-holes in the wing;

Chambers a few seconds later, still out of doors, being greeted by a woman in a smart dress-and-jacket ensemble;

Chambers and the woman sharing a laugh;

Chambers and the woman, going inside;

Chambers and the woman, nearly gone;

from the other side of the road, the arrival of more large, heavy cars at the Metropole.

———

Hardcastle didn't think much of Brighton so far. The fish and chips were double the price of the ones at home in Redcar, and the portion size was laughable. But the main thing was that everywhere was so hot and crowded: the piers were rammed with people; the beach a sea of bodies. Outside restaurants that smelled invitingly of beef gravy there were queues of sunburned people in their holiday clothes standing four abreast! In the end he turned inland, following a sign to the Pavilion, the site of Monday's meeting. He was curious to see it. But once there he met crowds again – albeit with an unusual free-range dairy-herd focus that, in all fairness, he couldn't possibly have anticipated.

Lurking outside the Pavilion – next to a sign that read 'Barber of the Year Contest Bank Holiday Monday, entrance 7/6' – was a boy of about seventeen. He had evidently just arrived, and was offering leaflets to anyone who would take them while shouting, 'Ruddy sham! Boycott the contest! Ruddy sham!' This was Rodolfo's fiery son Carlo. And as things turned out, it was an unfortunate meeting. If Hardcastle was an armed psychopath with an infinitesimally short fuse, Carlo was a brazen young delinquent who never backed down under threat.

'What's this rubbish, lad?' said Hardcastle gruffly, taking Carlo by the ear. 'What do you think you're playing at?'

'Get off!' Carlo shook himself free. 'This fake barbering contest on Monday, mate. It's a ruddy sham, and I'm not standing for it.' He raised his voice again. 'Boycott the contest! Ruddy sham!'

'Why do you say that?'

'It smells, that's why. There's something fishy going on here, and I want everyone to know.'

Now, any other man in this situation might have considered adopting a placatory tone and offering a ten-bob note, but not Hardcastle, even though the boy couldn't possibly know the true reason behind the bogus barbering extravaganza.

'Give me those leaflets. Now! Hand them over. And shut up.'

He made a move to grab Carlo's ear again, but the boy dodged. 'No. Get off.' But before he could shout 'Ruddy sham!' again, Hardcastle pulled out a gun and stuck it in his ribs.

Carlo froze. 'What are you doing? Is that thing real? Help! Help!'

'What's happening here?' said a passer-by.

'Help!' repeated Carlo.

'Hand them over!' Hardcastle repeated. 'Now!'

'Is that *a gun?*' yelped somebody.

It was at just this moment that Susan Turner innocently arrived in the Pavilion Gardens, obliged to divert there on account of the crowds on North Street. She dutifully carried the packet of photographs, which she had scrupulously not examined, perhaps because Inspector Steine had just insulted her by calling her nosy, but we will never know for sure. It didn't matter much, anyway, that she hadn't take a peek. She certainly wouldn't have recognised Mrs Groynes in them, consorting with the most dangerous criminal in England, and greeting him as an old friend. She wouldn't have known that by delivering these pictures to Constable Twitten, she would be placing in his hands all the evidence he needed to bring down the devious criminal charlady who'd been deceiving the police for years.

But Susan never did deliver that evidence. She was thinking about the case quite deeply, and perhaps not paying sufficient attention to her surroundings, when there was an outbreak of agitation in the crowd near the Pavilion.

'That man's got a gun!' someone yelled, and then there was confused movement, and a lot of mooing from startled cows, before people started running in all directions.

'Stay calm!' shouted the farmer. 'Stay calm around the cows!' But then the gun went 'Bang!' as Hardcastle grabbed Carlo's leaflets, shoved the boy to the ground and raced off.

'Oh, my God!' yelled the farmer, as the cows put their heads down and charged with a common goal towards Susan Turner, who alone had not fled the scene or climbed a tree.

She looked up with a frown. What was happening? Today really had been unlike anything in her life up to now.

'Can I help at all?' she called, reflexively.

But it turned out that she couldn't.

'Mind the cows!' was the last thing she heard in this world, along with the thunder of hooves.

Yes, thanks to a freakish coincidence – bringing together an out-of-town gangster with no impulse control; a kid with a grudge against a phony hair-cutting contest; a large bank-holiday-weekend crowd avid for novelty; an unfenced herd of cows in the middle of a major resort town; and an entirely unnecessary gunshot – poor Susan Turner was trampled to death by stampeding cattle.

It was a terrible shame. She had not only made a significant breakthrough in the case all on her own; she was also about to help Twitten expose the truth about Mrs Groynes. But on the other hand, we already know that her future life as a put-upon assistant producer at the BBC would have been sad and unfulfilled, so quite honestly who can judge what was best for her in the long run?

Eight
Sunday

When Twitten woke on Sunday morning, the first thing he saw – on the little dressing table in Mrs Thorpe's top-floor room – was the scrapbook pertaining to the death of Diana.

At first, he couldn't think what it was; then he couldn't remember why he'd brought it home. But as his thoughts began to clear he recollected the plan he'd made with Pandora Holden after the Dairy Maid Miss contest (inevitable winner: June Jackson, who had been resolutely unhelpful regarding police inquiries) to meet her today, and show her the pictures Officer Andy had taken of the Black Sheep Society all those years ago – namely, the athletic June, the absent-minded and untidy Diana, the brilliant Parvati, the tomboyish Wanda and the beautiful Pandora.

Judging by the level of daylight visible through the crack in the drawn curtains, it was still early, and he made no immediate move to get up, or even to check the hour. The interlude between sleep and waking was usually a very productive one for Twitten's clever-clogs brain, and he had learned to wait and let his mind wander before jumping out of bed. Lying here with his mind unfocused, he had found that puzzles tended to resolve themselves, and buried questions rise to the surface. This morning several images and memories were competing for precedence: a small golden terrier dog bolting up a staircase; a dying AA man lying on his back in some grass, feebly singing a music-hall song; a girl in a nightdress toppling backwards off a cliff edge into darkness; and a woman hitting her husband on the head with a frying pan, while Mrs Groynes stood beside her, explaining the significance of the choice of weapon. But just as these visions were happily commingling, and pressing towards an idea, he remembered that an as-yet-unidentified girl had been trampled to death by cows the previous afternoon, and he woke up properly, with a jolt.

Once dressed, he submitted to breakfast, but only to be polite. The wonderful Mrs Thorpe had insisted on getting up to supervise the making of it by Mrs Browning, the ever-reliable daily help.

'So I expect you're investigating these horrible murders, Constable?' Mrs Thorpe said, pouring tea into a finely decorated bone-china cup. They were sitting at a table in the sunny bay window, with its view across rooftops to the sea. Church bells were ringing. From this elevated position, the town of Brighton looked a lot more contained and manageable than it really was. You wouldn't imagine, for example, that young women could be trampled to death by herds of cattle down there.

'I bally well am, yes, Mrs Thorpe. Oh, thank you, that's lovely.'

'And what about this poor girl killed by the cows?'

'I'm afraid there's nothing to go on there. Apparently a street urchin was seen running off with her handbag in the melee, and as for identifying her by sight …' He trailed off, and pulled a face. 'We'll just have to wait for someone to come forward. She's sure to be missed by *someone*. I expect on Monday her employer will start asking questions, if nothing else.'

Mrs Thorpe shook her head sorrowfully, then decided to stop thinking about this disagreeable subject. She picked up a napkin, flapped it and placed it on her lap.

'But you're making good progress with the murder investigation?'

'Gosh, I wish I knew. With three victims, it's quite hard to know where to start. I had an initial theory concerning beauty contests, but unfortunately it didn't stand up to scrutiny.'

'It's the use of milk bottles that I don't understand,' she said.

Twitten made a rude scoffing noise, a bit like a snort. 'Join the bally club!' he exclaimed.

'I said to Mrs Browning – *milk bottles*?'

'I know. For a start, you'd have to carry them about and they're heavy. Also, they're very difficult to *wield*. They don't even smash easily. But I'm convinced the choice of weapon is significant, Mrs Thorpe. I heard a theory at the station that made a lot of sense. The milk bottle as weapon may *speak volumes* about who the murderer is.'

Mrs Thorpe looked puzzled, as well she might. 'You mean he's a milkman?'

'Oh. No. No, I don't mean that.'

'Everyone's saying it's a milkman, Constable.'

'Are they really?'

'Of course. It stands to reason.'

'Gosh, how simple-minded of them. No, I mean that by choosing such a prosaic, everyday object, the killer is uncon-sciously telling us that he's a person of negligible status. So not a criminal, or even a person – for example – in the business of rigging beauty contests for fraudulent personal gain.'

'So … a milkman?'

'Well, to be honest, we hadn't been thinking along those lines, but if the murderer does turn out just to be a bally milkman, Mrs Thorpe, we're going to look frightfully silly for not having rounded up all the milkmen to begin with.'

Twitten drank some tea. He was rather proud of the way he had referred – in vague terms – to *a theory at the station*, thus sidestepping the issue of Mrs Groynes being cleverer than him in matters of ratiocination. Sadly, however, the ploy hadn't worked.

'Was it your lovely Sergeant Brunswick who thought of that? The low status idea? He's so clever, isn't he? It was fascinating watching him work when he came to the house after poor Mr Braithwaite was killed. He learned so much of value in such a short time. I was literally agog with admiration.'

Twitten wasn't sure whether to laugh. Was she serious, saying such things about Brunswick? 'Er, no,' he replied cautiously. 'No, it wasn't the sergeant.' He was willing to believe Brunswick had impressed Mrs Thorpe with his detective abilities, but where had 'lovely' come from?

'The inspector, then?'

'Pardon?'

'Was it the inspector who said the clever thing about milk bottles?'

'Oh. No. It wasn't him either.' Twitten wished he'd never started this. Mrs Thorpe was like a dog with a bone.

She frowned. She was mentally calculating. Because if it wasn't the sergeant or the inspector, who else could it have been?

'Then who—?'

'It's just one of those theories that seem to bubble up communally, I suppose. Who can say where it came from?

I believe the great psychologist Carl Jung talked about a collective unconscious, although I don't suppose he meant it to be applied to solving murders, but – oh, thank goodness, here's Mrs Browning with my delicious bacon and eggs!'

While Mrs Browning delivered Twitten's beautifully cooked breakfast to the table, Mrs Thorpe poured tea for herself and added a slice of lemon, using special tiny tongs. Twitten really had fallen on his feet, getting digs here. In terms of service, it was better than the Metropole. Mrs Browning even came in on Sundays! On the other hand, it was becoming obvious that the inquisitive Mrs Thorpe expected to be kept in the loop in some way, and refused to be fobbed off. Was he a disappointment to her? Thinking about it, he supposed that for the past few years she had sat at breakfast with such glittering theatrical gossips as John Gielgud and Hermione Gingold. Having a tight-lipped police constable as her only guest must be a terrible comedown.

'Constable Twitten, there's something I need to ask you. Why didn't you mention the murders to me yesterday morning? You must already have known about them.'

Luckily, Twitten could answer this with perfect honesty. 'I did know by then, yes, Mrs Thorpe. Perhaps I misjudged the situation, but I was hoping to save your feelings, given – well, you know, given what happened to Mr Braithwaite.' He waved a hand at the walls of the newly repurposed breakfast room, which, just six weeks ago, had been covered in the bright arterial blood of a slaughtered playwright. 'I thought, if there's anyone I know who'd prefer not to think about one person slashing at another with murderous intent, and blood spurting all over the place, it's my wonderful landlady Mrs Thorpe.'

She smiled at the epithet 'wonderful', and magnanimously changed the subject. 'What's this? May I look?' she said, pointing to the scrapbook. 'Who's Diana?'

So Twitten – making a mental note never to bring evidence to breakfast again – handed the scrapbook to her, and without neglecting his excellent eggs and bacon, told her about Officer Andy and his obsessive private research into true crimes.

'Imagine being so fascinated by *murder*,' Mrs Thorpe shuddered, turning the pages. 'But I remember this story of the schoolgirl on the cliff. I read everything I could about it.'

'Did you? Why?'

'It was because everyone said she was such a clueless little thing. They kept saying she might have just fallen off, you see, and not been pushed. It made me think of those jolly hockeysticks school stories – you know, *Muriel Finds Her Spunk*, that kind of thing. There are bold girls who ride ponies and rescue people from wells and win at lacrosse to save the school, and then there's always one who doesn't quite keep up, and gets caught in the chapel after lights out. Diana was that sort.'

'I haven't read many girls' school stories, I'm afraid.'

'But you must have heard some of Cedric Carbody's funny skits on the wireless?'

'Not really. People keep mentioning them.'

'Well, it doesn't matter. But when I heard what the dead girl had been like, it struck a chord with me. I was much more the Diana type than anything else.' She lowered her voice, and raised an eyebrow. 'I was a very late bloomer, in fact, but I made up for it!'

She drank some tea. Twitten had finished eating.

'I'm afraid I have to go now,' he said.

Mrs Thorpe closed the scrapbook, but then opened it again. Something had caught her eye. 'This one's interesting,' she said, pointing at a glued-in photograph.

'What's that?' He rose and joined her, looking at the book over her shoulder. The picture showed children sitting side by side in a row of deck-chairs, with more rows behind. It was a bit fuzzy, but Twitten could clearly see the eleven-year-old Pandora there, laughing with friends.

'It's the children's playground,' said Mrs Thorpe. 'And look, isn't that Cedric Carbody sitting right behind the girls? The photograph must have been taken from the stage.'

Mrs Browning came in to collect Twitten's plate. Mrs Thorpe called her over. 'Mrs Browning, we're just looking at these old photographs of Brighton taken by Officer Andy, and this one caught my eye. I think it must be taken at the children's playground. Would you know?'

Mrs Browning was startled to be addressed out of the blue. 'Who, me, madam? You want me to … ?' she said, glancing at the door as if planning an escape.

'Yes. Come and take a look, if you would.'

'Ooh, well.' She hesitated. 'Well, madam, I could take a quick butcher's, I suppose.' With a show of reluctance, she joined them, wiped her hands on her apron and picked up the scrapbook. But when she held it up close to her face, her manner softened. Mrs Browning was evidently a very sentimental person, as well as short-sighted, and a bit of a cockney. (*Butcher's hook = look.*)

'Well, I call that proper lovely, madam,' she said at last, putting it down, sniffing loudly and producing a hankie from a pocket in her apron.

'We didn't mean to upset you, Mrs B,' said Twitten.

'No, I'm all right, dear. It's just such a lovely picture, that's all. All them talented boys and girls waiting to go up and give their all. Proper lovely, that is. Takes me right back.'

She started to clear the dishes away; Twitten stopped her. 'But where's the picture taken from?' he asked. 'Mrs Thorpe says from the stage, but how could Officer Andy have got up there to take it?'

'Well, Andy played the old Joanna for them, didn't you know?' (*Old Joanna = piano.*)

'Did he?'

'Ooh, he done it for years and years. And every boy and girl who sung a song or danced a dance, he knew them all! Not their names always; but he knew what they liked to sing. The man they called Uncle Jack stood at the side, conducting the audience with his cane, and Andy done the watchercallit … the accompany-ner-ment.'

'Accompaniment?' said Twitten.

Mrs Browning decided to rephrase. 'He done the old Joanna. Sometimes he'd start playing the kiddies' songs before they even got on the stage, he was so sure what they'd ask for!' She got the hankie out again. 'And now he's gorn!' she wailed. 'He's pushing up the daisies, ain't he?'

'I'm afraid so, Mrs Browning. Not literally yet, but certainly metaphorically. My breakfast was delicious, by the way.'

After his life-threatening ordeal outside the Pavilion on Saturday afternoon, you might suppose that young Carlo would come to his senses – at least to the extent of not putting himself in the way of dangerous criminals for the next decade or so.

Sadly, however, the incident of the gun-in-the-ribs merely strengthened his resolve. By the time he'd returned home on Saturday, he had acquired a firearm from a man in a pub near the railway station. It had cost him every penny he had. Coming home with it tucked into his waistband under his jacket, he seemed to see a policeman on every corner; and each time he spotted one, he consciously lengthened his stride, altered course, covered his face or turned his head away. It was a miracle that none of them apprehended him. Not since Richard Attenborough in the film of *Brighton Rock* had a young would-be felon looked so damp and bug-eyed with patent shiftiness.

'Carlo, you're not eating,' said his father at breakfast on Sunday.

'Let it go, Pa,' Carlo warned. The gun was in a suitcase under his bed, along with the famous rejection letter signed by 'Mrs P. Hoagland' – the woman he intended to seek out tomorrow and shoot.

Rodolfo sighed. He remembered when Carlo was such a happy child, sweeping the floor of the shop with a broom that was too long for him, and earning tips from the customers for running errands to the bookmaker's.

He had been such a nice boy before he learned to scowl.

At the House of Hanover Milk Bar on the seafront, the last preparations were being made for the grand opening. It was, clearly, commercially ridiculous to open a new business in August, just when the holiday season was nearing its end, but the manager Mr Shapiro had argued in vain on the subject. From the milk-marketing point of view, the grand opening in Brighton was part of a larger plan. After months of top-level debate at Dairy House in Mayfair, it had been decided that on Bank Holiday Monday the aggressive and unmelodic DRINKA PINTA MILKA DAY slogan would be unleashed on the world. So, on Monday afternoon, not only would the Milk Girl herself be present to open the new milk bar, and not only would there be a playful announcement of the winner of a Knickerbocker Glory competition, there would also be a 'surprise' visit from Mr Henderson's immediate boss from London HQ to announce the end to old-fashioned apologetic milk marketing. And if there happened to be anyone present who might be upset by this PR surprise, his feelings of betrayal would be entirely his own affair.

Having opened new businesses before, on Sunday morning Mr Shapiro had every confidence that everything was on track. Hand-in-hand with his wife, he surveyed the old bathing pavilion from the outside and nodded to himself. Everything was ready. Some excellent staff had been hired for the following day; the shiny chrome refrigerators were all installed; the ice cream was chilled to perfection; the Italian coffee machine worked; the new chrome chairs and tables had been polished; the interior walls had been painted a fashionable pistachio colour; the large plate-glass window had been replaced after the regrettable vandalism incident; Inspector Steine had reportedly sampled every Knickerbocker Glory in town – *twice* – in advance of the grand announcement of the winner.

The only question hanging over the event was the advisability of having cows in attendance, now that they had stampeded in a public park and killed someone. This horrific incident was being played down as far as possible, of course, and no blame had been attached to either the cows or the farmer. (We should feel sorry for this man, incidentally. Bringing cows into the centre of Brighton was a stupid idea, and he had opposed it from the start.)

But back at the House of Hanover, all seemed well.

'Well done, Dave, dear,' Mrs Shapiro said. 'It looks lovely, especially the green colour. I'd like that in the hall.'

'Thank you, Jenny.'

'I still think the name's a bit much.'

'What can I say, love? Out of my hands.'

'But I'll tell you what – I'll be glad when tomorrow's over.'

'So will I!' Shapiro produced the milk bar's door-keys from his pocket. 'May I treat you to coffee and a scoop, Mrs Shapiro?'

This had been their custom with other new businesses. On the day before the opening, they would go inside and 'play at milk bars' like children. So they went inside the House of Hanover, locking the door behind them.

'You sit there, Dave. I'll do it,' said Mrs Shapiro, reaching for a fresh white apron and slipping behind the counter. She picked up a little dish and a couple of wafer biscuits. 'Now, raspberry ripple or—?' But then she stopped. 'What's this?' she said.

'What's what?'

'It says – oh, Dave! It says *glass*!'

Shapiro let out a cry of disbelief as he leaped up to join her behind the counter. And together they read the handwritten sign that had been left on top of the serving area:

WARNING! SOME OF THIS ICE CREAM CONTAINS BLEED-
ING GROUND GLASS, DEARS! DON'T EAT IT!

'They've struck again, Jenny!' Shapiro wailed. 'But *who*? Who and *why*?'

———

In a small, steep street in Kemp Town, Graham Goodyear called ta-ta to his mother, quickly pulled shut the front door and set off downhill for the police station.

Since Friday he'd been aware that the police wanted to speak to him – presumably because of his connection to Barbara

Ashley. He felt bad that they'd missed him: he was happy to help in any way he could. Graham was a polite, respectable and somewhat phlegmatic young man, with – surprisingly, given his talent – no burning show-business ambitions. All the rumours about his scattering peas on top steps, and burying rivals under hundredweights of starchy vegetables, were based on cynical popular supposition. Being the star of the Ice Circus for a month was something he personally could take or leave.

'But it's Sunday!' his mum had protested, when he said he was reporting to the police station. She wanted to keep him at home, to tell him how brilliant he had been at replcing Buster Bond. Graham had flown around that ice rink; he had soared. If Buster Bond's absence turned out to be permanent, Graham would have two more weeks of glory before returning to his regular job.

'I was so proud!' she kept saying, giving him little hugs. 'My son, the star of the show!'

'I know,' he shrugged. 'But it's not worth getting carried away, Mum. Even if Bond's gone for good, it's only for a couple more weeks. Then things go back to normal.'

'I thought being in the show was your dream, Graham? It said so in the paper.'

'Yeah, but I told you before, Mum: I didn't say that. What I actually told them was that skating's harder work than portering! And the circus people are horrible! Those clowns are vile!'

'I don't believe it. Not the *clowns*?'

'Well, they are! They kept kicking the dogs yesterday. I'll be relieved to go back to work, Mum, I mean it. We have a really good laugh at the market.'

On his way to the police station, he tried to focus on Barbara. He wasn't sure there was much he could say about her, except that she'd been a tough girl to spend time with. Going out with her hadn't even been his idea. She had picked him out one day at the ice rink when they were both skating in an afternoon public session. 'You're brilliant, Graham Goodyear, you dark horse,' she'd said, excited, out of breath, and falling (quasi-accidentally) into his arms. And the next thing he knew, she was calling him her boyfriend, and putting her arm through his, and suggesting trips to the pictures, and encouraging him to give up his humble day-job to seek fame and fortune on the ice.

It had certainly been a relief to split up from her. For one thing, it had seemed that nothing he did was good enough for her; for another, he hadn't liked the way she quizzed him about his family background ('But *why* did your father leave you both?'), which made him feel disloyal to his mum.

But worst of all was the way Barbara never missed an opportunity to talk back to people in authority – who were, incidentally, usually men. It was intolerable. Every time she did it – to ticket collectors, policemen, shopkeepers, beauty-contest judges – it made Graham cringe. Girls were supposed to smile and simper, weren't they? If they felt insulted, they weren't supposed to say.

———

The day ahead for Twitten looked rather busy. Before leaving Mrs Thorpe's house, he reminded her that he would not be back that evening: he and Sergeant Brunswick would be keeping vigil at the new milk bar all night in advance of the opening.

'Well, I'm glad you'll have that brave and capable darling of a sergeant with you, Constable,' she said, 'in case anything does go wrong.'

'Oh. Thank you,' said Twitten, uncertainly. He had rather supposed that if anything 'went wrong', it was the magnet-for-bullets Sergeant Brunswick who'd be the one in need of protection. But how interesting to know that the sergeant was brave and capable now, as well as lovely and brilliant at detection and a *darling*. Was Mrs Thorpe actually in love with Sergeant Brunswick? Twitten genuinely hoped not, as it could not end well. Brunswick was not only younger than her, but attracted exclusively to brassy girls of nineteen.

Nevertheless, 'I'll definitely tell the sergeant you said so,' Twitten promised, as he trotted down the front steps and opened the gate.

But he carried on thinking about what she'd said, because it had come as such a surprise. Truthfully, since his arrival in June, Twitten had given Sergeant Brunswick's capabilities as a policeman very little consideration. It had been all too easy to dismiss the sergeant on a number of grounds, such as his aforementioned emotional instability, his obstinate blindness to the true nature of Mrs Groynes, his absurd over-confidence in his non-existent chameleon properties, and his consistent bad luck in getting shot in the leg.

And yet, after a day spent working closely with him, Twitten had to admit that those initial prejudices had now softened a little. Brunswick had many good qualities as a policeman. He was straightforward, and quick on the uptake, and (the best quality of all) he was driven by a proper desire to catch criminals. Also, there was something impressive about his lack of ego. Looking back, Twitten could remember several instances of the sergeant generously patting him on the shoulder and saying, 'Well done, son.' Where others might have taken umbrage at Twitten's success, or tried to claim it for themselves, Brunswick had always given credit where credit was due.

So it was a shame that at this precise juncture, just as Twitten was entertaining such kind, warm thoughts about Sergeant Brunswick, he discovered the existence of the police canteen. He happened to be walking close to the anonymous building where it resided just as Sergeant Brunswick emerged from an unmarked side door, licking his lips and rubbing his hands, and chatting to a fellow police officer about the quality of the breakfast kippers.

Confused, Twitten instinctively hid in a convenient doorway, and listened.

'You back in for lunch, Jim?' said the other officer.

'Roast beef day, are you kidding? Wouldn't miss it.'

'Might see you later, then.'

'Yes. Cheerio.'

Twitten tried to take this in, but couldn't. He felt oddly empty and weightless. *There was a canteen?* First no one told him about the pay parade, and now *this*?

He watched blankly as Brunswick crossed the road to the police station, where a man was waiting for him on the steps. Twitten needed to think about this, but at the same time the injury was so huge that he felt flattened by it. Looking up at the building, he realised that (faintly) he could hear plates being stacked, and cutlery being used. Faintly, he could hear men laughing and a wireless playing dance-band music. Faintly, he could smell bacon. *I have been here for nearly two months and Sergeant Brunswick never thought to tell me there's a canteen?*

'Constable Twitten?' said a voice behind him. He turned to find Ben Oliver there – the youthful crime correspondent of the *Argus*. Oliver smiled and indicated the door. 'Just off to your publicly subsidised breakfast, or on your way back?'

'Oh.' Twitten sighed and shook his head. 'Neither, actually.' He looked ruefully up at the building, but could say no more about it. *Even Ben Oliver knew about this bally canteen. I suppose everyone does.* 'No, I was just standing here ... thinking about something.'

'Are you all right?'

Twitten took a deep breath. 'Of course. Yes.'

'Fancy a cup of tea?'

'I'd bally love one. With five spoons of sugar, if possible.'

Oliver smiled, but didn't press for an explanation. 'Let's go in there,' he said, pointing to a tea shop. 'It's the only place that opens this early on a Sunday.' Then he patted his pocket and said, 'It's on the *Argus*.'

Once they'd sat at a corner table and given their order, Twitten decided to put the canteen out of his mind, especially when Oliver produced his notebook and said, 'So I was on my way to see you, obviously. I've tried to telephone half a dozen times since the events of Friday.'

This was news to Twitten. 'Well, we were out and about all day yesterday, of course, trying to piece things together.'

'And what have you got?'

'I'm afraid I can't tell you.'

Like all reporters, Oliver barely acknowledged the rebuff. His pen was still poised over his notebook. 'Look, Constable. I might have something for you. Are you aware that Barbara Ashley was accusing people of rigging the beauty contests?'

'Yes, of course,' said Twitten. 'She was obsessed, apparently. You must have talked to her parents.'

'I have. And I've been doing a bit of digging, and I think she might have been on to something. There's a man called Tony Sayle I'm trying to track down. Barbara Ashley seems to have threatened him, and there's a link to Carbody because Sayle was his agent – what's wrong?'

Twitten was pulling a face. This was difficult for him. He was under no obligation to help Oliver; also, strictly speaking, he ought not to share information with him. But on the other hand, he hated to see an intelligent person waste his time.

'Look. I really don't think the murders have anything to do with the beauty contests.'

'Right. Can I quote you on that?'

'Of course not!'

The tea arrived at this point, and Twitten gratefully poured it without waiting. Half of his mind was here with Oliver, being discreet about the progress of police inquiries; the other half was upstairs in that building across the road from the police station, where, in a parallel reality, he'd be waving hello to fellow officers, loading a tray with subsidised food, and being mothered, embarrassingly, by a kindly working-class woman at the till, with her hair tied up in a scarf. The works canteen was a boon to every job! It was a haven! Not knowing about it all this time had seriously impoverished his experience of working for the Brighton Police!

But the hardest part of all this was not, of course, the missed plate-loads of liver-and-onions; the missed gallons of sugary tea with little grease bubbles floating on the top. It was the stark realisation that Brunswick simply didn't like him.

'Twitten?'

'Sorry. What were we saying?'

'Look, OK, off the record, Constable, friend to friend, could you give me something? You know I can help. For example, what's that book there?' The reporter indicated the Diana scrapbook that Twitten had set down on the spare chair at their table.

Twitten hesitated. Was Oliver truly his friend?

'Would you mind putting your notebook away? It makes me nervous.'

'Of course.' Oliver made a show of putting the notebook on the floor, while squinting sideways at the labelled scrapbook. 'So,' he said, eyes bright. 'Tell me about Diana.'

Back at the station, the person who'd accosted Sergeant Brunswick outside on the steps turned out to be Rodolfo. He was in an anxious state about his son.

'It's this barbering contest, Sergeant.'

Brunswick moaned. 'Oh, not that again, Rodolfo. Flaming let it go, please.'

'I sometimes wish I'd never heard of it!'

'Blimey, so do I, I assure you.'

'But I'm worried about what Carlo might do!'

Brunswick didn't have time for this. There were bigger things going on in Brighton right now. Not only were there three murders to solve, but he'd just had a message that the House of Hanover Milk Bar had been targeted yet again by saboteurs, and that Graham Goodyear was waiting inside to be interviewed. On top of which, it was pretty hard to tear one's thoughts away from the as-yet-unknown woman who'd died yesterday by bovine misadventure. How could something like that *happen*? His auntie Violet had said she would never drink milk again! 'They said her own mother wouldn't know her after those cows had finished with her!' she'd gasped. Against such a background, the rights and wrongs of the admissions procedure to a barbering contest at the Pavilion did not come high on Brunswick's list of priorities.

However, he had always liked Rodolfo, and had noticed – with sadness – the recent, unmissable signs that Carlo was turning into a right little sod.

'Rodolfo, you know what I think about this flaming contest. You lot are all taking it much too seriously.'

The barber wrinkled his nose. 'My lot? What do you mean, my lot?'

'You barbers! I asked around, and do you know what? There's not a single Brighton barber who got in. Rejection letters all round.'

'Really?'

'Yes. So you shouldn't go taking it personally. Do you see? The whole thing is probably a flaming put-up job.'

'Look, please. I don't expect you to do much, Sergeant Brunswick.'

'That's just as well.'

'But couldn't you find the organisers and warn them? Isn't that your duty?'

Brunswick sighed. Once the D-word had been invoked, he knew he couldn't refuse.

'All right,' he said, grudgingly reaching for his notebook in an inside pocket. 'Have you got a name?'

'Yes.' Gratefully, Rodolfo handed over the original advertisement for the competition. 'There,' he said, pointing. 'Mrs P. Hoagland.'

'Hoagland?' Brunswick repeated. One of the men who'd been killed at the railway station in July had been called Hoagland. But that was presumably a coincidence.

'All right, Rodolfo,' he said. 'Leave it with me.'

Oliver left the tea shop first, leaving Twitten to sit alone for a moment.

'Are you sure you're all right?' the reporter had said, as he was leaving. But Twitten had bravely waved the question away, because 'all right' he certainly wasn't.

There are many people who say in such circumstances that they can't find the right words to express their feelings. However, being lost for words was rarely a predicament in which Twitten found himself. At this moment, he knew precisely the term for how terrible he was feeling: it came from the Greek, and it was *anagnorisis*. He was experiencing a moment of painful clarity – as when Oedipus realises in a ghastly flash that, thanks to his own arrogance, he has killed his father, married his mother, and generally pushed his luck.

'Look, as it happens, I can get hold of the old headmistress from Lady Laura Laridae,' Oliver had continued. It was just this youthful enthusiasm and energy that always beguiled Twitten, and won his trust. 'She sometimes sets crosswords for us. Brenda Stoater, her name is. She sets them under the name Mustella, which is Latin for "stoat". I think she left the school after the Diana incident.'

He waited for Twitten to say something, such as 'That's interesting', or 'Thank you'. But he didn't say anything at all.

'So-o-o,' Oliver resumed, 'if you can quiz Pandora Holden this afternoon, we could meet tonight, maybe, and compare notes? Oh, and I know the retired reporter who worked on this Diana story at the time. He might be able to help. He lives quite near here, so I'll go and see him first.'

He paused – again, to no purpose. 'But I notice you're not saying anything. Look, I don't want to intrude, Constable, but has your cat died?'

Twitten made an effort. 'I'm sorry, Mr Oliver. It's nothing, really. I mean, apart from being anxious that I've told you too much. But at the same time …' His voice trailed off. He had lost his thread.

'At the same time, you want to catch this murderer, Constable!'

'Well, yes. Exactly.' Twitten smiled, and took a deep breath. 'If it's the last thing I do as a bally policeman, I want that. I want that very much.'

Left alone, he poured another cup of tea from the pot, but it was stewed and disgusting, so he pushed it away and stared glumly out of the window, considering his position. Should he leave the force at once, perhaps? Walk out today and never look back?

It was awful. He wanted to weep. For most of his life, Twitten had known, deep down, that he wanted to be a policeman – so much so, that he had made the decision to defy his academic destiny. But look at him now. Sitting in a tawdry tea shop in Brighton, unable to solve a brutal trio of murders, being steamrollered by an ambitious crime reporter, and feeling sorry for himself because, basically, the other boys didn't like him. If he'd gone in for anthropology instead, he wouldn't be feeling like this. In academia, his clever-clogs brain would have been regarded as an asset, not a source of annoyance. But the biggest difference – which had never struck him before – was that, in academia, he'd be *in the right place*, and therefore he would have made friends.

While he was thus miserably sitting and thinking, Twitten finally noticed that opposite the tea shop, leaning against a wall, was a boy of secondary-school age, reading the *Beezer*. He looked familiar. Thinking about it, Twitten realised he had seen this boy before – many times – but always in exactly this pose: just leaning and reading, leaning and reading. This was quite suspicious, and Twitten would have gone out to question the boy about it immediately had he not noticed Ben Oliver's notebook, still on the floor. He picked it up and put it in his pocket.

'More tea, Constable?' asked the tea-shop proprietor. 'Only I'll have to start charging rent. Not that it isn't nice having you. We don't get many of your lot in here, on account of that famously cheap and filling and warm and welcoming police canteen of yours.'

'Hah!' said Twitten. 'I can imagine.' And he started to get up. But then something caught his eye and he paused.

'What is it, dear?' said the woman. 'What are we looking at?'

On the opposite side of the street, something was happening. The boy with the comic had looked up as a woman approached him. Then he'd broken into a grin and produced a large battered envelope from down the back of his shorts. The woman took it, and put it in her handbag. Then she patted the boy on the shoulder, and handed him a paper bag containing a quarter-pound of sweets. The woman was Mrs Groynes.

'That kid's always round here,' said the tea-shop proprietress, as the parties walked off in different directions while she piled teapot, cups and saucers on to a Coronation tea tray. 'He doesn't do any harm. Ooh, but come again, dear!' she called after Twitten. 'And tell all your policeman friends!'

Outside, he stood on the corner and opened Oliver's notebook. A few days afterwards, when he asked himself why he'd done that, the honest answer was that he merely wanted to see if he could decipher the shorthand. But once he'd understood the line of inquiry that Oliver had been working on, he was so shocked that his feelings of self-pity were at last displaced.

'Crikey,' he said to himself. Ben Oliver was clearly planning to denounce Inspector Steine, and traduce the proud achievement of the Middle Street Massacre!

Twitten flipped through the pages in horrified silence. In this notebook Oliver had jotted down (apparently in the dark) key lines from the famous film; on other pages he'd recorded his interviews with a source at Scotland Yard – a source who was far from flattering about Inspector Steine's famous policing *coup*. Twitten had never seen the word 'flukey' written in shorthand before, and it took him a while to work it out – which was just as well, as the source called Inspector Steine 'flukey' several times. Oliver had also spoken to a Fleet Street reporter working on a book about the massacre and its consequences, in which the angry offspring of murdered gang members were coming forward to claim that the whole débâcle had been engineered by the leader of a third gang, possibly with the collusion of a corrupt police force! Oliver had circled the word 'débâcle' and placed a tick beside it. Evidently it had struck a chord with him.

Twitten darted back into the tea shop, and replaced the notebook on the floor without being observed. Oliver was bound to come back for it. And then Twitten stood outside again, feeling lost and bereft, and a bit panicky. Should he go to the police station and confront Sergeant Brunswick with his canteen grievance, or should he run at once to Inspector Steine's house and inform him what was brewing at the *Argus*? Should he follow Mrs Groynes and demand to know what she had received from the child with the *Beezer*? Or should he just run away to France?

He looked down at the Diana scrapbook in his hand and made up his mind. He would visit Pandora Holden at midday, as planned, but do nothing else besides wander through the town. In every other option, people would argue with him, or not want to hear what he said. Brunswick would bluster lame excuses; Steine would refuse to listen, putting his hands over his ears; Mrs Groynes would tell him to mind his own business. But Pandora would call him Peregrine, and right now that counted for a lot.

Nine

At midday on Sunday, just as Constable Twitten was arriving at the Balmoral Hotel in Hove, the BBC's Home Service made an announcement.

'*And now a change to our schedule,*' said a starchy voice.

In millions of households across the country, the person standing nearest to the wireless set held up a finger and said 'Shhh, children' – because this was interesting, and needed to be heard.

'*It was with sadness that the Corporation learned yesterday of the death of the much-loved entertainer Cedric Carbody …*'

Listeners who were happily anticipating their weekly dance-band programme *Seaside Serenade* (this week from Bournemouth) would have to wait, apparently. They would be treated first to a twelve-minute talk by Carbody, previously aired in 1952.

This was the BBC's way of marking his sudden demise, in response to the many fans who had telephoned Broadcasting House to express their shock and sorrow. A disc recording of the classic 'A Difficult Term at St Winifred's' had been located in a basement and dusted off, and would now be played.

In many homes, this extra programme gave listeners pause. At his three-storey home in the Queen's Park area of the town, Inspector Steine stopped reading *The Riddle of the Sands* (his favourite book) and inserted a leather bookmark; in her flat on the London Road, Sergeant Brunswick's auntie sat down on a kitchen chair, smoothed her apron and poured a fresh cup of Ty-Phoo. At his hideaway hotel in Torquay, Gerry Edlin reached out an elegant arm to turn up the volume, smiling winningly at the other residents who were already putty in his hands. On Clifton Terrace, Mrs Thorpe settled herself on a Regency chaise longue in the bay window of her attractively decorated bedroom and took a sip of sherry. In the flat above Rodolfo's barber's shop in Hove, Miss Inman suspended the spring clean of her murdered brother's old bedroom. And at the Balmoral Hotel in Hove, Pandora greeted Twitten on the doorstep by grabbing his arm and rushing him inside to listen.

'What's happening?' said Twitten. 'Am I late?'

'Quickly, Peregrine,' said Pandora. 'It's just starting.'

'What is?'

'You said you'd never heard one of Cedric Carbody's talks,' whispered Pandora, as they took their seats with the other residents. Twitten recognised Mr Henderson, sitting in the best armchair, and nodded to him.

'Mr Henderson,' he whispered, removing his helmet.

'Shhh,' said the proprietor of the hotel. He waved Twitten towards a spare seat.

'Constable Twitten,' mouthed Henderson in reply, carefully making no sound.

'Shhhh!' said everyone else.

For the management at the BBC, incidentally, the decision to repeat this talk had not been a simple one. Monkeying with the schedule required top-level authorisation. An emergency meeting of pipe-smoking men in crumpled brown three-piece suits had been called on Saturday afternoon solely to determine whether a full fee would be payable under the terms of Carbody's original contract. Some of the pipe-smokers said yes; some said over their dead bodies. Some dared to suggest (absurdly) that the Corporation had a moral responsibility towards its loyal and feebly recompensed contributors, especially those who were murdered in the course of their work.

But when the legal director finally stated the official position, all discussion was over. This might sound harsh, he'd said, but by getting himself killed while technically representing the Corporation, Carbody had violated the terms of his contract. No fee was thus payable for this repeat. All future requests for payment from his estate would be blocked. It might even be possible to recover disbursements already made.

And so, against this caring background, 'A Difficult Term at St Winifred's' began, with the late Cedric Carbody affecting the falsetto voice of his legendary headmistress Miss Pritchard. Famously, he did not dress up in female garb for these talks, but he did perform them in front of an admiring audience, whose laughter came across the airwaves in hearty gales. In places you could hear the shuffling of pages. Occasionally, the falsetto slipped. But the main thing to strike any listener was the sheer merriment in Carbody's performance, as if every word he encountered – in his own script – came to him as a delightful, rib-tickling surprise.

'Girls [he began], many of you will be unastonished to hear that this has been … a Difficult Term. [Huge anticipatory laugh from the audience.] Ever since the first day back from the long vac when the small campfire set by Marjorie Whitlock next to the chem lab was caught by the breeze and all but consumed Miss Hopcroft's snuggery while sending poor Mademoiselle to the County General with first-degree burns, it is fair to say that St Winifred's has been … how can I put this? … "on the back foot".

'"For, when sorrows come, they come not single spies, but in battalions". No sooner had the embers cooled; no sooner had poor Mademoiselle's nerves been calmed with the reliable application of Dubonnet, and Miss Hopcroft comfortably installed *pro tem* in the potting shed, than the peace of our little clifftop world was assailed for a second time – no less sensationally – by a fiendish foreign plot to kidnap our spirited head girl Beryl Frensham.

'Ah, Beryl, Beryl, Beryl. [Big laugh.] Beryl, Beryl, Beryl, Beryl, Beryl. Not for the first time I say, well done, my dear, for beating off those ghastly krauts with your hockey-stick, and leaving them for dead in the boot hole. But a black mark – a very black mark indeed – for actually killing the unfortunate Miss Battersby [huge laugh] who unwisely attempted a rapprochement when your hockey-stick was, sadly, very much still in play and your indignant blood was up.

'Rest assured, Beryl, all those miles away in Holloway, that we think of you daily, wish you the best, and will mark the hour of your execution next Friday with the customary minute's silence.

'And on a sunnier note, you will be pleased to hear that when I dropped a line to Bennett and Dobbs, they provided a satisfactory replacement for Miss Battersby in an absolute trice! Thus, geography studies were disturbed by this regrettable capital offence of yours by the barest minimum.'

Carbody paused, beautifully. This was a masterly performance. Then he turned a page, sighed, and carried on.

'I shall not dwell on the *débâcle* that was Sports Day. [A shout of laughter from the audience.] The guilty party knows who she is. Order marks were duly given for the actual impaling of Lorna Hargreaves with a javelin, but I fear Lorna's parents are still demanding financial restitution for the punctured lung, and this might well prove the end of St Winifred's as we know it.

'"How much of this was my fault?" I ask myself. "Augusta, Augusta, Augusta. What have you done to deserve this difficult, difficult term?"

'The answer is, nothing. If pushed, I suppose I do regret lending my motorcycle and sidecar to Aileen Dunlop, who used it to abscond from justice, after masterminding a hashish-smuggling operation from her cubicle in Heliotrope Dormy. But in my defence, when she demanded the keys, she told me barefaced that she merely meant to purchase caramels in town with a five-shilling postal order sent by an aunt in Adlestrop.'

In all the sitting-rooms and kitchens where people were listening to this, there was a confusing mixture of emotions.

It felt wrong to laugh when the man was dead, but it also felt absolutely right. In the residents' lounge at the Balmoral Hotel, one woman was in a state of bent-double convulsion, laughing and crying at the same time, and hugging her knees.

'Last but by no means least, we must address the mystery of Diana's clifftop plunge.'

A huge laugh at this from the audience was met by a rather different reaction from two of the people in the Balmoral lounge. 'No!' Pandora gasped. And Twitten – scarcely knowing what he was doing – reached over and took her hand.

'How dear to us was Diana. A cornerstone of the Black Sheep Society of Ainsworth House, but so often – due simply to her ill-starred congenital slowness – out of step with the nimbler girls.

'Oh, Diana, Diana, Diana. [Laugh.] Diana, Diana, Diana, Diana, Diana. [Laugh building throughout.] When your classmates boldly broke the rules to delight the local hobble-dehoys by singing 'Let's Have a Tiddley at the Milk Bar' in a public arena [big laugh], you were the one left stranded outside the gates on the way back. When your friend Parvati lavishly buttered the stairs in the hope of incapacitating Matron, it was you who forgot, slipped and fell, and spent six days and nights in the san. When your athletic friend June held an unautho-rised archery competition on the school's front lawn, it was you who ambled athwart the whizzing arrows, munching a Cox's Orange Pippin, and risked at every nerve-shredding step a faithful re-enactment of the martyrdom of St Sebastian.

'And when – oh, dear! – a thrilling midnight assignation was made on the windy clifftop by a person who shall NOT be named [big laugh], it was you, Diana, who donned your *inad-equately soled plimsolls* [pause for laugh; laugh starts], followed at a distance, watched by gusty moonlight, slipped on the exposed chalk [laughter builds], shrieked: 'Oh, crikey! Not again!' [huge laugh] and took that final header into the dark.'

While everyone else roared with laughter, Twitten and Pandora looked at each other in horror.

'Poor Diana,' said Pandora quietly – which made everyone in the room laugh again. She fled the room, followed by Henderson, leaving Twitten torn as to what to do. He felt he should follow, but wasn't he obliged to listen to the rest of Carbody's sketch?

'On a happier note, the School Play was a tremendous success. Rarely has Mr Sherriff's *Journey's End* been performed with such unfettered joie de vivre. Meanwhile you will be pleased to hear that my own small efforts in the world of crossword-setting have met with some success …'

And so it went on, with Twitten transfixed, Pandora weeping in the arms of Mr Henderson in the dining room next door, and elsewhere Mrs Thorpe dabbing her eyes with a handkerchief at the loss of such a great artiste; Gerry Edlin loudly applauding (and getting his fellow guests to stand and applaud with him); Miss Inman grunting as she resumed the scouring of a wall with a Brillo pad; and Inspector Steine shaking his head in genuine sorrow at the sort of low offerings classed as entertainment by the listening British public, before removing his bookmark and returning to his Erskine Childers.

———

At the Metropole Hotel, quite a few of the stir-crazy conference delegates on the sixth floor happened to catch 'A Difficult Term at St Winifred's' – but only because there was sod all else for them to do until Monday.

They felt cheated. Chambers had promised them a proper Brighton weekend, with limitless alcohol, much dancing in nightclubs with scantily clothed women, narcotics aplenty, scrappy late-night violence in dark alleys, and possibly the thrills and spills of the greyhound track. Based on these expectations, most of them had left their drugs at home, and none had brought girlfriends. All had brought weapons. And as any villain will tell you, an idle knuckleduster hangs heavy in the hand.

So it is fair to say that a sense of frustration was building. And it would also be fair to say that the Carbody broadcast – with its camp, niche appeal – helped matters not one bit. Had a high-travelling crane-shot been available to pass along all the sea-view windows of the sixth floor of the hotel, it would have revealed one strung-out thug after another listening with an expression of offended disbelief, and then – enraged – jumping up and smashing the wireless set to pieces.

There were exceptions, however. In Room 615 all was quiet, and the wireless remained intact. This was because Mr Pickering (delegate for Essex and East Anglia) had died of septicaemia instantly on arrival, as a result of injuries inflicted by an enthusiastic Ipswich dominatrix the previous weekend.

(Looking back, it had been foolish of Pickering to travel. Blood poisoning is never to be taken lightly, and it was undeniable that he had felt, and looked, terrible all week. On the express from Victoria, he had presented such a corpse-like appearance that the other passengers in his compartment had opted to wedge themselves outside in the corridor.)

Meanwhile, in Room 608, occupied by Mr Shelby from the East Midlands, the wireless set was likewise spared, because a three-handed poker game had now been running, with curtains closed, for a full twenty-seven hours – and no one was ready to stop. Playing against Shelby in one of the most unevenly matched games of cards he had ever known, were Mr O'Brien from the neighbouring West Midlands, and Mr Baker (North West).

Both the Midlands boys were serious card-players and this was reflected in their winnings: they were coming out about equal. Baker, however – well, Baker was simply useless, and had already lost not only all the cash he'd brought to Brighton, but also his Bentley and the family home in the Wirral, not to mention two and a half legs of his favourite racehorse. Shelby and O'Brien could hardly believe their luck. Normally, on their home turf, these two were at daggers drawn over matters of demarcation – but a spirit of common amazement at their fantastic good fortune was bringing them closer by the hour.

What made Baker so bad at cards? It was – sadly – his 'tell', which his canny opponents had spotted in the first few minutes of play. It didn't take a genius to work it out, either. When Baker received a good hand, his eyes lit up and he smartly tapped his cards on the table, exclaiming 'Hah!' When he got a bad one, he frowned and said 'Oh'. At home, in his own casinos, people deliberately lost to Len ('Bang-Bang') Baker because – as his nickname implies – if they didn't, he might shoot them. It was a shame he had never realised this.

Finally, in Room 601, the last person not listening to Carbody's broadcast was, inevitably, the psychopathic Mr Hardcastle. In fact, Hardcastle made a point of never listening to the wireless, on account of having quite a few voices in his head already. So instead, he was hanging out of the window and aiming his gun at holiday-makers on the Promenade. He was in just this sniper-ish attitude – window wide open, one hip propped on the sill, cigarette clamped between his teeth, both arms extended for better control of the weapon – when, immediately after the Carbody memorial broadcast, Terence Chambers entered the room, with Palmeira Groynes at his side.

'Hardcastle, get down,' said Chambers, quietly.

The other man barely moved. It was too long-distance a shot with this sort of gun; he knew that. The woman he had in his sights – wearing a hot pink polka-dot dress and a yellow straw hat – might not be the person he hit when he pulled the trigger. But did it matter? Whoever copped it, the flap would be worth watching. And wouldn't it give that bitch in the hat a scare!

'Hardcastle,' repeated Chambers. From the dramatic decrease in volume of his voice, you could tell he was extremely angry.

'What now?' said Hardcastle, not lowering the gun.

Chambers swiftly joined him at the window, took hold of his standing leg and pulled.

'What the—?' Hardcastle grabbed the window frame for balance. 'Let go of me!'

Chambers leaned closer. 'I need a word with you, Hardcastle,' he whispered, with no trace of emotion in his voice.

Mrs Groynes, watching, gasped. When Terence Chambers dropped his voice to an *uninflected whisper*, you needed to start saying your prayers.

'Tell me about Diana, Miss Holden. Tell me anything you can remember.'

Twitten and Pandora were sitting together with Mr Henderson, post-broadcast, in the small dining room. All of them were reeling from what they had just heard. Twitten in particular had a lot of questions, but he slightly despaired of asking them. Pandora's wide streak of self-centredness was proving hard to miss. He knew that if he asked her something directly pertinent to the murder inquiry, she might very well answer, 'So how did you feel when you found out I was the Milk Girl?'

However, currently, most of the questions pertaining to herself *were* pertinent to the inquiry, so he let her talk.

'How could Mr Carbody know all that?' Pandora was saying now, rather than answering his question about Diana. 'He knew about me singing "Let's Have a Tiddley at the Milk Bar" at the children's playground! But no one knows that, Peregrine. I was so embarrassed, I never told anyone.'

'It was you?' said Henderson. 'Who sang that milk-bar song in public?'

'Yes!' Pandora blushed at the memory.

'I've never heard of it,' said Twitten.

'Really?' said Henderson, surprised. He not only knew all the songs extolling milk bars but had written most of them.

'It's just a funny old song.' Pandora shrugged. 'We found a record of it in the junior common room. It's not naughty or anything; it was a *dare*. We were always daring each other at Lady L. But it went wrong. I got the words all mixed up, and a couple of people in the audience booed, and then the man at the piano told me off for wasting everyone's time, and I felt awful. I hate being told off. I hate it!'

'The man at the piano was horrible to you?' repeated Twitten. 'That was Officer Andy, one of the murder victims.'

'Was it? Well, he made me cry. He said it was disrespectful to treat the talent show as a joke, and that as a well-brought-up girl I should know better. Everyone was uncomfortable, and June was furious, and then a girl got up – a local girl, I suppose; about my age, we didn't know her. She got up and told the man at the piano he ought to apologise to me for being so rude. It was really shocking, a girl talking back like that, and we were all told to leave – and because of that, someone informed Miss Stoater, the headmistress, and I got a detention with a hundred lines, and then the Stoat asked the whole school to explain the word "tiddley", but to be honest that was very funny, and made the whole thing better again, because of the way she said "Oh, Marjorie!" in such a tragic voice – a bit like Mr Carbody just now. Oh Marjorie, Marjorie, *Marjorie*. That was just the way she said it. In fact, everything he said was just like the Stoat.'

'Really?'

'But how could he possibly know about me singing? And what he said about someone making an assignation on the cliff and Diana following – where on earth did he get all that?'

———

Back at the Metropole, Mr Hardcastle from the North East was not reading the situation very well. He refused to relinquish the gun.

'You threatened a kid, Hardcastle,' said Mrs Groynes. 'You caused a bleeding stampede and someone died! My boy Shorty witnessed the whole thing. The bang, the thundering hooves, the screams, everything.'

'Look, that kid was threatening *us*,' said Hardcastle. 'You should be thanking me. I grabbed those from him.' He indicated a pile of hand-written flyers with the heading BOGOUS CONTEST on them. Mrs Groynes picked one up, scanned its contents, and then opened her handbag, as if to put it inside.

'Italian-looking, this kid?' she asked.

'Yes. I suppose so.'

She put her head close to Chambers, and spoke in a low voice. 'Barrow-Boy Cecil tells me he sold a gun last night to an Italian-looking kid at a pub near the station.'

'Oh, no,' said Chambers, under his breath. 'Oh … *drat*.'

'Now, I don't know who this kid is,' she continued, 'but if he turns up waving a gun tomorrow, and we end up surrounded by rozzers, I tell you, it'll be all this idiot's doing.'

Chambers shook his head wearily, and looked down into Mrs Groynes's open handbag, where a gun was nestling. He looked her in the eye and raised an eyebrow. She raised an eyebrow back. Years ago, when they worked as a team, they'd used this ploy a dozen times in sticky situations.

'What's going on?' said Hardcastle. 'What's in the bag?'

'Fancy a mint imperial, dear?' said Mrs G, holding out the bag to Chambers. 'It might help dissipate the tension, as it were.'

There was the slightest pause and then, 'Don't mind if I do,' said Chambers. 'Fancy one yourself, Pal?' Then he reached in, grabbed the gun and shot Hardcastle in the head before the man knew what was happening. The troublesome North East delegate dropped lifeless to the floor.

'Oh, well,' said Chambers, shrugging.

Mrs Groynes held out her handbag for the return of the gun. 'He certainly had that coming, Terry,' she said. 'Terry? You all right?'

'Mmm,' he said, distractedly. He was studying the position of the body. As it happened, the way people dropped to the ground when shot in the head was something Terence Chambers was particularly interested in. Sometimes, as a party-trick at home in Stepney, he would lay out ashtrays on the carpet to mark exactly where he anticipated a given person would land. 'What you doing, boss?' the intended murderee would ask, uneasily, as the process began.

Joining him to look down on Hardcastle, Mrs Groynes made a 'Tsk' noise and patted Chambers on the arm. 'Put it back, dear?'

'Oh. Right. Yes.' He surrendered the gun, pulled a regretful expression. 'This wasn't supposed to happen, Pal.'

'You did what you had to do, dear. He was a bleeding liability.'

'Yeah, but they're dropping like flies, what with Pickering and all.'

Mrs Groynes made another sympathetic 'Tsk'. 'I'm guessing you'd rather not tell the others that numbers are down from ten to eight, and that the whole East Coast of England north of London is presently rudderless and up for grabs?'

'You guess right, Pal.'

'Thinking of moving in yourself?'

'I am. I'm very fond of Southend.'

They turned to go, leaving Hardcastle where he fell.

'Eight out of ten left,' said Chambers, wearily, as they were leaving the room.

'That's still enough, Terry. But you had me worried for a minute there. I thought, He's only forgotten the old mint imperial trick!'

Chambers laughed, and was just about to say 'Never!' when a volley of shots rang out, and they both dived for cover.

'Oh, what *now*?' huffed Mrs G.

'Sounded like gunfire.'

'It's coming from there, Terry,' hissed Mrs Groynes, pointing to Room 608. 'That's Shelby's room.'

'Oh – *flip*,' said Chambers.

More shots followed, with the telltale sound of chairs falling over and bodies dropping to the ground. Chambers shook his head sorrowfully and sucked his teeth throughout. This was turning into a very testing day.

'Do we go in?' whispered Mrs G.

'Nah,' he said. 'No point.'

Finally, there was silence. Chambers and Mrs Groynes tentatively pushed open the door to find a darkened room featuring overturned chairs, a number of bloodied playing cards and bank notes, some IOUs with crude drawings representing parts of the equine anatomy – and three dead bodies.

'Don't look at *me*, dear; none of this is my doing,' said Mrs Groynes, opening the curtains.

It was pretty clear what had happened in Room 608. Shelby and O'Brien had finally exploited the Baker tell to its limit, and claimed the last leg of the racehorse, with fatal consequences. Exhausted, fraught and miserably racehorse-less, the North West had jumped up and shot the East Midlands; the West Midlands retaliated by shooting the North West; then the East Midlands (overexcited and fatally wounded) shot the West Midlands – not in retaliation, but because he couldn't resist the opportunity.

Then the sequence had been simply reversed, with the West Midlands shooting the East Midlands, and then expiring; the North West shooting the already lifeless West Midlands, just to be on the safe side; and the East Midlands shooting the North West twice before the gun dropped from his lifeless hand and he fell down.

So it was all quite neat, if otherwise far from satisfying from Chambers's point of view, as – at a stroke – it reduced the number of still-living delegates to the great Brighton Conference of 1957 from eight to just five.

'Oh, *number twos*,' said Chambers, with a small sigh. 'That's done it. We're in the doo-dah now.'

And so they were. Although nothing had been said overtly on the subject, there were definitely two classes of delegate present for this conference: the seriously big hitters with urban populations rife with villainy; and then the rest. As things now stood, of the big hitters only London and Brighton were still extant. With the East Midlands, West Midlands, North West, North East and Essex all out of the picture, the remaining fiefdoms being called upon to pool resources and resist the American mob incursions were:

the South West
the Scottish Borders

the Thames Valley
the Channel Islands
the Lake District

With the best will in the world, it was unlikely they were up to it, the main organisational demands in these five attractive regions being less concerned with protection rackets, narcotics and prostitution; more with:

cream teas
tweed manufacture
woollen carpets
tax avoidance
sublime poetic response to watery landscape.

'Why did we do this, Pal?' said Chambers, quietly, picking up a piece of paper marked, *I promise to pay the bearer one back leg.* 'Just remind me why.'

———

Elsewhere in Brighton, of course, people were unaware of the momentous happenings at the Metropole. Even visitors to the hotel had no idea what was occurring on the top floor. Downstairs in the bar, Ben Oliver was making notes, having just bought a drink for the retired *Argus* reporter who had worked on the Diana story, and now he was awaiting the arrival of Miss Stoater – crossword-setter and former headmistress of Lady Laura Laridae.

She had chosen to meet him at the Metropole rather than entertain him at her home, which was fair enough. Flipping with satisfaction back through his notebook, Oliver realised he was in a good position in regard to this murder inquiry.

If he helped solve it, he could take some of the glory. But if the case wasn't solved quickly, he could write his proposed piece condemning Inspector Steine as hopelessly ineffectual, and acquire stardom by another route. 'Win-win', we would call it today, because we have more words for things.

'Mr Oliver?' He looked up. He expected to see a handsome but square-cut woman of middle years in a capacious tweed suit and sensible lace-up shoes, possibly with a cameo brooch at her throat. Instead, the slim and shapely Miss Stoater wore a fashionable twinset in lavender blue with a light linen skirt and court shoes. Her hair was permed; her face powdered. She was forty-five at the outside. Oliver panicked. Had he called the wrong person?

But then she spoke. 'You wanted to talk about poor Diana, Mr Oliver,' she said, and her voice settled any doubts. She did at least still *sound* like a headmistress. 'I'm sorry I'm late, but something came on the wireless and I had to listen.'

'What was it?'

She waved the question away. 'Immaterial,' she said. 'Now, what exactly did you want to know?'

At Inspector Steine's house, there was a knock at the door. When he opened it, he saw a boy running away, and a small parcel on the doorstep.

'Hey, you!' he called. 'You, stop!'

But the boy made an obscene gesture and kept running, so the inspector picked up the parcel and took it through to the scullery where he knew his housekeeper kept a pair of scissors in a drawer. He opened the parcel to find a note signed 'From a well-wisher', a photograph of a vaguely familiar man standing outside the Metropole, and a loaded gun.

Steine looked at it all for a very long time. He kept saying to himself, 'I should call the police.' But then he kept remembering that he *was* the police, in which case the best thing he could do was think.

Sergeant Brunswick had spent the morning looking for Carlo on Rodolfo's behalf, questioning some of the tough street urchins who usually kept company with the boy. It was very depressing. Each of them found a more annoying way not to help. Despite being a fan of the cinema, Brunswick did sometimes regret the impact of films on kids' behaviour. When did they all learn not to smile? This was a very nice time to be a teenager: they should be rejoicing; there was no war on. Instead of which they looked at you as if they hoped you would drop dead.

'I understand Carlo was upset on his dad's behalf, on account of this barbering competition,' he told one darkly brooding lad on a butcher's bike, who was known to be Carlo's best friend. The boy wore his hair in a pompadour, and had a hand-rolled cigarette tucked behind one ear.

'First I've heard of it, you lousy woodentop,' came the curt reply, before the boy rode off, narrowly avoiding running over Brunswick's foot.

'Seen Carlo today?' he asked another.

'What's he done?'

'Nothing, as yet.'

'So why don't you coppers leave him alone!'

By the time he'd interviewed six of these churlish kids, Brunswick had had enough. He went back to the station, sat at his desk for a few moments, discovered that Barbara Ashley's ex-boyfriend Graham Goodyear had been and gone (he'd waited two hours), and then went to the canteen. Tonight he was on stake-out duty with Twitten at the new milk bar, so he'd better get some dinner and then a few hours' kip.

He noticed that someone had been using the typewriter in the office, and practising the words 'well' and 'wisher' on a piece of scrap paper, both with and without the hyphen. He took a quick look at it, screwed it up and dropped it in the bin.

Back at the Balmoral Hotel, Twitten waited until Pandora had exhausted all her many 'But *how*, Peregrine?' questions, and then produced the scrapbook.

'Miss Holden,' he said. 'I think I can answer the question of how Cedric Carbody knew about your tiddley-at-the-milk-bar song.'

'Really?'

'Yes. I believe he was present when you sang it.'

She took the book on to her lap. 'Oh, my goodness,' she gasped. 'That's us!'

'Yes, but more to the point, that's him.'

'This man here?'

'Yes.'

True to form, Pandora studied the picture, but rather than looking at the man indicated, ran a finger along the row of childish faces. 'This is so strange, Peregrine. The feeling that someone was spying on us.'

'I know, it must be.'

'Look at us. We're so wrapped up in ourselves, we have no idea someone's taking the picture; we don't know people are looking. There's June. She was fabulous! She always wore her school hat at that angle. It was wonderful to see her again yesterday at the beauty contest, although also a bit terrifying. And of course that one's Diana, looking the wrong way.'

'I know. Officer Andy seems to have collected every news-paper story about her, and she's nearly always a blur in the photographs. Officer Andy's sister said that he knew Diana personally, but I forgot to ask how. I was wondering: did she ever get up and perform?'

Pandora didn't answer. She was too excited. 'There's Gorgeous Graham!'

'Who?'

'Graham. That one, at the front.' She pointed, blushing again. 'We loved Graham. All of us. He was the local boy we had a crush on. Even Diana.'

'Do you mean Graham Goodyear?'

'Yes, I suppose. I mean, he was Mr Goodyear's son, so yes, I suppose. But how do you know about Graham?'

'He's someone we've been trying—'

'We only ever called him Gorgeous Graham, you see.'

'So I gathered.'

'He was a bit older than us, and he'd virtually left school already because, to be honest, he wasn't very bright, so he used to come up to Lady L sometimes on his father's milk-cart—'

'His father's *milk-cart*?'

'Yes. Mr Goodyear was our milkman.'

'Was he?'

'Oh, don't be a snob, Peregrine. There's nothing wrong with being the son of a milkman. Anyway, we'd wake up early on purpose and lean out of the dorm windows just in the hopes of glimpsing Graham. What's wrong, Peregrine? What have I said? We were only eleven; there was no harm in it.'

'It's not that.'

'It was a schoolgirl thing. We were mad about the garden-er's lad as well, and he had a *squint*.' Pandora laughed. 'There was a girl in the Lower Fourth who developed a crush on the Bishop of Chichester.'

'Of course. No, it's nothing. Go on.' But Twitten could hardly contain his excitement. Graham Goodyear's father was a milkman? This was *huge*.

'Well, while his father left the cart to make his deliveries to the kitchens, Graham would stay with the horse and give it a nose-bag. And Mr Goodyear was sometimes gone for quite a while, so we girls got a really good look. Graham was very, very handsome. There was something about the way the sun fell on his neck … Anyway, one day we dared Wanda to slip out of the side door and talk to him about the horse, and we didn't think she'd do it, but she did! She talked to a boy! And when she came back up to the dorm she reported that he was ever so sweet, despite not knowing his hocks from his withers (whatever that meant), and that he'd told her about the talent contests at the children's playground, and suggested she should come. That's why we went, really. Just to see Graham. We absolutely idolised him.'

'Why did he go there? It sounds like he wasn't a child any more himself.'

'That's true. I suppose they stretched a point.'

'He can't have skated?'

'No!' Pandora was confused by the question. 'No, of course he didn't skate, Peregrine. He used to sing.'

Twitten felt a strange wave of excitement wash over him. Could the facts in this case at last be coming clear?

'He sang songs? At the playground? Where Officer Andy played the piano?'

'Yes. Or just one song, actually. It was the same song every week. People expected it.'

Twitten bit his lip. 'Can you tell me … ?' he began, and stopped. He was attempting to remain calm. 'I mean, I don't suppose you remember which song it was, Miss Holden?'

'Yes, absolutely. It was "If You Were the Only Girl in the World".'

Twitten jumped up. 'Oh, flipping flips!' he exclaimed. 'So it was Graham flipping Goodyear! Flipping, flipping, crikey-flips!'

'What?' said Pandora. 'What have I said? Are you all right, Peregrine? I'm getting a bit worried about you.'

'Are you sure about the song, Miss Holden? Completely sure?'

Henderson, who had been listening to all this, intervened. 'Of course she's sure, Constable. She's not a liar. And I resent your attitude. Miss Holden isn't one of your suspects. She's helping you, and at considerable distress to herself.'

'Of course. I'm sorry. I can explain. But I just have to check … You are sure?' Twitten said this as gently as his agitated state would allow. 'You are absolutely sure about the song?'

'Of course. We all swooned, imagining he was singing it to us. He had a really good voice, and kept in tune right through to the end – when, to be honest, it went a bit flat. But you've got that look again, Peregrine. What's wrong? Honestly, this was years before I met you. I was a child. You seem very agitated, Peregrine.'

'No, I'm very well. Really. Could you give me a moment to think, please, Miss Holden?'

'Why?'

'Because I seriously have to think.'

Twitten closed his eyes, to concentrate. The milk bottles! The song! Graham's direct personal contact with all three of Friday night's victims – with the scoffing Cedric Carbody, with the piano-playing Officer Andy and with a local girl who talked back to people, who sounded a lot like Barbara Ashley, *who was, anyway, later to be Graham's girlfriend before she broke things off with him.* But the clincher was the song. Why else would Officer Andy sing that song with his dying breath, if it wasn't Graham Goodyear he meant to identify as his killer?

'Have I said something wrong, Peregrine?'

'Not at all. In fact, I think you've solved the case.'

Pandora flushed with pleasure. 'Have I? Me?'

'Yes. I think your Gorgeous Graham murdered three people on Friday evening.'

'Oh, no. Not Graham!'

'I'm bally well afraid so. He knew them all; he has a family connection to milk bottles; he has a lowly job with no influence in the world; he didn't appear in the ice show on Friday until at least half-past nine, so he had the opportunity to commit all three murders; and although I can't tell you how I know this, his connection to that bally song puts his guilt beyond all doubt.'

'Oh, no!' said Pandora. 'I wish I'd never told you. Now it will be my fault if he's guilty.'

Twitten decided not to argue with her, but made a mental note to look up the difference between solipsism, narcissism and infantile omnipotence once his reference books arrived from home.

'*Will* it be my fault, Peregrine?' she urged.

But Twitten refused to entertain the question. His mind was on more important things. Because if Gorgeous Graham Goodyear was guilty of these murders, there were still some serious questions to consider, such as *why* he had killed these people, and why he had killed them *now*.

Ten

Sunday night

By arrangement, Sergeant Brunswick arrived at the House of Hanover Milk Bar at 10 p.m., and looked about for Twitten. No one there. Was he the first? Had Twitten forgotten to come? Brunswick's spirits lifted at the thought.

'Over here, sir!' came Twitten's voice.

Brunswick huffed. 'Where? I can't see you.'

'The Punch & Judy booth, sir.'

Brunswick turned to see the red-and-white striped canvas tent used every day by Ventriloquist Vince. It looked strange silhouetted against the darkly glinting sea, its colours drained; it was weird, especially, to look at it and hear no terrifyingly aggressive shouting from a Greek-accented man with a swazzle in his mouth. Vince's show was as essential to the cheerful family Brighton seafront experience as the cockle stalls, the ice creams and the deck-chairs. No day was complete without the *Whack! Whack! Whack!* of Punch's stick against the head of his puppet-wife, with accompanying X-rated cries of '*I fucking kill you Judy, you brass! I not fucking joking!*' and '*Help! Help! I dying! I dead, mate. Punch, you bastard, look what you do, I fucking dead!*' But now, in the dark, all was quiet. The lifeless Punch & Judy theatre just rustled in the breeze, and Sergeant Brunswick shuddered.

'Inside the tent, do you mean, son?' he called, uncertain, hoping the answer was no.

'Yes, sir! Inside the tent. Although I think Mr Vince prefers the word "booth", doesn't he, sir? Hold on, sir.' There was a pause, and a scuffling noise, and then Twitten's face (with helmet) appeared in the Punch & Judy performance space. 'Here I am. I'm standing on a little stool.'

Brunswick crunched his way across the shingle, sighing. Despite his provident nap this afternoon, he still felt unprepared for an all-night session with Twitten. In fact, he was feeling pretty low. In the past couple of days, despite all the dashing about, he'd had a surprising amount of time to reflect on matters thrown up by the case. And in particular, it was the image of Officer Andy's bedroom-cum-crime-archive that dominated his mind's eye. He kept remembering Miss Inman opening the door, saying, 'I suppose you ought to see this.' And then those piles of scrapbooks in that darkened room; the smell of newsprint and fish-glue; the sheer unpleasant ghoulishness of it all.

Both he and Twitten had gasped aloud when they first saw inside the room. But while Twitten had rejoiced in the scrapbooks as a fabulous source of potential clues, the whole thing had depressed the hell out of Brunswick.

'Why?' he kept asking himself. Here was an AA patrolman who led a helpful and fulfilling life, rescuing stranded motorists. His was a simple, heroic existence that entailed, among other things, driving a beautiful brand-new Land Rover. His relationship with the motoring public was entirely enviable: when Officer Andy arrived at the scene, people literally cried with relief; when he left, they said, 'Our hero!' This man was, therefore, in all important respects, the opposite of a policeman, and had no need whatsoever to contaminate his life with the horrors of crime. But in his spare time, what did he do? He not only compiled private case files, but took the train to London and trailed after dangerous villains.

When you are a policeman, it's important to believe you are shielding the rest of the world from the need to know about evil and crime. When you find out that someone like Officer Andy actually *wants to know this stuff* – well, what's the point of it all? What is the flaming point?

'I just thought it was a good idea, sir,' Twitten continued, as the sergeant approached. 'I asked Mr Vince if we could use his Punch & Judy theatre for the stake-out tonight, and at first he swore a lot – and I mean it was truly bally shocking how much he swore. There were a couple of words I've honestly never heard in my life. But then I showed him a ten-shilling note and it was like a miracle, he completely changed his mind. The thing is, sir, it gives a very good view of the milk bar through the little eyeholes, and it will also protect us from the wind. The only trouble is, it's quite dark and stuffy in here and there's a lot less room than I expected.'

'How do I get in?'

'Round the back, sir.'

Brunswick opened the flap at the back of the booth, and ducked inside. In the gloom, he could make out – aside from Twitten – two low stools, some binoculars and a holdall. Then the flap closed, and all was blackness.

'What's in the bag?' he said, as he settled himself on one of the stools, hugging his raincoat around him.

'Well, it's quite good news, sir. There's a flask of tea and a packet of ham sandwiches, and two big slices of Victoria sponge wrapped in a tea towel. Mrs Thorpe insisted I bring it all. She was very concerned about us both being out all night, but I have to say, sir, she was particularly concerned about you.'

'Really?' said Brunswick. 'Why me?'

'Well, I don't fully understand the reason, sir, but she talks about you quite a lot.'

Brunswick tried to picture Mrs Thorpe. What mainly came to mind was the elegance of her Clifton Terrace house, and its panoramic view.

'You seem to have made a very good impression on her while investigating the Braithwaite killing, sir.'

'Oh.' This was nice to know.

'She baked the Victoria sponge herself, and she said, *Tell your lovely Sergeant Brunswick I wouldn't want him to go hungry.*'

'Blimey, did she?'

'Yes, sir. Her exact words.'

'She said *lovely*?'

'Oh, yes. And not for the first time.'

'I've only met her twice!'

'I know.'

'Well, thanks, Twitten. That's really cheered me up.'

'Oh, good. And I'm sure the cake will be terrific.' Twitten bit his lip. He felt the need to add something. 'But it does make me wonder, sir.'

'Wonder what?'

'Well … it's a bit awkward. But since Mrs Thorpe obviously doesn't stand a chance of your returning her feelings, would you like me to explain to her that you're really only interested in younger and brassier women, so she shouldn't waste her time?'

'*What?*' Brunswick was horrified. 'No, of course not. And what are you talking about, *brassy*? For God's sake, Twitten, what's wrong with you?'

In the darkness, Twitten pulled a face. 'But you *do* prefer younger women, sir. I mean, it's bally obvious. You went quite peculiar at the beauty contest last night, and none of the contestants was older than twenty-one.'

'Yes, I know. But—'

'And Maisie on the seafront is only nineteen.'

'Yes.'

'And as for Barbara Ashley—'

'Look, just don't say that to Mrs flaming Thorpe, all right? Just say thank you for the sandwiches and the Victoria sponge!'

It was strange, being in the dark like this. You would think, by now, that their eyes would have adapted, but in fact they could make out virtually nothing. Both of them listened intently for a while, as fast footsteps approached the milk bar, and then passed by.

'What are we expecting to happen, Twitten?'

'To be honest, I've no idea, sir. Whoever is conducting this campaign against the milk bar has vandalised the place in most of the usual ways already. Mr Shapiro told me they had to throw away all the ice cream today because of the threat of ground glass! I suppose the worst case would be someone setting the building on fire. But I still don't believe the attacks are about genuine opposition to the business, sir. I think someone wants an excessive police presence here tomorrow afternoon just to ensure that we're not somewhere else.'

'Well, I don't know about that, but the inspector has stepped up the numbers again.'

'Has he? Crikey. He keeps doing that.'

'I heard at the station. He telephoned in this afternoon. He's got virtually every copper in Brighton protecting the milk bar's grand opening now.'

Twitten sighed. 'Then whoever is behind this, their fiendish bally plan has bally worked.'

It occurred to him that now was the moment to tell the sergeant everything he'd learned today concerning the case, and the death of Diana. He should perhaps also tell the sergeant about what the *Argus* was planning. On top of which, he needed urgently to ascertain whether Brunswick had questioned Graham Goodyear. But the more he shared this tiny blind space with the sergeant, trying to talk normally, the more he choked on the one subject he really wanted to discuss with him.

'Sir,' he said. 'There's something I need to—'

Brunswick interrupted him. 'Here, have you still got your helmet on?'

Twitten put a hand to his head to make sure. 'Yes, sir. Why? I'm on duty, sir.'

'Well, take it off, son. If you like.'

'Oh, thank you, sir.'

Twitten removed the helmet and stowed it under his stool, and again, they sat in silence, despite having so much to talk about. Obviously, they should be planning what to do in the event of a dastardly saboteur turning up with a gallon of paraffin and a box of Swan Vestas. Obviously, they should be discussing the progress of their milk-bottle-murder investigations. But there was something so unusual about sitting here in the pitch dark, with a light sea breeze rustling the canvas, and the faint noise of fairgrounds and seafront traffic, and a jazz quartet on the West Pier, and above all the promise of delicious ham sandwiches, that Twitten decided it was now or never.

'Sir,' he said quietly. 'I'm afraid there's something I need to talk to you about. Something personal.'

'Really? Here, is it about that Milk Girl of yours? I could tell she liked you, son. The way she couldn't stop talking! Peregrine this; Peregrine that. She's mad about you, if you ask me. But in my view, you'd be better off with that Susan Turner girl; the cup of tea she made us was flaming out of this world.'

'I agree, sir. Hard to put one's finger on it, but that tea was bally outstanding. But it's nothing like that, sir. It's about – well, it's about the police canteen.'

'Ah.' Brunswick slumped on his stool. What could he say? He had known this moment would come.

'Yes. I found out, you see.'

'Ah, so you've found out about … ?'

'About its bally existence, sir, yes.'

'Ah.'

'The thing is, sir, I saw you coming out of the building this morning, talking about kippers with a fellow officer, and I put two and two together.'

'Oh. Well, look—'

'Up until then, I didn't know there *was* a police canteen, you see –'

'No, I suppose you—'

'– because you never mentioned it, sir. And of course there's no sign on the building, but no one else mentioned it, either, not anyone, not even Mrs Groynes, so presumably not telling me was a sort of station joke that I was the unconscious butt of, and everyone's been laughing at me for nearly two months, ever since I arrived.'

'Right. Well, give me a chance here—'

'For nearly two months, sir.'

'Yes.'

'I've been bringing sandwiches!'

'I know.'

Twitten waited for Brunswick to expand on his replies, but he didn't. The darkness between them remained impenetrable.

'The thing is, sir, I'm very hurt. I've been thinking about it all day. I mean, I'm pretty sure I've also made great strides towards identifying the Milk Bottle Murderer, and found out quite a few other significant things, such as that the over-promotion of milk is currently on such a preposterous scale it should be challenged in Parliament, especially now that it's actually killed someone, but all day I've been turning it over in my mind, you see, sir – turning over in my mind the simple, undeniable fact that you just don't like me, sir.'

'What? You can't—'

'It's all right, sir. It's an inescapable inference, and we all have to face up to inescapable inferences when they present themselves. And, luckily, I have a logical mind. I ask myself why you would keep such basic information from me, when it's the sort of thing you would normally tell a new recruit on their first day. I mean, casting your mind back to your own first day, sir, I expect someone took you to the canteen at lunchtime, didn't they, and bought you a cup of tea and showed you the ropes? And it was a bit intimidating to go there on your own at first, but then it quickly helped you feel that you belonged. As I say, it's a sort of automatic protective instinct to make a new person feel more at home.'

Twitten paused. He was aware he had the sergeant's full attention. 'So the logical deduction of your *not* doing that in my case, sir, is that you didn't like me from the start, and never grew to like me subsequently, and you'd rather I *didn't* feel like I belong, because then it would be more likely I would leave.'

'Look, son,' said Brunswick – but then stopped. He really had no excuses.

'I don't expect you to apologise, sir, but I felt you should know that I know – if you see what I mean. I had been thinking, after our work together yesterday, that we made a bally good team despite our personality and background differences, but now I know about your keeping the canteen a secret all this time, I realise I'm just not the sort of man you want as your constable. And I do understand that. It's been painful for me, but giving it some thought, I realise you would be much happier with a constable who was less well educated, or showed less initiative, and was from your own social class, or – if I may say so, sir – even lower.'

Brunswick didn't know what to say. How he wished the conversation had carried on being about Susan Turner's sensational cups of tea.

'I went to see your auntie this afternoon, sir.'

'What?'

'I said, I went to see your auntie, sir.'

'At the flat? But I was … How dare you do that? Now look—'

'You were asleep in your room, sir. I'm sorry. We made sure not to disturb you. But I just wanted to find out more about you, and identify where in your past this hostility towards me might spring from. Your aunt very kindly told me about all you did in the war, which sounds jolly harrowing, sir; and how you lost your parents when you were young; and how good you were at school.'

'You had no right to talk to my auntie, Twitten. And as for the death of my parents—'

'I suppose not, sir, but I felt I had to get to the bottom of a few things. In particular, I thought it would be helpful if I could explain this irrational compulsion of yours to go undercover, sir, which puts you in danger and usually doesn't achieve very much, and also angers Inspector Steine and often results in your being shot in the leg. I had a theory about your having such extremely low self-worth that you actually, deep down, hope to be killed.'

'Low self-worth? What are you flaming talking about? I can't believe this!'

'The technical psychological term is *low self-esteem*, sir. But I didn't want to burden you with it since it's not really in common parlance.'

'Common *what*?'

'But the point is I was right, sir! Once your auntie told me how your parents left you in a children's home and went to live in Worthing without you, and *then* died later on – well, then the whole death-wish thing made a lot of sense.'

Brunswick's head was spinning. 'They *what*?' he said. 'They went to *Worthing*? That's all wrong, Twitten. They died in a rail accident.'

'I mean, it's bad enough being orphaned, but such abandonment – it's virtually textbook, sir! And it perfectly explains your general tendency to self-sabotage, such as – well, case in point, such as your futile romantic interest in younger women.'

'Oh, shut up, now! Shut up about that.'

'The thing is, sir, such beautiful girls are bound to reject you, aren't they? But that's what you want – don't you see, sir? Because rejection is what you think you deserve!'

Twitten paused. He remembered now that Brunswick's auntie had whispered, *I know you want to help, dear, but whatever you do, don't tell Jim that his parents left him. He knows they're dead; he doesn't need to know they ran off.* But it was too late now; and it had been far too important a fact to omit. And after all, it's always better to know the truth, surely?

'But I notice it's me doing all the talking, sir, which is hardly fair when I'm asking you to explain why you don't like me. Would a lovely ham sandwich and a cup of tea from the flask help things along? Sir? Sir? Where are you going, sir?'

In one swift movement, Brunswick got up, opened the flap and went outside. This was more than he could stand – and more than he should be expected to stand. Low self-esteem? His own social class, *or even lower*? His mum and dad had *left him*? Hands thrust in his raincoat pockets, he bowed his head in misery and anger, and marched towards the sea. How many times, all through his life, had he revisited the moment of that door shutting, and him calling, 'Mummy! Come back, Mummy!' – and his auntie assuring him, every time, that it wasn't a proper memory; it had never happened? But he knew what he had heard. *We'll be all right now, Doris, without the kid.* That's what he'd heard his dad whisper outside the door. He had not imagined it. It was true.

'Sir?' called Twitten, lifting the flap and peering out. 'Are you all right, sir?' But Brunswick was nowhere to be seen.

Pouring the tea into a couple of cups (not easy), Twitten did wonder briefly if he had spoken out of turn. But on the other hand, how often was there a chance like this in life for a proper heart-to-heart? The sergeant was a patently unhappy man, whose limited understanding meant he would never fathom the source of his misery without this sort of expert intervention. What Twitten had just explained to him might take years to emerge in weekly psychoanalysis: looked at purely economically, the sergeant had just been saved a fortune. 'He'll thank me for this eventually,' Twitten said to himself. 'When he comes back, he'll definitely thank me.'

But Brunswick didn't come back. An hour passed, and the traffic and jazz-band noises grew fainter. The wind dropped. Seconds ticked by. Dogs barked. Twitten drank both the cups of tea, but resisted the ham sandwiches for as long as possible, applying his brain to various important unresolved questions, such as why Graham Goodyear would have wanted to kill those three people; what to do about Ben Oliver's upcoming article condemning Inspector Steine's role in the Middle Street Massacre; what Mrs Groynes was up to (because she was usually up to something); and whether talking so frankly to Sergeant Brunswick about his deepest formative emotional injury had been entirely motivated by a dispassionate desire to help.

At half-past twelve, Twitten consumed half the ham sandwiches. Unsurprisingly, they didn't make him feel any better about himself. Crikey, what had he done? He had said unforgivable things to Sergeant Brunswick just to get his own back! And at one o'clock, when Brunswick had still not returned, Twitten ate the rest of the sandwiches, with a little tear rolling down his cheek.

At two o'clock in the morning, Twitten woke from a light doze to hear a voice outside.

'Constable, are you in there?' It was Mrs Groynes.

'Yes! Yes, I am!' He was so pleased to hear her voice, he nearly burst into tears.

'Can I come in, dear?'

'Oh, please do, Mrs G. Come round the back.'

As she entered, it was hard to resist the urge to jump up and hug her – which was odd, of course, given who she really was, and what she was capable of.

'Now, what on earth's happened here?' she said. 'I thought the sergeant was supposed to be here with you, guarding this place, but he was in the bar at the Metropole earlier, looking like he'd seen a ghost, poor man, and ordering French brandies three at a time.'

'Oh, crikey. Is he all right now?'

'Search me. He left. But what happened here? Did you two have an argy-bargy?'

So Twitten told her what had been said between himself and Sergeant Brunswick at the start of the evening. He hoped, throughout his report, that she would make an effort to reassure him. But from her horrified exclamations of 'Oh, no!' and 'You didn't!' and 'The poor, poor sergeant!' it was all too clear what she thought about it.

'Well, one thing's for certain, dear. He'll never forgive you for saying all that.'

'No, I suppose not.'

'What the bleeding hell were you thinking?'

'I don't know. At the time, I was so pleased that I'd diagnosed what was wrong with him, psychologically speaking, that I didn't stop to consider how the information, after a lifetime of comforting denial, might come as a shock. But now I keep thinking, what if I was just paying him back for hurting my feelings over the matter of the canteen?'

Twitten wanted her to reassure him on this point, but she didn't. Instead, she settled on her stool, shaking her head. 'A bit tight-fitting in here, isn't it?'

'Yes,' said Twitten, miserably.

'Not much air, neither.'

'It's horrible. I wish I'd never thought of it.'

'Look. Do you want to know what I think?'

'Yes, please.'

'Well, for a start, you're not wrong about the sergeant wishing you were nothing like you are, dear. That was very perceptive of you.'

'Thank you.'

She laughed. 'I mean, bleeding hell, let's face it. No one wants an arrogant little pipsqueak like you working under them, do they?'

Twitten swallowed. 'No, I suppose not.'

'So, yes, the sergeant would have loved to have some impressionable lad working with him – and he'd have taken that impressionable lad straight to the police canteen and bought him a veal cutlet and spotted dick on his first day, no question. And he *is* sad and moody and self-sabotaging, as you put it. You've got that absolutely right.'

'Thank you.'

'Those girls who let him go near them are just having a laugh.'

'I know.'

'But what about putting the shoe on the other foot, dear? What about *you*?'

'What do you mean?'

'Well, if you're not his ideal constable, he's not your ideal sergeant either, is he? And you make that plain enough. You act on your own initiative *all the time*, dear. I mean, personally, I enjoy watching your clever-clogs brain go through the motions. I enjoy our little chats. But the way you take no notice of the chain of command at that station is shocking, dear. It is just *shocking*. If you worked for me and behaved like that, you'd already be vanished, dear, encased in concrete with just a little bit of hair sprouting out the top.'

'Ngh,' winced Twitten.

'You don't believe me?'

'Oh, crikey, Mrs G. I believe you.'

'But the irony is,' she continued, 'you're actually very lucky to have Sergeant Brunswick.'

'Am I?'

'Yes. He's an experienced policeman, and a good man, with a heart of gold. But when it comes to investigations he's always on the back foot, isn't he, thanks to your constantly going off following that so-called bleeding initiative of yours.'

Twitten was stung. 'We'd get nowhere if it wasn't for my so-called bleeding initiative, Mrs G.'

'Ah, well. You see? That's what you really believe. But what if you're wrong, dear? What if your faith in your initiative is actually the problem? What if it gets in the way of seeing things clearly – the way Sergeant Brunswick would see them if he got a ruddy chance?'

Twitten was glad it was too dark for him to see her face. He was having an appalling night.

'Do you think I should leave the police, Mrs G?' he said, quietly.

'No, dear! Of course not.'

Twitten let out a strangled snivelling noise. 'No one likes me!' he wailed.

'Oh, where are you? Come here.' She reached out and found him, and put an arm around his shoulders, and rocked him gently while he composed himself. '*I* like you, dear. I told you that when I had you at my mercy, didn't I? I said, *I like you, Constable*. And I keep offering to help you, don't I? I wish I'd helped more with this milk-bottle palaver, but you wouldn't believe what I'm dealing with right now, dear, elsewhere. It's been a bleeding nightmare.' She thought back to the Metropole, where five bodies representing most of the major conurbations of England were now piled in a heap in

Room 608, and where Terence Chambers would be awake and sitting very quietly in his own room, moving not a muscle of his face.

A long sniff indicated that Twitten had recovered himself. 'I'm truly sorry about what I said to the sergeant.'

'I know.' She sighed and took her arm away. 'Better now?'

'Yes. Yes, thank you.' He took a deep breath. 'Gosh, what a strange night, Mrs G. May I ask you something?'

'It depends.'

'Has it been you drawing all this adverse attention to the milk bar over the past couple of weeks?'

'Oh, that. Yes, of course.'

'I knew it!' As ever, it was nice to be right. 'Are you planning to burn it down tonight?'

'Oh, no. I need it to open tomorrow according to plan.'

'Well, I suppose that makes sense. My guess is that you want all the police here, so they won't be somewhere else?'

'I couldn't possibly comment.'

'Right. So Inspector Steine doesn't have to worry about being the judge of the Knickerbocker Glories?'

'He'll have a great day, dear. A special day. You mark my words.'

Twitten sniffed.

'Oh, blimey, you're not upset again, dear? Has it just occurred to you that no one's ever shown you the bleeding locker-room either?'

'You mean ... You mean *I've got a locker*?' This was too much.

'Yes, dear.'

'At the station?'

'Yes.'

'Somewhere I can put things I'm not using?'

'That's what lockers are for, usually.'

'I don't believe it!' Twitten huffed and shook his head. 'Look, I'm all right really, Mrs G. It's just – well, you're probably right. A bit. I do feel all the police work is up to me. And perhaps I shouldn't think of myself as the only intelligent policeman in the town. But there's so much I can't tell anyone – or I can't tell anyone except you! For instance, I found out yesterday that the *Argus* is planning to denounce Inspector Steine, saying the Middle Street Massacre wasn't a triumph after all, but a débâcle! And I know I should do something to prevent it, but I don't know what!'

'Blimey. Do you know *when* they're planning this article?' Mrs Groynes sounded so keenly interested that he could picture the look on her face: the alert, calculating expression she didn't bother to disguise when she asked at the station things like, 'So you're saying those silly bank vaults will be unlocked and unattended at *what* time exactly?'

'This week, I imagine. I think Ben Oliver will hang it on the inspector eating Knickerbocker Glories all over town when there's a dangerous killer on the loose.'

'So Oliver will be at the grand opening?'

'Oh, yes. He's bound to be.'

'Right. Good.' She sounded pleased. 'That's even better.'

'Better than what?'

'You'll see, dear. Leave this to me. Don't give it another thought. And meanwhile, I've got nowhere else I'd rather be, so why don't you tell me all about how the investigations are going? Did you find a person with no influence in the world who might be drawn to the milk bottle as a weapon?'

Half an hour later, Mrs Groynes sat back deep in thought. Twitten was relieved. Given how badly the night had gone so far, he'd expected her to poke holes in his logic, but she hadn't. She seemed to agree that Graham Goodyear was a good suspect – aside from such awkward facts as that people always spoke very highly of him, and that he had no discernible motive.

'It's only really the song that points to him, isn't it?'

'It is, I'm afraid. And since I can't tell anyone how I know about Officer Andy's swan-song, I do need a solid case against Graham, but I don't know where to start. I just keep trying to imagine myself back in that children's playground theatre, with Graham singing, and the schoolgirls swooning, and so on. But whenever I ask Pandora Holden to think about it, she finds a way of turning the subject back to *her* and—'

Twitten stopped. There was a noise outside. Someone was walking on the shingle, apparently in the direction of the Punch & Judy booth. Twitten and Mrs Groynes both held their breath.

'Twitten?' said a voice outside. 'Are you in there?' It was Inspector Steine.

'Yes, sir. Just a minute, sir!' He spoke quietly to Mrs Groynes. 'Shall I tell him you're here?'

'No, dear; I'll go,' whispered Mrs G. 'Keep him talking out the front for as long as you can.'

'Just a minute, sir!' called Twitten again.

'What do you mean, *just a minute*?' demanded Steine. 'Are you undressed in there, Twitten? Are you taking a bath?'

'No, no, sir. Of course not. It's just a bit untidy. And I'm afraid I took my helmet off. Also, there's a flask and a holdall …'

'Oh, for goodness' sake. A holdall? I'm coming in.'

'Yes, sir. Of course, sir. Round the back. But if you could just wait a moment ...'

'Nonsense.'

The canvas opened and – rather magically – when Inspector Steine ducked inside, Mrs Groynes had gone.

'What on earth has been going on here tonight, Twitten? I just had Sergeant Brunswick at my house, very much the worse for wear, handing me his blasted resignation!'

'I'm afraid the sergeant and I had a rather hurtful heart-to-heart, sir. It was all my fault.'

'And why does that not surprise me?'

Twitten, seated back on his usual stool, tried to compose himself and concentrate on talking to the inspector. But what with the lack of sleep, and the perpetual dark, and the surreal one-in-one-out nature of the night so far, it was difficult. Was he going to have to explain the police canteen revelation for a third time?

'It was about nothing, really, sir. I just happened to find out about the police canteen across the road from the station, and I've been here since bally June and no one had mentioned it to me, so I felt aggrieved.'

'Well, Sergeant Brunswick is the one feeling aggrieved now, so how do you explain that?'

'I believe I was tactless, sir. I used unfair psychoanalytical expertise to explain to him why he didn't like me.'

Steine huffed. He hated hearing words like 'psychoanalytical'; he also hated dealing with this sort of thing: settling disputes, or telling his men that his door was always open. Luckily, for the time being, something else Twitten had said had caught his attention.

'Hold on, Twitten, are you telling me you've been in Brighton only since June?'

'Yes, sir.'

'Good heavens, it seems like years.'

Steine got up, and then sat down again.

'Look, Twitten. I won't stay. I just came to say, make it up with Brunswick. That's all. Make it up. Buy him an ice cream, I don't know. Go and see one of his cowboy films with him, and pretend it doesn't bore you to death. I'm sorry you didn't know about the canteen, but if it makes you feel better, I didn't find out about it myself for four or five years. I mean to say, why is it in a different building? Why isn't there a sign on it, saying "Police Canteen in Here"? It makes no sense. So, has there been anything untoward happening here tonight?'

'No, sir. Nothing.'

'Good. Well, keep it up. I'll be off.'

'Yes, sir. Only ...' Twitten's voice wobbled.

'What's wrong?'

'Nothing, sir. But, well, I've been in here for about five straight hours now, sir. And I don't like to complain, but a lot of it has been quite stressful.'

Steine shrugged. He wasn't sure what Twitten wanted him to do about it. 'The nature of the job, I'm afraid, Constable. Did you put your helmet back on, by the way? I can't see a thing.'

'No, sir. I'm afraid I didn't.'

'Well, you have my permission to leave it off unless something happens.'

'Thank you.'

Again, Steine appeared to be ready to leave. But, again, he didn't go.

'By the way, Twitten, before I leave, I heard a name the other day. I thought perhaps I'd run it past you.'

'Yes, sir?'

'I honestly can't remember why it stuck in my mind, but I don't suppose you know of a Brighton man of violence called *Metropole Mike*?'

'No, sir. What does he do?'

Steine affected a casual laugh. 'He scoops people's eyes out, apparently!'

'Really? That's ghastly, sir.'

'Yes,' agreed Steine, thoughtfully. 'Yes, it is. By the way, Brunswick said something about some lovely home-made Victoria sponge … ?'

'I ate it, I'm afraid, sir.'

'Fair enough, Twitten,' Steine said, standing up again. And this time, when he stood up to go, he went – leaving Twitten alone, on his stool, in the pitch dark, without his helmet on, thinking about how much more pleasant this night might have been had he stuck to the subject of how two young women seemed to be in love with him.

Just before dawn, a dog sniffed its way inside the Punch & Judy booth and curled up beside Twitten. He patted its head, and stroked its ears, and in the end decided its name was Blakeney – he was slightly delirious by this point. When the dog lost interest and left again after ten minutes, Twitten felt more bereft than ever before in his life.

And then, just at sunrise, there came the sound of footsteps on the shingle. *This is it*, he thought, sitting perfectly still with his eyes closed. *If this is Sergeant Brunswick coming back to punch me in the face, or kill me, so be it, I deserve it.* But then he heard the voice of Mrs Groynes calling, 'Constable? How about some breakfast, dear?' – and the flap was opened, and the gloom lifted, and there was a smell of hot tea and sausage sandwich, and he stood up and stumbled out of the tent, yelling, 'Oh, Mrs Groynes! Thank God!' as if he had been trapped down a coal mine for thirty-eight days, rather than just spending a slightly fraught sleepless night on a beach.

'All a bit much, was it, dear?' she said, handing him a cup of tea. She had borrowed a tray from a nearby transport café where they knew her well. (She co-owned it, as it happened, with Stanley-Knife Stanley. It came in handy for money laundering.) 'Well, it's all right now. I put four sugars in. How about a lovely sausage sandwich?'

'That was the longest night of my life,' he said, when he'd gratefully eaten his sandwich and drunk his tea, and they were both sitting outside the booth on a breakwater, in the cool light of the rising August sun.

'What did the inspector want?'

'Oh.' Twitten thought back. It seemed so long ago. 'I think he told me off a bit about the sergeant. Yes, he did. And then it was a bit strange: he asked whether I'd heard of someone called Metropole Mike. But I hadn't. Have you?'

'Metropole Mike? I don't think there's any such person. Sounds made up to me.'

'Oh, well.' Twitten hung his head and looked at his hands. 'Thank you so much for coming back, Mrs G. I thought an all-night stake-out would be fun! But I can go home soon and get some sleep, I think. The regular police detail will be here from seven o'clock. And once this flipping grand opening is over, I can go back to thinking about the case.'

'As to that, dear, I couldn't sleep much myself, and I had a few thoughts. Do you want to hear them?'

'Of course, Mrs G. I seem to be going round in bally circles.'

'Well, first I thought about that song again. And it occurred to me that, from where Officer Andy was sitting on the stage, perhaps he'd connect the song not so much to Graham, who was up on the stage with him, singing it, as to the person in the audience he was singing it *to*.'

'Gosh, that's a good thought, Mrs G.'

'I know. And who was there every week facing the stage, listening to Graham sing, and beaming back at him, do you think?'

'I don't know. Schoolgirls who were in love with him?'

'Well, yes. But I wasn't thinking of them.'

'Cedric Carbody?'

'Think again.'

'His mum, perhaps?'

'Bingo, dear.'

'Graham's mum?'

'A woman who was famously dumped by a milkman.'

'Was she?'

'Oh, yes. Goodyear left her and went off with someone else. There was quite a stir about it at the time, because – and you'll like this – Mrs Goodyear smashed a lot of milk bottles in her fury.'

'So you think it might be her?' Twitten was excited. 'Mrs Goodyear, ambitious for her son, avenging any hurt to her darling Graham, and using milk bottles because she feels she has no influence in the world, and also because milk bottles represent a person who's hurt her?'

'I'm not saying it's watertight, dear. There's no blooming proof. But then I had another thought. Something's been niggling me ever since those first reports came in of the three murders. Why was Officer Andy out at that dodgy signpost? I mean, he was exactly the sort of person to step in and put it right. He'd have been outraged that someone was causing inconvenience to the great British motorist. But how did he know about it? The controller in the AA office didn't tell him on the radio, did he?'

'No. I was there the whole time with Mr Hollibon. There were no calls.'

'So who told him about that signpost? It wasn't chance that his murderer found him there. So was the murderer lying in wait, or was Andy followed from his last job? You never talked to Buster Bond's landlady up in Hassocks, did you?'

'No.'

'Well, I'd forget about going home to sleep.'

'What? No! I can't, Mrs G, I'm very tired.'

'Yes, you can, dear. Come on. One last push? If I were you, I'd get up to Hassocks at once.'

Eleven

Monday

The arrest of the Milk Bottle Murderer on Monday morning was something of an anti-climax. Newspapers referred to a 'Sensational Bank Holiday Dawn Raid', but truly it was nothing of the sort. Two uniformed officers (one of them Twitten) parked a police car in a quiet sun-filled street at half-past nine and knocked on a door; then they took the murderer peacefully away. No one saw it. The only point of interest was that, before knocking, the officers first removed two bottles of red-top from the doorstep, in case they gave the murderer any last-minute funny ideas.

Constable Twitten – exhausted from his dark night on the shingle, and also from the dash to Hassocks and back by police car – hardly had the strength to pronounce the words he had practised ever since Hendon. 'You are under arrest for the murders of Barbara Ashley, Andrew Inman and Cedric Carbody. You have the right to—' But he didn't get to finish. The culprit, who was dressed and ready, looked him up and down and said, 'Well, it took you long enough.' The arrest didn't even run to a thorough search of the premises. A box was shoved into Twitten's hands. 'All the evidence you need is in there.'

The police car dropped him back at his lodgings in Clifton Terrace, but he made it only halfway up the steps to the front door before his legs gave way. For a few moments, he sat there with his head in his hands.

'Constable, are you coming in? Are you all right? Oh, my darling, I've been dying to know, how was the sponge?' said Mrs Thorpe, opening the door.

He stood up, turned to face her, and made an effort. 'The sponge was delicious, thank you, Mrs Thorpe. And it was very much appreciated.'

'Where's the bag?'

'Ah.' He had no idea what had happened to the holdall she had given him. 'I'm sorry, Mrs Thorpe. I can't even remember the last time I saw it.'

'Oh, never mind. Are you all right? That's the main thing. Come in, my darling. Come in.'

The last thing Twitten could face was another of Mrs Thorpe's relentless interrogations. Once inside, he made a break for the stairs, but he'd achieved only the seventh step when she stopped him. 'So, did anything *happen* on the seafront?'

He would have loved to ignore the question, but he couldn't be rude. 'It's been a momentous night, Mrs Thorpe. A momentous night.'

'You caught them!'

Twitten had to think for a moment. 'Oh, you mean the milk-bar saboteurs? No. But on the plus side, I've just arrested the Milk Bottle Murderer –' he saw the question forming on her face '– and before you ask, I absolutely can't tell you who it is.'

He managed to attain the first landing before she stopped him again. 'Are you sure you're all right?' she called.

'I'm just very tired, Mrs Thorpe. I need to sleep.'

Fifteen minutes later, she knocked gently on Twitten's door and took in a cup of tea. He was asleep in his uniform, with his slippery chintz coverlet drawn over him. She placed the tea on his bedside table, then pulled the curtains more tightly together, and crept away.

———

When the three vans arrived for the setting up of the Barber of the Year competition at the Royal Pavilion, Sergeant Brunswick was outside, waiting. He wasn't in the best shape, having clearly not changed his clothes since yesterday, or had a shave. It seemed years since he'd last applied any Cossack ('for Men'). But he'd made a promise to Rodolfo, and even a person who's just found out that his self-esteem is so low that it amounts almost to a death-wish is obliged to keep his word.

'Excuse me, mate, I'm looking for a Mrs P. Hoagland,' he told the driver of the first van, showing his warrant card through the open window. The driver switched off the ignition, and gave him a blank stare.

Brunswick persisted. 'She's supposed to be in charge here.'

'What?' The man – in a businesslike flat cap and clean buff-coloured overalls – jumped down on to the gravel, and started opening the back of the van.

'Mrs who?' he said. 'We're a bit busy here, squire, can't you see? Ron! Open up!' This last was directed to a member of the crew, who produced a large bunch of keys from his overalls pocket and marched towards the Pavilion's main entrance.

'It's really important,' said Brunswick.

'So's this, mate. We've got to get this lot inside and set up before the bloody contestants arrive and start poncing about. It's been a nightmare getting here. We took a wrong turn on the road, and ended up at some village pond! Someone had turned the bleeding sign!'

'Well, I need to talk to her. Ask the others.'

'Oh, all right.' The man sighed, turned and shouted: 'Anyone heard of a Mrs Hoagland?'

'Mrs *P.* Hoagland,' corrected Brunswick – as if the initial would jog more memories.

'A Mrs P. Hoagland?' yelled the man.

But there was no reply, just the slamming of heavy doors and much muscular bustle, as six large barber chairs were unloaded and trundled through French doors into the vast Music Room. This was such an impressive operation that for a while the unshaven and emotionally wrung-out Brunswick just watched and admired it. The way each man performed his allotted task, without a word spoken, reminded him of the many heist movies he'd seen: one man laid down the protective sheets; another set up a generator and uncoiled electrical cables; another kept watch. Brunswick half expected a further man to start drilling through the floor while a colleague stood ready with an umbrella to poke through the hole. (Interestingly, had these hired minions of Mrs Groynes not been in Brighton this morning, posing as deliverymen, they'd have been in Shoreham drilling a hole through the ceiling of a fur emporium's cold-store in precisely this manner.)

'She might be with the contestants,' the man said, after he'd briskly passed Brunswick four or five times, ferrying equipment. 'This Mrs Hoagland of yours. Unlike us, the barbers got to stay in Brighton last night, so perhaps she did too. Here, you know it was *kids* who turned that ruddy signpost on the London Road? I'd have wrung their necks but we didn't have time. Bloody kids. Delinquents, the lot of them. Look at that one, there.'

'What one? Where?'

'There. If looks could kill, eh?'

Brunswick turned and looked. Peering round a shrub was a tough little face he knew very well. 'Carlo!' he called, and ran towards him. But the boy ran faster, cleverly circling the vans and then darting through the Pavilion's open doors.

'Hey, you!' shouted one of the men. 'After him, Sid!'

'No, no, I'll go,' said Brunswick. 'I know his dad. But look, if this Mrs Hoagland does show up, warn her she's in danger, all right?'

Back on the sixth floor of the Metropole Hotel, Mrs Groynes was well aware of the danger she was in – and it was from someone far more terrifying than young Carlo. Yesterday, Terence Chambers's summit conference had seemed in danger of collapse, and he had murmured about cancelling it. Today, at least, matters had clarified. When she knocked and entered his bedroom at ten o'clock, she found him eating a boiled egg in bed, while his boy Nicky was in the next room, running him a bath.

The good news, she told him, was that the barbering competition was set fair to go extremely well: the equipment had arrived; the barbers were ready; the winner's certificate already printed; even the protective sheets were (reportedly) beautifully laid. Newsreel cameras would be filming the event later in the day. In short, the bogus barbering side of things was going precisely to plan. On the other hand, the grand summit meeting at the Prince Regent's antique forty-seven-foot-long banqueting table had, unfortunately, met with fresh setbacks.

'What sort of fresh setbacks?' said Chambers, eyes narrowed.

'Well, put it this way,' she replied. 'We're going to need a shorter table.'

He groaned. 'How short?'

'Very short.'

'Oh, sweet Jesus, how many this time?'

'All of them, dear.'

'*What?*'

'Well, everyone except you and me. What can I say, Terry? I did argue they should be allowed to bring their dope and their women. Left to their own devices – well, they just went doolally tap.' (*Doolally tap = insane.*)

Chambers reached for his dressing-gown, and went with her to Room 606 (Channel Islands: tax avoidance), where five bodies lay, each with a gun in its lifeless hand.

'Was this you, Pal?'

'Me? What have I got to gain by rubbing out the bloke from the bleeding Lake District? I wanted this summit to *work*, Terry, and if I may say so, I have bust a gut to arrange it. If you hadn't come down, I had an extremely lucrative Russian sables job to be doing this weekend. But it's been like cooping up *wolves* here.'

Sighing, Chambers drew a gun from his dressing-gown pocket and shot them all again – West Country, Scottish Borders, Lake District, Thames Valley, Channel Islands – just to vent some of his annoyance. The man from the West Country said a faint 'Argh!' so, interestingly, had not been properly dead – but he was now. Nicky came running when he heard the shots, and it was just good luck that Chambers didn't shoot him too when he appeared unexpectedly in the doorway.

Chambers sat on the arm of a chair. He was very fed up. 'Oh, *knickers*, Pal. Whose idea was this summit thing, anyway?'

'It was very much yours, dear. I've always had better things to do. Those sables at Shoreham – well, that's a once-in-a-life-time go. Worth tens of thousands.'

'If Nicky and me get out of here today, can you and your boys get rid of the bodies?'

'Of course. West Pier.' She considered. 'What about the cars? Do you want any?'

'That's all right. You have them.' Chambers pursed his lips. 'They'll all come after me, you know.'

'I know, dear. From bleeding far and bleeding wide. Even from the Scottish Borders. You have to think fast, Terry. And if you're thinking of going abroad –'

'Abroad?'

'– there's a ferry from Newhaven this afternoon, as it happens.'

'No. I couldn't do that. What about my mum?'

'And I know a bloke at Shoreham Airport can fly you to Le Bourget at half an hour's notice, no questions asked.'

He looked at her. 'This *was* you, wasn't it?'

'For the last time, Terry, no, it bleeding wasn't. But you've got to think quickly, dear. These useless articles –' she waved a hand at the ugly heap of bodies that was so hard to equate with the areas of outstanding natural beauty from which they all hailed '– are going to be missed, gawd help us.'

Back at the Pavilion, in the deserted entrance hall, Brunswick called out for Carlo. This was a large building, and the boy could be anywhere. It was odd to see it like this: unlit, museum-like, with no one about. When the story of Brunswick's characteristic bravery was later told, one question was always asked: 'He went in alone knowing the boy was armed?' And the answer was: sorry, no, to be strictly accurate, Brunswick didn't know this yet. But when he did find out, he did not back down.

'Son?' he yelled. 'Come out, now, son. I'm not going anywhere without you. It's me, Sergeant Brunswick.'

No reply.

'Your dad's been cutting my hair for most of my life, son. I remember you as a tiddler. I used to give you sixpence at Christmas, remember? We can deal with this and get you home. Just tell me what's got into you.'

'Go away!' came the response.

There was no sign of the boy, but from the volume of his voice he was nearby.

'Look, son, we can talk about this.'

'I've got a gun here, rozzer!'

'*What?*' Brunswick was properly shocked. 'You're a kid! Where did you get a flaming gun?'

'Never you mind.'

'Now look, son, this is serious ...'

But again, Carlo was deaf to reason. There was the sound of youthful running footsteps: he was heading for the Banqueting Room and the kitchens. A door was opened and shut, and then there was silence save for distant bustling noises in the Music Room at the other end of the building.

Brunswick stood in the entrance hall, considering his options. The sensible thing would be to leave the Pavilion and telephone for reinforcements. But the result of that would be the definite arrest and trial of Carlo Innocenti on an arms charge, which would break his father's heart. So, in this great moment of truth, Brunswick asked himself what a lone, unarmed policeman with a character-defining abandonment complex would do in the circumstances, and the answer was: risk it.

'Give yourself up, Carlo.'

'No! Get back!' called a muffled voice.

The sergeant reached the door to the Banqueting Room, and stood beside it, taking deep breaths.

'I can hear you out there. Get back!' called the boy again. 'I'll shoot you through the door!'

'Carlo, you don't scare me,' Brunswick said quietly. 'I'm coming in.'

Twitten had been asleep only a couple of hours when Mrs Thorpe appeared at his bedside, and touched him on the shoulder.

'Constable, I'm so sorry; there's someone here to see you. He says it's very important.'

Twitten glanced at the time on his alarm clock and groaned. 'Who is it?' he rasped, thickly. One of his eyes had opened, but the other was still clinging to the possibility of more sleep.

'It's Gerry Edlin!' she trilled. 'From stage and screen! He's got information and a guilty conscience, apparently, and says it's very urgent. And he's *such* a lovely man. I've always supposed that he was, and he is! He pulled a florin out of my ear!'

A few minutes later, a bleary-eyed Twitten appeared in the breakfast room, and sat down at the table where Mrs Thorpe was gaily pouring Turkish coffee for her exciting guest. She'd brought out the rest of yesterday's sponge. Even in his unfocused state, Twitten noticed that his landlady was happier in this moment than he'd ever seen her before. A famous, good-looking and entertaining man was in her house, just like in the old days. He had no doubt been telling her hilarious (and unrepeatable) anecdotes about Lady Pru and Frank Muir.

'Constable.' Edlin stood up and extended an elegant hand. Even when dressed in a casual suit, he gave the impression of tuxedo, black tie and cabaret-style piano accompaniment. 'Constable, I apologise for rousing you from your bed, and I do hope you'll forgive me for not speaking sooner. I'm afraid I have acted badly.'

Twitten waited. He didn't want to appear rude, but he was far too tired to say 'Go on'.

'Coffee, Constable?' said Mrs Thorpe.

'Oh, crikey, yes, please. I don't know if Mrs Thorpe has explained, but I was up all night, Mr Edlin.'

'Yes, and I'm very sorry to disturb you. But I felt I had to set matters right. On Saturday morning, at the Metropole Hotel, I spotted a familiar face that alarmed me. It alarmed me so much, in fact, that once you'd interviewed us all at the police station, I'm afraid I caught the first train to Exeter.'

Twitten cast his mind back. 'Lady Pru said you seemed odd, didn't she? She said you were acting like you'd seen a ghost.'

'Well, I expect I was. The man I saw at the Metropole works for a notorious London gangster called Terence Chambers. And where this man goes, Chambers is never far away.'

'You're saying that Chambers is in Brighton?'

'Well, he was on Saturday.'

'Imagine, Constable!' breathed Mrs Thorpe, thrilled. 'On top of everything else, London gangsters!'

'Oh, crikey.' Twitten sat back in his chair. All weekend, he had neglected to ask an important question. If the bogus attacks on the House of Hanover Milk Bar were intended to divert attention away from something criminal, *what was that something*? He had heard about a consignment of very expensive fur coats being held at Shoreham this weekend. Was it anything to do with that?

'Did I do the right thing, waking you, Constable?'

'Of course, Mrs Thorpe. I just wish Mr Edlin had told me this two days ago.'

'But he was too frightened, isn't that right, Gerry?' said Mrs Thorpe.

Edlin, registering the unauthorised use of his first name with the merest arch of the eyebrow, took her hand. 'I was, Mrs Thorpe. I was petrified. Thank you for understanding.'

'Call me Eliza,' she said, breathily.

'Gladly.' His eyes widened. '*Eliza.*'

Twitten, ignoring this distasteful outbreak of middle-aged flirting, produced his notebook and flipped some pages. 'You asked about the possibility of Mr Carbody's murder being a *professional hit*, didn't you, Mr Edlin? I was struck by that at the time. So this was the reason?'

'Yes. I'm so sorry I didn't come clean. I've had dealings with Chambers once or twice, and he threatened my *fingers*, Constable.'

'Gerry's *fingers*!' echoed Mrs Thorpe, entranced. 'Isn't that horrible?'

'Mr Edlin. It would really help if you could remember anything said by this confederate of Terence Chambers. Did you hear him speak? You're very good at memory things, aren't you? You do them in your show. Did he say anything about fur coats, for example?'

'No, nothing about fur coats. But I did hear something. I don't think it concerned the milk-bottle murders, either, though.'

'Oh, that's all right. We know who did those.'

'You do? You know who killed Cedric? Who?'

'He's not allowed to say, Gerry!' gushed Mrs Thorpe. She really *loved* being in the know, this woman.

Twitten flipped open his notebook and licked his pencil. 'So, do you remember what you heard?'

'Yes, I remember precisely – even though it made no sense grammatically. He said – and this is word for word – "And when it's over on Monday, we *do groins*."' Edlin shrugged and laughed, raising his eyebrows meaningfully. 'I'd like to know how anyone *does groins*, wouldn't you?'

———

Down at the House of Hanover Milk Bar, Mr Shapiro was pretty happy with the ice creams, the tables, the bunting and the brass band, and he was resigned to the presence of the large red-and-white cow, whose name was Pansy. Evidently the milk-marketing supremo had insisted on the bovine element, so that was that.

The Milk Girl was due to arrive at two o'clock with a bigwig from the Milk Board and the faithful Mr Henderson. There would be a quick unveiling of a plaque, then a speech concerning the exciting way forward for milk marketing, then photographs with and without Pansy. Then, at half-past two, Inspector Steine of the Brighton Police would present an award in the shape of a gold-plated ice-cream scoop to the winner of the 1957 *Brighton Evening Argus* Knickerbocker Glory Competition.

Steine was already present, and seemed to think that his own job was by far the most important of the afternoon. In the past few days he had dutifully sampled Knickerbocker Glories all over town and come up with a shortlist of two contenders – a shortlist he refused to disclose. Only once or twice, incidentally, had he been aware of Ben Oliver watching him from outside and making notes, while an *Argus* photographer captured the incriminating images. The intended caption for these photographs was, of course, '*Inspector Steine: eating flaming ice cream at a time like this!*'

Just one element was troubling Mr Shapiro about this afternoon's upcoming festivities, but it was a big one. It was the fact that forty-five police constables had (on firm instruction from Inspector Steine) linked arms to form a cordon around the front of the building and were instructing the public to move along because there was nothing to see.

'Inspector Steine, we can't have this,' said Shapiro. 'This is a public event. We start in half an hour. There's a crowd of expectant people, and the way things stand they can't get anywhere near us.'

Steine sighed. 'It's a public event in a location that has been threatened on several occasions, Mr Shapiro. We talked about a police presence this afternoon. You agreed it would be a good deterrent.'

'Yes, but I didn't mean you should deter everyone from coming in!'

'Mr Shapiro—'

'I imagined one or two men mingling with the crowd and keeping an eye on things. I want people to come and buy ice creams and milkshakes and sandwiches, and to remember this as a happy day. One of your men just caught a little boy in swimming trunks trying to break through the cordon and threatened him with his truncheon!'

Steine didn't care. He was still trying to make up his mind between the Knickerbocker Glory from Luigi's (best fruit content) and the Grand Hotel's (better nuts). The Metropole's effort, with the best will in the world, had been inferior on every count: ice cream (watery), construction (sloppy), spoon (dirty), wafer (soft). Worst of all, the waitress had whisked away his glass before he had consumed the glacé cherry he had kept for last. There was no way, as a man of honour, that he could give this important award to Metropole Mike, whatever the consequences.

Mr Shapiro's thoughts, however, were not concerned with the merits of Knickerbocker Glories. 'Inspector, we could have a riot here at this rate!'

'Oh, pish.'

'Don't pish me.'

'I can and I will. A *riot*?'

'Look, it's a hot day. This event has been advertised all week, and people want to see the Milk Girl. A crowd has been forming for two hours. I can see juvenile delinquents out there, with quiffs. Things could turn ugly. Please disperse these men at once!'

'Well, I have my reasons, Shapiro. Very serious reasons.' Steine opened his briefcase, which contained the note from the well-wisher, the gun and the photograph identifying Metropole Mike. 'Have the mounted policemen arrived yet?'

Shapiro was aghast. 'You ordered horses?'

'Look, I am trying to prevent a bloodbath here. Or at least contain it. You'll understand later.'

Outside, there was movement, and a sound of cheering (and booing) as the cordon briefly broke ranks to allow Pandora Holden and Mr Henderson through, together with a red-faced Mr Hayes from Head Office. All of them looked flustered, and Pandora was in tears. It was the first time in her life that she'd been booed.

'What on earth is going on here, Shapiro?' demanded Hayes. 'Why are there so many police? It's extremely unpleasant.'

'Ask Inspector Steine, sir. I've demanded that he send the men away, but he won't listen.'

Hayes turned to Steine. 'This isn't a Cup Final, Inspector. It's the peaceful opening of a milk bar. *With a frightened cow.* Have you gone raving mad?'

Another movement outside, and more booing, announced more authorised arrivals, as Ben Oliver and his photographer were allowed in.

'Oliver, what are you doing here?' said Steine, annoyed. But before he could explain that this wasn't a place for a crime correspondent because *a crime was being averted,* the first stone was thrown by a member of the crowd outside. It was a fairly small one, and it bounced off the white summer helmet of a constable in the cordon, who staggered slightly but remained upright. Both inside the milk bar and without, there was a communal intake of breath.

'Bloody hell,' whispered Shapiro. 'That was close.'

'I agree. But no harm done,' said Steine. 'So I think—'

But then a second, and much larger, stone was hurled at the milk bar, over the heads of the police, and it was watched by everyone as it flew. Viewed from inside, it got bigger and bigger—

'Get down!' yelled Shapiro.

Then the stone crashed through the picture window and Steine was aware of glass shattering and a piercing scream from Pandora, and a violent surge in the crowd, and Mr Henderson shielding the Milk Girl under a table, and Shapiro shouting, 'This is all your fault, Steine! Write it in the paper, Mr Oliver. This was all his fault!'

'I resent that, Shapiro,' called Steine, from his own position on the floor behind the ice-cream counter.

But his words went unheard as the policemen outside reached for their truncheons, and the incident later known in Home Office files as the Utterly Preventable Milk-Bar Riot got under way in earnest.

As he raced along the seafront towards the Metropole, Twitten was aware of the unusually turbulent crowd noise emanating from the beach, but chose to ignore it. He was on a mission to warn Mrs Groynes. He had no plan, of course, and no weapon. All he knew was that she was in danger from the notorious Terence Chambers, and that he must save her if he could. Had he paused for a second, would he have reconsidered the impulse that drove him? After all, she was a very wicked and devious criminal; a world without Mrs Groynes would be a better one. Plus, an underworld assassination would be a fitting end for her.

And yet, as he ran along – past the busy cinema entrances and the colourful humbug shops and the packed, vinegary fish-and-chip restaurants – his mind kept returning to the way Mrs G had helped him in the past couple of days: coming to him with Officer Andy's dying words; nudging him towards asking the right questions about the Milk Bottle Murderer. Above all, she had comforted him in that flipping pitch-dark Punch & Judy tent and brought him a sausage sandwich when it was over. In exchange for that life-saving breakfast alone, he must warn her.

But he appeared to be too late. A worrying scene was unfolding outside the Metropole as he approached. Chambers and Mrs Groynes were standing on the front steps, with an unknown man confronting them, and a uniformed hotel doorman watching in patent horror. They both looked anxious, and Chambers had put up his hands. Mrs Groynes was evidently trying to reason with the man, but he was waving something at them, and it looked like a gun.

Twitten was too far away to intervene. He could only watch as Mrs Groynes swung her handbag hard into the man's face and yelled, 'Terry, run! Go where I told you! I'll deal with this!'

And Chambers fled. He crossed the road at full pelt, zigzagging through slow-moving coaches and buses, and threw himself down the steps towards the beach. Twitten ran to help Mrs Groynes, and to apprehend the man with the gun. 'Police!' he shouted and blew his whistle. But the man with the gun climbed into a large car with running boards and drove off. Meanwhile, the hotel doorman – whose assistance might have been useful at this point – fainted on the spot.

'I'm here, Mrs G!' Twitten called, panting as he ran. 'Who was that? Who was threatening you? Where did Chambers go? Are you all right, Mrs G? Are you all right?'

———

While chaos reigned at the House of Hanover Milk Bar, all was dark and quiet in the Royal Pavilion Banqueting Room, which was shuttered against the daylight. The only things the two scenes had in common were: a) people hiding under tables, and b) firearms in irresponsible hands.

'Where are you, son?' called Brunswick.

'Stop calling me that, I'm not your son,' came Carlo's voice (from under the table). 'And I'll shoot you if you come any closer, so back off!'

'Hah!' said Brunswick, with feeling. He pulled out a chair and sat down. He felt strangely calm. If this was to be the day he gave his life in the line of duty, at least it was in an interesting location. 'Look, tell me why you're doing this.'

Carlo said nothing, partly because he had only contempt for people as old and square as Brunswick, but also because, if he was honest, he had largely forgotten why he was doing this. Also, he felt a bit silly being on all fours underneath a table, despite the slight tactical advantage.

'All right. If you're not going to tell me why *you're* here, I'll tell you why I am. How about that?'

'What? Leave off. You've got a screw loose, you have. You're mental.'

'Well, you might be right.' Brunswick laughed. 'Here, have you ever heard of low self-esteem, Carlo? I hadn't heard of it myself before last night. I thought all that sort of thing was claptrap, I really did. But now I've heard of it, it's funny, I can't flaming well stop thinking about it.'

'What's that got to do with me and my gun?'

'I'm not sure. But I'll tell you why I've got it, shall I? This low self-esteem of mine. My parents, you see, apparently they didn't love me. In fact, they blooming upped and left me.' He laughed again. 'Blimey! Whoo, blimey, I said it out loud! I can't believe I said that, Carlo! Whoo!'

Under the table, the boy closed his eyes and physically cringed. It would be fair to say that no other conversational topic would have made him quite as uncomfortable as this one.

'Whereas *you*, you see – well, your mum died, that's true, but your dad loves you more than anything, doesn't he? He'd do anything for you. So that's why I keep thinking, There's no way *Carlo* can have this low self-esteem thing, is there? But that's what you seem to have, son! I mean, that's why you went and got yourself a gun!'

Carlo was bewildered. He'd seen any number of black-and-white films in which tragic mixed-up juvenile delinquents curled their lips and aimed guns at policemen. Always the coppers came slowly towards them, saying 'Give me the gun, Johnny' to a crescendo in the hopped-up music, while the camera moved closer and closer to the delinquent's sweaty brow and huge pupils. Then there was the inevitable *bang!* – and the next thing was either the noose or the electric chair, depending on the film's country of origin. Just Carlo's luck to get this clueless loony, who took no interest in cinema.

'Aren't you going to say, *Give me the gun, Carlo?*'

'Do you want me to?'

'Well, yeah.'

'You want me to say, *Give me the gun?*'

'Yeah.'

'Would you give it to me if I asked, though?'

'Of course not.'

'No point, then. It would be a charade. No, I've had it with all that. The thing is, son, if I survive this afternoon, I might be leaving the police.'

'Stop it. Stop talking.'

'It was last night I made the decision.'

'Oh, God. Shut *up!*'

'You see, it was explained to me why I keep putting myself in danger. I always thought it was because I was brave! Well, that's a laugh. It turns out I actually *want* people to shoot me.' Brunswick laughed again. 'Work that one out, eh? I even want *you* to shoot me – you! It's what I think I deserve. Ha! What a game, eh? Just like you think you deserve to be hanged for killing this Mrs P. Hoagland that you've never even met. It's not about her, you see, son, is it? This Mrs Hoagland, whoever she is. It's all about you.'

There was a knock at the door, which made Brunswick jump.

'Are you all right in there? Did you find the kid?' It was the barber-chair delivery man, calling from outside. 'We're not authorised to use that room, you see. The door should have been locked.'

'Give us a minute!' Brunswick called back. Then he peered under the table in the gloom and for the first time came face to face with Carlo, who was – startlingly – on his knees just three feet away, with the gun pointed straight at Brunswick. The sergeant didn't flinch. 'Look, son, shall I ask this bloke to telephone for an ambulance, or are we going to be all right?'

The boy shrugged, insolently, but he was well out of his depth.

'I'll tell him to get the ambulance, then?'

'Well.' The boy shook his head. 'Yes.'

'Yes?'

'I mean, I don't know. Leave me alone, you're confusing me, you weirdo.'

'Better be on the safe side, then,' said Brunswick, and called, 'Here, mate!'

'Yeah?'

'Could you call for an ambu—'

'No!' said Carlo. 'Stop. Don't do that.'

'An ambulance?' the man called back. 'Okey-dokey!'

'No!' called Carlo.

'Look, we'll need one if you're going to shoot me, son. It stands to reason. Even if you kill me.'

'No, don't get one. Tell him not to.'

'Why?'

'Just don't get one, I said. Here, you win.'

And the boy, deflated, handed over the gun.

———

'Oh, thank gawd you're here, dear,' gasped Mrs Groynes, as Twitten escorted her back inside the hotel. 'I know you've had a trying weekend yourself, but you wouldn't believe what Chambers has been up to. I wanted to tell you all along, but I was too scared. Quick, get in the lift. You need to see this.'

A couple of minutes later, they were on the sixth floor, and Mrs Groynes had produced a key. 'Come and see, dear. Come and see what Terence Chambers has done. And I warn you, it's not a pretty sight.'

At this point, it might be useful to remember that just three days earlier, Twitten had complained of the amount of carnage he'd personally witnessed since arriving in Brighton. He had felt so oppressed by the number of people he'd seen shot in the head (three), that he had devised a 'rest cure' for himself consisting of 'rounds', so that he could experience the 'subtle diurnal rhythms' of the town. As he had declared to the AA's Mr Hollibon on Friday evening, 'I can't help feeling that another brutal murder in Brighton by an unknown hand with complicated motives would just about finish me off!'

So when the door to Room 606 was opened to reveal the ten dead and stiffening bodies of the (former) summit delegates, it was fair enough that Twitten let out an actual scream, and needed to be slapped. Then he opened his eyes and screamed again, and Mrs Groynes hit him quite hard – after which he finally gathered his wits enough to ask, 'Who the flip are they, Mrs G? What the flip happened here? I mean, *what the flip?*'

'It was Chambers, dear.'

'Oh, my God. How many are there?'

'Ten.'

'*Ten?*'

'He invited them all here and then killed them. He's gone stark raving mad, dear. This will stir up all sorts in the national criminal community. You can't imagine.'

'But who are they all?'

'Big cheeses, all of them. Villains from every part of the country. Look, this'll help; I've typed a list.'

'What?'

'Here.' She produced a sheet of paper from her handbag.

'Thank you. But hang on, *you typed a list?*'

He took the paper from her, and stared at it. It was in the form of a table headed: 'Killed by Terence Chambers, Bank Holiday 5 August at Metropole Hotel', with five columns headed 'Name', 'Age', 'Address', 'Fiefdom' and 'Misc.' Every box had been helpfully filled in.

'I'll explain later. But right now, you've got to follow him, dear. He's scared that someone's already after him, so I told him to head for that House of Hanover place on account of all the coppers there, and demand protective custody. Would you recognise him?'

Twitten thought back to the umpteen images of Chambers pinned up in Officer Andy's bedroom. 'Of course. I recognised him just now. But I nearly forgot why I was here in the first place. To tell you what someone overheard on Saturday morning: that Chambers planned to kill you today, *once it was over.*'

'Oh, I knew all about that, dear.'

'You did? Oh, thank goodness.'

'But thank you anyway. Now go on, and take the list with you. Go!'

Chambers had indeed been scared by what had happened outside the Metropole, when a man with a strong Geordie accent had approached him and pulled a gun.

'This is for Hardcastle,' the man had said. But before he could shoot, Palmeira had sloshed him with her bag, and told Chambers to run. Once across the road, he threw himself down the steps to the beach and sprinted along the Lower Promenade towards the House of Hanover Milk Bar where – as Palmeira had predicted – there was so much police presence that Hardcastle's man wouldn't dream of following. 'What you want to do is get inside as quick as you can,' she had told him. 'The inspector's my man, and always has been. You'll be safe once you're on the other side of the cordon. Just say you're *from the Metropole*, and he'll understand. It's our code, dear. Our code for: Look after this bloke and I'll see you all right.'

So he obeyed her instructions, forcing his way through the rioting crowd, and it will be no surprise that this was the last thing Terence Chambers ever did.

'He says he's from the Metropole, Inspector,' said a red-faced constable, holding Chambers back from the relative calm of the milk bar.

'Oh, my God,' said Steine, under his breath. The moment of truth had arrived. 'Let him in.'

'Yes, I'm *from the Metropole*,' said Chambers, meaningfully, walking towards Steine.

'Thank you, yes. I heard.'

Inspector Steine did not act at once. While Chambers stood waiting, and the riot continued to rage outside, Steine quickly opened his briefcase, re-read the note from the well-wisher and studied the photograph again. Then, when he was completely satisfied, he took out the gun and shot Terence Chambers, twice, in the chest.

'Oh, *fuck*,' said Chambers, as he fell.

'What are you doing?' yelled everyone else.

'You fucker,' said Chambers, expiring. And then he was still. He had fallen in an interesting star shape, as it happened, but sadly there was no one present who cared enough about such things to take note.

'Well, I hope I never have to do anything like *that* again,' said Steine, putting down the gun. 'I am happy to explain my reasons, but right now I suppose someone had better arrest me.'

Outside, the sound of the gunshots had a salutary effect. Most of the rioters ran off with their hands over their heads, while others (who perhaps had more experience of such situations) stood still, with their hands raised. The police cautiously lowered their truncheons. *Was it over?* Pansy the cow took the opportunity to release a stream of hot urine, which made everyone look around. But there was no question: the riot was over, and inside the House of Hanover Milk Bar, all was tensely quiet.

Ben Oliver stared. 'That was Terence Chambers!' he whispered, excitedly.

Steine frowned. He had no idea what Oliver was talking about. The man he had killed was Metropole Mike, and it was self-defence based on information received. 'Look, before you start, I had to do that. I can explain. The gun isn't mine. I got this note—'

'You killed Terence Chambers right in front of me!' shouted Ben Oliver, running over. 'I can't believe it! I can't believe it!' He was very excited. 'Quick, Phil. Take the picture! Inspector Steine has just wiped out the most villainous man in England. This is huge. Huge! Is there a phone here, Shapiro? I need to call my editor!'

Twitten arrived, breathless, and took in the scene. 'Is that Chambers?' he gasped. 'Oh, crikey, is he dead?'

'The inspector shot him.'

'What? The inspector?' This was difficult to process. 'Did you, sir?'

'Yes, but I can explain, Twitten. This man is not—'

'Oh, well done, sir. Bally well done!'

'But listen—'

'I can't believe it! I can't believe you did that! Where did you even get the gun? You never carry a gun!'

'Twitten, calm down. And for the last time, will someone *please arrest me*?'

'But this couldn't be better, sir. I mean, for you. It will make your reputation all over again, sir! Killing Terence Chambers, after he's just wiped out *the ten top villains in the country*—'

'Is that why he was in Brighton?' asked Oliver, quick on the uptake as always. 'He's been wiping people out here?'

'I just saw the bodies, Mr Oliver. Ten! From places like Manchester and Birmingham and – a bit weirdly – Truro and Saint Helier. It's a bally bloodbath. They're on the sixth floor of the Metropole. What a great story for you, Mr Oliver. All those men destroyed in one go, and then the perpetrator *shot by Inspector Steine*. It's like – well, I have to say, it's like the Middle Street Massacre, only better.'

'Look,' said Steine, firmly, and getting everyone's attention. 'Look, I can see you're all excited, but that simply *isn't what just happened*.'

'Isn't it, sir?'

'No!'

Twitten gave the inspector a meaningful look. 'Well, personally, I can't wait to see the film they make about this, sir.

You, alone, shooting the infamous baddie – it's like bally *High Noon*!'

Everyone looked at Steine, and then down at the corpse of Terence Chambers, and then back at Steine. He still hadn't quite grasped the situation, but slowly it was dawning on him.

'Look, I don't know where you even got the idea …' he began, but then he trailed off and stopped talking, a quizzical expression on his face. Certain words were finally beginning to penetrate his mind – such as:

It will make your reputation all over again.

It's like the Middle Street Massacre, only better.

It's like bally High Noon.

Calmly, he replaced the well-wisher's note (that read: *Shoot Metropole Mike before he can shoot you; it's your only chance to preserve the integrity of the Knickerbocker Glory Competition*) in his briefcase and snapped it shut.

'No, you're right,' he said. 'Of course you are. I was just being modest.'

'Oh, bally well done, sir.'

'This man is the notorious London thug Terence Chambers and no one should arrest me – obviously – because I shot him in the line of duty. Now, all these people he just killed at the Metropole Hotel – I don't suppose anyone's got a list of their names and addresses?'

Twelve

Subsequently

Alone in her cell for a full day before being questioned, the Milk Bottle Murderer had plenty of time to contemplate both her past and her future.

Did she regret braining three people with milk bottles and then stabbing them in the chest and neck with the broken shards until they were dead? Well, no – partly because those three people were the poisonous Cedric Carbody, the interfering Andrew Inman, and the shameless Barbara Ashley; and partly because she was insane.

Had it been a tricky and messy way to dispose of one's enemies? Hell, yes. She had ruined three pairs of perfectly nice court shoes.

Wouldn't a gun have been easier? Definitely. But for Brenda Stoater, former headmistress of Lady Laura Laridae, there was a supremely obvious reason for using milk bottles as her weapon of doom: that her long-term inamorato, with whom she had once shared the romantic clifftop liaison that led to the tragic death of the schoolgirl Diana, was Mr Goodyear the milkman.

'She was probably a bit mad from the night of Diana's death onward,' Twitten explained to Mrs Groynes on Tuesday morning. 'She resigned from her post straight after the tragedy, of course, but no one suspected she had any direct responsibility for what had happened. It was clever of her to take up the profession of crossword-setting, though, once in civilian life. It was hiding in plain sight.'

'Are they all mad, then? Crossword-setters?'

'Oh, definitely. Mad but harmless. That's quite well known.'

'Fancy having a romantic liaison at midnight when you're a milkman,' reflected Mrs G, shaking her head. 'He'd have had to get up again in four hours' time.'

Naturally, the swift and efficient capture of the Milk Bottle Murderer had been eclipsed somewhat in the public's mind by the sensational Bank Holiday happenings at the milk bar. When Twitten arrived at the police station first thing on Tuesday, he had to fight his way through reporters, none of whom cared about the arrest of Miss Stoater. Most of them were waving mimeographed copies of Mrs Groynes's handy list of Metropole casualties. In the end, the national and international coverage of the event would be huge. By an amazing stroke of luck (or was it?), the newsreel camera crew that had come to Brighton to film the barbering contest was tipped off by a passing street-boy carrying a rolled-up comic. 'Here, you lot,' he yelled. 'Get down the seafront! Shootings and all sorts! And I think I saw Diana Dors in a fur bikini and all!' The cameras were thus able to capture the sensational footage of Inspector Steine in the House of Hanover Milk Bar, gun in hand, that later became iconic.

'I'll tell you exactly what happened,' said Steine, with impressive dignity. (He had got his story straight by the time they arrived.) 'This man was Terence Chambers and I shot him.' The footage was such a success with the public that when a compilation of Pathé News 1957 highlights was screened nationwide at the end of the year, Inspector Steine's 'and I shot him' clip was right in the mix with the launch of Sputnik, Bill Haley and the Comets playing at the Dominion Theatre, Harold Macmillan's 'never had it so good' speech, and the momentous introduction of glove-puppet Sweep to the ever-popular *Sooty Show*.

'Where did all the boxes go?' asked Twitten, as he accepted his first cup of tea from Mrs Groynes on that Tuesday morning. All the surfaces that since Saturday had been heaped with the haul from Andy Inman's bedroom were now – very noticeably – clear, tidy, and freshly polished.

'Which boxes do you mean, dear?'

'The ones with Officer Andy's true-crime scrapbooks.'

'Oh, no one wanted those messy things cluttering up the place, did they? I came back 'specially and got rid of them last night. Look!' She waved a hand. 'It's like they never existed.'

'Those scrapbooks were evidence, Mrs G.'

'I know. But look at it this way: you've got your murderer, and she's confessed, so the way I see it, those scrapbooks would only confuse matters.'

Twitten took a sip of his tea. 'So I'm guessing they contained material that could incriminate you and your associates?'

'Bleeding tons of it, dear.'

Twitten sighed. There was no point arguing. If the books were gone, they were gone. At least he'd preserved the Diana one. He would give it to Pandora.

'Jammie Dodger with that cuppa, dear?'

'Oh, that would be lovely, thank you.'

'Here you are, dear. Take the tin.'

It was always strange when a case was solved. There seemed so much to talk about, so many questions to ask; but at the same time, if you were Twitten, you could usually work out a lot of it for yourself. For instance, it was clear enough in retrospect that absolutely everything that had happened over the Bank Holiday weekend on the sixth floor of the Metropole and at the House of Hanover Milk Bar had been contrived by Mrs Groynes with the intention of exterminating her rivals, pinning the atrocity on Chambers, ensuring he got shot immediately, and making Inspector Steine the hero of the hour. Twitten was not a cynic by nature, but he had learned recently one pragmatic life lesson: if it benefits Mrs Groynes, look no further for the cause.

'Aren't you going to ask me how long I was planning all this, dear?'

'No, I don't think so,' said Twitten, munching a biscuit. 'I assume it was months.'

'Bleeding *months*, dear.'

'When did you type that list?'

'Two weeks ago.'

'Mm. Well, I'm glad you decided to give the inspector all the bally glory. You've made him very happy.'

'Are you kidding? I didn't do it for *him*. The last thing I need is for him to be replaced by someone with a bit of brain.'

'I know, but—'

'Him being safe in his job is essential to my continued success, dear!'

'I know, but—'

'The day he goes, I'm finished.'

'I know, but what I'm trying to say, Mrs G, is that you've made him very happy nevertheless. So, unconsciously, I think you wanted to do a kind thing.'

'Unconsciously? Me?'

'Everyone has an unconscious mind, Mrs Groynes.'

'Even me, dear? Are you sure?'

Twitten took another sip of tea. 'Even you.'

———

For Sergeant Brunswick, Tuesday morning was even stranger than it was for everyone else. Usually he celebrated the successful close of a case in a hospital bed at the Sussex County, with a brown paper bag of South African grapes and a copy of the latest *ABC Film Review*, reading about Tony Curtis. It was very odd to wake up at home, uninjured, and then walk into town. Was he disappointed to miss both the arrest of Miss Stoater and the shooting of Terence Chambers? Not in the circumstances. The way he had handled Carlo, and delivered the boy back to his father unscathed, had given him the nerve to go home and raise a difficult subject with his auntie Violet. She finally told him everything. Today he felt as if a great cannonball of pent-up grief had dropped out of his body and rolled away.

'Sergeant Brunswick, is that you?'

He was crossing North Street when it happened. He turned and saw a handsome woman in smart clothes. It was Mrs Thorpe, Twitten's attractive widowed landlady who – if reports were to be believed – had set her cap at his lovely superior officer.

'Good morning, Mrs Thorpe,' he said, smiling. 'Can I help you?'

'Yes, please. If you wouldn't mind.' She hesitantly smiled back at him, but then, unable to maintain the gaze, looked down to search her handbag and produced a packet wrapped in greaseproof paper, tied with string. 'Are you on your way to the police station? It's just that the constable forgot to take his sandwiches this morning. I don't suppose you could take him to them – I mean, take them to him?'

'Oh, of course. His sandwiches,' said Brunswick. 'Don't worry, madam. I'll make sure he gets them.'

'You'd think there would be a canteen, wouldn't you? For all you strapping men!'

'Um, yes. I suppose there ought to be. Thank you for the cake on Saturday night, Mrs Thorpe. That was very kind.'

'Oh, my pleasure.' She beamed at him, and then, instead of saying goodbye, she did something unexpected: she put a hand to her neck as if suddenly mildly flustered, or a bit embarrassed, or overwhelmingly sexually attracted, or possibly all three. Brunswick smiled again, waiting. He could feel his own face reddening too.

'Was there something else, madam?'

'Yes. I just wanted to say … Well, the constable. I just wanted to say, he's very – he's very young.'

Brunswick laughed. 'Oh, I know! He makes me feel about a hundred.'

'But it's easy to forget. How young he is. He speaks without thinking. Anyway—' She reached out a gloved hand and touched the sleeve of Brunswick's raincoat. 'I just wanted to say that, being so very young and new to things here, he's lucky to have someone as manly as you to look up to.'

And on that bombshell, she turned and walked away on her classy high heels, leaving Brunswick clutching a packet of cheese and pickle sandwiches with the word 'manly' hanging in big letters in the air around him.

In terms of positive milk marketing, the opening of the House of Hanover Milk Bar had just one thing in its favour: Pansy the cow didn't kill anyone. In all other respects, it was a disaster. The highly important Mr Hayes had no opportunity to announce his new national slogan; the beautiful Milk Girl barely escaped injury and disfigurement; Mr Henderson decided in the heat of the action it was now or never to tell Pandora he was in love with her – which merely shocked and upset her, and added to the ghastliness.

On Tuesday morning, Pandora woke to find a note had been pushed under her bedroom door. It was from Hendy, saying he was catching an early train back to London, wishing her luck in the future, and apologising for everything. She felt a brief pang, but that was all. There was packing to do. Her anxious parents were already en route from Norfolk to pick her up. And although they weren't likely to arrive before midday, she vacated her room by ten o'clock: the impulse to put Brighton behind her was powerful.

Leaving Peregrine Wilberforce Twitten, however, was harder to contemplate. She kept picturing his arrival at the milk bar – running in just after Chambers was shot and then explaining everything. He had been so quick to see the bigger picture! From her own position under a table, Pandora could have sworn that the inspector had shot the man not knowing he was this famous Chambers person. In fact, didn't he even try to deny it? Didn't he keep saying at first that someone should arrest him? But the main thing was: everyone had been in confusion until Peregrine ran in waving a list of dead villains, when suddenly all became clear.

It was Twitten who'd looked after Pandora in the aftermath of the preventable riot. He had escorted her back to the hotel, and ensured she got a hot drink before going straight to bed. He had called her parents and explained that she was shaken but unharmed, and that she was – great news – giving up being the Milk Girl forthwith, and would never, *ever*, be asked again to pose as if milking a cow.

'What I'm wondering myself, Professor Holden,' he'd said on the telephone to Pandora's mother, 'is why everyone's so obsessed with milk anyway. It's all milk, milk, milk. But surely milk is just an opaque fatty bovine mammary secretion? I'm thinking of conducting some research on the subject, seeing how people react to calling a spade a spade, as it were.'

'Ah, you are a loss to academia, Mr Twitten; I always said so,' came the approving reply. 'But it's also possible that you think too much.'

Elsewhere the repercussions of the weekend were felt differently. At the BBC in London, for instance, no one noticed Susan Turner was missing for several days, thanks to the well-established institutional heartlessness. When she failed to return to work after two weeks, it was assumed she must be terribly ill, so her employment was terminated. At the House of Hanover Milk Bar, business boomed, thanks to the rich ghoulish seam in the British psyche. At the Royal Pavilion, the regular staff unlocked the building on Tuesday to find a number of barber's chairs abandoned in the Music Room, but otherwise no sign that anything had occurred there. Outside, on the (former) Pavilion Lawns, the farmer loaded his cows on to trailers, leaving a scene of such devastation to those pretty gardens – churned-up mud, noxious puddles and denuded tree trunks – that for the next three weeks, veterans of the First World War would burst into tears when they saw it.

And at the *Argus*, all sleep was cancelled until further notice, with edition after edition hitting the streets.

'A bit of a different fucking story now, Oliver!' the editor chuckled, at least twice a day.

'Suits me, sir!' said the harassed reporter, barely glancing up from his steaming typewriter.

This was a fine example of how journalism works – as all the *'Steine Must Go'* copy was subtly re-pointed to suit the headline *'Brighton Knew He Had It in Him'*. Thus, the incriminatory pictures of Steine eating-flaming-ice-cream-at-a-time-like-this were now captioned to show what a cool waiting-game he had played: the great policeman yet again calmly dipping a long-handled spoon in a tall glass while dangerous lowlifes gunned each other down. With the film of the Middle Street Massacre fresh in his mind, Oliver was able to draw detailed parallels with the events of the recent Bank Holiday, and also speculate on who would play the devilish Terence Chambers in the inevitable sequel (in the end, it was Richard Todd, cleverly cast against type; he won Best Supporting Actor at the British Academy Film Awards in 1959).

The biggest problem the *Argus* faced was what to call the milk-bar incident. It needed a name. On Monday evening, a brainstorming session in the editor's office got rather heated. The chief subeditor was convinced there was mileage in wordplay on 'deserts' and 'desserts' (as in, *'Top Villain Gets His Just Desserts!'*) – but he was repeatedly howled down, and in the end, Oliver mentioned Twitten's *High Noon* reference and *'High Noon at the Milk Bar'* was agreed upon. The fact that the shooting had occurred at about a quarter to two was cleverly elided, and in later years nearly everyone who'd been present was happy to say that they'd noticed the hands of a non-existent wall-clock pointing precisely to twelve when Chambers entered and met his doom.

Back at the police station on Tuesday morning, Twitten and Brunswick sat at their desks, each drinking a welcome cup of post-interrogation tea, while Mrs Groynes bustled with her feather duster in the inspector's office with the door open. Rarely in the annals of police work had an interview with a murderer gone so smoothly.

'So she confessed to it all, is that right?' Mrs Groynes called to them.

'She did indeed, Mrs G,' said Brunswick. 'She's been very co-operative. She isn't sorry, though.'

'No, she's quite proud of the killings,' agreed Twitten. 'But then we have to remember she's mad, which is a factor.'

'Did you ask her why she did it?'

'Oh, she told us without much prompting,' said Twitten, ruefully. 'It was all for lust, she said, and I'm afraid she didn't spare the anatomical details. She might regret her confession when it all comes out in court. It will sound like stuff from a novel by James M. bally Cain.'

'Blimey, Mrs G, you should have heard it,' laughed Brunswick. 'She looks such a lady! And there she is, swooning over Goodyear's hairy arms and heroic war wounds! She's abso-flaming-lutely potty about him.'

'Poor woman,' said Mrs G. 'How are the mighty fallen.'

Twitten nodded his agreement. It pained him to see a clever person lose her mind through mere physical attraction. 'It seems that when he used to bring his horse and cart up to the school – while Miss Holden and the other girls were ogling his son Graham from their dormitory windows, and admiring how the sun fell on his neck – Mr Goodyear would lug a crate of milk round to the kitchens and Miss Stoater would be lying in wait.' He shuddered, and flipped open his notebook. 'She'd be waiting in a *baby-doll nightdress* for a spot of *wooing*.'

'Wooing?' queried Mrs G, feather duster raised. 'You sure that's the *mot juste* here, dear?'

'The sergeant and I were quite satisfied with wooing, weren't we, Sergeant? Given everything else we were hearing.'

'I'll say.'

'Anyway, of course one night they had this midnight wooing assignation on the cliffs, and Diana followed them in her daft plimsolls and slipped, and Miss Stoater was almost demented by feelings of guilt. She felt it was all her fault. She was just about able to bear it while she believed Mr Goodyear loved her with an equal, exclusive passion; in fact, she's borne it for years—'

'But then it turned out,' said Brunswick, enjoying himself, 'that he was wooing all over the place.'

'Was he?' gasped Mrs G in mock horror. 'And him a milk-man?'

Twitten nodded. 'She found out two weeks ago that Mr Goodyear had not been faithful at all. He'd even been wooing young *Barbara Ashley*! And for Miss Stoater something snapped. Her guilt over Diana's death finally overwhelmed her; also her terror of anyone finding out she'd been there and seen the fatal fall. Cedric Carbody was her cousin; he had always used her, without asking, as a source for his school-story parodies, and he had dropped plenty of hints that he had guessed precisely what had happened on the night of Diana's death. He put the business of the slippery plimsolls in the broadcast that was repeated on Sunday.'

'*Nothing was sacred*,' said Brunswick.

'Precisely, sir. And you remember the death-threat letter sent to him at the BBC, Mrs G?'

'No, dear. You forget, I was mainly busy elsewhere this weekend, looking after my visitors.'

'Of course. Well, Miss Stoater had written a letter to him a year ago – anonymously, and with purposely bad grammar, warning him to stay away from Brighton – but the BBC, being unbelievably heartless, never told him. Meanwhile Officer Andy had been openly investigating the unsolved case of Diana, and was tailing Mr Goodyear. And Barbara Ashley was Miss Stoater's youthful rival, plain and simple.'

Mrs Groynes stopped dusting, and addressed the sergeant, smiling. 'How does it feel to share your dead girlfriend with a bleeding Romeo of a milkman, dear?'

'She wasn't my girlfriend, Mrs G. We hadn't even gone out.'

'But you raise a very good point, Mrs G,' said Twitten. 'Miss Stoater told us that Miss Ashley harboured a strange – possibly unique – sexual preference for older men with firearm injuries, such as suffered by Mr Goodyear in the war.'

'*Did* she now?' said Mrs Groynes, head on one side. 'Well, it takes all sorts.'

'Yes, but unfortunately this interesting fact, which come to think of it might have helped the investigation, had never come up in the course of our inquiries.'

Twitten looked pointedly at Brunswick, but he merely pulled a face. In no circumstances would he ever repeat the eye-watering stuff Barbara Ashley had unleashed on him within minutes of their first meeting.

'Are you sure she didn't mention this unusual sexual preference to *you*, sir?'

'To me? Are you joking?'

'Even though you yourself are an older man, relatively speaking, with a history of being shot in the leg?'

Brunswick shrugged. There was no way he was conceding this point.

Mrs Groynes finished dusting in Inspector Steine's office and came back in.

'Do you know what I want to know?' she said, as she collected their cups on her tea-tray. 'I mean, this all fits together very well, I'm not saying it doesn't. You deserve bleeding medals, the two of you. But I wonder if – and you'll think I'm silly – I wonder if there was a *special song* or anything?'

'Ah!' said Twitten. 'Thank you for reminding me, Mrs G. I did ask about that, and the answer is yes.'

Brunswick frowned. 'Yes, what was that all about, Twitten? Asking her if Mr Goodyear ever sang to her? You completely lost me there.'

'Oh, it was just something Mrs Groynes and I were talking about the other day. About how Graham always sang "If You Were the Only Girl in the World" in the shows at the children's playground. We wondered why.'

'That's right, dear.'

'Well, it turns out that he sang it because it was his father's signature song. It was what you might call a family favourite.'

'No!'

'But if you recall, it was *years ago* that Graham used to sing it at the children's theatre. Whereas Mr Goodyear whistles it *to this day* while out on his rounds – and Officer Andy, who had been following Goodyear Senior and observing him, worked out quite recently that it wasn't *just* his favourite tune.'

'No, dear?'

'No. It was code!'

'Code for what?'

'I'm afraid it was Mr Goodyear's way of asking the woman of the house, "May I come in? Is the husband out of the way? Is a spot of wooing on the cards?"'

'Well, I never.' Mrs Groynes was clearly impressed. 'And did Officer Andy tell poor Miss Stoater that?'

'He did. It was very cruel of him. He told her that every time Mr Goodyear would start whistling "If You Were the Only Girl in the World" outside certain houses, the front doors would open and he'd be ushered inside.'

'Blimey.'

'So, you see, that explains why, as he was dying of his wounds, Officer Andy tried to – er – oh.' Twitten stopped, overcome with confusion. 'Oh, crikey, sorry. What am I talking about? Sorry.' He took a deep breath, while his mind raced. *You're not supposed to know about this!* 'So that's the whole bally story, Mrs G. Could I have another of your lovely cups of tea?'

Brunswick looked puzzled. 'You all right, son?'

Mrs Groynes raised her eyebrows. She looked amused.

Twitten bit his lip. 'Sorry,' he said again.

Brunswick was mystified. 'Are you all right, son? You were just saying about the song explaining something about when Officer Andy was dying. But I don't understand. Was someone else there?'

Twitten shot a look of panic at Mrs Groynes. 'Um?' he said. Unpractised in guile, he hadn't the first idea how to get out of this awkward situation. Should he pretend to faint?

'Um?' he began again, his eyes swivelling. But Mrs Groynes stepped in.

'Toasted teacake, Sergeant, dear?' she asked, casually patting Brunswick's shoulder.

The question hung in the air, and Twitten held his breath. Would it work? Would Sergeant Brunswick refuse, for once, to have his thoughts derailed by the offer of food?

'Oh. Well,' said Brunswick. 'Thank you, Mrs G, a toasted teacake would be lovely.' But Twitten could see that the danger hadn't quite passed. Was that a flicker of a thought crossing the sergeant's face? 'But hang on, I was just asking—'

'Dollop of strawberry jam with it, dear? I've got a brand-new jar. Tell you what, you can do the honours. There's always a nice big strawberry on the top.'

'Ooh, well, lovely, thank you. Strawberry jam!'

'You're very welcome, dear. And I'd say you bleeding deserve it after all you've been through.'

And thus was the crisis averted.

The disappearance of Buster Bond was finally confirmed on the Tuesday by the Ice Circus management, and Graham Goodyear officially stepped into his skates until the end of the run. Mrs Goodyear was aware of all the usual snide remarks about Graham nobbling anyone who stood in his way, but she knew the truth about her dear son: that he was a very nice person who wouldn't hurt a fly. Naturally, speculation flew about what had happened to Bond. Those who knew about his unsavoury night-time activities supposed that he had been murdered by some local hoodlum whose girlfriend he had forced his attentions on.

Not for decades did the truth come to light, when Giuseppe Savoretti of the ice-clown troupe admitted on his deathbed in Old Naples, Florida, that one of his brothers had shot Buster Bond on the ice. Speaking to a reporter from the *Naples Tribune*, he explained that it had been a case of straightforward retribution. Bond was the man who'd ratted to the authorities about them using an underage family member in the act. When they found out, they killed him. Initially, Giuseppe said, Buster Bond's body had been cunningly crammed inside the miniature fire engine used in their act, but they'd had to think again when the Russian woman's poodles kept sniffing round it and barking.

Up at Hassocks, Bond's landlady Mrs Lester was convinced that her daughter June had driven Mr Bond away – especially as June had packed a bag on that Saturday night and left for London with just her trophy for winning the beauty contest (a disappointing silver cream jug in the shape of a cow) and her worryingly short and effeminate boyfriend. But Mrs Lester could at least console herself that she had helped the police by identifying the woman who'd been tailing Officer Andy on the night that he died. It was her testimony to Twitten early on the Monday morning that had led straight to the arrest.

'Officer Inman had just finished with Mr Bond's car,' she had told the sleep-deprived Twitten, 'and Mr Bond had driven off. And then one of my neighbours came and told us about this misleading road-sign he'd passed on his way home. Officer Inman said it was probably kids that had turned it, but that he would set it right. It was only as he was leaving that I spotted a van following him with a woman at the wheel. And as it moved off, I could hear the rattle of milk bottles. It was unmistakably Miss Stoater from June's old school.

'June didn't want me to come forward, but I knew I should have, and I'm only sorry I didn't do it straight away. She has always been a very forceful girl! But are you sure you shouldn't be in bed, Constable Twitten? You look terrible.'

When the Holdens arrived in Hove to pick up their daughter, Twitten was there, too. With all this darting around town for the past few days, he was seriously thinking of requisitioning a pushbike.

'Blakeney! Is that you?' he said, in surprise, as a small golden dog scampered up the path, then straight past him and up the stairs. It transpired that the Holdens had been travelling for an hour before realising that Blakeney was hiding under the back seat of their car. But once his presence was noted, his excited tail-wagging certainly brightened their journey. Before this, King's Lynn had been the extent of the little dog's travel ambitions. Cadging a lift all the way to the South Coast was beyond his wildest dreams.

'Mummy!' said Pandora, bursting into tears. 'Please take me home. I want to go home.'

But the Holdens were tired from the long drive, and they were also intrigued to see Twitten again, and to hear his account of all that had happened. On their way to Brighton – stopping at little parades of shops – they'd become increasingly aware of the incident now widely described as '*High Noon at the Milk Bar*'. Had their daughter really been present when a notorious London gangster was shot dead? Who could have imagined that becoming the Milk Girl would expose her to such things? Thank goodness she was off to Oxford in a couple of months' time. The blood-soaked revenge plays of Aeschylus and Euripides would seem positively tame by comparison.

'You look so different with your short hair, Peregrine,' said Pandora's mother. 'I wouldn't have known you.'

'No one seems to like it,' he admitted. 'Mummy actually let out a scream. But, as I said to her, my old schoolboy style would look bally strange with the uniform.'

All of them laughed except for Pandora. 'Perhaps you'd grow it back,' she said, 'if enough people asked you to.'

'Oh, I shouldn't think so,' said Twitten.

'What brought you here, though?' asked Pandora's father. 'We were saying in the car, we'd had no idea where young Mr Twitten's bizarre career decision had taken him. What made you choose Brighton?'

'Oh.' Twitten blushed. 'It wasn't a choice, as such, sir. I'm here because no one else would have me.'

The Holdens looked at each other. 'Are you joking?' asked Pandora's father.

'I'm afraid I'm bally serious, sir. I was transferred several times before I came here in June. At Scotland Yard I lasted less than a week.'

'Why was that?'

'Oh, it was my bally cleverness, of course! It kept making people uncomfortable. You see, I can't help spotting things that my police colleagues have missed, and instead of being grateful, they get furious and annoyed, and refuse to work with me, or neglect to tell me where the lockers are, which is possibly the most hurtful thing of all. It's human nature, apparently, but in my opinion it's very small-minded and unconstructive, not to mention the bane of my bally life.'

'So you're here because Inspector Steine is a bigger man who appreciates your cleverness?'

'Oh, no, sir! Hah!' Twitten laughed at the very idea. 'That's hilarious, sir.' The Holdens, shocked, exchanged glances.

'No, quite the opposite!' Twitten continued, cheerfully. 'I annoy Inspector Steine, too, all the bally time. But fortunately he is very wrapped up in his own concerns, you see. That's the difference here.'

Twitten was pleased to talk about this with people who would understand. 'Inspector Steine is an inveterate solipsist, you see, which in a way is bally fascinating to observe at close quarters. Over the past weekend he genuinely thought that his own judging of an ice-cream competition was the most important thing going on!'

Twitten laughed again. 'Also he has a phenomenal capacity for denial and self-deception, which of course is a bit disappointing in one's superior officer, but at the same time his consistent obtuseness does help maintain a dubious status quo vis-à-vis the blatant criminal activity operating within the town, so, truthfully, it has its uses.'

The Holdens looked stunned.

'Well, you've certainly chosen an interesting career, Peregrine,' said Pandora's mother, at last.

'Thank you. But, ooh, I just thought. Have you finished your Cook Islands book, yet? Does Father have a copy? I'd love to see what conclusions you eventually drew from all that data.'

'Oh, heavens, no,' laughed Pandora's father. 'We're still collating.'

Twitten tried not to betray how shocked he was at their glacial progress. He failed.

'Cleverness takes many forms, Peregrine,' said Pandora's mother, gently. 'It's not all about quickness. But that's what we used to discuss when you were staying with us, wasn't it? If you don't mind my saying, that's where your own capacity for self-deception comes in.'

A few minutes later, Twitten waved them off – the Holdens, Pandora and the stowaway dog whose owner, back at the railway station in Norfolk, had been informed by telephone of his latest long-distance escapade. Twitten had given Pandora the Diana scrapbook and promised to visit her in Oxford. On parting, she begged him to stop addressing her as 'Miss Holden', and he shrugged and said he would do his best.

As he left the hotel, he noticed across the road a large advertisement with Pandora's face on it – her cheeks shining with youthful energy as she raised a glass filled with white liquid. 'You'll Feel A Lot Better If You Drink More Milk' it read. But this was the end of an era, surely? There had been

High Noon at a milk bar, as well as a riot involving criminal damage. A herd of startled red-and-white ruminants had shockingly killed a young woman destined to be buried in an unmarked grave. A milkman's frightful dalliances had led to the murder of three people who'd been slain by milk bottle. And as for the beauteous Milk Girl – she had gone home to Norfolk, never to return.

They hardly saw the inspector that day at the station, so busy was he in his newfound fame. Interestingly, the more he talked about the shooting, the more he seemed to have committed it while in full possession of the facts.

'Of course, we knew about that pile of bodies at the Metropole,' he said. 'That's why I shot him. Terence Chambers had, in an insane murdering spree, just butchered ten villains aged between forty-two and sixty-five, some of them with distinguishing marks, hailing from every corner of the country.'

In the office, when Twitten returned from saying goodbye to Pandora, he found Mrs Groynes with her feet up and a cigarette in her mouth.

'Oh, good, it's you,' she said, not moving. 'I have created a monster; can you imagine how that feels?'

'You knew exactly what you were doing, Mrs G.'

'Well, I suppose that's true.'

Twitten sat down. Even after a full night's sleep, he was still tired. 'I just said goodbye to Pandora,' he said. 'It was bizarre. She burst into tears.'

'She's keen on you, dear. The sergeant said that girl from the BBC had a crush on you too. You ought to call her up. And you remember that posh girl Phyllis who was in the

Brighton Belles? I hear she's joining the bleeding police on account of you.'

'That's nonsense, Mrs G.'

'You've got something about you, dear. I mean, obviously *I* can't see it.'

'Oh, please.'

'All right, dear. Have it your own way.'

'It was funny just now,' he said, thoughtfully. 'I used to think Pandora's parents approved of me, but when I merely outlined some of Inspector Steine's personality faults – just stated what they were – they seemed horrified. I think they wanted me to praise him, just because he's a man of superior rank.'

'They're fools, then.'

Twitten looked around. There was something missing. 'May I have a cup of tea, please, Mrs G? When I came in you didn't make me one.'

'Oh, all right.' She stubbed out her cigarette in an ashtray and stood up, stretching. 'Usual sugars?'

'Yes, please.'

While he waited, he picked up a sheet of paper. It was a mimeographed copy of Mrs Groynes's list, which was rapidly becoming a famous document. According to this, Norman Hardcastle, aged fifty-six, ran all criminal affairs in the North East, lived in ostentatious grandeur at the Hotel Splendide in Redcar, and (under the heading Miscellaneous) had a reputation as a 'bleeding psycho'.

'What's so interesting about this list, Mrs G, is that no one's asking who drew it up.'

'I know.' She put down his tea.

'It's even typed on Brighton Police Station headed notepaper.'

'I know. I couldn't resist it. But I just couldn't risk them taking days and days to identify the bodies; I needed all the information to come out at once. And I have to say, you played your part in that, dear, so thank you very much.'

'How many of them did you kill personally, Mrs G?'

'Me? None. But I did help a bit by sowing discord and what have you. Giving them packs of cards. The septicaemia victim, obviously, was a separate case. Poor sod took care of himself.'

'Fortunate that there were those newsreel cameras in town, and that they got wind of what was happening at the milk bar.'

'Fortunate, did you say?'

'Ah. I beg your pardon. Is the word "brilliant"?'

'That's nearer to the right word, certainly.'

'And who was the man threatening you and Mr Chambers outside the hotel when I came along?'

'One of my boys. I must remember to send him a turkey at Christmas.'

'Why did you do it, though, Mrs G? Why did you want Chambers out of the picture so badly? I thought you used to be a team?'

'He was losing it, dear. You need to be a *bit* mad in this business, but he'd gone bleeding loco. He'd started shooting family members just to see where they landed on the carpet.'

'Gosh. Do you mind if I write to my father about that? He'd be bally fascinated.'

'Be my guest, dear.'

'Thank you.'

How easily they talked together, he and Mrs Groynes.

'Will you move in on London now?' he asked.

'Oh, no, dear. I wouldn't touch it. Imagine having to bribe the police! It's hand over fist up there. That's why Terry trusted me about going down to that milk bar and handing himself in. I said I'd fixed the inspector! I said he was *in my pocket*, dear. I said, *he's expecting you*. I told him to say: *I'm from the Metropole.'*

She laughed at the naivety of a villain believing that the only way to fix a policeman was with money.

'Down here I've not bribed the police once, dear! But Terry would never have understood how you can keep a trio of policemen in the palm of your hand just by supplying them continuously with tea and biscuits, dear – or buying them a life-saving sausage sandwich from time to time, or giving their daft careers a well-timed boost when they seem to be on the slide.'

'And how did you get the inspector to do it? I assume you supplied the gun?'

'Of course. I sent him a picture of Terry, and a note from a well-wisher saying that the man who presents himself and says *I'm from the Metropole* was prepared to kill because he cared so much about winning a bleeding ice-cream competition!'

'And the inspector fell for that?'

'Of course he fell for it.'

Mrs Groynes lit another cigarette, and blew a perfect smoke-ring. 'He's a very, very stupid man, dear. Or have you already worked that out for yourself?'

Brunswick took Twitten to the canteen that day, and ordered egg and chips twice while Twitten scouted for a recently wiped (i.e. still wet) table near a window. The place was busy with helmet-less police officers drinking tea and smoking; a few were playing cards. One or two nudged each other when they saw Twitten. Embarrassed, he looked away. He felt nervous.

This was the first time he and Brunswick been alone together since the horrors of Sunday night in the Punch & Judy tent. An enormous bally scene was definitely on the cards, friendly egg and chips notwithstanding.

He supposed they would eat first and talk afterwards, but no, Brunswick launched straight into it before even sitting down. 'Look, son,' he said, arriving with a tray, which he proceeded to unload. 'About storming out the other night, I shouldn't have done it.' He set down a plate of egg and chips, with a clunk. 'It was unprofessional, leaving you on your own.' A cup of tea was sloshed into the saucer. 'I got upset, that's all.' Cheap cutlery cascaded on to the table. 'So let's put it behind us, all right?'

It was only after this performance, when Brunswick had sat down, that Twitten responded. He was well aware how blatantly the sergeant was avoiding eye contact, and he was having none of it. This stuff was jolly important, and needed to be talked about man to man.

'It was my fault, sir. If you could just look at me for a moment, sir? I gave it a lot of thought afterwards and – could you just look at me, sir?'

But it was no use.

'Bread and butter?' asked Brunswick. 'Salt and pepper?'

'No, thank you. You see, if you would just—'

'Red sauce? I could get you some. Hold on. I'll go and—'

'No, thank you, sir. Please don't bother.'

'Brown?'

'No.'

'Well, tuck in, son, before it gets cold. There's a good lad.'

'Of course, sir.' Twitten picked up his knife and fork and tasted a chip. He immediately regretted refusing all the condiments.

'Look, son,' said Brunswick, stirring sugar into his tea and watching it swirl. 'I know you'd probably like to yak about this till the cows come home, but I'd rather not. And you know what they say, son.' At last, he raised his face and looked Twitten in the eye. 'Least said, soonest mended.'

Twitten physically shuddered at this platitude: there was scarcely a saying in the English language he disapproved of more. But he governed his urge to argue and said, 'Right, sir. If that's what you want. We shan't discuss it.'

'Here, I forgot,' said Brunswick, changing the subject and spearing a chip. 'There's a packet of sandwiches for you in my desk.'

'Really? Why?'

'I bumped into your landlady this morning and she asked me to bring them in. It was what made me think of doing this: bringing you here for your first canteen hot dinner.'

'I do hope you didn't say anything to her about what I told you? About her doomed romantic fixation?'

'Of course I didn't, Twitten!' Brunswick pierced his egg, which was undercooked. 'What do you take me for? But I think you're right, though. About her. She called me "manly", to my face.'

'Gosh, sir.'

'What age do you think she is?'

'Forty-one. I checked the electoral register. She's awfully nice, but she has a distinct weakness for gossip, so my advice would be to brush up a few anecdotes. She also loves anything to do with the world of theatre and film, so your subscription to *Picturegoer* will be a bally godsend.'

Brunswick finished his egg and chips, and pushed his plate away. And then, to Twitten's alarm, he stood up and held out his hand for shaking. Aware that other people were watching, Twitten stood up too, and took it.

His mind raced. Was Brunswick at last preparing to apologise for not telling him about the canteen and causing the rift between them? Was he going to set things straight? Was he going to say, 'You're wrong, you know, son. I do like you, Twitten; I always have'?

'Look, I'm only going to say this once,' said Brunswick, quietly, as they shook hands. He seemed to be working himself up to some sort of declaration. Twitten gulped.

'Thank you, sir. Say what?'

'Look,' said Brunswick. 'This isn't easy for me.'

'No, sir. Of course.'

'I wouldn't do this for just anyone.'

'Understood, sir.'

'Well, you remember that acronym they taught you at Hendon about people being wrong about not knowing anything?'

Twitten frowned. 'Do you mean WANKA, sir?'

Brunswick winced. 'Shhh, yes, that's the one. I didn't say anything at the time, but I think those blokes at Hendon were having you on.'

'Really?'

'Yes. It's a bad word, son.'

'Is it?'

'Yes, it is.'

'A *bad word*?'

'Yes.'

'But why would they play a trick on me like that?'

'I don't know, Twitten.' Brunswick patted him on the shoulder. 'But is it possible they just didn't like you?'

Then the sergeant picked up his coat, paid the cashier and headed for the door, leaving Twitten to resume his glorious first canteen meal alone.

Back in the office, he was gently opening Brunswick's desk drawer and withdrawing the packet of sandwiches when Mrs Groynes came in.

'You going back on your rounds later?' she asked.

'I thought I would, actually. After I've written my report.'

'Good for you, dear.'

She whistled the tune to 'Wunderbar' while flapping her duster out of the window. For someone who had just ruthlessly eliminated eleven rivals in the world of organised crime, she was giving an excellent impression of a woman with nothing on her conscience. Twitten sat down at the typewriter and fed two sheets of paper (with fresh carbon paper sandwiched between) on to the roller. He took a deep breath, and cracked his fingers.

But before he could start, Mrs Groynes sat down.

'I've been meaning to say, dear.'

'Yes?'

'You didn't notice what happened today, did you? It was quite big, but it seemed to pass you by.'

Twitten frowned. He couldn't think of any landmarks today besides, of course, visiting the canteen for the first time, taking the startlingly unguarded confession of a headmistress-cum-murderess, and discovering that even at his beloved Hendon he had been universally unpopular. A childhood chant kept running through his head: *Nobody likes me, everybody hates me, I think I'll go and eat worms.*

But that wasn't what Mrs Groynes was referring to. 'It was that business over Officer Andy's dying words, dear.'

'Oh, that. Gosh, I did feel awkward, Mrs G!'

'I could tell.'

'You did brilliantly with your teacake ruse. But I don't see how it was momentous. It was just bally awful.'

'You covered up for me, dear.'

'Did I?'

'Yes. You could have told the sergeant how I'd passed on that information to you – *which I'd heard from one of Chambers's underlings*. You could have used it against me, but you chose not to. You made a choice, dear, and I saw the whole thing written on your face.'

Twitten cast his mind back. It was true that he hadn't spoken up, but had he made this so-called choice to support Mrs Groynes? Surely not. 'He wouldn't have believed me, Mrs G, that's all. And I wouldn't have known where to start.'

'That's all? Are you sure?'

'Yes. I mean, I think so. Gosh, I hope you don't think I was colluding with you, because I wouldn't bally do that.'

'Perhaps not consciously, dear.' She twinkled at him. 'But as a clever-clogs of my acquaintance recently said to me, everyone has an unconscious mind, dear. Even you.'

She let this sink in for a moment, and then – with the consummate skill he had always admired – changed the subject. 'So you've been to that bleeding canteen at last, then?'

'Oh, yes. The sergeant took me. We had egg and chips.'

'And how was it? Did it measure up to expectations?'

Twitten pulled a face. 'Truthfully? I'd rather not say.'

'I bet you wouldn't. But go on. There's nobody here but us chickens.'

'Well, truthfully … it was bally awful.'

Mrs Groynes laughed. 'So it turns out you hadn't missed anything all these tragic months not knowing about it?'

'No. In my opinion, only someone with very low self-esteem and a profound abandonment complex would derive any comfort from it whatsoever.'

'As bad as that!'

'I was about to explain this to Sergeant Brunswick, but unfortunately he decided to leave. I'll certainly tell him if he invites me there again, though.'

'Will you, dear?' Mrs Groynes looked at him with genuine delight. 'You'd say that to him, after everything that's passed between you?'

'Yes. Of course.'

'That's my boy,' said Mrs Groynes, patting him on the back. She lit a fresh cigarette.

Twitten began to type, but then stopped. He had thought of something.

'Ooh, but I meant to say, Mrs G.'

'Yes, dear?'

'Something good did come out of all the painful and divisive revelations of the past few days.'

'What's that, then?'

'I located my locker!'

She smiled.

'And I can't tell you how bally useful it is!'

She reached for her mop.

'Good for you, dear,' she said, as she started to swab the lino. 'Bleeding well good for you.'

Acknowledgements and Author's Note

Authors should never admit they enjoy writing books. It strips away the mystique. However, it would be silly for me to pretend that I don't love writing this series. I wholeheartedly appreciate the opportunity, and I thank everyone at Raven Books for their support and professionalism, and especially I thank my editor Alison Hennessey, who is terrific. Raven is a great list, and I'm very proud to be on it.

I realise that it's not always a good idea to specify how one's plots or characters are inspired by real events, because it can backfire. "So everything in *The Man That Got Away* was *true*?" exclaimed a recent interviewer, pointing accusingly at my last Acknowledgements page. "I thought you had *made it up!*" Naturally, I didn't know what to say. For one thing, I was sure I had made up a substantial part of it.

But why bother with research if you don't draw inspiration from it? A degree of authenticity is what one strives for, after all. When I was just starting work on *Murder by Milk Bottle*, I told an audience in Lewes (situated between Brighton and Eastbourne) that I was currently musing on a tiny news story I had read. Just before the Bank Holiday in August 1957, motorists were inconvenienced on the road to Eastbourne by a mischievously turned road-sign. I said I was very drawn to this detail, but wasn't sure yet how to use it. After the event a woman of mature years came up. "That road sign that was turned?" she said, in a confidential whisper. "That was *me!*"

If it's a mistake to use research, though, I have boobed again. In 1957, there was – in reality – a striking amount of milk promotion going on in Brighton. The local paper was awash with milky references. A herd of cows really did graze on the Pavilion lawns, and there were many milk-related events. Meanwhile, the DRINKA PINTA MILKA DAY campaign, launched in 1957, famously went on to become one of the greatest advertising successes of all time. A caption in the *Brighton Evening Argus* really did shockingly (but hilariously) refer to some Dairy Princess beauty queens as "lactic lovelies". When I discovered this – bending over a microfilm reader at The Keep (Brighton's excellent local history archive) – I was so excited I nearly fell off my chair.

The celebrities on *What's Your Game?* are clearly inspired by real showbiz types of the period; meanwhile, the childish way Inspector Steine is cold-shouldered backstage before the show is (sadly) based on the author's own jaw-dropping experience. The larger-than-life Cedric Carbody has elements of various real people, but because his work as a comic broadcaster had to be good enough to convince, his "skits" are firmly – and with great affection and admiration – based on the work of the wonderful Arthur Marshall (1910-1989), who I'm sure was never unpleasant to anyone in his life.

Lady Laura Laridae occupies the position on the cliffs east of the town that is actually occupied by Roedean, but has nothing else in common.

The House of Hanover Milk Bar is located in the real-life Milkmaid Pavilion, which in recent years was given an upper floor as the Alfresco restaurant (it's now something else).

The Sports Stadium in West Street – with its huge rink, and massive audiences for both ice shows and ice hockey – did exist, but has long gone, and many people living today in the city of Brighton and Hove have no idea it was ever there. It was probably better known as SS Brighton, and was demolished in 1965.

The Regent Ballroom and Cinema occupied the position on the corner of North Street and Queen's Road where we now find Boot's.

The children's playground, with its little theatre, is now a distant memory, but a snatch of the talent show (fronted by the real-life Uncle Jack) can be seen in the charming film *Brighton Story* (1955) which is available on line courtesy of the British Film Institute. The young boy belting out, "If You Were the Only Girl in the World" was, of course, the most direct inspiration for this book. I couldn't get it out of my head.

Finally, readers will have noticed that the location of the police station in these books is rather vague, and that the building itself is only partially described. There are steps outside, and some cells in the basement, and a staircase, and a locked cupboard, but that's it. Brightonians will know that the real police station at that time occupied the lower section of the stately old Town Hall in what is now Bartholomew Square – but somehow I have always resisted using that building, while still happily locating the station in the same part of town. However, anyone curious about the old station can see it in dramatic action in Val Guest's police procedural film *Jigsaw* (1962), much of which is shot on location. It's almost as if the film-maker's main intention was to preserve the police station premises – both inside and out – for the benefit of future novelists.

But while I have resisted using the station in the old Town Hall per se, I loved the fact that the canteen was in a different building. I am indebted to David Rowland's excellent *On the Brighton Beat: Memoirs of an Old-Time Copper* (2006) for this and other useful information, such as the position of various police boxes around the town and also the existence of weekly pay parades. Another book by Rowland – *Bent Cops: The Brighton Police Conspiracy Trial* (2007) deals with the real-life corruption uncovered in the Brighton police in the autumn of 1957 – but this sorry tale was, of course, less useful to me. As we know, no such tawdry palm-greasing was required in the Twitten/Mrs Groynes universe.

Read on for the new instalment of Lynne Truss's thoroughly entertaining crime series

PSYCHO BY THE SEA

One

If the disappearance of Barrow-Boy Cecil aroused no suspicions at first, it was for one very good reason: since the beginning of the month, Brighton had been subject to constant, drenching rain.

The September seafront was grey and deserted; striped shop-awnings sagged and flapped; street drains backed up; overexcited schoolboys wrote rude words, backwards, on the steamed-up windows of the trolley-buses. No wonder that the town's dodgy street characters, one and all, turned up their jacket collars, pulled their sodden headgear tighter to their heads, and raced indoors (through puddles) to sit it out.

Any visiting academic engaged in studying the Petty Criminal of the South Coast of England could have had a field day in the cheaper cafes and milk bars of Brighton during this unlooked-for monsoon season. Even the respectable Lyons tea room towards the top of North Street was full of minor hoodlums. In every establishment it was the same: damp, disgruntled men and boys (some with livid facial scars) sat around formica-topped tables in loose, taciturn groups, waiting with charmless impatience for the pubs to open at half-past eleven while their clothes steamed unpleasantly.

Conversation was scant. Each man nursed a cup of strong tea, smoked roll-ups down to the stub, miserably totted up halfpennies dug from deep trouser pockets, or idly polished a flick-knife blade with a handkerchief – or at least until the proprietor yelled 'Oi!' from behind the counter.

It would have been madness for Barrow-Boy Cecil to be out. 'See the bunny run, madam?' was his perpetual patter, as he wound up the plastic mechanical toys on his felt-lined pedlar's tray and waved a showman's hand, as if the world offered nothing more splendid than their stiff, arthritic hopping. 'See the bunny jump, sir! Only half a crown! See the bunny jump!' Well, what sort of idiot holiday-maker would be in the market for a cheap, foreign-made clockwork toy in weather like this?

But there was another good reason. Cecil's regular pitch was at the Clock Tower – a location that tended to bear the brunt of inclement conditions, what with its being a major crossroads, exposed to winds whipping straight up West Street from the sea. In some ways it was an excellent spot, providing a 360-degree vantage point for a trusted lieutenant in a well-organised criminal gang headed by a woman cunningly posing as a charlady at the police station. It made him the visible hub of the organisation; almost its talisman. 'What's the lay, Cecil?' Mrs Groynes would traditionally ask, smiling, as she stood in front of him at least twice a week, pretending to purchase a bunny for a favourite niece. Alternatively, if she needed him to act as an urgent bush telegraph, she would get hold of young Shorty (trusted juvenile messenger) and hiss, 'Get this to Cecil. He'll tell the others.' So there was no gainsaying the topographical advantage of Cecil's position, but there was also no denying that it was dismal when the wind blew hard from the south and the rain came down like bullets.

So, that's why no one missed him initially. There were four perfectly good reasons for Barrow-Boy Cecil to be absent from the streets. In the first place, there was zero passing trade; second, standing in his usual place, it would be like having buckets of water chucked in your face; third, he secretly received a regular substantial stipend from Mrs Groynes anyway, so the revenue from the bunnies concerned him little.

But the fourth factor was probably the clincher: in conditions like these, the bunnies not only blew about on the flimsy tray suspended from Cecil's neck; their mechanisms seized up, and they toppled over onto their backs, making a heart-breaking noise (*Fzzzzz, fzzzzz, fzzzzzzz* ...), with their little legs kicking feebly at the air.

Sergeant Brunswick was the first to ask where Cecil was. For several years the sergeant had, deludedly, been passing money to the bunny-man every couple of weeks in return for information about criminal activity in the town. Sometimes this outlay was later reclaimed from petty cash; more often, it came from the sergeant's own pocket (he wasn't very clever about money). It was only ten shillings, but you could buy quite a lot for that: two tins of salmon; sixty cigarettes; several quick haircuts from Rodolfo the Barber on Western Road. However, if the sergeant wished to throw his money away on Cecil, it was up to him, and it made him feel he was doing his job properly.

For his own part, Cecil quite relished the comic role of underworld 'grass'. Sometimes, alone in the evening, he practised in a mirror tilting his hat forward, tapping his nose, and speaking shiftily out of the side of his mouth. At one point he toyed with having a toothpick clamped between his jaws, but it turned out to be almost impossible to say 'See the bunny run' with your jaws clenched. Also, for proper authenticity, you had to manoeuvre the stick from one side of your mouth to the other, and the first time he tried this he nearly swallowed it.

But Cecil didn't assume the role of double-agent for his own entertainment. It was entirely for the benefit of the gang. For Mrs Groynes's purposes, this 'informer' arrangement was a reliable means of sending the police (in the person of Sergeant Brunswick) on well-timed wild goose chases when she had important criminal business to conduct.

'Word is you should keep an eye on that new Buy Rite supermarket, Sergeant,' Cecil would murmur, conspiratorially (head down, lips exaggeratedly lopsided, like Popeye), as he picked up a toy, wound it up, and placed it on the tray. Then, loudly, with the usual flourish of the arm, 'See the bunny run, sir? Lovely, innit? Lovely bunny, sir! Only half a crown! See the bunny jump, look!'

'Good man, Cecil,' Brunswick would murmur in reply, and then announce for the benefit of anyone passing, 'I'll take that pink one, mate.'

'Pink one? Good choice, sir. Look here, sir, on the bottom. Made in Hong Kong, only the best!'

Then the sergeant would hand over a folded ten-bob note, put the toy in his pocket, and walk off without any change, glowing with achievement, while Cecil called 'See the bunny run, madam?' at a fresh member of the public.

And usually the information paid off – but only because it was a fair bet in this town that if you set out to uncover criminal activity in any location, you would succeed.

Acting on Cecil's insider dope, Brunswick (taking several men with him) would lie in wait at the new supermarket and, sure enough, apprehend a couple of unwashed kids smuggling tins of peaches up their moth-holed jumpers. What Brunswick had so far failed to notice was that, invariably, just as he triumphantly grabbed a scarpering juvenile delinquent by the ear and said 'You're nicked, sonny!' (to gratifying cheers from female shoppers), a high-end jeweller's shop in another part of town was successfully raided by masked villains.

Meanwhile Brunswick's desk drawer was filling with wind-up bunnies, as testament to his acumen and perseverance as a police detective. When she was alone in the office, Mrs Groynes sometimes turned from her special locked cupboard – filled with gelignite, armed-robbery equipment, hot jewellery, and gold bullion – and opened the sergeant's drawer, just to see the bunnies. They always made her smile. Much as she liked Sergeant Brunswick personally, there was no escaping the tragic fact that he was, basically, *such easy meat*.

Still, it was Brunswick who was the first to notice that the bunny-man was missing. 'Barrow-Boy Cecil hasn't been around much lately,' he observed on this dismally wet Tuesday morning in September, hanging up his soaked hat and mackintosh to drip on the lino, and gazing in despair at his sodden, half-ruined shoes. 'I hope he's all right.'

The overhead lights were on in the office, and heavy rain drummed at the window. Mrs Groynes, a lit cigarette in one hand, was waving a feather duster along the tops of picture frames (mostly for effect), while young Constable Twitten was absorbed in a book. It was quite cosy. The air smelled of cocoa-flavoured biscuits, fresh from the packet.

But before Brunswick could properly relax, he nodded at the inspector's empty room.

'The inspector … ?' he said carefully. 'Still *elsewhere*?'

'Thank Christ, yes, dear.'

'You're sure?'

Twitten chipped in, without looking up from his book. 'The inspector is still in London, sir.'

Brunswick narrowed his eyes. Something was different. 'It's very quiet.'

This was true. No phones were ringing.

'Oh, I got them to deal with all his calls at the switch-board,' said Mrs Groynes.

'Blimey, you've got some nerve, Mrs G!' said Brunswick, impressed. The fierce female telephonists at the station were notoriously unaccommodating to requests of this sort. They also had surprisingly well-developed arm muscles from all the reaching across each other to connect the jacks to the board. Once, without properly thinking it through, he had asked out a petite redhead from the switchboard and over their first drink in the saloon bar of the Cricketers pub she had challenged him to arm-wrestling, with embarrassing results.

'Oh, they don't scare me, dear. I said if they put one more call through to this office, I'd rip the wire out of the bleeding wall. I said the bags of post piling up are bad enough.' As if to prove the point, she kicked an unopened sack of fan letters that stood against the wall with a dozen others. 'All this interest is on account of that shocking Chambers business last month, of course,' she sighed, shaking her head as if this vague 'Chambers business' was a regrettable train of events with which she'd had nothing to do (when she had in fact engineered the whole thing). 'Cup of tea, then? Come on,

Sergeant, there ain't nobody here but us chickens. Take the weight off those massive plates of yours.'

Brunswick exhaled with relief and sat down. Naturally, everyone was very pleased that the psychopathic London villain Terence Chambers had been shot dead in Brighton last month, making the world a better place; and yes, they were proud that Inspector Steine was the man who pulled the trigger. But had the shooting marked the end of anything? No, it had been more like the flaming beginning. Because afterwards came ... the *accolades*.

It started just a day or two after that momentous Bank Holiday Monday, when the inspector came bursting out of his office with the news.

'Men! Men! Listen!'

'Yes, sir?'

'I'm receiving the Silver Truncheon award from the Commissioner of the Metropolitan Police!'

'Ooh, well done, sir. Well deserved, sir.'

'Bleeding well done, dear.'

'Thank you. I'm very excited. It's the highest honour bestowed—'

'We know, sir.'

'I know too, dear. Good for you.'

'I am absolutely overwhel—'

'Cup of tea to celebrate?'

'—med. Oh. Well, yes. Yes, please.'

But it didn't stop there. It escalated.

'Men! Men! You won't believe it!'

'Gosh, sir. What is it now, sir?'

'They want me to be a guest on *Desert Island Discs*! Roy Plomley just telephoned personally! I nearly fell off my chair!'

'That's flaming marvellous, sir. Well done.'

'I know. It's a huge honour.'

'Yes, sir. Bally well done.'

'Men! Men! You won't believe it! I've been invited to the Palace!'

'Men! Men! They want me to appear on something called *The Sooty Show*!'

'Men! Men! If I am willing to lend my name to Brylcreem, which is apparently a hair preparation of some description, they'll pay me a fee of five hundred pounds!'

Much as Brunswick and Twitten tried to say 'Congratulations, sir!' with consistent gusto, it soon grew hard to do so. Inwardly they groaned with each fresh salute to Inspector Steine's greatness. One evening, when Brunswick and his auntie sat cosily at home watching *Panorama*, a handsome young man with a guitar started singing a witty topical calypso about Inspector Steine, 'Cleaning the Streets of Bright-on', and Brunswick was so upset he burst into tears.

But there was more to it than having to offer constant congratulations. For those who knew Inspector Steine well, to observe him on the receiving end of so much hero-worship was seriously alarming. The big question was: *could he cope?* After all, it takes strength of character to treat fame with the contempt it deserves, what with the natural temptation to measure one's own self-worth by it. Many great men have fallen victim to hubris. What hope could there be, then, for Inspector Steine – a man of small achievements, feeble intellect, and no self-knowledge whatsoever?

So this was why Brunswick was relieved to find the inspector out of the office, and was free to remark (again) that Barrow-Boy Cecil hadn't been seen lately, causing Twitten to stop reading for a moment and look up at Mrs Groynes. Knowing full well that the bunny-seller was, secretly, one of this ersatz charlady's most trusted gang members, he was keen to observe her response.

She didn't let him down. 'Barrow-Boy *who*, dear?' said Mrs Groynes, still flicking the feather duster with one hand and dropping fag-ash on the floor with the other.

'Cecil,' said Brunswick. 'You know, Mrs G. *See the bunny run*? By the Clock Tower.'

Mrs Groynes frowned, as if trying to place the name. 'Oh, yes. Tall cove with a tray. Ain't he out and about, then?'

'Not that I can see.'

Twitten closed his book. 'I can't imagine how a chap like him actually makes a living, can you, Mrs G?' he asked, in a conversational tone. 'Even if he sells the bunnies at two shillings and sixpence each. I wonder sometimes whether such colourful Brighton street characters in fact obtain the bulk of their income from other, more nefarious sources.'

Mrs Groynes reached over to pat him on the shoulder. 'You're asking the wrong bleeding person, dear. Now, how about that cup of tea, Sergeant?'

'Ooh, yes, please,' said Brunswick, idly picking up the *Police Gazette*. 'The thing is, it's been at least a week since anyone clapped eyes on him. I hope he hasn't got that flaming Asian Flu everyone's talking about. The doorman outside the Essoldo said he saw Cecil talking with a glamorous young woman—'

But at this point, unfortunately, all talk of Cecil abruptly ceased. With a cup of tea in the offing, more important matters had come up.

'Kettle, sir!' interrupted Twitten urgently, jumping to his feet. 'Sir? Sir? The electric kettle!'

Kettle? What was going on? Why was Twitten so excited by tea-making all of a sudden? But then Brunswick remembered. 'Right, son. Yes!'

'Give me strength,' said Mrs Groynes. Year after year she had made the tea for this lot and no single bugger had taken the remotest interest. But now? Good grief. Rolling her eyes, she withdrew her hand from the kettle's switch.

'Go on, then, Constable. Do the honours.'

Twitten blushed. 'May I?' he breathed. 'May I *again?*'

And so the electric kettle was switched on by the good graces of the constabular digit, and all three of them stood in silence to watch it in action.

The cause of all this unusual excitement was that Mrs Groynes had lately acquired an up-to-the-minute electric kettle that *turned itself off once it had boiled*. Formerly, she had made tea using water from an enormous hot-water urn that she trundled, clanking, along the corridor from the lift on a rickety steel trolley. This urn was distinctly old-fashioned: the fact that it provided the requisite hot water for tea-making was utterly dull and unremarkable. Whereas who could fail to be thrilled and transported by the sheer novelty of this shiny, futuristic kettle, with its little switch that sprang out – with a wondrous 'tock' noise – once the boiling process was complete? Truly, making an everyday hot beverage was now like living in the twenty-third century!

All conversation was suspended while the appliance noisily heated to a boil on its special new tin tray. Both Twitten and Brunswick were tense. Would the switch duly pop out when the time came? They listened to the sound of the water starting to rumble and bubble, and looked at each other. Would it? Would it ever? The kettle was by now boiling fiercely. Hot steam was issuing from the spout. *Would it? Shouldn't it have done it by now?* But then, just when they started to think that the mechanism must have failed (and that it was time to call the fire brigade), 'Tock!' it went, and the boiling subsided, along with their groundless fears.

'Gosh,' sighed Twitten, sinking back onto his chair.

'Blimey,' exclaimed Brunswick, with a chuckle.

'And about bleeding time, dears,' muttered Mrs G, as she poured the water into the prepared teapot, and gave the contents a stir.

At Gosling's Department Store, on the London Road, the weeks of rain had been highly beneficial. Sales of swimwear and sunglasses might have dropped abysmally, but the sales of umbrellas had soared, along with stewing steak, tapioca, warm vests, jigsaw puzzles and the new (huge) fifteen-inch television sets.

Gosling's was one of several department stores in the town, the most prestigious and central being the mighty Hannington's in North Street. Like its competitors, Gosling's took what you might call a 'gamut-running' approach to retail lines (or 'indiscriminate' if you were being unkind), and dealt in everything from Dutch lard to fur coats, bedroom furniture to dog meat, surgical appliances to coach trips. Promotional signs were displayed everywhere: KEPEKOOL REFRIGERATORS! CHILPRUFE THERMAL UNDERWEAR! EASICLENE OVENS! (In the exciting consumer boom of the mid-fifties, brand names adopted an ostentatiously *faux-naïf* approach to spelling.)

It was a bustling, lively sort of shop, arranged over four floors. Many Brightonians preferred Gosling's to the more sedate Hannington's, because in the London Road store there was always something entertaining to gawp at. The original Mr Gosling (known to staff as Mister Edward) had founded the shop in 1912, and laid a foundation of good service; his forty-three-year-old son (known as Mister Harold) was more of an extrovert, and although he was a cheapskate by nature, his retail instincts were excellent.

Since Mister Harold took the helm, Gosling's had become *the* place to go on a rainy day. Every morning in the kitchen-ware department, a high-heeled woman with a tiny waist and pencilled-on eyebrows (and an unfortunate pained expression suggestive of a headache) demonstrated how to make such fashionable dinner-party staples as crabmeat puffs and chocolate chiffon. In the record department, customers could listen to LPs of their choice in little booths lined with soundproof pegboard, thanks to the modern-day miracle of speaker-wire. And in the dairy section of the food hall, little cubes of exotic cheese (such as Edam) were offered on sticks by a blonde teenaged girl from Patcham dressed up in a rough approximation of Dutch national costume. For people who had recently endured a drab decade of post-war rationing, the invitation from Gosling's to sample a morsel of seafood canapé, then listen to the latest Pat Boone and scoff free cheese from the Netherlands, was almost unbearably exciting.

It was in Gosling's that Mrs Groynes had purchased the electric kettle. For reasons that will become apparent, she received a discount there. But it was Inspector Steine who had paid. In a rare access of munificence (on the day he discovered he was to receive the Silver Truncheon, which came with a cheque for a hundred pounds), he had searched his mind for ways to share his good fortune with his immediate staff. But what did they like? What were their interests? He considered each of his men in turn, trying to picture them in their leisure hours – and, interestingly, came up with nothing. In the end, he decided to consult the charlady, calling her into his office for a private conversation.

'Well, dear,' she said, when he had put his proposal to her, 'I wish I could say this needs a lot of thinking about, but I'd be lying. If you ask me, the sergeant would like nothing better than a trip to one of them poncey film studios up London way.'

Sitting back in her chair, she produced cigarettes and an expensive-looking lighter from the deep pocket of her flowery (but deeply ugly) pinny, and lit up a Capstan Full Strength. Tilting her head back, she took a satisfying drag.

Steine was mystified. 'What poncey film studios?'

'Oh, come on, dear. You know. Pinewood, Shepperton, Merton Park; one of those. And as for Constable Clever Clogs, I can promise you he'd love you for ever, dear, if you got him a year's membership of that bleeding London Library he's always banging on about.'

'Really? Are you sure?' Steine pulled a face. Film studios and a library? Personally, he hated the sound of both of those things.

'See this?' From the pocket of her pinny Mrs Groynes produced a page torn from a film magazine. It featured a competition, with the words 'WIN A TRIP TO FABULOUS PINEWOOD' across the top in red lettering. 'The sergeant goes in for this every bleeding month, dear.'

'No!'

'Yes, and it's not free. You have to send a postal order. It's a proper scam, of course, but he can't see it, bless him. If you look in his desk, you'll find he's got several postal orders ready, *and* a stack of ready-addressed envelopes, so he can post off his entry the minute the competition opens.' She shook her head knowingly. 'As if that would make a blind bit of difference.'

'Good heavens.'

Steine took the page and perused it, frowning. Evidently, entrants to this competition were required to study a series of studio photographs of somebody called Patricia Neal and list them in order of 'loveliness'. He sighed. Here was proof enough that it was a bad idea to dig beneath the surface of the people you worked with. 'And what on earth's the London Library?'

'Ah,' shrugged Mrs G, 'search me, dear. But I'm guessing on the available evidence that it's a library up London. Constable Clever Clogs is always after some obscure book or other, and I've heard him on the dog-and-bone nagging his poor old mum to make him a member of it.'

'I see.' Steine considered what he had heard, wrinkled his nose, and came to a decision. 'Well, thank you for those imaginative suggestions, Mrs Groynes, but I can't think of anything I want to encourage less than Sergeant Brunswick mooning over more actresses, or Twitten with his head in more books.'

'That's a shame, dear. You could have made them very happy.'

'Even so. My first instinct was new silver-plated whistles.'

She let out a laugh of surprise. 'Oh, my good gawd. *Whistles?*'

'Yes.' He refused to be mocked by the charwoman. 'Whistles coated in silver, and *engraved*. So they will be very special.'

'They'd still be bleeding whistles, dear.'

'Yes. But look, Twitten and Brunswick are both policemen, Mrs Groynes. The whistles will be engraved with the date of my shooting Terence Chambers. In their old age, Brunswick and Twitten will explain to their grandchildren that they were fortunate enough to be in Brighton at the time of the momentous event, even if they didn't actually play a part in it, and weren't in fact present when I heroically pulled the trigger.'

'Right, dear. Well, you know best.'

'Thank you.'

'But in that case, can I put in a request for one of them new electric kettles that switch theirselves off?'

'A new what?'

'Kettle, dear. That turns itself off. It would benefit everyone, but it would also save me wrestling with that bleeding tea-urn for the rest of my life, risking life and limb.'

Steine brightened. This was more like it. 'It turns itself off? How?'

'Well, I'm no thermo-bleeding-physicist, dear, am I?'

'Well, no.'

'But as I understand it, it's got a bi-metallic strip in the rear of the kettle—'

'Bi-metallic?'

'Made of two metals.'

'Ah.'

'And this strip is cunningly exposed to the steam rising from the water, and due to the steam this metal expands to a point where it knocks the switch out, thus turning off the element, stopping the boiling process, and saving everyone in the area from a gruesome fiery death.'

Steine looked impressed, but also a bit thoughtful. 'Mrs Groynes, how do you—?' he began.

'But don't listen to me, dear,' she interrupted, laughing. 'What do I know about technological advancements in domestic appliances and whatnot? Hovercrafts, dear?

Araldite? The many-worlds interpretation of quantum mechanics? Ha, I mean to say!'

And so she had trotted along to Gosling's to buy the recently launched Russell Hobbs K1 model, with the revolutionary automatic shut-off. As she sailed through one of the pairs of swing doors on London Road, greeting the uniformed doorman holding it open, and tucking the customary ten-shilling note into his hand, she reflected that Brunswick and Twitten would sadly never know how close they had come to gaining their hearts' desires. If Constable Twitten ever so much as entered the stately catalogue hall of the London Library in St James's Square (where she had herself been a member since 1945), he would set up home there for the rest of his life. If Brunswick once saw inside a film studio, it would be much the same story, but with busty actresses being the attraction, instead of dusty tomes. However, neither of them knew that she had made such wonderful suggestions on their behalf, and it was better that they didn't. If there was ever a woman who whole-heartedly maintained that *what you don't know can't hurt you*, it was, obviously, Mrs Palmeira Groynes.

On her way through Gosling's to buy the kettle, she had said a discreet hello to various gang members who'd been in place in the store for months, posing as everything from migraine-victim cookery demonstrator to carpenter-cum-handyman. She had come up with the plan the previous Christmas, and had been patiently slotting the pieces into place all year. In all her days in the business of crime, the upcoming Gosling's Christmas Job was the one that had excited her most. It was masterly. It would go down in history as the cleverest and cleanest (and most lucrative) commercial robbery ever carried out in Great Britain.

As she handed over a five-pound note to the sales assistant in Domestic Appliances, she watched with particular pleasure as he took a canister from a basket behind him, unscrewed its lid, and placed inside it the handwritten note of sale and the money. He then posted it into the shop's vacuum-activated tube system, where it was immediately sucked away. He smiled at Mrs Groynes, and she smiled back pleasantly. He then wrapped the purchase for her in paper and string, while they waited for the cashiers in the far-off basement 'tube room' to send the canister back.

It was quite a good idea for stores such as Gosling's to keep no cash on the shop-floors. Less tempting for opportunistic criminals; also, of course, less tempting for light-fingered staff. Some of the shops in town used an overhead pulley-system for transporting cash that involved a very entertaining pull-down catapult mechanism and a network of overhead wires. But Gosling's had lately taken down the untidy and obtrusive wires and opted for the more discreet vacuum tubes that ran next to (and sometimes through) the walls. It was a quieter system, and much neater. The local engineers who had installed it (on the cheap) promised it would go wrong only if a) someone accidentally posted a French baguette into it, or b) it sucked a cashier's arm off up to the shoulder.

Most customers had no idea where the canisters went. To them, it was a delightful mystery. But Mrs Groynes knew all about the tube room, where a row of seated girls and women dealt with every sale in the store – opening the canisters, entering the purchases in ledgers, calculating the change, and sending the canisters back, with the notes of sale stamped 'PAID'.

The thing was, one of these tube-room girls was Denise Perks, aged nineteen, orphaned older sister of Shorty the messenger boy, trainee gang member, and well on her way to becoming Mrs Groynes's deputy. (We will be hearing much more of Denise.)

'I see a lot of myself in you, dear,' Mrs Groynes told the girl once, when she was only fifteen and working as part of a whizz mob at the railway station (picking pockets). 'Just don't fall in love with someone pretending to be a bleeding war hero, and nothing can stop you getting to the top.'

It was good advice, and the cool-headed Denise had resisted falling in love with anyone. She was far too focused on her job. Having worked at Gosling's for only three months, she was already in charge of a team of twelve, and earning an extra seven and six a week. Right now, she was efficiently placing Mrs Groynes's change (one shilling and fourpence) in the canister and posting it back through the appropriate tube, thankfully without getting her arm sucked off, not even up to the elbow.

Back at the office, with the kettle duly boiled, Twitten returned to his book. It was very absorbing. These had been excellent weeks for him: Inspector Steine's absence and an unusual drop in violent criminal activity (due, as he was fully aware, to the understandable exhaustion of Mrs Groynes after all the shenanigans over the Bank Holiday weekend) meant that for several weeks Twitten had not been obliged to stand over a single bullet-riddled corpse.

But how best to take advantage of this little holiday? By reading, of course. True, under orders from the inspector, he had reluctantly started reporting for driving lessons on week-days from a brisk police instructor, which were going far from well ('*Left foot, Constable! I said left, that's the accelerator! Eyes on the road! Mind that pram! What the blazes is wrong with you?*'), but mainly he'd embarked on a great reading spree at his desk, often with a sharpened pencil in his hand and a zealous gleam in his eye.

Lately, he had been reading a newly published book called *The Hidden Persuaders*, and he had rarely read anything that excited him more. It was so bally relevant to the modern world! It explained so much! He couldn't wait to describe it to everyone, and persuade them to look at the world in a new way – which was presumably why Mrs Groynes had taken the sergeant aside and warned him, 'Whatever you do, dear, don't ask the constable about that book of his. He's bleeding bursting with it.'

Brunswick, meanwhile, had also enjoyed the period of calm, by daring to turn his attentions elsewhere for a change. Very tentatively, and without much conviction, he was courting Twitten's attractive forty-one-year-old landlady, Mrs Thorpe.

'Please, Jim. Call me Eliza,' she had urged him warmly, on their first date, but somehow he couldn't do it. Any younger woman he could call by her first name automatically, but not Mrs Thorpe. She was older than him, for a start, and her late husband had been a general. She spoke beautifully, and was firmly middle class, with a nice house in one of the most desirable terraces in Brighton. Admittedly, her house had recently been the location of an upsetting and grisly murder (a playwright horribly slain with the general's regimental sword), but it had also for years played host to eminent stars of stage and screen. By striking contrast, Brunswick had received his education at the London Road Academy for Orphans, Waifs and Foundlings, and had joined the army at thirteen. He owned two decent suits, had never held a bank account, and he lived with his auntie in a flat above a bicycle shop.

So he couldn't call this woman Eliza, but he did enjoy her company, and he was intrigued (or, more honestly, pleasantly disturbed) by her undisguised interest in him physically. In all Brunswick's dealings with women up to now, the attraction had flowed emphatically in the other direction, with gum-chewing girls rejecting each romantic advance with 'No, Jim. Not interested!' Or 'Mind my nylons! These cost two and eleven!' He had experienced, in his miserable love life, a great deal of being pushed in the chest (and he had also shelled out for a lot of replacement hosiery). So he was naturally confused by Mrs Thorpe's strange erotic attraction to him. She throbbed with it. He once took her hand to help her out of a taxi and she was so thrilled by his manly touch, she started to hyperventilate.

But things had not progressed easily. They had seen a few films together; drunk a few frothy coffees. It was only when they went to see a new stage production of a comedy called *The Reluctant Debutante* at the Palace Pier Theatre that things moved on slightly. They would both always remember that particular evening. As they walked back uphill from the Clock Tower towards Mrs Thorpe's fine house on Clifton Terrace, they discussed the merits of the cast.

'I preferred Wilfrid Hyde-White in the original production, I'm afraid,' said Mrs Thorpe.

Now, Brunswick might have been hurt by this. After all, he'd paid for the tickets. Women weren't supposed to be critical of something a man had spent good money on. At certain levels of society, such an ungrateful remark would earn a woman a smack on the kisser. But Brunswick was deeply pleased by what Mrs Thorne had said, because he agreed with it. The chap in this production hadn't been a patch on Wilfrid Hyde-White.

'You saw it last year, then?' he said. 'At the Theatre Royal?'

'Yes. But why do you—?'

'I was there, too!'

'Oh, I see.'

'You're the first person I've ever told. I mean, I can hardly talk much at the station about light-hearted stage comedies about rich people. When the inspector's about, I have to read my monthly *Plays and Players* on the sly, tucked inside the *Police Gazette*.'

'Well, wasn't he good? Freddie, I mean.'

'Good? He was flaming brilliant!'

'Apparently they've cast Rex Harrison for the film,' she said matter-of-factly. 'But I can't quite imagine that, can you?'

Brunswick stopped walking, and looked at her. What an amazing woman this was. She knew about Rex Harrison being cast in *The Reluctant Debutante* in the part that belonged by right to Wilfrid Hyde-White? Who else would care about this but him? Who else would have an informed opinion? Who else would refer to Wilfrid Hyde-White as *Freddie*?

'James?' she said, puzzled.

And then, on a romantic impulse, he took her in his arms. As he pulled her close, she received the full force of his pungent after-shave – Cossack ('for Men') – but being well versed in acceptable feminine behaviour, she cleverly masked the gag reflex.

'James?' she said again, raising her face to his, and not breathing.

'Mrs Thorpe!' he exclaimed, and kissed her.

———

If we have started with a pause, it is deliberate. Because, back at the police station, the days of peace are about to end. Later on, all those present will remember how agreeable things were on this seemingly humdrum rainy Tuesday in the middle of September. Mrs Groynes is having a sit-down, while Brunswick whistles softly to himself, scanning the latest *Picturegoer*, and Twitten makes another scholarly note with a pencil. All is well in their world. The kettle makes comforting contracting noises as it cools. A clock ticks. Everyone has forgotten about the minor mystery of Barrow-Boy Cecil's disappearance – everyone apart from Mrs Groynes, who is reliably quick at putting two and two together.

———

But beyond the police station, key events are taking place – events that will require someone to put two and two together, plus two, and two, and two, and two, and two. At the tiny Polyfoto shop in Western Road, for example, the manager returns from his lunch hour and finds the door hanging open and the place ransacked. Cameras have been stolen from the portrait studio at the back; furniture has been knocked over; storage boxes tipped out on the floor.

'Len?' he says, a quiver in his voice. He can't work this out. Has Len the Photographer done this? Has he gone berserk after ten years of taking pictures in here?

And then the manager turns round and sees Len lying unmoving on the marbled lino with blood puddling around his head. The sight makes him yelp and stagger. Then he picks up the telephone and asks the operator for the police.

———

At about the same time, Ben Oliver of the *Brighton Evening Argus* receives a phone call from a woman with a strong Germanic accent who refuses to give her name. She is evidently in distress, but wants to tell him something important. She says she is a psychiatrist who's been working for several months at an unnamed hospital for the criminally insane in the county of Berkshire (clearly she means Broadmoor), attempting to treat an inmate with a history of extreme violence.

'They von't tell me any-zing,' she gasps, 'but I know some-zing hass happen. I sink he hass escape!'

Oliver raises an eyebrow. This news is interesting, but he doesn't see what the *Argus* has to do with it. 'Can you give me his name, please?'

'Of course,' she says, trying to calm herself. 'His name iss Chow-tza. Geoffrey Chow-tza. C-H-A-U-C-E-R.'

Oliver, who has just switched the phone receiver to his left ear in preparation for making notes, pauses, and briefly considers just hanging up at once. *Geoffrey Chaucer?* 'But that's the name of … well, that's the name of Geoffrey Chaucer, madam. English poet.'

'I know! Ve talk of ziss coincidence many time, belief me.'

Bemused, Oliver picks up a pen. He has to admit it's all been a bit slow recently in the crime-correspondent world, since the killing of Chambers by local hero Inspector Steine in August. Oliver has been so stuck for decent stories that he's been working towards a somewhat lame feature about an American academic who's been in town studying 'crowd behaviour' (whatever that is). He might as well establish the facts about this escaped Chaucer character, such as they are.

So he makes a note. 'Broadmoor?' he writes. 'Escape. Geoffrey Chaucer – REALLY?' Then he draws a circle around 'REALLY?'

'And why are you telling me this, exactly, madam?' he asks.

'Because he iss obsess wizz killing polizemen, and in particular he has grudge – "grudge"? Iss this correct?'

Oliver considers. 'You mean, a grudge against someone?'

'Precisely. It iss a grudge against a policeman in your own town of Brighton!'

Oliver finally sits up straight. 'Please tell me your name, madam.'

'*Nein, nein*, not important. But you must alert ze police! Geoffrey kills policemen, and not only zat! He cut off head and boil in bucket!'

'Ugh,' says Oliver, who is now making proper notes in shorthand. 'Why don't you alert the police yourself?'

'Why? You zink I not try? Zey never answer ze telephone!'

'And this policeman? I assume we're talking about Inspector Steine?'

'*Jah! Natürlich!*' says the woman. 'His name is Steine.'

'Oh, my goodness.'

'Yes! And if I were zis Inspector Steine, I would run at once for ze hill!'

In the tube room at Gosling's Department Store, it has been a very busy day, and Denise Perks is at full stretch, dealing with umpteen canisters a minute. If anyone had only heard of repetitive strain injury in the 1950s, she'd have been able to take this shop to the cleaners. The dozen girls working alongside her today are fast, too, but it speeds things up if Denise, as supervisor, takes each canister out of the basket as it arrives, unscrews it, and passes the contents to one of the others for processing.

It is just after lunch when she takes one such canister, and tips out something unexpected: a severed human finger with a ring on it, plus a small heap of crushed plastic, and a note that reads:

DON'T TELL MRS GROYNES ABOUT THIS
OR SHORTY WILL BE NEXT

This is an unpleasant surprise, to say the least.

'Oh, my God!' Denise exclaims, unable to moderate her reaction. In her defence, you don't see a human body part fall out of a canister every day.

'Something wrong, Miss Perks?' says one of the other girls, looking up.

'No, no!' she says quickly. 'Keep working.'

But Denise recognises the ring. It belongs to fellow gang member Barrow-Boy Cecil! What is happening? Has someone kidnapped him? Are they truly threatening Shorty? As her mind races, she recognises the significance of the shards of brightly coloured plastic mixed with springs and a little key. They are parts of a clockwork bunny.

Unaware of all this activity elsewhere, Twitten continues to read, and is so absorbed that he hardly notices the arrival of Mr Lloyd, the station's permanently miserable post-delivery man who daily, with a lot of wheezing and grumbling, dumps one of the large sacks of letters for Inspector Steine just inside the door. Today, Mr Lloyd pointedly pauses at the doorway, hand on handle, clearly waiting for the others to pay him attention.

It has been observed by many employees of Brighton Police Station that the notably dandruffy Mr Lloyd can never just shuffle in, make a delivery, struggle for breath a bit, collect the outgoing post from its designated pigeonhole, and shuffle out again: he always has to start a conversation. This is not because he is sociable by nature. Being the long-standing shop steward of a major union, he is a professional troublemaker who tirelessly angles for any affront or infringement (or misspoken word) worthy of protest, rebuke or even industrial action. As a consequence, people are very careful around him and speak little. He once attempted to call the whole branch out on strike because a boy in the pay office called him 'Mr Death Rattle' (in a whisper) when he was twenty yards away.

'Now I've got here something for young Constable Twitten,' he says, locating a large envelope in the top tray of his trolley but not passing it over. He wheezes a few times, while he gets his breath. 'But I have to tell you (*wheeze*) this is highly irregular, and I am in two minds (*wheeze*) what to do about it. Deliver it or not? In fact, should I even be touching it?'

He holds the envelope and stares at it, as if deciding.

'You see, a *very* pleasant and polite young lady handed it in at the front desk as I was setting out on my rounds and said it was urgent. So ... (*multiple wheezes, for dramatic effect*). So, seeing as it was not received into the building via the agreed union-approved channels ... well.'

Brunswick and Mrs Groynes look at each other, but say nothing. They know better than to interrupt this display of union muscle. Twitten opens his mouth to speak, but Mrs Groynes says 'Shh, dear', so he closes it again.

They all look at each other. Twitten looks (quite hard) at Mr Lloyd; Mr Lloyd looks challengingly at Mrs Groynes; Mrs Groynes looks steadily at Brunswick; Brunswick looks at Twitten. It's like a stand-off without the guns, and then – in a flash – it's all over. Because the telephone in the inspector's office loudly rings ('Oh, my good gawd,' yelps Mrs G, clutching her chest), and an unknown woman of grave proportions, in a mauve tweed suit and small bottle-green felt hat, appears in the open doorway, blocking it entirely. Mr Lloyd slings the envelope at Twitten, and smartly turns to go.

'Steine's office?' demands the dragoness, entering.

Confusion reigns. This woman is very intimidating. 'Um, yes,' says Twitten, standing up. 'May I help you?'

'I'm the inspector's new SECRETARY. Miss LENNON. And I have brought whistles as a gift.'

Stopping only to slam two silver-plated whistles in front of the startled Brunswick and Twitten, she strides into Steine's office and answers his phone.

'The office of Inspector STEINE,' she booms. 'Miss LENNON speaking. How may I HELP you?'

While the postman quickly wheels his trolley out, Brunswick and Mrs Groynes exchange anxious glances while Twitten, absent-mindedly, opens the envelope, unaware that the contents will threaten to alter the course of his life.

'What just happened?' hisses Brunswick. 'Who's Miss flaming Lennon? Why is the phone ringing again?'

'I don't know, sir,' says Twitten, bewildered.

He draws out the contents of the envelope and is bewildered further. It seems to be a photograph of Terence Chambers outside the Metropole Hotel in the company of Mrs Groynes. Twitten gapes. He says, 'Oh, crikey.' He looks up at Mrs G and then back at the picture. This is enormous. He has in his hand incontrovertible evidence of Mrs Groynes's true criminal nature! He can use this to expose her, at last! *Oh, crikey*, he thinks. *Oh-crikey-crikey-flip!*

'What have you got there, dear?' says Mrs Groynes, moving closer.

'Nothing,' he says. 'Nothing.' Quickly sliding the photograph back into the envelope, he pathetically picks up the whistle, saying, 'Gosh, look, Mrs G.'

'At what? It's a bleeding whistle, dear. You said "crikey".'

'Yes, but … oh, look, it's engraved in tiny letters. Is yours the same, Sergeant Brunswick, sir?'

Miss Lennon emerges from Steine's office and stands looking at them all, big hands on ample hips. They all shrink back; they can't help it.

'I'd like a cup of tea with TWO SUGARS, please, Mrs Char. But you must get rid of that kettle, it's against regulations and a serious FIRE HAZARD.'

No one says anything. They are too shocked. *Did this woman just call Mrs Groynes 'Mrs Char'?*

She pulls on the locked door of Mrs Groynes's stash-cupboard.

'And I'd like the key to this AT ONCE, or I'll get the station carpenter to come up tomorrow and open it BY FORCE.'

Newport Community
Learning & Libraries

Also available by LYNNE TRUSS

A SHOT
IN THE DARK

A CONSTABLE TWITTEN MYSTERY

WINNER OF THE CRIMEFEST LAST LAUGH AWARD

Brighton, 1957. Inspector Steine rather enjoys his life as a policeman by the sea. No criminals, no crime, no stress.

So it's really rather annoying when an ambitious – not to mention irritating – new constable shows up to work and starts investigating a series of burglaries. And it's even more annoying when, after Constable Twitten is despatched to the theatre for the night, he sits next to a vicious theatre critic who is promptly shot dead part way through the opening night of a new play.

It seems Brighton may be in need of a police force after all...

'This is crime fiction turned on its head
– a giddy spell of sheer delight'
Daily Mail

'Funny, clever, charming, imaginative,
nostalgic and gently satirical'
The Times

'A perfect summer read'
Guardian

Order your copy:

By phone: +44 (0) 1256 302 699 · By email: direct@macmillan.co.uk · Delivery is usually 3–5 working days.
Free postage and packaging for orders over £20. · Online: www.bloomsbury.com/bookshop
Prices and availability subject to change without notice. · bloomsbury.com/author/lynne-truss

Also available by **LYNNE TRUSS**

THE MAN THAT GOT AWAY

A *TIMES* CRIME NOVEL OF THE YEAR

The Brighton Belles are on hand to answer any summer holidaymaker's queries, no matter how big or small. The quickest way to the station, how many pebbles are on the beach and what exactly has happened to that young man lying in the deckchair with blood dripping from him?

Constable Twitten has a hunch that the fiendish murder may be connected to a notorious Brighton nightspot and the family that run it, but Inspector Steine is – as ever – distracted by other issues, not least having his own waxwork model made, while Sergeant Brunswick is just delighted to have spied an opportunity to finally be allowed to go undercover...

'A knockabout farce of mayhem and murder ... A feast of black humour'
Daily Mail

'Lynne Truss is clearly having a great time – and so does the reader. There is a smile, giggle or guffaw on every page'
The Times

'A worthy follow-up to *A Shot in the Dark* ...
One looks forward with glee to this quick-learning constable's future adventures'
Wall Street Journal

Order your copy:

By phone: +44 (0) 1256 302 699 · By email: direct@macmillan.co.uk
Delivery is usually 3–5 working days. · Free postage and packaging for orders ove
Online: www.bloomsbury.com/bookshop
Prices and availability subject to change without notice
bloomsbury.com/author/lynne-truss

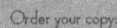

Ringland

Library

13 8 4